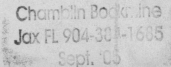

Mary Jo Putney

Petals

in the Storm

A SIGNET BOOK

SIGNET
Published by New American Library, a division of
Penguin Group (USA) Inc., 375 Hudson Street,
New York, New York 10014, USA
Penguin Group (Canada), 90 Eglinton Avenue East, Suite 700, Toronto,
Ontario M4P 2Y3, Canada (a division of Pearson Penguin Canada Inc.)
Penguin Books Ltd., 80 Strand, London WC2R 0RL, England
Penguin Ireland, 25 St. Stephen's Green, Dublin 2,
Ireland (a division of Penguin Books Ltd.)
Penguin Group (Australia), 250 Camberwell Road, Camberwell, Victoria 3124,
Australia (a division of Pearson Australia Group Pty. Ltd.)
Penguin Books India Pvt. Ltd., 11 Community Centre, Panchsheel Park,
New Delhi - 110 017, India
Penguin Group (NZ), cnr Airborne and Rosedale Roads, Albany,
Auckland 1310, New Zealand (a division of Pearson New Zealand Ltd.)
Penguin Books (South Africa) (Pty.) Ltd., 24 Sturdee Avenue,
Rosebank, Johannesburg 2196, South Africa

Penguin Books Ltd., Registered Offices:
80 Strand, London WC2R 0RL, England

Published by Signet, an imprint of New American Library, a division of Penguin Group (USA) Inc. The book previously appeared as a Signet book in a substantially different form under the title *The Controversial Countess* and later appeared in a Topaz edition under its present title.

First Signet Printing (as *Petals in the Storm*), November 1999
10   9   8   7   6

PUBLISHER'S NOTE
This is a work of fiction. Names, characters, places, and incidents either are the product of the author's imagination or are used fictitiously, and any resemblance to actual persons, living or dead, business establishments, events, or locales is entirely coincidental.

The publisher does not have any control over and does not assume any responsibility for author or third-party Web sites or their content.

To Nic, who may well be
the only professor of economics in America
who reads and enjoys my books

Of the numerous books consulted for the background of this story, the author wishes particularly to acknowledge *Wellington: Pillar of State*, by Elizabeth Longford, *The Foreign Policy of Castlereagh, 1812–1815*, by Sir Charles Webster, and *The Reminiscences and Recollections of Captain Gronow* (Viking Press edition, 1964).

Chapter 1

"What the devil is going on here?"

It was the battle cry of an angry husband; Rafe would have recognized it anywhere. He sighed. Apparently there was going to be an untidy emotional scene of the sort he most loathed. Releasing the delightful lady in his arms, he turned to face the man who had just stormed into the drawing room.

The newcomer was about Rafe's height and of similar age, somewhere in his mid-thirties. Though he probably would have looked pleasant under other circumstances, at the moment he seemed ready to commit murder.

Lady Jocelyn Kendal cried, "David!" and stepped forward with pleasure, then stopped dead at the expression on her husband's face. Tension throbbed between them like a drum.

The silence was broken when the newcomer said in a low, furious voice, "It's obvious that my arrival is both unexpected and unwelcome. I assume this is the Duke of Candover? Or are you spreading your favors more widely?"

As Lady Jocelyn rocked with the impact of the words, Rafe said coolly, "I'm Candover. I'm afraid that you have the advantage of me, sir."

Visibly wrestling with the urge to throw his wife's guest out, the other man snapped, "I am Presteyne, husband of this lady here, though not for long." His hard gaze returned to Lady Jocelyn. "My apologies for interrupting your amusements. I'll collect my belongings and never trouble you again."

Then Presteyne left with a wall-rattling slam of the door. Rafe was glad to see the back of him; though an expert in all forms of gentlemanly sport, brawling with a furious husband of military bearing was not high on Rafe's list of pleasures.

Unfortunately the scene was not yet over, for Lady Jocelyn folded onto a satin chair and began to weep. Rafe regarded her with exasperation. He preferred to conduct his affairs lightly, with mutual pleasure and no recriminations, and would never have touched Lady Jocelyn if she hadn't told him that her marriage was in name only. Clearly the lady had lied. He remarked, "Your husband doesn't seem to share your belief that the marriage is one of convenience."

She lifted her head and regarded Rafe blankly, as if she had forgotten that he was there.

Irritated, he asked, "What kind of game are you playing? Your husband doesn't seem the sort of man to be manipulated with jealousy. He may leave you, or he may wring your neck, but he won't play that kind of lover's game."

"I wasn't playing a game," she said unevenly. "I was trying to discover what was in my heart. Only now do I know how I feel about David, when it is too late."

Rafe's irritation faded in the face of her youth and vulnerability. He had once been equally young and confused, and the sight of her misery was a vivid reminder of how disastrous love could be. "I'm beginning to suspect that under your highly polished surface beats a romantic heart," he said dryly. "If that's true, go after your husband and throw your charming self at his feet with abject apologies. You should be able to bring him around, at least this once. A man will forgive the woman he loves a great deal. Just don't let him find you in anyone else's arms. I doubt he would forgive you a second time."

Her eyes widened. Then, in a voice on the edge of hysterical laughter, she said, "Your sang-froid is legendary, but even so, the reports do you less than justice. If the devil himself walked in, I think you would ask him if he played whist."

"Never play whist with the devil, my dear. He cheats." Rafe lifted her icy hand and gave it a light farewell kiss. "Should your husband resist your blandishments, feel free to let me know if you want a pleasant, uncomplicated affair." He released her hand. "You'll never get more than that from me, you know. Many years ago I gave my heart away to someone who dropped and broke it, so I have none left."

It was a good exit line, yet as he looked into the girl's lovely face, he found himself saying, "You remind me of a woman I once knew, but not enough. Never enough."

Then he turned and walked away, out of the house and down the steps into the civilized confines of Upper Brook Street. His curricle was waiting, so he swung up and took the reins.

The part of him that laughed at his own vanities found mocking amusement in how well "The Duke" had carried off the scene. The Duke was Rafe's private name for the public image he had spent a dozen years crafting and polishing. As The Duke, he was the perfect, imperturbable English gentleman, and no one played the role better than Rafe.

Everyone needed a hobby.

Yet as he turned the corner into Park Lane, he was uneasily aware that he had shown a little more of himself than was comfortable. Fortunately Jocelyn was unlikely to spread the story, and Rafe certainly wouldn't.

He pulled the curricle up in front of his Berkeley Square house, gloomily thinking that he would have to start looking for a mistress again. In the weeks since he had ended his last affair, he had been unable to find a woman who caught his fancy. In fact, he had begun to wonder if he should give up on the compliant matrons of his own class and hire a courtesan. It would be simpler to keep a professional mistress, but such females were usually greedy and uneducated, and not infrequently diseased. The prospect did not enthrall him.

That was why he had been pleased when lovely Jocelyn Kendal had delicately informed him that she had entered into a marriage of convenience, and was interested in diversion. He had always admired her, but had kept his distance because it was strictly against his code to tamper with innocents. During the weeks he had been in the country he had thought about her with mild anticipation, and as soon as he returned to London he had called on her. Alas, in the interval since the lady had issued her discreet invitation, she seemed to have become an adoring, if confused, wife. Rafe must look elsewhere.

In an effort to relieve his depression, he congratulated himself on a narrow escape from what could have been a sticky affair. He should have known better than to become involved with such a bantling-brained romantic. In truth, he *had* known better, but she was really quite refreshing, the most appealing woman he had met in years. She was rather like . . .

He cut the thought off sharply. The main purpose of his early return to London was not dalliance, but a message from his friend Lucien, who wanted to discuss a business matter. The fact that the Earl of Strathmore's business was spying meant that his little projects were usually quite interesting.

Rafe's rank gave him access to the highest levels of society wherever he went, and over the years that fact had made him a useful part of his friend's far-flung intelligence network. Rafe's specialty was acting as a courier when official channels were not sufficiently private, but he had also conducted several discreet investigations among the rich and powerful.

As Rafe drove the curricle into his stable yard, he hoped that Lucien had something damned distracting this time.

Lucien Fairchild watched with amusement as the Duke of Candover made his way across the crowded drawing room. Tall, dark, and commanding, Rafe so exactly fitted the part of an aristocrat that he might have been an actor rather than the genuine article.

Since he was also theatrically handsome, it wasn't surprising that the gaze of every female in the room followed him. Idly Lucien wondered who would be next in the long line of glittering ladies who had shared Rafe's bed. Even Lucien, whose business was information, had trouble keeping track.

By Lucien's count, Rafe had used his famous icy glare to intimidate three encroaching nobodies as he crossed the room. Yet when the duke finally reached Lucien, his cool social smile warmed. "It's good to see you, Luce. I was sorry that you couldn't get away to Bourne Castle this summer."

"I was sorry, too, but Whitehall has been a madhouse." Lucien glanced across the room and gave an unobtrusive signal to another man, then continued, "Let's find a quieter place to catch up on the news." He led Rafe from the drawing room to a study at the back of the house.

They both took seats, and Rafe accepted a cigar from his host. "I assume that you have some devious task for me."

"You assume correctly." Lucien used a taper to light Rafe's cigar, then his own. "Do you fancy a trip to Paris?"

"Sounds perfect." Rafe puffed his cigar until it was burning evenly. "I've been feeling bored lately."

"This shouldn't be boring—the journey concerns a lady who is being a bit troublesome."

"Even better." Rafe drew in a deep draft of smoke, then let it trickle slowly from the side of his mouth. "Am I to kill her or kiss her?"

Lucien frowned. "Certainly not the former. As to the latter"—he shrugged—"I leave that to you."

The door opened and a dark man entered. Rafe rose and offered his hand. "Nicholas! I didn't know you were in London."

"Clare and I arrived just last night." After shaking hands, the Earl of Aberdare dropped casually into a chair.

As Rafe took his own seat, he observed, "You're looking particularly well."

"Marriage is a wonderful thing." Nicholas grinned mischievously. "You should take a wife yourself."

His voice dulcet, Rafe said, "An excellent idea. Whose wife would you suggest?"

After the other men laughed, Rafe continued. "I trust that my godson is also prospering."

It was an effective diversion. Nicholas's face immediately acquired the doting expression of a proud new father, and a description of young Kenrick's amazing progress followed.

The men in the study were three-quarters of a group that had been nicknamed the Fallen Angels in younger, wilder days. Friends since Eton, they retained the ease of brothers even when years passed between meetings. The absent member was Lord Michael Kenyon, who was Nicholas's neighbor in Wales. After the infant's achievements had been duly admired, Rafe said, "Did Michael come with you so that we could have a Fallen Angels reunion?"

"He isn't quite ready to travel, though he's convalescing with amazing speed. Soon he'll be as good as new, barring a few more scars." Nicholas chuckled. "Clare insisted on nursing him herself. Talk about an irresistible force and an immovable object! I think that my stubborn little wife is the only person on earth who could have kept Michael in bed long enough to heal properly. Now that he's better, I thought that Clare needed a holiday, so I brought her to town."

"Trust Michael to return to the army as soon as Napoleon broke out of Elba," Lucien said acerbically. "Since the French didn't manage to kill him in Spain, he had to give them another chance at Waterloo."

"Michael never could resist a good fight, and Wellington needed every experienced officer he could get," Rafe said. "But I hope that this time the war is over for good. Even Michael's luck might run out eventually."

The words reminded Lucien of the purpose of the meeting. "Now that you're both here, I'll get down to business. I asked Nicholas to join us because during his travels on the Continent, he occasionally worked with the woman I mentioned earlier."

The other two men exchanged glances. Rafe said, "I've always suspected that you might have been helping Lucien during your rambles through Europe, Nicholas."

"Gypsies can go anywhere, and I often did. Obviously you were pressed into service as well." Nicholas gave Lucien an amused glance. "You certainly play your cards close to your chest, not even letting Rafe or me know about each other. I'm surprised that you're talking to both of us now. Have we suddenly become more trustworthy?"

Even though he knew he was being baited, Lucien bristled. "In my business, it's merely good policy not to tell anyone more than they need to know. I'm bending that particular rule tonight because you might know something that could help Rafe."

"I gather that the lady in question is one of your agents," Rafe said. "What kind of trouble is she causing?"

Lucien hesitated, considering the best place to start. "I assume that you've been following the peace conference in Paris."

"Yes, though not closely. Weren't most of the issues settled at the Congress in Vienna?"

"Yes and no. A year ago the Allies were willing to blame the wars on Napoleon's ambition, so the Vienna settlement was fairly moderate." Lucien pulled the cigar from his mouth and eyed its glowing tip with disfavor. "Everything would have been fine if Napoleon had stayed in exile, but his return to France and the battle at Waterloo put the cat among the diplomatic pigeons. Because a large part of the French population supported the emperor, most of the Allies are now out for blood. France will be treated far more harshly than she was before Napoleon's Hundred Days."

"That's common knowledge." Rafe flicked the ash from his cigar. "Where do I come in?"

"There's a tremendous undercover struggle for influence in these months until the new treaties are settled," Lucien said. "It wouldn't take much to upset the negotiations, perhaps to the point of war. Information is critical. Unfortunately, my agent, Maggie, whose work has been invaluable, wants to retire and leave Paris as soon as possible, before the conference is finished."

"Offer her more money."

"We have. She's not interested. I hope that you can persuade her to change her mind and stay at least until the conference is over."

"Ah, we're back to kissing," Rafe said with an amused gleam in his eyes. "I gather that you want me to sacrifice my honor on the altar of British interests."

Lucien said dryly, "I'm sure that you have other means of persuasion. You are a duke, after all—she may be flattered that we're sending you to France to talk to her. Or perhaps you can appeal to her patriotism."

Rafe's brow furrowed. "While I'm flattered at your opinion of my charm, wouldn't it be simpler to have one of your diplomatic people who is already in Paris deal with the woman?"

"Unfortunately, there is reason to believe that a member of the delegation is ... unreliable. Secret information has been getting out of the British embassy, and it has caused problems." Lucien scowled. "Maybe I'm seeing shadows where none exist and there is no traitor, merely carelessness. But this business is too vital to risk working through unsafe channels."

"I'm getting the sense that you're worried about something more than the normal diplomatic wrangling," Rafe said.

"Am I that obvious?" Lucien said wryly. "You're quite right—I've been getting disturbing reports that suggest a plot to disrupt the peace negotiations, possibly end them altogether."

Rafe rolled his cigar between his thumb and forefinger as he tried to think of a single deed so disruptive that the Allies would be thrown into chaos. "Is it an assassination plot? All the Allied sovereigns except the British Prince Regent are in Paris, along with Europe's leading diplomats. Killing any of them could be disastrous."

Lucien exhaled a smoke ring that formed an improbable halo above his blond head. "Exactly. I hope to God that I'm wrong, but my sixth sense says that serious trouble is brewing."

"Who is the assassin, and who is the target?"

"If I knew that, I wouldn't need to be talking to you now," Lucien said gloomily. "I've only heard hints, gleaned from half a dozen sources. There are too many hostile factions, and too many possible targets. That's why information is so critical."

Nicholas said, "I heard that there was an assassination attempt on Wellington in Paris last winter. Could he be the target this time?"

"That's one of my worst fears," Lucien said. "After his victory at Waterloo, he is the most honored man in Europe. If he were to be assassinated, God only knows what would happen."

Somberly Rafe considered his friend's words. "Which is why you want me to convince your lady spy to keep sending you information until the plot is uncovered, or the conference ends."

"Precisely."

"Tell me about her. Is she French?"

Lucien made a face. "The plot thickens. I met Maggie through someone else and I know almost nothing about her background, but I've always thought she was British. Certainly she speaks and looks like an Englishwoman. I never probed further, because what mattered was that she hated Napoleon and looked on her work as a personal crusade. Her information was always good, and she never gave me a reason to distrust her."

Hearing the unspoken reservation, Rafe said, "But something has happened that makes you question her reliability."

"I still have trouble believing that Maggie would betray us, but I don't know if I can trust my own judgment. She can convince a man of anything, which is one reason she is so effective." Lucien frowned. "The situation is too grave to take anything for granted, including her loyalty. Now that Napoleon is on his way to St. Helena, she may be feathering her nest by selling British secrets to the other Allies. Perhaps she's in a hurry to leave Paris because she's earned a fortune through double- or triple-dealing and wants to escape before she is caught."

"Is there any evidence that she's disloyal?"

"As I said, I always assumed Maggie was an Englishwoman." Lucien glanced at Nicholas. "You knew Maggie as Maria Bergen. Recently you wrote me a letter, and rather than mention her by name, you discreetly referred to her as 'the Austrian woman you had worked with in Paris.'"

Nicholas straightened in his chair, expression startled. "You mean that Maria is actually English? I find that hard to believe. Not only was her German flawless, but her gestures, her mannerisms, were Austrian."

"It gets worse," Lucien said with reluctant amusement. "I became curious, and made inquiries of other men who had known her at earlier stages of her career. The French royalist knows that she is French, the Prussian says that she is a Berliner, and the Italian is willing to swear on his sainted mother's grave that she is from Florence."

Rafe couldn't help laughing. "So you are no longer sure where the lady's loyalties lie, if indeed she can be called a lady."

"She's a lady, no doubt about that," Lucien snapped. "But whose lady is she?"

Rafe was surprised by the vehement reaction, for Lucien was not sentimental where his work was concerned. Mildly Rafe said, "What should I do if I find that she has been betraying the British—assassinate her?"

Lucien gave Rafe a hard glance, not sure if the remark had been a jest. "As I said earlier, it's not a killing matter. If she's untrustworthy, simply inform Foreign Minister Castlereagh so that he won't rely on what she says. He may want to use her to feed false information to her other masters."

"Let me see if I have this straight," Rafe said. "You

want me to seek the lady out and persuade her to use her skills to uncover any assassination plots that might be afoot. In addition, I must ascertain where her loyalties lie, and if there are grounds for suspicion, I warn the head of the British delegation not to rely on her work. Correct?"

"Precisely. But you'll have to move quickly. The negotiations won't last much longer, so any conspirators will have to strike soon." Lucien glanced at Nicholas, who had been listening in silence. "Based on your dealings with Maggie in her Maria Bergen disguise, do you have anything to suggest?"

"Well, she's undoubtedly the most beautiful spy in Europe." Nicholas went on to contribute his evaluation of the woman, but the ensuing discussion resolved nothing.

Finally Rafe said, "The information we have is nothing if not contradictory. Obviously your Maggie is a superb actress. I'll have to play the situation by ear and hope that she proves susceptible to my famous charm."

As they all got to their feet, Lucien asked Rafe, "How soon will you be able to leave?"

"Day after tomorrow. The most beautiful spy in Europe? The prospect sounds quite stimulating." There was a gleam in Rafe's eye as he stubbed out his cigar. "I promise that I shall do my utmost for king and country."

They all returned to the party and mingled with the other guests. After he had done enough socializing to seem normal, Rafe was impatient to get away, but it occurred to him that he had forgotten to ask what the so-beautiful Maggie looked like. Since Lucien had disappeared, Rafe went in search of Nicholas.

Seeing his friend step into a curtained alcove, Rafe followed. Yet when he pushed aside the curtain, he halted, one hand clenching the edge of the drapery.

In the shadowy alcove, Nicholas and his wife Clare

were in each other's arms. Not kissing; if that had been the case, Rafe would have smiled and left without a second thought. But the sight that met his eyes was simpler, yet more disturbing.

Clare and Nicholas were resting against each other, eyes closed, his arms circling her waist, her forehead against his cheek. It was a tableau of perfect trust and understanding, and far more intimate than the most passionate embrace.

Since his presence had not been noticed, Rafe silently withdrew, his face tight.

It wasn't good to be too envious of one's friends.

After a day of frenzied preparation, the Duke of Candover was ready to leave England. He would be traveling fast, taking only one carriage, his valet, and a wardrobe that would do justice to his rank in the most fashionable capital in Europe.

As the clock struck midnight, he sat down in his study with a glass of brandy and leafed through the day's correspondence to see if there was anything urgent. Near the bottom of the pile was a note from Lady Jocelyn Kendal. Or rather, Lady Presteyne; since she was now very married, he must stop using her maiden name. In the note she thanked Rafe for his good advice in sending her back to her husband, extolled the joys of a happy marriage, and urged him to try it himself.

He smiled a little, glad to hear that matters had worked out. Underneath her beauty, famous name, and extravagant fortune, Jocelyn was also a very nice girl. If she and Lord Presteyne were both raving romantics, perhaps they would stay happy indefinitely, though Rafe had his doubts. He raised his glass in a solitary toast to her and her fortunate husband and drained the brandy, then smashed the glass into the fireplace.

The toast came from the heart, yet his smile went awry as he contemplated the shattered results of his uncharacteristic gesture. A man known for savoir faire would have been wiser to refrain. All he had to show for the moment was one less crystal goblet and a nagging sense of loss.

He poured another glass of brandy, then settled back in the wing chair and surveyed his library with a jaundiced eye. It was a beautifully proportioned room, a symphony of Italianate richness. In all of Rafe's vast holdings, there was no spot he enjoyed as much. That being the case, why the devil did he feel so depressed?

Wearily he recognized that the only way to cure his morbid mood was by giving in to it. Jocelyn wasn't the issue; if he had wanted the girl that much, he could have married her.

What disturbed Rafe was the way she had reminded him of Margot—beautiful, betraying Margot, dead these last dozen years. There was little physical resemblance, but both women had had a bright, laughing spirit that was irresistible. Whenever he had been with Jocelyn, he had found himself remembering Margot. She had moved him as no other woman ever had—and since he could never be that young again, no other woman ever would.

As he sipped his brandy, he tried to think objectively about Margot Ashton, but it was impossible to be rational about his first love. First and last, actually; the experience had cured him forever of romantic illusions. But at the time, the illusion had seemed very real.

Margot was not the most beautiful woman he had ever known, and certainly not the wealthiest or best-born. But she had had warmth and charm in lavish abundance, and she had sparkled with matchless vitality.

Bittersweet images flooded his mind. The first time he saw her; the first hesitant, miraculous kiss; lengthy sessions over a chessboard, when the formal moves had masked a deeper, more passionate game; the interview with a gently amused Colonel Ashton when Rafe haltingly had asked for her hand.

Most vivid of all was a morning when they had met in Hyde Park for a dawn ride. A light rain had been falling as he trotted through the quiet Mayfair streets, but the sky cleared as he entered the park. Ahead of him, arching through the dawn-bright air, had been an intensely colored rainbow. As he admired it, Margot had emerged from the mist at the foot of the rainbow, riding a silvery gray mare like a fairy queen from legend.

She had laughed and held out her hand to him, a living treasure at rainbow's end. Even then he had known that the magical image was a mere trick of weather and light, but it had seemed like the deepest reality he would ever know.

A fortnight later the affair ended, and so did his illusions.

His deepest regret came from the knowledge that it was his own jealousy and anger that had ended their engagement. If he had possessed at twenty-one the cool composure he developed later—if he had been able to accept her deceitfulness—he could have had her friendship for all these years.

For when all was said and done, her companionship was what he missed most. He knew that time had enhanced his memories, for no woman could possibly be as desirable as recollection painted her. But he had never stopped missing the way Margot had shared his laughter, or the impact of her changeable eyes meeting his across a room with such intimacy that he would forget that the rest of the world existed.

His reverie ended when the stem of the goblet in his hand snapped, cutting his fingers and splashing brandy across his lap. Scowling at the mess, he stood up. He'd had no idea the stems were so fragile. The butler would sulk for days when he discovered that the set of crystal goblets was now two short.

Rafe rose and headed upstairs to his bedchamber. A little self-indulgent melancholy was poetic, but he was beginning a hard journey early the next morning. It was time to bury thoughts of youthful foolishness and get some rest.

Chapter 2

"NO!"

Though the perfume bottle whizzed by his temple with no more than two inches to spare, Robert Anderson made no attempt to dodge, knowing that Maggie had an excellent aim and no real desire to damage him. She was merely, so to speak, sending him a message. With her usual good sense, she had chosen to throw the bottle of cheap scent given to her by a purse-pinching Bavarian with poor taste.

Robin smiled at his companion. Her magnificent bosom was heaving and her eyes flashed sparks; gray ones today, because of the silvery robe she wore. "Why don't you want to meet this duke that Lord Strathmore is sending? You should be flattered that the Foreign Office is taking such an interest in you."

A spate of Italian profanity was his answer. He tilted his blond head to one side and listened critically. When her outburst was over, he said, "Very creative, Maggie, love, but it isn't like you to slip out of character. Surely Magda, Countess Janos, should swear in Magyar?"

"I know more profanity in Italian," she said loftily. "And you know perfectly well that I never slip out of character with anyone but you." Her look of aristocratic dignity gave way to an impish chuckle. "Don't think you can change the subject, which is the Most Noble, the Duke of Candover."

"So it is." Robin studied his companion thoughtfully. They had known each other for a long time, and though the relationship was no longer an intimate one, they were still the best of friends. It was unlike her to be temperamental, even when she had been acting the part of a volatile Hungarian noblewoman for two years. "What do you have against the duke?"

Maggie sat down at her vanity table and lifted an ivory-backed brush, then began pulling it through the tawny waves of hair that fell over her shoulders. Scowling into the mirror, she said, "The man's a prig."

"Does that mean he didn't adequately appreciate your charms?" Robin said with interest. "Strange— Candover has the reputation of being quite the lady's man. I can't believe that he would ignore a tasty morsel like you."

"I am nobody's tasty morsel, Robin! Rakes are the biggest prigs of all. Pious hypocrites, in my experience." She tugged viciously at a knot in her hair. "Don't try to pick a new fight until we've finished with the current one. I refuse to have anything to do with the Duke of Candover, just as I refuse to continue spying. That part of my life is over, and no one—not you, not the duke, not Lord Strathmore—can change my mind. As soon as I take care of a few matters of business, I will be leaving Paris."

Robin came to stand behind her. Taking the brush from her hand, he began pulling it gently through her thick, dark gold hair. It was odd how they still shared some of the intimacy of husband and wife, though they had never married. He had always enjoyed brushing her hair, and the faint sandalwood scent took him back to the years when they had been impassioned young lovers, challenging the world with few thoughts for the future.

Maggie was looking stonily into the mirror. Her eyes were now a cold gray, not sparkling as they had been earlier. After several minutes of brushing, she began to relax.

"Did Candover do something dreadful?" he asked quietly. "If it would upset you to see him, I won't mention it again."

She chose her words carefully, knowing that Robin was uncomfortably adept at detecting hidden meanings. "Though he *was* rather despicable, it was a long time ago and it wouldn't bother me to see him. I simply don't want another man nagging me to keep doing what I don't want to do."

Robin's gaze met hers in the mirror. "Then why not meet him once to tell him that? If you want to wreak a bit of vengeance for past injuries, a fitting punishment would be to look your seductive best. You can drive him mad with longing while you turn down his request."

"I'm not sure that would work," she said dryly. "We parted on rather poor terms."

"That makes no difference—he's probably been thinking lustful thoughts of you ever since. Half the diplomats in Europe have let state secrets fall from their lips while struggling for one of your smiles." Robin grinned. "Wear that green ball gown, heave an alluring sigh as you refuse his request, then glide gracefully from the room. I guarantee it will cut up his peace for at least the next month."

She regarded her reflection thoughtfully. While she had a great deal of whatever it was that drove men mad, she was not convinced that Candover would succumb to her charms. Still, anger and lust were closely related, and Rafael Whitbourne had been very angry indeed at their last meeting. . . .

A slow, wicked smile curved her lips. Then she threw back her head and laughed. "Very well, Robin, you win. I'll meet with your ridiculous duke. I owe

him a few nights of ruined sleep. But I guarantee he
won't change my mind."

Robin dropped a quick kiss on the top of her head.
"Good lass." In spite of her protests, if she saw
Candover there was a chance that she could be persuaded to continue her work for a while longer. And
that would be a very good thing.

When Robin left, Maggie did not immediately sum-
mon her maid to complete her toilette. Instead, she
crossed her arms on the edge of the vanity and laid her
head on them, feeling sad and tired. It had been foolish
to agree to see Rafe Whitbourne. He *had* behaved very
badly, yet even then she had seen how his cruelty had
come from pain, and she had been denied the pleasure
of hating him.

Nor did she love him; the Margot Ashton who
thought the sun revolved around his handsome head
had died over a dozen years before. Maggie had been
many different people in the ensuing years, as Robin
had taken her under his wing and given her a reason to
go on living. Rafe Whitbourne was only a bittersweet
memory, with no relevance to her present self.

Love and hate were indeed opposite sides of the
same coin because both meant caring; the true opposite
was indifference. Since indifference was the only feeling Rafe could rouse in Maggie now, minor forms of
revenge were not worth the effort. She just wanted to
be done with this phase of her life, with deceit and
misdirection and informers.

Most of all, she wanted to accomplish the task that
had been delayed too long, then go home to England,
which she hadn't seen in thirteen years. She would
have to start over again, this time without Robin's protection. She would miss him bitterly, but even her
loneliness would contain relief; the two of them knew

each other too well for Maggie to reinvent herself if he was near.

She lifted her head and propped her chin on one fist while she regarded herself in the mirror. Her high cheekbones made her a convincing Magyar, and she spoke the language well enough so that no one had ever doubted that she was Hungarian. But how would Rafe Whitbourne see her after so many years?

A wry smile curved her full lips—lips that had had at least eleven pieces of bad poetry dedicated to them. Apparently the man could still arouse some emotion in her, even if it was only vanity. She studied her image critically.

Maggie had never been a great fancier of her own appearance, for her face lacked the classic restraint of true beauty. Her cheekbones were too high, her mouth too wide, her eyes too large.

But at least she looked little different from when she had been eighteen. Her complexion had always been excellent, and riding and dancing had kept her figure shapely. Though there was more fullness to the curves, no man had ever objected to that. Granted, her hair had darkened, but instead of becoming dull tan as blond hair often did, it was now the shade of rippling, golden wheat. Overall, she decided, she looked better now than when she and Rafe had been engaged.

It was tempting to imagine that he was fat and balding, but the damned man had the sort of looks that would only improve with age. His personality was another matter. Even at twenty-one he had not been free of the arrogance of wealth and rank, and the intervening years would only have made him worse. By this time, he must be insufferable.

As she resumed dressing for dinner, she told herself that it would be amusing to try to pierce his smugness. Yet she could not rid herself of the uneasy feeling that meeting him would prove to be a mistake.

* * *

The Duke of Candover had not been in Paris since 1803, and there had been many changes. Yet even in defeat, the capital of France was the center of Europe. Four major sovereigns and scores of minor monarchs had come to glean what they could from the wreckage of Napoleon's empire. The Prussians wanted revenge, the Russians wanted more territory, the Austrians hoped to roll the calendar back to 1789, and the French wanted to save themselves from massive reprisals after Napoleon's insane and bloody Hundred Days.

The British, as usual, were trying to be fair-minded. It was like trying to mediate a discussion between pit bulls.

In spite of the plethora of rulers, "the king" always meant Louis XVIII, the aging Bourbon whose unsteady hand held the French throne, while "the emperor" always meant Bonaparte. Even in his absence, the emperor cast a longer shadow than the physical presence of any other man.

Rafe took rooms at a luxurious hotel whose name had changed three times in as many months, to reflect changing political currents. Now it was called the Hotel de la Paix, since Peace was an acceptable sentiment to most factions.

He had just time to bathe and change before going to an Austrian ball where Lucien had arranged for him to meet the mysterious Maggie. Rafe dressed carefully, mindful of his friend's suggestion that he charm the lady spy. Experience had taught him that he could generally get what he wanted from women with a debonair smile and some earnest attention. Frequently, the ladies offered a good deal more than he wanted to accept.

Every inch The Duke, he went to the ball, which was a glittering assemblage of the great and notorious of Europe. Guests included not only all the important monarchs and diplomats, but hundreds of the lords, ladies, sluts, and scoundrels who were always drawn to power.

Rafe wandered about, sipping champagne and greeting acquaintances. But under the surface gaiety, he sensed dangerous undercurrents swirling. Lucien's fears were well founded—Paris was a powder keg, and a spark here might set the continent ablaze once more.

The evening was well advanced when he was approached by a young Englishman with fair hair and a slight, elegant figure. "Good evening, your grace. I'm Robert Anderson, with the British delegation. There's someone who wishes to meet you. If you'll come with me?"

Anderson was shorter and younger than Rafe, with a face that seemed vaguely familiar. As they snaked their way through the crush, Rafe surreptitiously examined his guide, wondering if this man was the weak link in the delegation. Anderson was so good-looking as to be almost pretty, and gave an impression of amiable vacuity. If he was a cunning, dangerous spy, he concealed it well.

They left the ballroom and went up a stairway to a door-lined corridor. Stopping outside the last door, Anderson said, "The countess is waiting for you, your grace."

"Do you know the lady?"

"I have met her."

"What is she like?"

Anderson hesitated, then shook his head. "I'll let you discover that for yourself." Opening the door, he said formally, "Your grace, may I present Magda, the Countess Janos." After a respectful bow, he left.

A single branch of candles cast a soft glow over the small, richly furnished room. Rafe's gaze went immediately to the shadowed figure standing by the window. Even though her back was turned to him, he would have known that she was beautiful by the confidence in her graceful carriage.

As he closed the door, she turned to face him with a slow, provocative movement that caused the candlelight to slide tantalizingly over the curves of her lush figure. A feathered fan concealed most of her face, and one wheat gold curl fell charmingly over her shoulder. She radiated sensuality, and Rafe understood why Lucien had said that she could cloud a man's judgment. As his body tightened in involuntary response, he had to admire how well she understood the power of suggestion.

Less subtly, her décolletage was low enough to rivet the attention of any man not yet dead. If Rafe was required to sacrifice his honor in his attempts to persuade the lady, he would do so with great pleasure. "Countess Janos, I'm the Duke of Candover. A mutual friend asked me to speak with you on a matter of some importance."

Her eyes watched mockingly above the fan. "Indeed?" she purred, her words spiced by a Magyar accent. "Perhaps it is of importance to you and Lord Strathmore, Monsieur le Duc, but not to me." Slowly she lowered the fan, revealing high cheekbones, then a small, straight nose. She had creamy rose-petal skin, a wide, sensual mouth. . . .

Rafe's inventory stopped, and his heart began hammering with stunned disbelief. It was said that everyone had a double somewhere in the world, and apparently he had just met Margot Ashton's.

Struggling to control his shock, he tried to compare the countess to his memories. This woman appeared to be about twenty-five years old; Margot would be thirty-one, but she might look younger than her age.

Surely the countess was taller than Margot, who had been only a little above average height? But Margot's bearing and vitality had made her appear taller than

she actually was. It had been a surprise how far he had
had to bend over the first time he kissed her. . . .

Sharply he retreated from his chaotic emotions and
forced himself to continue his analysis. This woman's
eyes seemed to be green, and she had an exotic, foreign look. But she was wearing a green gown, and
Margot's eyes had been changeable, shifting from gray
to green to hazel with her mood and costume.

The resemblance was uncanny, and there were no
differences that could not be ascribed to time or faulty
memory. He had the wild thought that this might be
Margot herself. Though she had been reported dead,
perhaps a mistake had been made; news was often
mangled as it traveled. If Margot had been living on
the Continent all these years, she might no longer have
the air of an Englishwoman.

Yet the countess's behavior implied that they were
strangers. If she was Margot, she must surely recognize him, for he looked much the same. If so, he
couldn't believe that she wouldn't acknowledge him, if
only with a curse.

Instead, she stood with a faint, amused smile during
Rafe's lengthy inspection. The silence had gone on too
long, and as the supplicant, it was up to him to make
the next move.

He fell back on The Duke, who was never at a loss
for words. With a deep bow, he said, "My apologies,
Countess. I was told that you were the most beautiful
spy in Europe, but even so, the description did you less
than justice."

She gave a rich, intimate laugh. Margot's laugh.
"You speak very prettily, your grace. I have heard of
you also."

"Nothing to my discredit, I hope." Rafe decided that
it was time to use his vaunted charm. Stepping toward
the countess, he smiled and said, "You know why I am

here, and it is a serious business. Let us not stand on formality. I would prefer that you use my given name."

"Which is?"

If she was Margot and this was an act, she was performing it superbly well. His smile showing signs of strain, he lifted her hand and kissed it. "Rafael Whitbourne. My friends usually call me Rafe."

She snatched her hand back as if he had bitten it. "Surely a rake should not have been named for an archangel."

At her words, Rafe's doubt vanished. "My God, it *is* you, Margot," he said in a wondering voice. "You are the only one who ever dared mention my lack of similarity to archangels. It was a good quip; I've used it myself many times. But how the devil did you come to be here?"

She gave a languid flutter of her fan. "Who is this Margot, your grace? Some vapid little English girl who resembles me?"

Her denial triggered a surge of the greatest anger Rafe had known in years. He could think of only one sure way to determine the identity of the woman in front of him. With a swift movement, he closed the distance between them, drew her hard against him, and kissed her mocking mouth.

It was Margot; he knew it in his bones. Not only because of the way her body curved into his, or the familiar softness of her lips, but because of a unique, elusive essence that was unmistakably hers.

Even without that recognition he would have known, because he had never met another woman whose touch produced such a blaze of desire. As passion burned through him, he forgot why he was in Paris, forgot the reason for this embrace, forgot everything but the miracle in his arms.

Margot shivered, and for an intoxicating instant she yielded, her body pliant and her mouth opening under his. The years seemed to fall away. Margot was alive, and all was right with the world for the first time in a dozen years. . . .

The moment was over almost before it began. She tried to pull away, but he held her tight a little longer while he explored her mouth and marveled at how little she had changed in this particular way.

When she shoved violently against his chest, he reluctantly released her. She stepped back, her eyes blazing with such rage he thought she might strike him. To himself he acknowledged that she had the right to be angry, and he would have made no effort to avoid a blow.

Instead, in a mercurial change of mood, she laughed with genuine amusement. In her natural English accent she said, "I had you guessing, didn't I?"

"You certainly did." Glad to see a flash of the old Margot, Rafe studied her face, still not quite believing she was real. Why the devil hadn't Lucien told him who the spy was? Then he remembered that none of the other Fallen Angels had met Margot. Not knowing Maggie's real name or background, Lucien had no reason to make a connection between her and Rafe. Trying to sound collected, Rafe said, "Please forgive the impertinence, but it seemed the best way to establish your identity."

"Forgiveness is not my policy," she said flippantly, donning her worldly mask again. It was not an improvement.

She went to the sideboard where glasses and an open bottle of Bordeaux stood. After pouring two glasses of wine, she handed one to Rafe. "Our kind hosts have provided everything a misbehaving couple might want. A pity to waste it all. Pray be seated." She sat in one of the solitary chairs, pointedly ignoring the velvet sofa.

As he settled in the other chair, she said, "Why

should I have been hard to identify? I am said to be well preserved for a woman of my advanced years."

" 'Age cannot wither her . . .'?" He smiled faintly as he quoted the line. "That in itself is a cause of confusion—you scarcely look older now than at eighteen. But the real reason I had trouble deciding if you were Margot Ashton was that you were supposed to be dead."

"I am no longer Margot Ashton," she said, her tone edged, "but neither am I dead. What made you think I was?"

Even now that he knew she was alive, he needed to school his expression before he spoke. "You and your father were in France when the Peace of Amiens ended. It was reported that you were both killed by a French rabble on their way to offer their arms to Napoleon."

Her smoky eyes narrowed with an expression he couldn't interpret. "The news of that reached England?"

"Yes, and it caused quite an uproar. The public was outraged that a distinguished army officer and his beautiful young daughter were murdered simply for being British. However, since we were already at war with the French, no special diplomatic sanctions were possible." He studied her face as he drank his wine. "How much of the story is true?"

"Enough," she said tersely. Setting down her glass, she got to her feet. "You are here to try to persuade me to continue my services to England. You will appeal to my patriotism, then you will offer me a substantial amount of money. I will reject both. Since the outcome is already determined, I see no reason to waste my time listening to you. Good night, and good-bye. I hope you enjoy your stay in Paris."

She started toward the door, but stopped when Rafe raised his hand. "Please, wait a moment."

Now that he knew that "Maggie" was Margot, part of his job was done. She was certainly English, not French, Prussian, Italian, Hungarian, or any other role she chose to play.

Beyond that, he flatly refused to believe that she would ever betray her country. If British state secrets were being sold, it was not by her. But he was uncertain how to proceed. Given the resentment Margot obviously felt for him, Lucien could not have made a worse choice of envoy. "Will you give me ten minutes?" he asked. "I may surprise you with something you don't expect, Margot."

For a moment, the issue waved in the balance. Then she shrugged and took her seat again. "I doubt it, but go ahead. And kindly remember that I am not Margot. I am Maggie."

"What is the difference between the two?"

Her eyes narrowed again. "None of your bloody business, your grace. Please say your piece so that I may leave."

Though it was hard to continue in the face of such hostility, he had to try. "Why must you leave Paris at this particular moment? The new treaty will be negotiated and signed before the end of the year. It may be only a few more weeks."

She made a dismissive gesture. "That argument was used on me at Boney's first abdication. The Congress of Vienna was supposed to be over in six or eight weeks, and lasted nine months instead. Before it was finished, Napoleon had returned and once more my services were indispensable."

She lifted her wineglass and sipped. "I am tired of postponing my life," she said with a trace of weariness. "Bonaparte is on his way to St. Helena to preach his destiny to the seagulls, and it is time for me to take care of some long overdue business."

Sensing that her mood had changed, he risked asking another personal question. "What kind of business?"

She stared down at her glass, swirling the wine. "I will go first to Gascony."

Rafe felt a prickle at the base of his neck as he guessed what she had in mind. "Why?"

She looked up at him, her face expressionless. "To find my father's body and take it back to England. It has been twelve years. It will take time to find where they buried him."

Though he had guessed correctly, he took no pleasure in it. The wine tasted bitter on his tongue, for he must speak of something he would have preferred to keep private. "There is no need to go to Gascony. You won't find your father there."

Her brows drew together. "What do you mean?"

"I happened to be in Paris when news of your deaths arrived, so I went to the village in Gascony where the murders had taken place. I was told that two fresh graves belonged to *'les deux Anglais,'* and assumed that you and your father were buried there. I arranged to have the bodies returned to England. They are in the family plot on your uncle's estate."

The worldly veneer dissolved and she bent over, burying her face in her hands. Rafe wished he could comfort her, but knew that there was nothing she would accept from him.

He had envied the friendly, loving relationship between Margot and her father, so different from the distant politeness between Rafe and his own sire. Colonel Ashton had been an affable, direct soldier, less interested in seeing his daughter a duchess than in seeing her happy. His death at the hands of a mob would have devastated her.

After a long silence, Maggie raised her head. Her eyes were unnaturally bright, but her face was composed. "The second coffin must have been Willis, my father's orderly. He was a small man, about my height. The two of them ... gave a good account of themselves when we were attacked."

She stood and crossed to the window, pushing the heavy brocade drapery aside to gaze down into the boulevard. Her haunted image was reflected in the dark glass. "Uncle Willy was almost a member of the family. He taught me how to shoot dice and cheat at cards. My father would have been appalled if he had known."

A faint smile crossed her face, then vanished. "I'm glad that Willis is in England—he would have loathed the thought of his bones spending eternity in France. I was going to take his body back as well, but you have made that unnecessary."

She turned to face Rafe, no longer hostile. "Why did you do it? It couldn't have been easy."

Indeed it hadn't been, even for a young man of wealth and determination. Rafe had come to France with the secret hope of finding Margot. Even when war threatened to break out again, he had postponed his departure.

Then, just as the Peace of Amiens ended, news of their deaths at the hands of a mob had reached Paris. A sensible man would have instantly returned to London to avoid being interned for the duration of the war. Rafe, who had not been sensible where Margot was concerned, had instead sent his servants home and made his way across France alone, using his excellent French to pass as a native.

It had taken weeks to locate the graves. Because of the danger, he had taken the lead-encased coffins over the Pyrenees into Spain rather than risk crossing France again.

The two coffins had been reinterred at the Ashton family estate in Leicestershire. With his own hands Rafe had planted daffodils on the smaller grave, because he had met Margot in the spring and daffodils always reminded him of her. He would not speak of that. The action was not only maudlin and sentimental, but vaguely laughable since hindsight now showed that he had acted under a misapprehension.

He wondered where Margot had been when he was in Gascony. Injured perhaps, or a prisoner in the local jail? If he had searched, could he have found her and brought her home? But that also was no longer relevant, so he said merely, "There was nothing else I could do for you. It was too late for apologies."

After a long pause, she asked, "Why did you feel it was necessary to apologize?"

"Because I behaved very badly, of course." He shrugged. "The more time passed, the worse my behavior looked."

Maggie took a deep, slow breath. She should have known this interview would not go according to plan. Rafe Whitbourne had always been able to find the vulnerable spots in her. That sensitivity had been welcome when they were young and in love, but it was intolerable now that love was gone. She hated losing her control in front of him.

When she was sure her voice would be even, she looked directly at him and said, "I am obligated to you." Cynically she wondered if he would try to use her sense of duty to persuade her to stay in Paris.

Instead, he said, "There is no obligation. I suppose I did it for myself as much as for you."

His quiet disclaimer bound her as nothing else could have. Resigned, she said, "You can tell Lord Strathmore that I will stay and continue working until the conference is over and the treaty is resolved. Is that satisfactory?"

He wisely refrained from any show of triumph when he answered. "Very good, especially since there is more at stake here than routine information gathering. Lord Strathmore has a special task for you."

"Oh?" Maggie returned to her chair. "What does Strathmore want me to do?"

"He has heard hints of a plot to assassinate one of the major figures here at the peace conference. He would like you to investigate as quickly and thoroughly as you can."

Maggie frowned, personal considerations forgotten. "Just three weeks ago a plot to assassinate the king, the tsar, and Wellington was exposed. Could that be the source of the rumors?"

"No, Lucien was aware of that affair, and this seems to be separate. What makes this new conspiracy so dangerous are indications that it originates in the highest diplomatic circles of the conference. Not only will it be harder to detect, but it means the conspirators have better access to their targets." Rafe reached inside his coat and pulled out a folded and sealed sheet of paper. "Lucien sent this to explain what he knows."

Maggie accepted the note and made it disappear. "Did you read what he wrote?"

His brows arched. "Of course not. It was sent to you."

"You'd never make a spy."

Rafe's voice was silky, but for the first time emotion showed through. "Quite true. I could never match your talent for deceit and betrayal."

Maggie whipped herself upright in the chair, her kidskin slippers slapping to the floor as the room pulsed with the unspoken past. For a moment her fury threatened to spill out, but years of hard training stood her in good stead and she managed to master herself. "No, I'm sure you couldn't," she said acidly. "When your fairy godmother waved her wand over the ducal crib, the special gifts she bestowed were stubbornness and self-righteousness."

Their gazes locked—two angry, passionate people determined to give nothing away. Rafe was the first to

regain his control, probably because he needed her
more than she needed him.

Shrugging off the insult, he said, "No doubt you are
right—I never claimed to have an admirable character.
To return to business, do you think Lucien is right to
be concerned? He is going mostly on guesswork." His
long fingers toyed with the stem of his goblet. "Of
course, Luce is a brilliant guesser. You're closer to the
situation. What's your opinion?"

Glad to leave the charged emotions that kept surfac-
ing, Maggie said, "I've heard nothing in particular, but
there has been a surprising silence from the radicals. It
isn't like them to give up as long as there are still
young men left to die for their revolutionary ideals."

Curious about another point, she continued, "You
use Lord Strathmore's first name. You know him
well?"

"Very. You used to tease me about being part of a
group nicknamed the Fallen Angels. Luce was another
member. Since I was a little older than my friends, I
finished at Oxford and went to London a year earlier.
Luce and the others were still at university when you
had your London Season."

Maggie had only met Lord Strathmore twice during
the years she had worked with him, but he had left a
strong impression. It was strange to learn that he was
a close friend of Rafe's. The world was indeed a small
place. "As I recall, the four of you acquired the nickname because of some unholy combination of angelic
looks and diabolical deeds."

She had hoped to disconcert Rafe, but he only
smiled slightly. "Both the looks and the deeds were exaggerated."

Her hand tightened around the handle of her fan.
The deeds might have been an exaggeration, but not
the looks. Rafe had been glorious at twenty-one; now
maturity had added power to his tall frame, character

to his face, and authority to his presence,. Though she recalled that his dark coloring had come from an Italian grandmother, she had forgotten how dramatic a contrast his clear gray eyes made.

She wished she were immune to his attractions, but she wasn't. What made it worse was that she was no longer an innocent girl; she was a woman, and she knew something of passion. And of longing . . .

Thank God she wouldn't need to see Rafe again; he was having a terrible effect on her concentration. Getting to her feet, she said, "I'll start investigating immediately. If I hear anything important, I'll notify my contact in the British delegation. Now if you'll excuse me, there are some people I must talk to."

He stood also, his expression wary. "There is one more thing: Lucien wants you to work with me on this, not with the delegation."

"What!" Maggie exclaimed. "Why the devil should I waste time dealing with an amateur? If there is a conspiracy afoot, time is critical. At the risk of insulting your grace's consequence, you would only get in the way."

Rafe's lips tightened, but he kept his voice level. "Lucien suspects that someone in the British delegation is either careless or treacherous, and this matter is too important to take chances. He wants you to report to me. We've set up a temporary courier service between here and London to keep him informed. If events warrant it, I'll go directly to Castlereagh or Wellington."

"How nice to know that Strathmore trusts them," she said with heavy sarcasm. "However, I prefer to work in my own way."

"I am not in a position to compel you," Rafe said gently, "but for the sake of the task at hand, do you think you could manage to choke down your repugnance and work with me? It won't be for very long."

Maggie glared at him, suppressing the desire to pour

the rest of her wine over his head to see if that would disturb his impenetrable calm. Unfortunately, there was no compelling reason not to work with him except for her personal distaste, and like it or not, she was under a heavy obligation to him. Through slightly gritted teeth, she said, "Very well, I will let you know whatever I find."

After she set down her wineglass and opened the door to leave, he said, "Let me give you my direction."

She smiled at him wickedly. "No need. I already know where you are staying, the names of your groom and valet, and the number of pieces of luggage you brought." Having finally managed to produce a surprised look on the Duke of Candover's face, she added sweetly, "Remember, information is my business."

Maggie felt rather pleased as she left. At least she had gotten the last word for tonight.

A pity it wouldn't be the last word with him forever.

Chapter 3

After Maggie swept from the room, Rafe released a long, exhausted breath. For years he had cherished romantic memories of the girl he had loved and lost, with occasional speculations about what might have been. It was jarring to have that nostalgia shattered by the very real presence of the former beloved, now alive, impudent, and dismayingly competent.

He finished his wine, then set the glass on the sideboard. For all the haunting flashes of Margot Ashton, this woman was a stranger, hardened and unpredictable in ways he would never understand. The girl he had loved no longer existed, and he wasn't at all sure he liked this Maggie with her cool, polished surface and her prickliness. She acted as if he had been the one to betray her so many years ago, not vice versa.

He sighed and stood up. Most truths had more than one aspect; perhaps her memories of the incident were different from his. It didn't matter now. It takes youth to risk the appalling dangers of total love, and Rafe knew that he was no longer capable of that.

But he had been wrong on one point; he had thought no woman could be as desirable as his memories of Margot. As it turned out, she was even more alluring than he remembered. It had been difficult to keep his hands to himself even when she was spitting insults.

As he stepped into the corridor to return to the ball, he reminded himself that he was not in Paris to romance her, reminisce with her, or to make childish taunts, no matter how great the provocation. What mattered was the conference, and the lives of the men who were trying to build a lasting peace.

Before proceeding to her next rendezvous, Maggie stepped into a dark side passage for a moment to regroup her forces. Leaning against the wall and closing her eyes, she mentally went through the profanity that she knew fluently in five languages.

Damn Robin for talking her into meeting the Duke of Candover, damn Rafe Whitbourne both for his impenetrable coolness, and for that shattering kiss that proved that Margot was not as dead as Maggie had thought. Most of all, she damned herself for the faint, irrepressible anticipation she felt at the thought of seeing him again.

She reminded herself furiously that a kiss meant nothing to him. He must have participated in hundreds over the years. Probably not hundreds but *thousands*.

Which was why he was so very good at kissing . . .

The thought revived her fury. She was all the way down to Slovakian curses before she could laugh at herself and resume her journey. Her destination was another assignation room, a near-twin of the one she had just left. She entered without knocking and found Robin sprawled on the sofa with a glass of wine in his hand, for all the world like a lover eagerly awaiting a lady. Which was, after all, more or less the truth.

He started to rise, but she waved him back. "No need to get up." She moved his feet from the sofa so she could sit down next to him, wanting the comfort of his familiar presence.

As he interpreted her expression, the look of fatuous vacuity he cultivated changed to amused intelligence. "Dare I ask how your confrontation with the duke came out?"

She sighed. "You and he win. I'll be staying through the end of the peace conference, no matter how long it takes."

Robin gave a soft whistle of surprise. "How did Candover accomplish that? If he has found some miraculous technique to persuade you, I should ask him what it is."

Maggie chuckled and patted his hand. "Don't bother, my dear. His method was not one that anyone else could use." Her brief amusement faded. "He happened to be in France when my father and Willis were killed, and he arranged to take the bodies back to England. They have been buried at my uncle's estate the last dozen years."

Robin looked at her narrowly. While it was good that she was staying, this new fact suggested a myriad of interesting questions. How well had Maggie known the duke, and were there implications here that might affect his own plans? Keeping those thoughts to himself, he asked, "Is it possible that he lied about that, to convince you to stay here?"

Maggie was startled by the question; it had never occurred to her to doubt Rafe's word. She did not pause to reconsider before shaking her head. "No, he's one of your proper English gentlemen, without enough imagination to lie."

Robin grinned, looking irresistibly boyish. "Haven't I convinced you yet that not all Englishmen are gentlemen?"

"You, Robin, are sui generis, absolutely one of a kind. The fact that you are English is a mere accident of birth." Maggie smiled at him affectionately. In spite of all his strenuous objections to the contrary, Robin was completely a gentleman, more so than Rafe Whitbourne had proved to be.

Over the years she had often wondered about Robin's background. She suspected that he was the illegitimate son of a noble house, raised and educated among gentlemen but forever an outsider in the ranks of polite society. That would explain why he showed no desire to return to his native land. But she had never asked for confirmation, and Robin had never volunteered. Though in many ways they were very close, some subjects were not discussed.

"Your suggestion to tantalize the duke with my irresistible body was a dead loss, by the way," she added wryly. "It wouldn't have mattered if I were as beautiful as Helen of Troy, or as ugly as Madame de Staël. The duke's noble mind is above such crass matters as lust, at least when he is engaged on His Britannic Majesty's business." His kiss, after all, had only been a way to confirm her identity.

"He merely has superhuman control. Seeing you in that gown tempts me to lock the door and overpower you with kisses myself."

Maggie glanced away, not wanting to deal with what lay beneath his teasing tone. "Before I return to England, I'm going to acquire an entire wardrobe of gowns that come up to my throat. It's tedious to have men always talking to one's chest rather than one's face."

Serious again, Robin said, "Why did Candover do something as extraordinary as returning your father's body to England? It must have been very difficult to arrange."

"I imagine it was." Maggie was reluctant to tell even Robin her history with the duke. Choosing part of the truth, she said, "He and my father were friends." Before Robin could inquire further, she went on, "For your sins, you can now learn about the urgent project Candover dropped onto our plates."

Succinctly she outlined what Rafe had said about a possible plot hidden in Parisian diplomatic circles. At the end, she produced the paper Lord Strathmore had sent, and she and Robin read it together.

"If Strathmore is right, this is deadly serious," Robin said soberly. "There have been other conspiracies, but always by insignificant people far from the centers of power. This plot looks different."

"I know," she said thoughtfully. "I can already think of several names to put behind this conspiracy."

"So can I, all men who will be impossible to accuse without rock-solid proof, even if we were sure ourselves."

"After you and I have both checked with our informants, it may reduce the number of possibilities."

"Or it may increase them. All we can do is get to work and hope for the best." He glanced at the letter again. "You're disobeying orders—according to this, you should have nothing to do with anyone in the delegation save Castlereagh and Wellington. What if I'm Strathmore's weak link?"

"Nonsense," she retorted. "He means the regular delegation, not you. You've worked with Strathmore longer than I have."

As Robin got to his feet, he shook his head with mock sorrow. "I see that all my lessons have been wasted. How many times have I told you not to trust anyone, even me?"

"If I can't trust you, who can I trust?"

He dropped a light kiss on her cheek. "Yourself, of course. I'll leave first. Shall I come by tomorrow night so we can discuss our findings?"

She nodded and watched him don his low-level diplomat's face. Every delegation was cursed with junior officers who had better family connections than wits, and Robin looked like one of those: ineffectual and too handsome to have a brain. In reality, of course, he had a mind like Saracen steel, highly polished and razor sharp. It was he who had taught her how to gather and analyze facts that might be of value, as well as how to cover her own tracks and avoid suspicion.

But he was wrong on one count, she thought as she prepared to return to the ball. At the moment, she was not at all sure she could trust herself. Her life was no longer entirely under her own control, and she didn't like it one bit.

Downstairs, the ball churned on exactly as Rafe had left it, with too many costumes, scents, and languages struggling for notice. Seeing nothing that encouraged him to stay, he started working his way across the room toward the exit.

Because of the crowd, he had no warning before coming face-to-face with Oliver Northwood. Rafe was hard-pressed to conceal his shock. Bloody hell, it only needed this!

The other man did not share his feelings. "Candover!" Northwood said jovially. "Splendid to see you. I had no idea you were in Paris, but of course, half the *ton* has come over. Too many years trapped on our island, don't you know."

He laughed heartily at his own wit and offered his hand, which Rafe accepted without enthusiasm.

Northwood was a beefy blond man of medium height, a younger son of Lord Northwood and almost a caricature of the hearty country squire. The first year that Rafe had been on the town, when his closest friends were still at Oxford, he had moved in the same circles as Northwood. Though not close, they had been on amiable terms, until Northwood's disastrous role in ending Rafe's engagement. Rafe knew it was irrational to blame the other man for what had happened, but he had done his best to avoid him ever since.

Unfortunately, there was no way to avoid him now. "Good evening, Northwood," Rafe said with what patience he could muster. "Have you been in Paris long?"

"I'm with the British delegation, been here since July. M'father thought I should get some diplomatic experience." Northwood shook his head mournfully. "Wants me to settle down and take a seat in Parliament, make myself useful, y'know."

Parisian diplomatic circles were small, so they would be running into each other often. Rafe resigned himself to being civil. "Is your wife here with you?"

He was unprepared for the ugly glint that came into Northwood's eyes as he looked across the room. "Oh, Cynthia's here. A sociable female like her wouldn't miss the opportunity to ... make so many new acquaintances."

Following the direction of the glance, Rafe saw Cynthia Northwood at the edge of the ballroom, in earnest conversation with a dark, handsome British infantry major. Even at this distance Rafe could see how absorbed they were in each other, as if they were alone instead of in the midst of a crowd.

Knowing better than to comment, Rafe returned his gaze to Oliver Northwood and decided to start gathering information. "How are the negotiations going?"

Northwood shrugged. "Hard to say. Castlereagh plays everything very close to his chest, y'know, don't let us underlings do much except copy documents. But I'm sure you've heard that the first problem—what to do with Napoleon—has been taken care of. They were thinking of exiling him to Scotland, but decided it was too close to Europe."

"St. Helena should be far enough away to reduce the opportunities for mischief. But one can't help thinking that it would have been simpler if Marshal Blücher had been able to capture Bonaparte and shoot him out of hand, as he wanted to."

Northwood laughed. "It certainly would have, but once the emperor surrendered to the British, we were stuck with preserving his wretched hide."

"One has to admire the man's effrontery, not to mention his cunning," Rafe agreed. "After calling Britain the most powerful, steadfast, and generous of his enemies, there was no way the Prince Regent could throw him to the wolves, even though most of the British people would cheerfully see Boney in hell."

"Instead, he retires at British expense to an island that is supposed to have one of the best climates in the world. Still, if he'd stayed on Elba I wouldn't be here in Paris now." Northwood gave a man-to-man chuckle. "It certainly is true what they say about the Parisian ladies, isn't it, Candover?"

Rafe gave one of his coldest stares. "I've only just arrived and have no opinion on the subject."

Immune to the setdown, Northwood glanced toward a side door in time to see Maggie return to the ball, her golden hair shimmering above the provocative green gown. She looked every inch the highborn trollop. Northwood stared, his jaw slack. "Say, would you look at that blond doxy! Must have been upstairs with some lucky devil. Think I'd have any success if I asked her for an encore?"

It took Rafe a moment to register that Northwood was referring to Maggie. He had never thought of her as blond, a word that conjured up thoughts of pale anemic maidens. Maggie's glowing cream-and-gold vitality was too vivid for such an insipid description. When he did realize who Northwood meant, Rafe felt a powerful urge to use his fists to wipe the smirk off his companion's face.

He held his breath until the impulse faded, then said, "I doubt it. I met the lady earlier, and she struck me as particular in her tastes."

The implied insult also bounced off Northwood's impenetrable skin. "Tell me about her." He frowned as Maggie disappeared into a clump of Austrian officers. "You know, she looks familiar, but I can't quite remember ..." He snapped his fingers. "That's it! She reminds me of an English girl I knew years ago. Margaret, no, Margot, something."

Rafe's stomach turned. "Do you mean Miss Margot Ashton?"

"Yes, she's the one. You were after her yourself, weren't you? Was she as good as she looked?" The coarse laugh left no doubt about the kind of relationship that Northwood assumed Rafe had had with Margot.

Rafe took another deep breath. Had Northwood always been this vulgar, or had he gotten worse with the years? Icily he said, "I wouldn't know. I barely remember Miss Ashton. Didn't she die a year or so after her come-out?" He made a pretense of studying Maggie. "I suppose there is some resemblance between them, but the lady you are admiring is Hungarian— Magda, the Countess Janos."

"Hungarian, eh? I've never had a Hungarian. Will you introduce me?"

Deciding that if he didn't leave in the next ten seconds, he would do Northwood serious bodily harm, Rafe said, "Unfortunately I have a pressing engagement, but I'm sure you can find some other mutual acquaintance. If you will excuse me ... ?" He was on the point of escaping when someone latched on to his right arm. With a sense of tired inevitability, he looked down into Cynthia Northwood's wide brown eyes.

"Rafe!" she exclaimed. "How delightful to see you here. Will you be staying in Paris for a while?"

Cynthia was an attractive young woman with dark curls, a heart-shaped face, and an expression of misleading innocence. Her firm grip prevented Rafe's escape. Besides, she had been his mistress for a time and they had parted amiably, so he could hardly repulse her.

"Yes, I've taken apartments and intend to stay

through the autumn, perhaps longer." Gently he disengaged his arm. "Pray have a thought for my valet. He is so protective of my coats that I'm surprised he actually lets me wear them."

"I'm sorry," she said apologetically. "It comes from being in Paris, you know. People are so much more demonstrative here. I'm afraid it is contagious."

"Is *that* your excuse?" her husband asked nastily.

Rafe felt the tension as the two glared at each other. Knowing that he absolutely must escape before they started a public scene of the sort he most detested, he made the barest of farewells, then slid away into the crowd. This time he made sure that no one could catch his eye.

Outside in the warm night air, he gave a sigh of relief. Since it was still early, he decided to dismiss his carriage and walk back to his hotel. It would be interesting to see what Napoleon had done to the city. More important, he needed time to get his disordered thoughts under control.

First Margot—it was still hard to think of her as Maggie—whose very presence was a disruption and a reminder of things best forgotten. And as if that wasn't enough, the Northwoods. The evening might have been designed by the devil in a farcical mood.

But it was hard to be amused by a farce that made him feel as if he had been kicked in the stomach. As he walked unseeing toward the Tuileries, events came back to him with the clarity of yesterday rather than thirteen years before.

He had loved Margot Ashton with uncritical adoration, awed and humble that a girl who could have her choice of London's most eligible men had chosen him. They had behaved discreetly in public since their engagement had been unannounced, but he had spent every possible moment with her. She had seemed as happy in his company as he was in hers.

Then had come that fatal bachelor party in June. He could remember the name of every young man in the group that night, could recall with excruciating accuracy how Oliver Northwood had drunkenly described relieving a girl of her unwanted virginity in the garden during a ball some days earlier. Rafe had scarcely paid attention, until the end, when Northwood had let slip the girl's name: Margot Ashton.

Most of the young men were admirers of Margot, and after a stunned moment, one of them had shushed Northwood, saying that it was ungentlemanly to speak so of a young lady. But the damage had already been done.

No one present knew of the engagement, so they thought nothing of it when Rafe excused himself a few minutes later. The green tinge of his face was attributed to the quantity of claret he had drunk, and he was forgotten as soon as he left the room.

Outside, Rafe had made it no farther than the street when he fell to his knees and began retching. Feeling as if his very guts would spew out, he thought of Margot's body under that drunken sot, her full lips kissing his, her long legs entwined . . .

The vision had burned on his brain with nauseating clarity. He had no idea how long it was before someone said, "You all right, lad? I'll call a chair for you." The Samaritan helped him to his feet, but Rafe had refused further aid, heading blindly down the street as if he could outrun his imagination.

He had spent the rest of the night walking the streets of London, heedless of his direction. More than once lurkers in the shadows considered the richness of his attire, balanced it against the expression on his face, and decided to let him continue unmolested on his journey. The young gentleman might be worth a pretty penny, but his dead gray eyes threatened disaster to any thief foolish enough to try to collect it.

Inevitably, he had ended up at Margot's house early the next morning, just before she left for her dawn ride. They had not planned to meet, but he had joined her unannounced before.

She had greeted him with delight despite his disheveled evening attire. An emerald-colored veil had floated over her wheat gold hair as she danced across the salon for a welcoming kiss, her changeable eyes green in the early morning, her laughing face brimming with life.

Rafe had pulled violently away, unable to bear her touch. Then he told her what he had learned, heaping abuse on her golden head. He knew her passionate nature, and only his idealistic desire to bring her a virgin to the marriage bed had prevented him from taking what she had so casually given to another man.

How many others had there been? She was much sought after; had he been the only one too foolish to sample her luscious flesh? Had she accepted his offer among so many only because he was heir to a dukedom? On those early morning rides, could he have mounted her as well as his stallion if he had had the temerity to ask?

Margot made no attempt to deny it. Had she offered the feeblest of defenses, he would have grasped it with craven gratitude. If she had wept and begged his forgiveness, he would have granted it, even knowing that he would never be able to trust her again.

He would have beggared himself of his whole life's pride if she had given him the barest reason to do so.

She had merely listened, her creamy complexion turning dead white. She did not even ask the name of the man who had revealed her wantonness—perhaps there were so many men that it didn't matter. Instead, she had said calmly that it was fortunate that they had discovered each other's true natures before it was too late.

Her reaction had been a death knell, for Rafe had been unable to suppress a desperate hope that the story was untrue. In that instant, something in him had withered and died.

Though they were not officially engaged, he had given her a Whitbourne heirloom ring, which she wore on a chain around her neck. When she finished speaking, she pulled it from between her breasts, breaking the gold links in her eagerness to be free. Then she had hurled the ring to the floor at Rafe's feet with such force that the large opal cracked.

Murmuring that she did not wish to keep her horse standing any longer in the cool air, she had walked out with her head held high, no emotion visible. He had never seen her again. Within days, she and her father had taken advantage of the newly negotiated Peace of Amiens and left for the Continent.

As the months passed, Rafe's fury and sense of betrayal were gradually overcome by his longing for Margot. He found himself waiting with hope and pain for the Ashtons to return to England. After almost a year of agonizing, he had gone to France, determined to find her again. If he had succeeded, he would have begged her to marry him.

Then in Paris the news had come that it was forever too late. The only thing he could do to make amends was bringing the bodies of her and her father back to England.

As time passed, Rafe had convinced himself that it was fortunate that she had died before he could abase himself to her. The thought of being married to a woman before whom he was so helpless was not a pleasant one.

The Seasons and the Beauties had come and gone since then, and few remembered the glorious Margot Ashton who had been so briefly the toast of London. Rafe had learned to take his pleasures from the skilled and willing married women of his set, kissing lightly and letting go gracefully. Not for him the tawdry problems of getting birds of paradise out of the lovenest when they were loath to go; he saw no reason for a man to pay for a mistress when there were so many volunteers available for the price of a few compliments and an occasional bauble.

Rafe had taken particular pleasure in cuckolding Oliver Northwood. Cynthia Browne had been a pretty, happy girl, the daughter of a prosperous country squire. It had been considered an excellent match for her to marry the younger son of a lord. Oliver had been attractive in a bluff, blond way, and she had not realized the kind of man she was getting.

After learning of her husband's gambling, drunkenness, and whoring, she had bitterly decided to play the same game. Though she was not promiscuous by nature, she had started taking lovers of her own. It was tragic, really; with a loving husband she would have been a devoted wife and mother. Instead, she gave herself to any man who wanted her.

Rafe had been quite willing to oblige. Not only was Cynthia attractive, but the affair fulfilled an ignoble desire for revenge. Though Northwood would never know how his indiscretion had shattered Rafe's life, there was still satisfaction in paying the man back by bedding Northwood's wife.

The affair had not lasted long, for Cynthia's desperation had made Rafe uncomfortable. He had disengaged himself gracefully, as he was so skilled at doing. In the years since, he had sometimes seen Cynthia socially, and been pleased to see her regain her equilibrium, no longer holding herself cheaply.

There had been recent rumors linking her with a soldier, perhaps the major she had been talking with at the ball. Rafe wondered if she really loved the man, or if she was using him as still another weapon in her war with her husband.

Her tactics seemed to be working. Oliver Northwood was apparently the sort of man who would chase anything in skirts, but was enraged when his wife claimed the same freedom to amuse herself. One of them would probably end up murdering the other.

As he went up the steps to his hotel, Rafe swore that he would not let himself get caught in their crossfire. Paris promised to be unpleasant enough without that.

Chapter 4

Even before her eyes opened the next morning, Maggie remembered her encounter with Rafe Whitbourne, and shuddered. Impossible man! Usually she admired calm English control, but the same trait infuriated her in Rafe. Whatever warmth and spontaneity he had had as a young man had obviously dissipated over time.

She lay still in bed, listening to the sounds of early morning—the creak of a cart, occasional footsteps, the cry of a distant rooster. Ordinarily she rose at this hour, had a cup of coffee and a hot croissant, and went for a ride out at Longchamps. This morning she simply groaned and pulled the covers over her head, burrowing farther into the feather mattress as she planned a busy day of spying.

Half an hour later, Maggie rang her maid Inge for breakfast. As she sipped strong French coffee, she jotted down the names of the informants she wished to contact first.

While it was popularly supposed that a female spy gathered information on her back, Maggie scorned that method as too limited, tiring, and indiscriminant. Her technique was different, and as far as she knew, unique: she had formed the world's first female spy network.

Men with secrets might be cautious with other men, but were often amazingly casual in front of women. Maids, washerwomen, prostitutes, and other humble females were often in a position to learn what was going on, and Maggie had a talent for persuading them to confide in her.

Europe was full of women who had lost fathers, husbands, sons, and lovers in Bonaparte's wars. Many were glad to pass on information that might contribute to peace. Some wanted revenge as much as Maggie did; others were impoverished and desperately needed money. Together, they made up what Robin called Maggie's Militia.

Vital documents could be put together from scraps in trash baskets, important papers were sometimes left in the pockets of clothes sent for washing, men bragged of their deeds to their conquests. Maggie cultivated the women who had access to such data, listening to their joys and sorrows, sometimes giving them money to feed their children even when they had no information to sell.

In return, they gave her loyalty beyond anything that could be purchased. None had ever betrayed her, and many had become friends.

Since losing her father, Maggie had spent the largest part of her time in Paris, disguised as a humble widow with drab clothing and a mob cap over her bright hair. When the Congress of Vienna was called, she had resumed her natural appearance and gone to Vienna as the Countess Janos, where she had moved among the diplomats at their own social level.

When Napoleon had escaped from Elba and reclaimed his crown, she had immediately returned to her post in Paris so she could send information to London. After Waterloo, most of the diplomats and hangers-on from the Congress had convened again in Paris, so she had resurrected the countess and rented a house worthy of her rank. But she was getting very tired of being someone other than herself.

Over the years Robert Anderson had played many

parts. He had helped her become established in her covert career, and had channeled the money that enabled her to live comfortably and pay her informants. He had also created her lines of communication, not easy when Napoleon's Continental System had closed almost all European ports to the British. At various times information had been sent through Spain, Sweden, Denmark, even Constantinople.

Of necessity, Robin had traveled extensively. Maggie guessed that sometimes he carried vital messages to England himself, crossing the Channel secretly with smugglers. He spent about a third of his time with Maggie, with months passing between visits. His work was far more dangerous than hers, and she was always relieved when he reappeared, jaunty and intact.

For most of those years they had been lovers. Even in the beginning, when she had been in desperate need of his kindness, she had known that what she felt for him was friendship and gratitude, not romantic love. Yet she had drifted along, enjoying the warmth and physical satisfaction they found together. He was her best friend, the man she trusted most in the world, the brother she had never had.

Then one day, three years before, she had woken up with a powerful conviction that friendship was not enough, and that the time had come to end their intimacy. She owed Robin so much, and cared for him so deeply, that it had been wretchedly difficult to say that she no longer wanted to share his bed.

But he had always been the most considerate of lovers, and he had made it easy for her. After she had made her halting statement, he had gone very still for a moment. Then he said calmly that of course he didn't want her to do anything that made her uncomfortable.

They were still friends, they had continued to work together, and he had still lived with her when he was in Paris. The only difference was that he had a separate room.

The fact that Robin had accepted the change in their relationship with such good grace confirmed that he also viewed her more as a friend than as a life's partner. Though he had offered to marry her shortly after he had saved her life, she knew that he had been relieved when she had turned him down.

Still, though she never doubted that she had done the right thing, her bed had been cold and lonely. No doubt that was why Rafe looked so blasted attractive.... Hastily she changed the direction of her thoughts.

Robin had recently emerged from the murkier pools of spying to join the British embassy as a clerk. Maggie assumed that his identity was known to Lord Castlereagh, but the rest of the mission probably thought he was merely an agreeable rattle of no particular ability.

She was glad that he was nearby, and not only because she enjoyed his company. Given the possible threat to the peace negotiations, his remarkable talents were needed.

After deciding on her plan of action, Maggie donned her inconspicuous widow costume and set off to visit her most useful informants. If her women knew what to look for, they should be able to add to Maggie's sketchy knowledge. And if she was lucky, her friend Hélène Sorel would soon be back in Paris and able to assist in the task.

Over pot-au-feu, a long baguette of bread, and a jug of wine, Maggie and Robin discussed what they had learned in the last twenty-four hours. Splitting the last of the wine between them, she said, "We're agreed then?"

"Yes, the three men we have decided on are the most likely masterminds, though we'll have to watch half a dozen more." Robin ran a tired hand through his fair hair. "Even then, we may not have the right man."

"Well, it's the best we can do. I suppose we could warn the guards around the most important persons, but there have been so many other plots that everyone is already cautious."

"True." Robin studied Maggie's face. There were shadows under the changeable gray-green eyes, as if she had slept badly. "I have an idea you're not going to like."

Maggie's mouth quirked up. "I have disliked the majority of your ingenious ideas over the years, so don't let that stop you."

Refusing to respond to her teasing, he said, "I think that you and Candover should pretend you are lovers."

"What!" Maggie banged her glass down so hard the wine sloshed out. "Why the devil should I do a mad thing like that?"

"Hear me out, Maggie. Our suspects are all senior officials who divide their time between fighting over the treaty and attending salons and balls with the rest of the diplomatic corps. The best way to approach them is by going to the same places."

"Can't you do that?"

"I'm not important enough. A junior clerk would be out of place at the more exclusive functions."

"Why can't I go by myself?"

Robin said patiently, "Maggie, you're being unreasonable. It was bad enough going to that Austrian ball alone—if you do it again, it will be assumed that you are looking for a lover. You'll spend all your time fighting off men who are interested in you for nonpolitical reasons."

"I have had ample experience dealing with that!"

Ignoring her interjection, he continued, "Candover is a perfect escort. He's important enough to be invited everywhere, yet he has no official government position. And, of course, he's a friend of Strathmore's and here to help us investigate this conspiracy. If you and he go about together, you can go anywhere and talk to anyone without rousing suspicion."

Fighting a valiant rearguard action, Maggie said, "Do you think it's really necessary for me to do this, Robin?"

"Your intuition is the best weapon we've got." He caught her eye, trying to impress his opinion on her. "Time and again you have felt there was something wrong about a person we had no reason to suspect, and have been proved right. In the absence of hard evidence we are going to need every advantage we have, which means you must get well enough acquainted with our suspects to develop an opinion, and perhaps pick up some clues. But you can't do that unless you get close to them."

"You're right," she said reluctantly. "If I knew them well, they wouldn't be on our list because I would already have an excellent notion of their innocence or guilt. But I don't know if I can make convincing cow-eyes at Candover. I'm more likely to throw a glass of wine in his arrogant face."

Robin relaxed, knowing he had won his point. "I'm sure that someone with your magnificent acting skills can do a good job of draping yourself over the duke. In fact, I should think most women would envy you the job."

Ignoring her snort, he added, "Besides, this investigation might be very dangerous, much more so than your usual sort of work. We're talking about desperate men, and time is running out for them. The Allied rulers are all anxious to finalize the treaty and return to their kingdoms. They should be gone by the end of September at the latest, so if anything is going to happen, it will be in the next two or three weeks."

"So?" she prompted.

"If someone suspects you, your life could be for-feit," he said bluntly. "Candover might not be a profes-sional agent, but he looks like he'd be useful in a fight. Since I can't be near you most of the time, I'll feel bet-ter if he is."

"Since when have you decided that I am incapable of taking care of myself?" she snapped.

"Maggie," he said gently, "no one is invulnerable, no matter how clever he—or she—is."

Her face paled at the reference. Robin didn't like re-minding her of the circumstances of their first meeting, but wanted to ensure that she would be cautious. He knew from experience that Maggie was brave to the point of recklessness.

After a moment she gave him a resigned smile. "Very well, Robin. Assuming Candover can be con-vinced to cooperate, he and I shall become an object of gossip. We will be seen everywhere, and will appear so enraptured that no one will suspect us of having a use-ful thought in our heads."

"Good." He stood. "Time to go. I have to meet someone who never lets himself be seen by the light of day."

Maggie rose also. "Since time is in short supply, I'll pay a visit to Candover and explain his dire fate to him. But if he objects, I will give you the job of con-vincing him."

Robin shook his head. "I think it better that he not know of our connection. You know the first rule of spying."

" 'Never tell anyone anything he doesn't need to know,' " she quoted. "I suppose you're right. Candover is an amateur at these games, and the less he knows, the better."

"Let's hope he proves to be a talented amateur." Af-ter a light farewell kiss, Robin was gone. Maggie closed the door on him with a sense of vexation. Here he was, worried about her safety, when she expected that what he was doing was twice as dangerous.

She shrugged and climbed the stairs to her room. If she had been of a nervous disposition, she would never have lasted long as a spy. Far better to spend her time wondering how she was going to tolerate so much time around Rafael Whitbourne.

In stage-mad Paris, the playhouses were an accurate barometer of public opinion, so Rafe decided to spend the evening at the theater. It was a disquieting experience.

All playhouse managers had been ordered to admit free of charge a certain number of soldiers from the armies of occupation. Unfortunately, what had been intended as a goodwill gesture had resulted tonight in brawling in the pit between Frenchmen and Allied soldiers. Though no one had been badly injured, the performance had been disrupted for almost half an hour. Another English playgoer had casually mentioned that such disturbances were not uncommon.

Rafe was in a somber mood when he returned to his rooms. In spite of Lucien and Maggie's fears, he had not truly believed that the battered nations of Europe might go to war again, but the incident at the playhouse had convinced him. He had the sense that stormclouds were gathering, and there was a very real risk of another cataclysm.

Lost in thought, Rafe entered his bedchamber. He was about to ring for his valet when a cool voice emerged from a shadowed corner.

"I'd like a word with you before you retire, your grace."

The voice was unmistakable—honey with a touch of gravel—and he identified his visitor even before his eyes had adjusted to the dim candlelight. Maggie was casually sprawled across a chair, dressed entirely in

dark men's clothes, her bright hair covered by a knit
cap and a black cloak tossed across the bed.

Rafe wondered how the devil she had gotten in, but
refused to give her the satisfaction of asking. "Are you
practicing to be a Shakespearean heroine—Viola, perhaps?"

She gave a peal of laughter. "Actually, I rather fancy
myself as Rosalind."

He removed his coat and dropped it over the sofa. "I
assume you have a reason for being here that is different from what a man usually expects on finding a
woman in his bedchamber."

The remark was a mistake. Giving him a dagger
look, she said, "You assume correctly. There are several matters we must discuss, and this seemed the
quickest and most private way."

"Very well. Care to join me in some cognac?" When
she nodded, he poured them each a glass, then took a
chair at right angles to his visitor. "What have you discovered?"

She absently swirled the brandy around in her glass.
"My sources indicate three principal suspects, and several minor ones. They are all prominent men, the sort
usually considered above suspicion. Each of them has
the ability and the motivation to plan this kind of conspiracy."

"I'm impressed by your efficiency." He took a sip of
brandy. "Who are your suspects?"

"In no particular order, they are a Prussian, Colonel
Karl von Fehrenbach, and two Frenchmen, the Count
de Varenne and General Michel Roussaye."

"What would their motives be?"

"The Count de Varenne is an Ultra-Royalist, a close
associate of King Louis's brother, the Count d'Artois.
As I'm sure you know, d'Artois is a fanatic reactionary. He and his emigré friends want to wipe out every

trace of revolutionary spirit in France and take it back
to the ancien régime."

She made a Gallic gesture of exasperation. "Of
course that is impossible—one might as well try to
hold back the tide—but they won't accept that.
Varenne has spent the last twenty years skulking
around Europe on dubious royalist business. Some of
his past projects qualify him for our list."

"I see." Her high cheekbones were impossibly dramatic in the candlelight, and strands of golden hair escaped from the hat to glow around her face, softening
the starkness of her garb. With an effort, Rafe forced
himself to concentrate on her words. "If this plot
comes from the Ultra-Royalists, who do you think the
target would be?"

"This may sound farfetched," she said hesitantly,
"but perhaps Varenne might try to kill King Louis himself so that the Count d'Artois would take the throne."

Rafe whistled softly at the idea. It was an ugly
thought, but given France's current instability, he supposed that anything was possible. "What about the
other Frenchman?"

"Roussaye is a Bonapartist. He was born the son of
a baker, and he fought his way up to being one of
France's top generals. He's tough and brave, and dedicated to Napoleon and the revolution. Currently he is
on Talleyrand's staff, dealing with questions relating to
the French army."

"Who would be his most likely target?"

She shrugged. "From his point of view, almost any
important Allied official would do, because that would
result in a much harsher treaty. If anything happens to
the leading voices of moderation, the radicals will get
all the humiliation they want."

"And Europe might be at war again within a year or
two." Rafe frowned. "Wellington would be the best
target. Not only is he universally revered, but it's com-

mon knowledge that he won't take precautions because he thinks it would be cowardly to seem to value his life too much."

"Even a charmed life may eventually run out," Maggie said dryly. "If anything happens to him, Britain will be baying after France's blood as loudly as the Prussians are."

"Speaking of Prussians, what about Colonel von Fehrenbach?"

Maggie finished her cognac, then got up to refill their glasses. Rafe admired the way her skin-tight pantaloons clung to her shapely hips and legs. In the old days, when she had always dressed like a lady, he hadn't known how much he was missing.

Unaware of his scrutiny, Maggie sat down and said, "Von Fehrenbach is a typical Prussian, which means that he hates the French in a pure, uncomplicated way. Von Fehrenbach was an aide to Marshal Blücher, and is presently a military attaché with the Prussian delegation."

"Do all Prussians feel such hatred for the French?"

"It's easier for the British to behave with restraint than the other Allies," she said obliquely. "Considering how horribly the nations of Europe have suffered, it's no wonder the Prussians and Russians and Austrians are determined to make France pay. France has sowed the wind, and now she is reaping the whirlwind."

Knowing her personal reasons for hatred, Rafe asked, "How do you think France should be treated?"

Maggie looked up, her gray eyes cool and steady. "If Napoleon stood before a firing squad, I would pull a trigger myself. But someone must stop the hating, or there will be no end to it. Castlereagh and Wellington are right: destroying France's pride and power will create another monster to rise up and fight again. If anything happens to either of them . . ." She shrugged eloquently.

Rafe took her meaning. "They and Tsar Alexander are all that stand between France and a vengeful Europe. Do you think von Fehrenbach might want to assassinate one of those three?"

"I think he would be more interested in striking at Talleyrand and Fouché," she answered. "They are Frenchman who served both the Revolution and the royalists, and now they are leading the French negotiations against the four Allies. An honest Prussian must despise them for being turncoats."

"Now that you've given me a lesson on the politics of the conference, what do we do about it?"

Maggie felt her stomach clench; what had seemed reasonable when she talked with Robin now looked like appalling idiocy. "Investigations are being made behind the scenes, but it's also necessary to observe our suspects more closely. I have a talent for spotting villains, so I might be able to guess which is our man if I can talk to each of them."

Surreptitiously she wiped a damp palm on her thigh. "Distasteful as the idea is, it's expedient for you and me to pretend to be having an affair. That way we can mingle with the diplomatic corps at the social events where so much of the unofficial negotiating takes place. You will be invited everywhere, and you can take me as your mistress."

His dark brows rose with unholy amusement. "That makes sense, but do you think you can bear so much of my company?"

"I can bear whatever is necessary," she said tersely, "no matter how distasteful I find it."

Her mood did not improve when he laughed aloud. "A palpable hit! But it illustrates my point. Do you think you can restrain yourself from sinking your claws into my unworthy flesh?"

She got to her feet, saying blandly, "In public, my

behavior will be all one could expect of a brainless, infatuated female."

"That being the only kind that would be interested in me?" He stood also, a smile lurking in his gray eyes. "What will you be like in private?"

Maggie swore at herself for leaving such a wide opening. She had been trying to treat this interview as if they were both professional spies, with no past history, but that was no longer possible. She and Rafe had once known each other painfully well, and that awareness throbbed between them.

She wanted to bolt, for she knew that he was dangerous to her. Not physically, even though he stood only a yard away and towered over her; the damned man would never have had to use force in his life. All he had to do was smile that lazy, entrancing smile, exactly as he was doing now. . . .

Refusing to back away, she said crisply, "There won't be any 'private.' This is strictly a business arrangement."

"If you think this is only business, you're a fool, and that I can't believe," he replied. "Like it or not, you're going to have to deal with the fact that there is this between us." He stepped forward and smoothly drew her into his arms.

Even when she realized that he was going to kiss her, she couldn't seem to move. Turbulent feelings surged through her when their lips met—an instinctive desire to run for her life, a deeper instinct to melt into his arms.

And in the back of her mind, a cool, rational voice said that Rafe was right; if they were going to be convincing lovers, they must seem comfortable with each other. That wouldn't be possible if she jumped like a frightened rabbit every time he touched her.

It was all the excuse she needed to kiss him back. She slid her arms around his neck and pressed close. In spite of the years that had passed, the warmth and strength of his hard body were hauntingly familiar, as was the texture of his tongue and his faint, individual male scent. But then she had been an innocent and he had been a tender, protective young suitor. Now they were both adults, experienced in the ways of passion, and desire crackled like heat lightning.

He made a soft sound like a groan and cupped her buttocks, pulling her tightly against him. He wanted her as much as she wanted him, perhaps even more. The knowledge gave her a feeling of power. He had started this, so it was her choice when to end it. But not just yet, not when his touch was searing away the cold and loneliness.

She gasped involuntarily when he caressed her breast. Her nipple tightened and a heated tide began flowing through her limbs. He began to unfasten the buttons of her shirt. The way her breasts ached for his touch told her that she dared not let this continue, or she would be urging him to the bed. After an instant to collect her strength, she spun away, putting half a dozen feet between them before he had time to react.

He moved to come after her, his face raw with longing. She stopped him with a sharp chop of her hand that was unmistakable dismissal. In her coolest voice, she said, "It's a nuisance to be attracted to a person one doesn't particularly like, but that can be used to help our masquerade. If you look at me like that in public, no one will realize that our affair is pretense."

Rafe stopped in his tracks. In the instant before his controlled mask clamped into place, she saw anger, and perhaps reluctant admiration, in his eyes.

Neither of those emotions showed in his voice when he said with matching coolness, "If you react like that the next time I kiss you, the affair will become quite genuine."

"I won't deny that I find you attractive, but passion

is not my master, so you had better accustom yourself to frustration." She smiled maliciously. "If you think that being with me will put too great a strain on your self-control, I suggest that you make arrangements with one of the hotel chambermaids. No doubt one of them will be happy to relieve your frustration."

"I can do better than a chambermaid," he said dryly. "And don't worry about my self-control. I have yet to meet a woman who could turn me into a lust-crazed savage."

Deciding that it was time to conclude her business, she pulled a paper from an inside pocket and handed it to him. "Here are the names and descriptions of seven other men who are possible suspects. Read it and destroy it before you go out tomorrow morning. I didn't mention them because I don't want to confuse you with too much information, but all should be observed carefully if you chance to meet one."

Rafe glanced at the paper. Sorbon, Dietrich, Lemercier, Dreyfus, Taine, Sibour, and Montcan. He set the list aside to study later.

Maggie said, "There's a reception tomorrow night at the British Embassy to honor the Prussian delegation. Von Fehrenbach will be there, so we should go. I live at 17 Boulevard des Capucines. Can you call for me about eight o'clock?"

"I'll be there. Try to be punctual." Unable to resist asking a question that had been nagging him, Rafe added, "Incidentally, what does your husband think of your activities?"

"My *what*?"

"Count Janos, of course."

The tension in the room eased as Maggie's eyes began to brim with laughter. "Oh, my darling Andrei!" She clasped her hands before her heart and gave a nostalgic flutter of her lashes. "He was matchless. Utterly beautiful in his Hussar uniform, and *such* a pair of shoulders!"

"Is the matchless count still among the living?"

"Alas, his noble life was lost at the Battle of Leipzig. Or perhaps it was at Austerlitz."

"Those battles were nine years apart," he pointed out. "Did you misplace him for all that time, or merely decide that you didn't suit?"

Maggie waved her hand airily and lifted her cloak, swirling the dark folds around her shoulders. "Ah, well, they say that spending too much time together is bad for a marriage."

"Do they, indeed?" he said with dry humor. "Why do I have the feeling that you are no more a countess than I am?"

Maggie was heading toward the window, but she flashed an impish smile over her shoulder. "I, at least, have the possibility of becoming a countess, which is more than you can say," she said flippantly.

As she pushed the drapery aside, Rafe said, "Wouldn't it be easier to leave by the doorway?"

"Easier," she admitted, "but I have a reputation to maintain. Good night, your grace." As her dark figure slipped behind the draperies, a faint breeze eddied into the room.

Rafe strolled to the window and looked out. She had vanished, but there were stout vines growing up the wall. It would present no great challenge to an active person.

He shook his head in amusement and dropped the drapery. She was a beguiling witch who wanted to drive him mad, but two could play at that game. His lips curved into a smile. She might think that she was too strong to be swept away by passion, but he was not so sure.

It promised to be a most interesting few weeks.

* * *

The Englishman had been blindfolded for his trip through the Paris streets, and he suspected that the carriage had driven in circles to confuse him. His jaw clenched whenever he thought about the upcoming meeting. The man who had summoned him was known only as Le Serpent. Like the snake he was named for, he was regarded with fear and loathing by those few people who knew of his existence. The Englishman knew it was dangerous to make Le Serpent's acquaintance, but without risk there would be no reward.

The shabby hackney rumbled to a halt. How long had they been circling—fifteen minutes? Thirty? Time was hard to judge when one was helpless.

A whiff of fresher air entered the malodorous hackney when the door opened. The silent escort grasped the Englishman's upper arm and jerked him out of the carriage and across a narrow strip of pavement, indifferent to the fact that his blindfolded charge stumbled and nearly fell.

They entered a building, descended a closed stairway, then walked along a narrow, echoing passage. After a very long walk and a climb up more stairs, the escort stopped. There was the sound of a turning knob, then the Englishman was thrust into a room. He raised one hand to remove the blindfold, but stopped at the sound of a sibilant voice that was clearly disguised.

"I would not advise you to do that, *mon Anglais*. If you saw my face, I should have to kill you. That would be a great waste, for I have better uses for you."

The Englishman dropped his hand, demoralized by being blind and alone. It was impossible even to guess the nationality of his dangerous employer; considering what a political stew Paris was, the bloody man could be anything.

Trying to sound confident, the Englishman said, "Don't waste my time with threats, Le Serpent. You must like the information I give you, or you would not be paying me for it. And you must want more, or you wouldn't have asked to meet me in person for the first time."

There was a throaty chuckle. "The tidbits you gave me in the past were useful, but they were trivial compared to what I need from you now. Over the next few weeks, I want complete information on the movements of Lord Castlereagh and the Duke Of Wellington, plus daily reports on what the delegation is doing."

"I'm not in a position to know all of that."

"Then find someone who is, *mon Anglais*."

The menace in the silky tone was unmistakable. Not for the first time, the Englishman wished he had never gotten involved in this. But it was too late for regret: Le Serpent knew far too much about him. Wanting to put the best face on this, he said, "It will cost extra to learn more. Most of the staff won't talk at all, and those who do are expensive."

"You will be reimbursed for expenses, as long as they are legitimate. I will not pay for your whores and gambling."

Sweat formed under the blindfold as the Englishman wondered if Le Serpent knew about the money skimmed from the sum provided to pay lesser informants. It had been unwise to appropriate some for his own use, but if he hadn't paid that particular gambling debt, he might have lost his position with the delegation. Tersely he said, "You need have no fears on that score."

"How comforting," Le Serpent said with unmistakable irony. "Send your reports the usual way. Remember, I want daily information, for matters are becoming critical. You will be informed when I need to see you again. Now go."

As the escort came and led him from the room, the Englishman speculated about what was brewing. If he knew what Le Serpent had in mind, the information could be very valuable.

The danger lay in the fact that he wouldn't know where to sell it unless he discovered who the snake was. But when was profit without danger?

Chapter 5

After Inge had dressed her for the reception, Maggie dismissed the maid and studied her reflection with clinical detachment. She wore a striking coral pink gown that guaranteed that she would be noticed. Gold chains wound around her neck, and her shining hair was twisted into an elaborate knot high on her head.

Thinking that she looked too formal, she loosened a single ringlet. It drifted delicately across the bare skin of one shoulder in a subtle invitation for a man to wonder what it would be like for his lips to trace the same path.

She gave a nod of satisfaction; she had found the perfect balance between lady and trollop.

It wasn't yet eight o'clock, which gave her time to think about Rafe. It was important to understand her feelings before they began their charade, because she found that her emotions fluctuated wildly when she was near him. She kept swinging from exasperation to anger to amusement, and that was dangerous. The project they were undertaking was too important to be endangered by personal issues.

She must not make the mistake of allowing any more kisses. Above all, she must not challenge him, or he would feel compelled to prove his virility. It would be safer to tease a tiger.

Granted, Rafe had acted very badly when he ended their engagement, but she had not been without blame in the affair. He had made amends for that particular sin when he had taken the bodies back to England. It was an odd, generous gesture to make on behalf of a woman he had once claimed to despise. But whatever his motives had been, he had balanced the scales between them.

She would try to pretend they had met just two days before. She would accept him as an attractive, enigmatic man who shared her goal of uncovering a dangerous plot: no more, no less. A pity he was so handsome, because that complicated matters. He was used to getting what he wanted, and he obviously wanted her. Partly, she supposed, it was simply because she was there, and partly because he had *not* had her all those years ago.

Men were like fishermen; they never forgot the one that got away.

Over the years, she had become very familiar with Rafe's type. A complete lack of response would intrigue him since he was accustomed to women falling into his arms. Therefore, her best approach would be friendliness, tempered with a wistful regret that business prevented her from getting on closer terms with him. That should flatter him enough to salve his ego.

Her reflection looked back at her, cool, glamorous, and self-possessed. That image was her armor in the covert wars she had fought, and it was very effective. Though the features were identical, it was not the face of Margot Ashton, daughter of Colonel Gerald Ashton and fiancée to Rafael Whitbourne.

Maggie felt a wave of sadness. Where had she gone, that impetuous girl who had been so disastrously honest, and who had been so unable to control her temper when it mattered most? Gone to where all youth and innocence went.

Luckily Inge chose that moment to announce that the duke had arrived. Maggie lifted her chin and turned away from her mirror. After living so long among the French, she was developing their deplorable habit of morose philosophizing. Thank God she had been born an Englishwoman, with all the pragmatism of her race.

Looking ridiculously handsome, the duke wore his impeccably tailored black evening clothes with the same graceful unconcern that he would have bestowed on his oldest riding garments. If he was impressed by Maggie's flamboyant appearance, it showed only in the faint lift of a dark brow. As he offered his arm, he murmured, "Is this the same urchin who scrambled out of my bedroom window last night?"

Maggie relaxed as she took his arm. As long as Rafe behaved, it shouldn't be hard to stay on amiable terms with him. "You have urchins in your bedroom, your grace? Of which sex?"

As they stepped out through the door, a hint of a smile played around his mouth. "It was hard to say. Alas, I didn't have the opportunity to investigate more carefully."

His carriage was resplendent in gleaming black and burgundy, the four black horses perfectly matched and the Candover crest lacquered on each door. Rafe handed Maggie in, then settled on the seat opposite as the carriage set off.

As they began clattering through the streets, she said, "You had best call me Magda. I suppose you could use Maggie, since you are English, but *never* call me Margot. It might raise questions, which could be dangerous."

"It will be hard not to call you Margot, but I'll do my best." He smiled a little. "Strange—when you were English, you had a French name. Now that you are claiming to be Hungarian, you think of yourself as a good British Maggie."

"If only that were the least of my oddities," she replied with an exaggerated sigh.

"Dare I ask what the others are?"

"Not if you value your longevity, your grace," she retorted.

He was unsure what had caused her change of attitude, but it was a relief to find Maggie in this relaxed, teasing mood rather than bristling defensively. "You really must call me Rafe, my dear, since we are supposed to be on terms of intimacy."

"Never fear. I will be so convincing that even you will have trouble remembering that this is a charade." Changing languages, she said, "We should speak French now."

Rafe listened with interest. "Is that French with a Magyar accent that you are speaking?"

"Of course! Am I not a Hungarian countess?" She continued with a different accent. "Of course it's a pity to waste my pure Parisian"—she changed again—"but as long as I don't speak with an English accent, I will not disgrace myself."

It was startling to hear her switch between three different modes of speech. Rafe could tell that the Parisian and English-accented versions were flawless, and was willing to take the Magyar one on faith. "How the devil do you do that?"

"It's a knack I was born with, like musical pitch," she explained. "I can duplicate any accent after hearing it spoken. Once I start using it, I will continue in the same mode until I consciously choose to use another. Here I will restrict myself to Magyar-accented French, since that is how people know me."

"It's quite a gift," he said admiringly, "and it explains why a Prussian, an Italian, and a Frenchman all swore to Lord Strathmore that you were one of their nationals."

"Really?" She laughed. "That shows the drawback of having an ear for languages. It's not good to have too many identities—there's always the risk of meeting someone from an earlier incarnation."

They halted in the line of carriages waiting to discharge passengers in front of the magnificent, torch-lit British embassy. Soon they were among the crowd in the receiving line. The Duke of Wellington had bought the building a year earlier from the Princess Borghese, Napoleon's notorious sister Pauline.

As they progressed down the line, Maggie stood on her toes and whispered seductively into Rafe's ear, "A sculpture of the Princess Borghese was done by the great Canova. When one of her friends asked how she could bear to pose in the nude, she smiled innocently and said that it was no problem at all, because there was a fire in the studio."

Determined to play the game as well as Maggie, Rafe slid his arm under her shawl and caressed the smooth skin of her arm as he murmured, "Were all the stories about the princess true?"

She gave a shiver that he thought was not just acting, then chuckled richly and fluttered her eyelashes. "Very true. They say she conquered as many men as her brother, but her methods were much more . . . shall we say, intimate?"

As Maggie continued her scandalous commentary, he admired her sparkling eyes and full, kissable lips. Any onlookers would see them as a perfect tableau of intoxicated new lovers. It was easy to be convincing since he had been simmering ever since that maddening, delicious kiss the day before.

He guided her forward with a hand at the back of her slim waist. After exchanging greetings with Wellington, the Castlereaghs, and other dignitaries, they joined the chattering crowd in the main reception hall. Maggie stayed close, one hand tucked in Rafe's elbow as they made their way around the room.

He knew most of the British aristocrats present, and

she seemed to know everyone else, for there were numerous salutations and kisses for the dearest countess. The better part of an hour was spent in meeting people and sipping champagne.

Rafe noticed how men examined him with curiosity or envy, trying to determine how he had won such an enchanting creature. It was equally amusing to see how women studied him, and then gave Maggie the same kind of glance.

How did Maggie contrive to look so exotic and un-English? Certainly she had those bold Eastern cheekbones, and she used her hands with Continental verve, but it was more than that.

When she pressed against him in the crush, he caught a haunting whiff of the scent she wore. It explained part of her aura; not for her the delicate floral fragrances of England. Instead, she wore a complex, spicy blend that hinted of silk roads and Persian gardens. Scent was a primitive but powerful form of identification, and to be around her was to think of the mysteries of the Orient.

Maggie was as convincing as she had promised; she almost had Rafe himself believing that they were engaged in a torrid affair. The coral silk dress caressed her magnificent figure so lovingly that he desired to do the same. When her smoky, laughing eyes met his, or when she snuggled against him, he was tempted to whisper that it was time they sought a place of greater privacy. He would have suggested that to any other woman who made his blood race as she did; more than once he had to remind himself that this was only a charade.

When he looked away in an attempt to cool his rampaging male urges, he saw that there was a method to the way Maggie was steering him across the room. Though she stopped to introduce Rafe frequently, they drew ever closer to a tall man in the uniform of a Prussian colonel.

The colonel stood unmoving in a circle of silence, his back against the wall. His blond hair was so fair that it appeared almost white in the candlelight. He would have been handsome if his face hadn't held chilly distaste for the people around him. Occasionally he nodded to someone, but he made no attempt to join in the frivolity.

Rafe said quietly, "That's von Fehrenbach?"

"Yes." When she turned her face up to reply, their lips almost met, and she flinched away from him.

Ignoring that brief, telltale withdrawal, he asked, "Do you know him?"

"Not really. I was introduced to him once, but he avoids most social gatherings. He wouldn't be here tonight if this affair wasn't in honor of Marshal Blücher."

When they were close enough, Maggie gushed, "Colonel von Fehrenbach! What a pleasure to see you again." Extending her hand, she said, "I am Countess Janos. We met at the last Russian review of troops, you'll recall."

The colonel didn't look as if he remembered, but he bowed politely over her hand. As he straightened and got a better look at the plunging coral neckline of her gown, his expression thawed a little. Rafe was glad to see that the man was human.

When Maggie introduced her companion, the colonel gave a slight, stiff bow. Rafe felt chilled when he looked into von Fehrenbach's pale blue eyes. The colonel looked as if he had gone into hell, and not come all the way back.

Maggie glanced across the room at Prince Blücher. "What a privilege it must be to serve the field marshal. We shall not see another like him."

Von Fehrenbach nodded gravely. "Indeed. He is the bravest and most honorable of men."

Artlessly she continued, "Such a pity that people do not fully appreciate the part he played at Waterloo. For all of Wellington's brilliance, who knows what might have happened if Marshal Blücher hadn't arrived when he did?"

Rafe wondered if Maggie might be overdoing her enthusiasm, but von Fehrenbach was regarding her with definite approval.

"You're very perceptive, Countess. Wellington had never faced the emperor before, and it is not impossible that Napoleon might have turned defeat into victory."

Rafe felt a prickle of chauvinistic irritation. Wellington had never been defeated in his entire career, and the battle of Waterloo had already been won by the time Blücher had arrived at seven in the evening. However, he wisely kept his mouth shut.

Still admiring, Maggie continued. "They say the marshal was told he would never reach Wellington in time, and that he should not even try."

"That is true," the colonel confirmed with signs of animation. "But the marshal refused to listen to such talk. Though ill, he led the march, swearing that he had given his word to Wellington, and nothing in heaven or hell would stop him."

"Were you with him?"

"I had that honor. The marshal was an inspiration, a true soldier and a man of complete integrity." Von Fehrenbach's eyes chilled. "Not like these wretched lying French."

Maggie gestured vaguely. "Surely not all the French are devoid of honor."

"No? With a king who fled his own capital and slunk back in the baggage train of the Allies? With turncoats like Talleyrand leading them?" The colonel's words began to spill out in an angry torrent. "France rose up behind the Corsican when he returned from Elba, and she deserves to be punished. Her lands should be divided and given to other nations, her people humiliated, her very name wiped from the map of Europe."

Rafe was startled by von Fehrenbach's intensity. The colonel was clearly a dangerous man, quite capable of destroying any Frenchmen that crossed his path.

Maggie said softly, "Have we not learned anything in two thousand years? Shall there be only vengeance, with no place for forgiveness?"

"You are a woman," the colonel said with a dismissive shrug. "It is not to be expected that you would understand such things."

Deciding that he had been silent long enough, Rafe interjected, "I do not suffer from the countess's failing in that regard, but I agree with her that vengeance may not be the best course. To humiliate a losing opponent is to make an implacable enemy. It's better to help him rise and keep his dignity."

The cold blue eyes shifted from Maggie to Rafe. "You English and your obsession with sportsmanship and fair play," he said with contempt. "That is all very well with boxing and games, but we are talking about war. It was the French who taught my people what we know about savagery and destruction, and it is a lesson we have learned well. Would you be so fair-minded if your lands had been burned, your family murdered?"

The other man's obvious anguish caused Rafe to back away from what he might have said. "I would like to think that I would try, but I don't know if I would be successful."

The tension eased and von Fehrenbach retreated behind his impassive mask. "I am glad to hear you admit doubt. Every other Briton in Paris seems to think he has all the answers."

It could have been taken as an insult, but Rafe let the comment pass. He touched the back of Maggie's right arm, silently questioning whether it was time they left.

Before either of the three could move, a woman joined them. She was small, with a sweetly pretty face framed in soft waves of brown hair. Her rounded body was more sensual than elegant, but her blue satin gown showed the unmistakable style of a Frenchwoman.

"Hélène, my dear, you are looking very well. It has been too long," Maggie said warmly.

After a swift glance at the colonel, the newcomer kissed Maggie's cheek. "It's a pleasure to see you again, Magda. I've only just returned to the city." Her voice had the same sweetness as her face.

Maggie introduced her to the two men as Madame Sorel. After offering her hand to Rafe, the French-woman turned to the Prussian. "Colonel von Fehrenbach and I are acquainted."

The colonel's face pokered up even more, if that was possible. In a voice that could only be described as forbidding, he said, "Indeed we are."

Sensing the tension, Rafe wondered if Maggie knew what lay between her friend and the Prussian.

Before Madame Sorel could reply, von Fehrenbach said, "If you will excuse me, I must attend Marshal Blücher. Ladies, your grace." He nodded, then made his escape.

As she watched the ramrod-straight back vanish into the crowd, Maggie exclaimed, "Good heavens, Hélène, what did you do to that man to make him bolt like a cavalryman?"

Madame Sorel shrugged, the movement causing a charming ripple of curves. "Nothing. I have met him several times at various functions. He always glares at me as if I were Napoleon himself, then walks away.

Who knows what might be on his mind? Except that he has no use for anything or anyone French."

Studying her friend with shrewdly narrowed eyes, Maggie said, "But he is a fine figure of a man, no?"

Hélène said dryly, "He is not a man, he is a Prussian." After exchanging a few more remarks, she took her leave with a charming smile.

Rafe watched her swaying walk with male appreciation. When she was out of earshot, he asked, "What was going on there that I did not understand?"

"I'm not sure," Maggie said thoughtfully, "though I might hazard a guess." Glancing up at him, she said, "I'll be back in a few minutes."

As she headed for the ladies' retiring room, Rafe compared her walk with Madam Sorel's, and decided that while the Frenchwoman was well worth watching, it was amazing Maggie didn't have crowds of men following her down the street.

His pleasant thoughts were interrupted by the regrettable Oliver Northwood. "Congratulations, Candover, you're a fast worker. Three days in Paris and you've captured the countess." Northwood's words were jovial, but his beefy face was malicious. "Not that she's hard to capture, for a man who has the price."

Turning to give Northwood his most frigid stare, Rafe said, "I thought you were unacquainted with the lady."

"After you told me her name, I made inquiries. No one knows much except that she's a widow, she's received everywhere, and she has expensive tastes." He winked meaningfully. "She's very good at getting others to pay for her pleasures."

Rafe should have buried his fist in Northwood's gut. Instead, to his disgust, he found himself asking, "What else did you learn about her?"

"She's said to be worth every penny of her price, but

then, you would know that better than I, wouldn't
you?"

It was the vulgarity that disturbed him, Rafe decided. After all, Maggie was a spy, and what better
way to get men to talk than over a pillow? She had to
support herself, and it was doubtful that the British
government paid her enough to maintain that house or
that wardrobe. Behaving like any other highborn tart
who expected jewels in return for her favors was a
splendid way of concealing her deeper purposes.

Odd how it was easier to think Maggie was a whore
than to believe she would betray her country.

Maggie was seated at one of the mirrored vanity tables when the only other lady in the retiring room said
in English-accented French, "Isn't Candover a splendid
lover?"

Maggie swiveled around in astonishment to stare at
the young woman sitting at the neighboring vanity table. In her chilliest tone, she said, "I beg your pardon."

"I'm sorry, that was dreadfully forward of me," the
girl said remorsefully. "But I saw you with Candover
and it seemed from the way you were acting that,
well . . ." She finished with a vague wave of her hand.
Her face was flushed, as if she was only now realizing
how outrageous her comment had been.

Amusement replaced Maggie's irritation. "I assume
from your comment that you have personal experience
of his grace's skills?"

The girl ducked her head in agreement. She must be
at least twenty-five, not really a girl, but her guileless
air made her seem younger. "My name is Cynthia
Northwood. Rafe was . . . very kind to me earlier in my
marriage, when I needed kindness."

Intrigued, Maggie asked, "And now your marriage is
better and you longer need kindness?"

"No," Cynthia said, her wide brown eyes hardening,

"now my marriage is nothing to me, and I have found kindness elsewhere."

Maggie sighed inwardly. It was one of the curses and blessings of her life that people felt compelled to tell her their innermost secrets. Even total strangers like this artless chit seemed to assume that she would offer good advice, or at least an understanding ear.

A talent for getting people to talk was an asset to a spy, but did she really want to hear about the Duke of Candover's amorous prowess from his former mistresses? In an effort to head off more confidences, she said, "I am Magda, Countess Janos, but perhaps you know that already."

"Oh, yes, everyone seems to know you. I've been admiring you since you came in. You have such presence. You and Rafe are the handsomest couple here. He seemed so absorbed in you, not like he is with most women."

How could one be insulted by such a naive tribute? Nonetheless, Maggie said severely, "Mrs. Northwood, don't you know how improper such remarks are?"

Cynthia flushed again. "My wretched tongue! My mother died when I was very small, and my father always encouraged me to speak my mind in the most unladylike manner. And . . . and my friend Major Brewer likes it, too. He says I'm not missish, like most women. Truly, I mean no insult," she said earnestly. "But I am very fond of Rafe, and he looked happy with you. I don't think he is happy very often."

Intrigued against her better judgment, Maggie said, "Surely Candover has everything a man could want: birth, wealth, intelligence, enough charm and address for three men. What makes you think he is not happy?"

"He always seems a little bored. Perfectly polite, but not really caring about what he does. Of course," she added sadly, "perhaps that was just how he was with me. I know he never thought I was interesting, I was nowhere near intelligent enough for him. He only got involved with me because he had nothing better to do at the time."

Maggie listened to Cynthia's speech with horrified fascination and a certain respect. Perhaps there was more to the girl than had been first apparent. "Mrs. Northwood, you really should not say such things to a stranger."

"No, I shouldn't. But I have been doing wrong things ever since I arrived in Paris, and I have every intention of getting worse before I get better." With a lift of her chin, she added, "Countess Janos, I am sincerely sorry if I have embarrassed you. I hope you will believe that I wish both you and the Duke of Candover well. I wish everyone well, except my husband."

Then she left, not without a certain dignity.

Maggie shook her head as she thought over the strange conversation. If ever she had seen a young woman headed for trouble, it was Cynthia Northwood.

Chapter 6

Rafe was quite capable of administering a setdown that would dismiss even so thick-skinned an oaf as Oliver Northwood, but he refrained. Northwood was obviously waiting in hopes of an introduction to Countess Janos, and Rafe had a perverse, unhealthy desire to see how Maggie would react when unexpectedly confronted with her first lover. Assuming that Northwood *had* been the first, as he had claimed.

With his advantage of height, Rafe could see Maggie making her way through the swirling crowd, pausing sometimes to greet acquaintances. It was all casual, until she stopped to talk with a fair-haired man in the center of the room.

Ordinarily Rafe would have thought nothing of it, but his perceptions had been heightened by his present mission. For a moment Maggie's social mask slipped and intense concentration showed on her face. Then she continued her progress.

The fair-haired man had his back to Rafe, but when Maggie moved away, he turned to gaze after her. With surprise, Rafe identified Robert Anderson, the British embassy underling who had introduced Rafe to the mysterious lady spy. Lucien had told Maggie not to deal with anyone in the delegation except the men at the top, so why had she been talking to Anderson with such earnestness?

Rafe wished he could remember who Anderson reminded him of. The fellow had struck Rafe as negligible on their first meeting, but when he had looked after Maggie, there had been an expression of shrewd capability on his face.

As a smiling Maggie came to his side, Rafe wondered if this foray into spying was making him overly fanciful. Soon he would be suspecting everyone and everything. No wonder Maggie had been prickly and suspicious in their first meetings. After years in the shadowy world of intelligence gathering, she must have forgotten what normal life was like.

Maggie laid one hand on Rafe's arm and raised her smoky eyes to his. "Are you ready to leave, *mon cher*? Things are sadly flat here, and I can offer better amusement at home."

"Anywhere you wish to go, Magda, my love." Rafe covered her hand with his own. "But first, let me introduce you to an admirer. This is Oliver Northwood, of the British delegation. Northwood, Countess Janos."

Maggie's control was admirable. Though Rafe watched her closely, her only visible reaction to Northwood was a faint tightening of her lips. Of course, she probably knew that he was in Paris and that they would meet sooner or later, so she had mentally prepared for this encounter.

Or had she had so many lovers that the first meant nothing? Very few of Rafe's old mistresses could have disconcerted him. Why should Maggie be any different?

Why indeed, except that he wanted her to be different?

Northwood bowed and said ingratiatingly, "It's a great pleasure to meet you, Countess. I have indeed been admiring you from afar."

Maggie acknowledged his words with a cool nod. It had taken her several moments to recognize him. As a young man he had not been without a certain boisterous charm, but the years had coarsened him. Or rather, his actions over time had indelibly shaped his face. His eyes reminded her of slugs—cold, damp, and slimy. She did not offer her hand.

He must be Cynthia Northwood's husband. Poor Cynthia. She would have been too young and innocent to realize the kind of man she was marrying.

Northwood said with heavy gallantry, "Our little northern island is incapable of producing beauties such as you."

From the twitch of Rafe's lips, Maggie gathered that he was amused by the wrongheadedness of Northwood's compliment. Smiling sweetly, she said, "You are too hard on your countrywomen, Mr. Northwood. I have just met one who is the fairest of English roses. Such a lovely complexion, and such a forthright manner!" Drawing her brows together, she added, "But surely she said her name was Northwood, Cynthia Northwood?"

His expression soured. "My wife is held to be a good-looking female."

"You are too modest on her behalf, monsieur." Smiling brilliantly, she continued. "It's been a pleasure to meet you. I trust our paths will cross again. But now we must be leaving."

Deftly she removed Rafe and herself from the reception.

When they were safely alone in his carriage, Rafe said with sardonic admiration, "It's an education to watch you work, whether you're coaxing a man to talk, or depressing his aspirations."

"Mr. Northwood is a common type. Unfortunately." She carefully peeled off her long gloves. "His wife offered her felicitations on my choice of lovers."

Rafe sighed inwardly. Though he had always rather enjoyed Cynthia's forthrightness, he wished she had held her tongue this time. "I'm sure she meant well."

By this time thoroughly tired of the Northwoods, he asked, "What does your intuition tell you about Colonel von Fehrenbach?"

In the brief flare of a streetlamp, he saw a grave expression on Maggie's face. "It should be obvious why we consider him a major suspect. What were your impressions?"

"He certainly hates the French enough to be dangerous, and with his military background he would be a skilled, formidable adversary. And yet"—Rafe paused, trying to define his perceptions—"he makes no attempt to disguise his feelings. Surely a conspirator would be more circumspect?"

"Perhaps. Perhaps not," she said reflectively. "He might be so angry that he wouldn't care what happened to him after he accomplished his goal."

"Do you think he is our man?"

The silence was so long that Rafe wondered if she was going to answer. With a hint of steel in his voice, he said, "Maggie, for the sake of our mission I will let you drag me around like a fur muff to disguise your interrogations, but do not treat me like a backward child when we are alone. Like it or not, we are in this together, and there is a greater likelihood of success if we share our information and surmises."

"Is that a threat, your grace?" Her voice was lightly mocking. "If I don't choose to lay bare my thoughts, will you beat me until I change my mind?"

"I have a better way of persuading you than that," he replied with deliberate ambiguity.

"If Cynthia Northwood was correct in her praise of your abilities, I suppose that means you intend to overpower my feeble female brain with kisses." The sarcasm was blistering.

"Not at all. All I have to do is appeal to your sense of fairness, the inbred Achilles heel of Britain."

After a moment of surprised silence, she laughed out

loud. "Rafe, your talents are wasted. You should have become a negotiator like Castlereagh. You certainly know how to take advantage of an opponent."

"We are not opponents," he pointed out. "We are partners."

"I must admit that I have trouble remembering that." She paused, then said, "Despite von Fehrenbach's anger, I don't think he is our man. He's not the sort to plot in secret; he would think it ignoble. He might walk up to Talleyrand and shoot him in the heart, but I doubt that he would lower himself to conspire with others. Though the colonel is like a wounded, dangerous bear, I don't think that he is the one we seek."

"Tell me about Madame Sorel."

"Hélène is a widow with two daughters. Her husband was a French officer who died at Wagram. She was left comfortably off, and is received in the best Parisian society. We've been friends for years, and I trust her."

"Would you care to guess why von Fehrenbach reacted to her presence so vehemently?"

"I think the reason is very simple, and not at all political."

Rafe accepted that without comment. "If you're right about von Fehrenbach, one of the Frenchmen is the most likely villain."

"If I am right." Maggie's voice took on a note of bitterness. "But it's not unknown for me to be wrong."

Things can be done in the darkness that would be impossible in the light. Rafe impulsively reached across the seat to take her cool, tense hand in his own. He neither knew nor cared what memories brought that tone to her voice. All that mattered was that she had carried burdens too heavy for even the broadest of shoulders, and that she was feeling that weight.

Her fingers tightened convulsively around his, though she made no other acknowledgment. Her hand warmed, became more relaxed. For the first time, Rafe felt that the barriers between them had gone down. Perhaps they would get along better if they didn't talk to each other.

When they reached her house, Maggie released his clasp to pull her cashmere shawl about her shoulders. As Rafe helped her from the carriage, her mouth quirked up. "You see yourself as a fur muff?"

He smiled. "Or some other useless, ornamental object carried only for display." He turned and dismissed his carriage.

Maggie gave him a hard look when he followed her into the house. Before she could comment, he said, "If we are to maintain the illusion of an affair, I can't drop you at your doorstep and leave. After a suitable interval, I'll walk back to my hotel. It isn't far from here."

She accepted his reason with an unflattering lack of enthusiasm. "I suppose it's necessary."

They went into the salon and she poured brandy for them both. Then she kicked off her sandals and curled up on one of the sofas. "Should I have asked Cynthia Northwood how long you must stay to uphold your reputation? Perhaps I should make up a bed in one of the spare rooms, since no one would expect to see you before morning."

He refused to be drawn. "I'll slip out the back door in an hour or so. After all, it would be a blow to both our reputations if I left too soon."

Wandering across the room, he found an antique chess set on a small game table. The chess pieces were designed as a medieval court. The smooth enameled figures were about three inches high, and each was a sculpture with individual, hand-drawn features.

Rafe picked up the white queen, an exquisite golden-haired lady riding a white palfrey, then glanced at Maggie. The resemblance was undeniable. The queen, the most powerful figure on the board.

Setting the piece down, he lifted the black king from the opposite side of the board. His dark face arrogant and hawklike, the king brandished a sword from a rearing charger. Rafe studied the figure for a moment, wondering if he imagined its resemblance to himself. The kings were the ultimate objectives in chess, but had relatively little power themselves.

It was not unlike the game he and Maggie were playing, with the white queen in charge and the king standing by. But they were on the same side, weren't they?

He lifted the fair-haired white king. The face was cool and enigmatic, and it took little imagination to see the figure as Robert Anderson. If it was an omen, it was a disturbing one.

Rafe set down the white king. "Care for a game of chess? At the reception, you promised me better amusement at your home."

Maggie rose gracefully and joined him at the chess board. "If you wish. You'll find that my playing has improved a bit. Shall we toss a coin to see who plays white?"

Traditionally white moves first, an advantage, but Rafe picked up the white queen again, admired the proud chin, then handed it to Maggie. "She could only be yours."

They sat down and began. In younger days, Maggie had played with a wild brilliance that occasionally brought victory, but more often led to defeat against Rafe's more thoughtful style. Now they were evenly matched. He was interested to see that she still played boldly, but with a much keener eye for strategy.

An hour passed where the only words were an occasional compliment on a good move. When the clock struck eleven, Maggie looked up in surprise. "At the risk of seeming a poor hostess, I must ask you to leave. We can finish the game another day. I doubt that anyone is watching the house, but just in case, I'll show you to the rear door where you can slip out unobserved."

Rafe followed her through the halls, admiring the house. Though not exceptionally large, it had been designed to feel spacious and every detail was perfect. It was very much the home of a gentlewoman, reinforcing the idea that it was not supported on a spy's wages. He wondered acidly how many lovers were contributing to the establishment.

When Maggie turned to face him at the back door, Rafe was surprised to see how small she seemed in her stocking feet. The top of her head scarcely reached his chin. She looked young and soft and utterly desirable, and the air between them seemed charged with possibilities.

Once Margot Ashton had looked up at him with just such an expression in her eyes. For a moment Rafe's world tilted as the past and present crashed together. He desired her with all the passionate intensity of twenty-one; he wanted to bury his face in tangles of golden hair, to discover one by one the mysteries of Margot's laughing, elusive spirit and lush body.

It was a painful moment of disorientation, and his only salvation was that the present-day Maggie was unaware of it. A faint tremor went through him as he fought the desire to draw her into his arms. Experience told him that it would be better to play a waiting game. She desired him; allow time for her desire to grow. If he moved too quickly, she would become antagonistic instead.

He bid her a polite good night, and hoped that it was a trace of disappointment that he saw in her eyes. Then he walked down the steps, crossed the stable yard, and turned left into a narrow, deserted alley.

He was far too restless to retire tamely to his apartments. He considered going to the Palais Royale to find a card game or a woman, but the prospect did not appeal. Deciding to walk, he headed toward the Place Vendôme.

Maggie was irresistibly on his mind. Even when she was eighteen her innocence had existed only in his mind, so it should be no surprise to learn that she had joined the company of women who collected expensive tributes in return for their favors. It was very common where women had greater beauty than fortune. He didn't think it would be fair to call her a courtesan; she had merely found a practical way to combine business and enjoyment.

At least she also had goals beyond her own pleasure. Presumably she chose her lovers both for wealth and for the information they could provide. In bed with a woman like Maggie, a man might say anything and not care, nor remember it later.

He entered the octagonal Place Vendôme, which was nearly deserted at this hour. In the center was an enormously tall pillar that Napoleon had erected to commemorate the Battle of Austerlitz. The bronze spiral that twined up the column had been made by melting down the twelve hundred cannon Bonaparte had captured at that battle. Not surprisingly, the Prussians wanted to pull the column down.

His mouth twisted. It was hard to care about politics when his mind was disabled by lust. He might as well face the fact that he wanted Maggie for a mistress. Though it was true that he had bedded women that could be considered more beautiful, he had never known one who was so alluring.

In spite of her protests, she was not indifferent to him, and this evening her hostility seemed to have lessened. It was time for them to put aside the past and enjoy each other as they were now, without recriminations or complications.

Instead of sparring with her, he would make a

straightforward offer. Perhaps part of the reason she had been so adamant about keeping her distance was because she didn't want to give away what usually was a source of profit.

Well, he was a reasonable man, and recognized that Maggie had to support herself. Though he had never paid for a mistress before, he was willing to make an exception in her case. In fact, he was prepared to be extremely generous. If she agreed to a long-term arrangement, he would even consider making a permanent financial settlement, so she would have some security for the future.

He turned decisively and headed back to the Boulevard des Capucines. Though it was late, he returned to the alley behind her house, hoping for some sign that she was still awake, perhaps as restless as he was himself.

As he scanned her windows, he saw a stealthy figure coming along the alley from the other direction. Rafe stepped farther back into the shadows so that he wouldn't be seen.

Instead of passing by, the other man stopped and looked around warily. Rafe flattened himself against the wall, glad that he was wearing dark clothing.

Apparently satisfied that he was unseen, the stranger climbed Maggie's back steps and knocked at the door. It swung open immediately. Maggie was standing inside, illuminated by a lamp in her hand. She had changed to a flowing dark robe and her bright hair was loose around her shoulders, like the white queen.

Her visitor bent to kiss her, and Rafe stayed to watch no more.

The stealthy newcomer was Robert Anderson, the white king himself. No wonder she had talked to him with such intensity at the reception; they had been setting up an assignation.

Rafe was coldly furious without quite understanding

why. He knew that Maggie had lovers, so why should it anger him to see one entering? It certainly wasn't jealousy; he hadn't felt jealous about a woman since . . . since he was twenty-one, and Margot had betrayed him with Northwood.

He swore out loud, rejecting the idea. His anger was not a result of jealousy, but concern for his mission. Maggie had been told not to associate with the lesser members of the British delegation, yet she was defying Lucien's orders.

This was a dangerous, complicated business, and getting more so by the hour. Rafe stalked the streets until long after midnight, thinking hard about the new development.

Since Maggie was an expert at espionage, he had assumed that she would not make foolish errors of judgment. That had been careless of him. While he still refused to believe that she would deliberately betray her country, in the future he would be more skeptical of her actions.

Though her affair with Anderson might be irrelevant to the business at hand, it was safer to assume the worst. Women were just as susceptible to misjudging bedmates as men were. If Anderson was a traitor, he might be using Maggie exactly as she had used countless other men.

By the time Rafe reached his hotel, he had decided on a strategy. He knew enough of Maggie's stubborn independence to be sure that if he asked her not to see Anderson, she would laugh in his face. Rafe would have to become her lover so that he would have more influence over her. Then he would tell her to get rid of Anderson—and any other damned men she had on her string.

He had wanted to bed her for purely physical reasons. Now that desire was reinforced by a need to secure her loyalty. For the sake of their mission, he was

prepared to use every weapon he had to gain the upper
hand with Maggie.

How convenient that in this instance, duty would
march with pleasure.

He didn't doubt that ultimately he would be successful; he had never failed to win a woman he really
wanted. But he would have to move very carefully.
Since time was critical, he daren't risk antagonizing
her. Rather than make a straight financial offer, he
would first soften her resistance with expensive gifts.

He also decided that he should develop some information sources of his own. A wealthy lord has many
employees; it took Rafe only a few minutes to think of
two clever, discreet, and trustworthy Frenchmen who
worked for him.

Before going to bed, he wrote a letter to his agent,
summoning both men to Paris immediately.

Robin looked tired and worried, which was unusual,
so after giving him a welcoming kiss Maggie insisted
that he join her in a midnight supper. They sat at the
kitchen table and worked their way through pâté, sliced
squab, and sundry other delicacies that had been left by
Maggie's cook.

When they finished, he pushed the remnants aside.
"Nothing like good food to restore one's optimism.
Did you learn anything useful this evening?"

Maggie described her encounter with Colonel von
Fehrenbach, ending with her conclusion that he was
probably not the man behind the conspiracy. "Now it's
your turn, Robin. What has happened to worry you?"

He ran his right hand restlessly through his hair. It
was a paler blond that Maggie's and looked silvery in
the candlelight. "An informant told me that someone
has been making discreet inquiries for a brave fellow
who would like to bring down 'the Conqueror of the
Conqueror of the World.' "

Maggie bit her lip. The Parisians had hung that nickname on the Duke of Wellington after his victory at Waterloo. It was appropriate, since Bonaparte had gotten into the habit of thinking himself the Conqueror of the World, and Wellington had most certainly cleared up that bit of hyperbole.

"So they really are going for Wellington," she said with depression. "They could hardly make a better choice for stirring up a hornets' nest. Were there any indications of who was making the inquiries?"

"Only that it was a Frenchman, which fits with the conclusion you reached tonight." Robin polished off the last slice of pâté. "How are things going with Candover?"

Maggie shrugged and traced a pattern on the table in a few spilled drops of wine. "You were right, he's an excellent cover for my inquiries. He's perceptive, too—he reached the same conclusion about von Fehrenbach that I did. But I'm concerned . . ." Her voice trailed off.

"About what?"

"Though he's been cooperative so far, tonight he made a remark about me dragging him around like a fur muff to disguise my activities." Robin chuckled, but she said seriously, "For the moment it amuses him to play this game. I don't doubt his patriotism, but I'm afraid of what he might do when he is no longer amused."

Robin's eyes narrowed. "What do you mean?"

"Only that he is used to being in charge, and doing exactly what he wants. The man is no fool, but if he gets all lordly and pigheaded at the wrong time, it could cause serious problems."

Robin's blue eyes crinkled slightly around the corners. "I rely on you to keep him in line."

Maggie leaned back in her chair, suddenly exhausted. "You overrate my abilities, my dear."

"I doubt it." He pushed back his chair and got to his feet. "I'll be going along now. Who will your next target be?"

"I hope to intercept the Count de Varenne within the next day or two. He lives outside of Paris, but he is a habitué of the king's court and attends many social events. I should be able to further my acquaintance with him soon."

Maggie followed Robin to the back door. When he gave her a good-bye kiss, she put her arms around him and rested her head on his shoulder. She had a sudden, intense desire to ask him to spend the night with her. Not only did she yearn for the warmth and fulfillment of lovemaking, but perhaps he would be able to drive thoughts of Rafe from her mind.

But she said nothing, for using Robin in such a way would be unforgivable. Nor would it be more than a temporary cure for what ailed her. Sadly she said, "When will this be over, Robin?"

He was touched by the note in her voice. For a moment, Maggie sounded like the girl she had not been able to be for too many years. He put his arms around her, holding her tight for a little longer than was wise. "Soon, my dear. Then we can all go home to England."

She looked up at him, her eyes widening. "Do you want to go back to England, too?"

"Perhaps." He gave a teasing smile. "I shall lie down until the feeling goes away."

Then he was gone. Maggie bolted the door after him, thinking that it was the first time Robin had ever shown any desire to see his homeland. Even he, with his eternal energy and good nature, must be weary of the endless deceit, and the tension that was a constant companion.

In that case, she was quite justified in having a few tears of exhaustion in her eyes, wasn't she? After all, she was only a woman.

Chapter 7

The next afternoon was hot, and most of the fashionable ladies who had come to St. Germain lolled under
shade trees, leaving the walks private for Maggie and
Hélène. Maggie was glad that her friend had requested
this meeting, for there was much to discuss.

They spent some time exchanging the usual pleas-
antries of friends who hadn't seen each other in a
while. Hélène had just returned from taking her two
young daughters to their grandmother's home near
Nantes, where she had stayed several weeks before returning alone to Paris.

Though she wanted her daughters out of harm's way,
Hélène herself felt an obligation to contribute what she
could to the cause of peace. Until terms for a treaty
were settled, information was critical, and she was well
placed to hear rumors. She knew that what she learned
was passed to the British, and her love for her country
was so strong that she chose to do what some would
call treason.

The two strolled along the garden paths in their
wispy muslin dresses, for all the world like any other
ladies of leisure. Only when they were well clear of
possible eavesdroppers did Maggie ask, "Have you
heard anything of special interest? Your note implied
urgency."

"Yes." Hélène's brow furrowed. "I have heard that
someone is plotting to assassinate Lord Castlereagh."

Maggie inhaled sharply. "Where did you hear that?"

"One of my maids has a brother who works in a gambling hell at the Palais Royale. He heard two men talking very late last night, careless from too much wine."

"Could the brother identify the men?"

Hélène shook her head. "No, the light was poor and he only overheard a fragment of conversation while serving someone at the next table. He thought that one was a Frenchman and the other probably a foreigner— German or English, perhaps. The Frenchman asked if the plan was set, and the other man said that Castlereagh would be out of the way within a fortnight."

Maggie was silent as she tried to assimilate this new piece of information. Was this the same plot that she was pursuing, or a separate one? She felt as if she were trying to find a needle in a cellar at midnight. As they entered a new path between bright flowerbeds, she briefly outlined what little she knew of the conspiracy.

Hélène's face became bleak as she listened. "It sounds very dangerous. With so many troops of all nations around, the slightest spark could set France into flames again."

"I know," Maggie said grimly. "But other such plots have failed. God willing, this one will too." Shifting the subject, she asked, "What do you know of Colonel von Fehrenbach?"

Hélène's softly rounded face was shadowed under her lacy parasol and her voice gave no clue to her thoughts. Though the two women were friends, each had her secrets. "Not very much. We've met several times at social events. He is like many of the Prussian officers—angry, and determined to see France suffer."

"Forgive me if I seem to pry, Hélène," Maggie said hesitantly. "But is there anything between you two?"

"He sees me and thinks of everything he hates," her

friend said in a colorless voice. "Apart from that, there is nothing."

"Do you think he might be involved in this plot?"

"No, he is an uncomplicated man and would have no use for plots." With a wintry smile, Hélène added, "Not unlike my late husband Etienne, going forward bravely, unperturbed by doubt or common sense. Do you have reason to suspect the colonel?"

"Not really. Von Fehrenbach is well placed to do mischief, but my assessment agrees with yours. Still, if you should see him again and observe anything suspicious, you will let me know?"

"Of course." Hélène gestured at an unoccupied bench under a chestnut tree. "Shall we sit while you tell me about that magnificent Englishman you have attached?"

Maggie felt strangely unwilling to discuss Rafe. "He is rich, bored, and in Paris. For the moment he fancies me." She brushed a stray leaf from the wooden bench before sitting. "There is nothing else to tell."

Hélène's dark eyes studied her skeptically. "If you say so."

It was time to change the subject again. Maggie asked, "Do you know anything about Cynthia Northwood? Her husband Oliver is a member of the British delegation."

Waving her flat reticule like a fan to stir the heavy air, Hélène thought for a moment before replying. "She is one of life's heedless innocents. She is having an affair with a British officer, a Major Brewer of the Guards, and she doesn't care who knows it. Having met her husband, I can see why she has strayed, but she shows no discretion whatsoever. Why do you ask about her?"

"No reason, really, except that yesterday she was telling me a great many things one doesn't usually say to a complete stranger." Maggie frowned. "She's unpredictable, and because she is connected to the British delegation she might become involved in something she doesn't understand."

"You're right—Mrs. Northwood is just the sort to blurt out secrets unthinkingly. But if she and her husband are on bad terms, she would probably not have access to important information."

"True, but we can't afford to ignore any possibility. Can you find out something about her associates, besides her major?" After Hélène's nod, Maggie continued, "Also, do you know anything about Count de Varenne?"

Her friend gave her a worried glance. "Yes, and none of it is good. That one is dangerous. Is he involved with your plot?"

"Possibly. Do you know where I might casually meet him?"

"He is often at Lady Castlereagh's evening salons. Be careful, my friend, when you meet him. They say he writes his name in blood."

In spite of the afternoon's heat Maggie felt a shiver along her spine. Firmly she told herself that she was only reacting to Hélène's melodramatic phrasing.

If Castlereagh and Wellington were the targets, Varenne should be dropped from the list of likely candidates. Still, for the sake of thoroughness, she wanted to meet him. Rafe was taking her to the theater tonight. Afterward they could go to the salon at the British embassy and hope that the Ultra-Royalist count was there.

But if Varenne was uninvolved, why did thinking of him give her a nagging sense of danger?

When Rafe called to take Maggie to the theater, she entered the salon in a shimmering, silver gray dress that reflected hints of blue and green in its folds. She was so lovely that it hurt to look at her. He took a slow, deep breath. Patience was not going to come easily.

"Sorry to keep you waiting, your grace. Shall we be on our way?" The honeyed voice was friendly and intimate.

Rafe was impressed at how calm his reply sounded. "You're looking particularly lovely tonight, my dear. I shall be the envy of every man in Paris."

She gave a sorrowful shake of her head. "I'm disappointed, your grace. Surely a gentleman with your reputation for address can offer more imaginative flattery."

"I speak only the truth, Countess," Rafe replied as he escorted her through the door. "Flattery would be useless with a woman of your acuity."

She gave him a mischievous smile. "My apologies for underestimating you. Clearly you flatter on a higher level. A woman who is often complimented on her appearance much prefers to hear lies about her intelligence."

Grinning, he helped her into his carriage. It would take every ounce of wit and charm he possessed to seduce her; he hadn't felt so alive in years. Having more money and more women than he knew what to do with had become a bloody bore, and the harder she made him work, the sweeter the prize at the end.

As the carriage rattled down the Boulevard des Capucines, Maggie spoke, her teasing gone. "The plot is thickening. I have a reliable report of a threat against Lord Castlereagh within the next fortnight."

"The devil you say!" Lechery vanished as Rafe listened to the meager facts that Maggie had. Briefly he wondered who her informant had been—another patron of the gambling hell, over a pillow this afternoon?—but shoved the thought aside for more serious considerations. "Perhaps I can visit that club later this evening, after I leave you off."

"It's not likely to do much good. You can hardly ask

the people who work there the names of the two men discussing assassination last night."

"True, but the fellows might be regular customers. If I make a few critical comments about Castlereagh or Wellington, one might strike up a conversation with me."

At her continuing silence, he added, "I'm not wholly incapable of subtlety, you know."

"I suppose not," she said, clearly not convinced. "I presume you know enough to go armed? There are French officers who make a point of insulting foreigners in the hopes of starting a duel. As an Englishman, you will be fair game. Not as good as a Prussian, but still appealing to a belligerent Frenchman."

"I am touched by your concern for my continued existence."

"Don't flatter yourself, your grace," she said tartly. "I merely dislike losing a chess partner in the middle of a game."

He couldn't tell whether it was sarcasm or humor that laced her voice.

She added, "If you do get forced into a duel, pistols would probably be a better choice. Most of the French officers are capital swordsmen, and it's a rare foreigner who can best them."

Rafe was about to ask why she had faith in his marksmanship when he remembered a long-ago afternoon when they had shot at wafers together in a friend's private pistol gallery. She must remember his skill. Margot had been equally good, the only woman he had ever met who could shoot as well as a man. It was one of many things her father had taught her, treating her as if she had been a son instead of a daughter. One of the many things that made her different from any other woman he had ever known.

The carriage pulled up in front of the theater. Maggie attracted a great deal of attention from gawkers as Rafe helped her from the carriage. She played up to it, casting flirtatious smiles around her. No one watching would ever imagine that she was a cold-blooded spy rather than a hot-blooded tart.

He escorted her upstairs to their private box. The play was excellent, and for whole minutes at a time Rafe forgot serious thoughts in the humor of Molière's *Tartuffe*.

But as the performance progressed, he became increasingly aware of Maggie's closeness. After the second act began, he casually laid his arm across the back of her chair, not quite touching her, but close enough to feel warmth from her skin.

He was pleased to see her lean forward, as if absorbed in the play. It wasn't Molière that put that flush on her high cheekbones; she was as aware of him as he was of her, and he guessed that she didn't trust herself to relax against him. Good. He let his fingertips drift across her bare shoulder.

She shivered, and her hand tightened on her folded fan. He wondered how far he could go before she called a halt. Not much further, he suspected. He rested his arm on the chair again. Gradually she relaxed and leaned against the padded chair back, her shoulders barely grazing his arm.

It was a pleasant game. He was considering massaging the nape of her neck when a growling sound emerged from the pit. Instantly alert, Rafe withdrew his arm and leaned forward to look over the railing of the box. The growl became a rumble, and he saw men shoving each other below.

The actors tried to shout their lines over the increasing noise, but cries of *Vive le Roi!* began warring with *Vive l'Empereur!* The next actor who spoke was pelted with pieces of fruit, and the whole cast bolted for the wings.

Some members of the audience raised white ban-

ners, signifying support for the king. When Bonapartists began brandishing violet flags, Rafe realized that a
brawl was in the making. One of the most frightening
experiences of his life had been when he was caught in
a London street riot, and the mob below was heading
in the same dangerous direction.

The royalists outnumbered the Bonapartists, and one
by one the violet flags were ripped apart. One brawny
fellow with an imperial eagle banner was dragged
down, disappearing under brutal kicks and punches. A
woman screamed, her voice abruptly cutting off. The
cries of *Vive le Roi! Vive le Roi!* became a harsh,
threatening chant that made the walls and ceiling vi-
brate.

Rafe looked across to see Maggie silently staring
down. She was utterly impassive, only the tight set of
her lips indicating concern. As he studied the calm pro-
file and flawless golden hair, he had a sudden, horrifying vision of Maggie surrounded and pulled down by
rough men. The scene was so vivid that for a moment
it blurred the reality of the theater. She was fighting
frantically, but there were too many attackers and she
disappeared beneath vicious hands.

The shocking image gave Rafe a frantic urge to take
Maggie away before violence engulfed the whole theater. He grabbed her arm and half lifted her from her
chair. "Come on," he snapped. "We're getting out of
here."

He swept her toward the back door of the box. The
tumult drowned out the sound of his voice, and at first
she resisted. Rafe was on the verge of swinging her off
her feet and bodily carrying her through the corridor
when she capitulated.

Other patrons were beginning to empty out of the
boxes, but Rafe was quicker. He looped his arm around
her waist and hustled her down the nearest staircase.

Halfway to the ground floor, their way was blocked

by two ruffians who were racing upward. The men stopped, their eyes gleaming at the sight of Maggie.

Without waiting to see whether the men would attack, Rafe threw a savage fist into the belly of the nearer one. His victim made a hoarse, squawking sound as he tumbled against his fellow.

While the two men struggled to save themselves from falling down the steps, Rafe caught Maggie's hand and pulled her past them. No longer protesting, she lifted her skirts with her free hand and ran swiftly beside him, her fingers tight on his.

The stairs came out into a deserted passage. The sounds of the riot came from the right, so they turned and continued left until they reached a side exit.

Outside, they found that both aristocrats and common people were pouring from the theater. A man was running down the boulevard screaming for the Guards. Fortunately, Rafe's carriage was waiting nearby. He bundled her inside, and within a few moments they were heading away from the theater.

Maggie's skirts rustled as she settled herself in the corner of the carriage. Rafe's heart was still pounding. The threat to her safety had roused the most primitive of protective responses in him, and he still felt shaken on her behalf. On impulse he moved across the seat and put his arms around her, needing to reassure himself that she was all right.

She gave a kind of shiver, then turned her face up, her mouth seeking his. Their tongues touched, and suddenly they were kissing with frantic intensity. She slipped her hands under his coat and began kneading his back, her nails digging deep into the muscles.

Dimly he realized that the brush with danger had unleashed something in her, something dark and primal that roused him to equal madness. They sank into the deep, velvet-cushioned seat. Her exotic scent filled his nostrils, intoxicating him. He buried his face in the warm curve of her throat, kissing her beating pulse. The sound of her rough breathing filled the coach.

Remembering that she had always had exquisitely sensitive ears, he trailed kisses upward, along the line of her jaw, until he could tease her lobe with his teeth. She gasped and stiffened, her head arching back and her legs separating so that his knee slipped between hers. They twisted against each other as their bodies instinctively sought a closeness impossible in the cramped quarters.

Their mouths came together again and they shared the same heated, hungry breath. Her breasts crushed against his chest, soft and lush. He ran his open hands down her sides, over her slim waist to the delicious fullness of her hips.

The carriage shook as it hit a hole, almost throwing him to the floor. He lifted himself a little, bracing his shoulder against the side panel and one foot against the base of the opposite seat. She adjusted herself to his new position, her pelvis pressing against his.

Her thigh was firm and shapely, and as he stroked downward he discovered that her skirt had worked its way over her knee. He heard the whisper of silk as his fingers skimmed over her stocking-clad calf. If he had been reasoning, he would have moved more slowly, but he was beyond reason. He caressed upward, over the ribbon of her garter to the bare, warm flesh of her inner thigh.

She sucked her breath in, then drew her head away from his. "Enough!"

As he looked into her stark eyes, Rafe became very still. The glow of a streetlight showed that there was still desire in her face, but her wildness had faded.

The same was true of him. Though passion burned through his veins—ye gods, how it burned!—the madness had subsided. He was profoundly unnerved to realize how thoroughly he had lost control of himself.

Instinctively he retreated. Though his body ached to complete what they had begun, he made no attempt to persuade her to continue. Very carefully he lifted himself away and sat on the facing seat. His muscles vibrated with tension.

Maggie pushed herself upright and tugged her skirt down over her bare legs. "What was that about?" Her unsteady tone belied the banality of her words.

"A brush with danger often provokes a passionate desire to celebrate life," Rafe observed, trying to sound detached, as if they hadn't just been on the verge of ripping each other's clothing off. He was grateful that the darkness concealed his embarrassingly obvious state of arousal.

"The danger wasn't that great." Satisfied that her gown was straight, she began checking her hair. "Such scenes are not uncommon. The royalists are trying to intimidate the rest of France now that they have the upper hand. It's called the White Terror. If we had stayed in our box and waved white handkerchiefs, we would have been quite safe."

"While I admire your aplomb, no one is ever entirely safe during a riot," he said dryly. The horrific image of Maggie under attack flashed through his mind again, and he shuddered. If she had been alone, a white handkerchief would have been a poor defense against men like those on the stairs. "Since you seem to have more courage than sense, I feel responsible for keeping you intact, at least until you find our assassin."

She pulled out a hairpin and reattached a loose lock. "A pity to miss the rest of such a fine play. Luckily I've seen *Tartuffe* before, and leaving early means we will reach Lady Castlereagh's evening salon in good time."

He wanted to laugh at the absurd way they were

both ignoring that spectacular outburst of passion. "What, no maidenly vapors?"

"They would be singularly inappropriate since I am not a maiden," she said sharply. She drew a deep breath before continuing. "I've heard that Count de Varenne often attends Lady Castlereagh's evenings. While it's unlikely that an Ultra-Royalist would be behind our plot, I would still like to meet him." After a moment's thought, she added, "I was warned that he is a thoroughly dangerous man."

"I'll bear that in mind. Is he likely to challenge me to a duel, too?"

"No, I believe he is more the knife-in-the-back type."

"Sounds like a charming fellow. Remind me to keep my back to a wall if we encounter him." The uneasiness Rafe had felt at losing control began to fade, leaving him pleased with the progress he had made. Maggie was coming closer and closer to yielding; he didn't doubt that very soon she would be willing to accept him. And soon after that, he would make sure that she got rid of her other lovers.

Satisfied with his conclusions, he stretched his long legs as far as possible in the limited space. "Lead on. I hope that Lady Castlereagh has a good supper planned. There's nothing like a riot to put an edge on a man's appetite."

Chapter 8

As the carriage rumbled down the boulevard toward the British embassy, Maggie's hands were locked so tightly in her lap that her fingers must be white inside her gloves. She wondered if her voice had betrayed her near-panic at the theater riot.

The episode had brought back all her worst nightmares in hideous detail, and she had been so paralyzed by fear that she could hardly move when Rafe had dragged her from the theater. There had probably been little real danger—she routinely carried both a white and a violet handkerchief in her reticule, just in case—but panic was immune to reason.

While she would have forced herself to stay in the theater rather than give in to her fears, it had been a relief to go along with Rafe. Most of the time Maggie would fight hammer and tongs if a man tried to compel her against her will, but not tonight, not in the face of that seething brawl of mad humanity.

It had been profoundly comforting to have his strong arm around her, and pure pleasure to watch him dispatch those two ruffians so deftly. All in a day's work for the Duke of Candover, of course. He hadn't even wrinkled his perfectly tailored coat, and he had betrayed no more concern at the riot than if a mule cart had blocked his carriage.

She admired his imperturbability. Most of the time she could match it, but not when a mob brought back the horrifying scene that had killed her father and Willis, and changed her life forever.

She tried not to think of their impassioned embrace, even though her body throbbed with frustration. The attraction she had always felt for Rafe had reacted explosively with her fear to produce a shattering degree of need. Though he had responded fiercely, he had stared at her as if she were a stranger when they had separated. Dear God, what must he think of her?

The thought produced a wintry smile. His opinion of her was already so low that her acting like a wanton probably made no difference. A good thing they had been in a cramped carriage, or heaven only knew where it would have ended.

Disaster, that's where it would have ended.

Her hands had almost stopped trembling by the time they reached the British embassy on the Rue du Faubourg-St.-Honoré. As Rafe helped her from the carriage, she smiled and said with her most ravishing Hungarian accent, "Lady Castlereagh's evenings are very splendid, with some of the best conversation in Paris. One may see anyone here."

Inside, Lady Castlereagh herself greeted them. Emily Stewart was not renowned for beauty or wit, but she was a kind woman, and she and her brilliant husband were devoted to each other. "Good evening, Candover, how charming to see you." She extended her hand. "I trust that Magda has been making you feel welcome in Paris?"

He bowed over her ladyship's hand. "She has indeed. The countess even found a theater riot for me this evening, so I should be well informed about the events in Paris."

"Unfair, your grace," Maggie said indignantly. "You chose the theater. I thought perhaps you arranged the riot as an alternative to the farce."

"Unfortunately, one needn't look far for disorders,"

Lady Castlereagh said wryly. "Nightly mobs in the Tuileries gardens, duels almost daily between French and Allied officers. There have been disturbances at each of the four theaters where I have boxes, and they are the staidest playhouses in Paris." She glanced at the door and saw another party arrive.

"I must excuse myself now, but I hope to speak more with you later. Was there anyone either of you particularly wished to meet? There's quite a crowd this evening."

"Is the Count de Varenne here, Emily?" Maggie asked.

A small line appeared between Lady Castlereagh's brows, but she said merely, "You're in luck, he arrived a few minutes ago. Over there, in the far corner, talking to the Russian officer." She nodded and left to attend to her hostess's duties.

The splendid reception room was crowded with people, and a dozen languages could be heard, though French predominated. Lord Castlereagh and the British ambassador, Sir Charles Stuart, were part of a group that included Prince Hardenburg, the Prussian foreign minister, and Francis I, Emperor of Austria.

Negotiations were at a critical phase now, and the key figures were striving night and day to reach agreement. With the support of Wellington, Lord Castlereagh's plan for an army of occupation was slowly coming to be accepted among the Allies.

Maggie's eyes lingered on Castlereagh for a moment. He was a tall, handsome man, reserved in public, but generous and unassuming in private. The foreign minister was known for both intelligence and irreproachable integrity, and his death would be a tremendous loss.

Her jaw tightened; he would not become a victim of political terror if she could do anything to prevent it. She glanced at her escort and found the duke also gaz-

ing at the British minister, thoughts similar to hers reflected in his face. Sensing her regard, he glanced
down and for a moment their eyes met in perfect
agreement.

There were a number of Britons present and Rafe
knew them all, so it was easy to progress indirectly toward their quarry while they exchanged greetings with
fellow guests. Maggie studied the count as they drew
closer. He was in his late forties, a powerfully built
man of middle height with great elegance and an air of
authority.

Mentally she reviewed what she knew of him. The
last of an ancient family, he had been involved in royalist attempts to regain control of France ever since the
Revolution. Circumstances had made him a dangerous
and devious man, and he unquestionably had the
knowledge to organize a conspiracy.

For the last decade he had been governor of a Russian province for the tsar. Napoleon's defeat had
brought the count home, and he was now in the pro-
cess of restoring his estate outside of Paris to its
former splendor. As one of the most influential Ultra-
Royalists, he was thought likely to be chosen soon for
an important government post.

As they drew nearer to the count, Maggie was
pleased to see that the Russian he conversed with was
Prince Orkov, whom she had met several times before.
Tucking her hand firmly in Rafe's elbow, she drew him
up to their quarry at a lull in the conversation, cooing,
"Prince Orkov, so delightful to see you again. Surely
the last time we met was at Baroness Krudener's?"

Prince Orkov's eyes lit up with uncomplicated male
pleasure. "It has been too long, Countess," he said as
he bowed over her extended hand.

Introductions were performed all around, but
Maggie's bright social smile froze when her eyes met
those of the Count de Varenne. Most men stared at her

with obvious physical appreciation. Occasionally that was a nuisance, but lust was normal and passion was warming. Varenne's gaze was pure ice, the cold, dispassionate evaluation of a buyer contemplating a possible acquisition.

For a moment she was off-balance. She could deal with any variety of passion, whether love or anger or hatred—she had liked Rafe better in the days when he had had emotions—but the count seemed like a man who stood apart from such human weakness.

Though uncertain of the best way to question him, she plunged in with a smile. "I have heard of you, Monsieur le Comte. It must give you great pleasure to be restored to your country and your estates after so many years of exile."

He paused, his black eyes flatly opaque, then said in a dark, whispery voice, "Satisfaction, certainly. Pleasure may be too strong a word."

She nodded sympathetically. "France must seem sadly changed, but now you and your royalist compatriots have the chance to rebuild that which was destroyed."

His mouth twisted. "We shall never be entirely successful with that, for too much has changed in the last twenty-six years. The misguided idealism of the radicals has wrecked France. Jumped-up bourgeois pretend to be aristocrats, the true nobility had been decimated or impoverished. Even the king himself is only a shadow of his distinguished ancestors. Who could look at Louis the Eighteenth and see the Sun King?"

His soft voice was peculiarly commanding, and Maggie wondered if she imagined the undertone of threat. "You seem very pessimistic for a man of the ruling party. Do you think matters are truly so desperate?"

"Difficult, Countess, but not desperate. We have

waited a long time to reclaim our patrimony. We shall not lose it again." His gaze ran over her again, coolly dismissive. "If you will excuse me, I am expected elsewhere." With a polite nod to the others, he left the group.

Rafe and Prince Orkov had been discussing horses, that topic of universal and unending interest to the male half of the species. When she turned back to them, Rafe said, "The prince has invited us to a ball he is giving two days hence. Are we free to accept?"

Assuming that someone on the guest list would be of particular interest, Maggie said cordially, "We accept with pleasure, Your Highness. Your entertainments are legendary."

The prince took her hand and caressed it in a way that warned Maggie not to let him get her alone. "Your presence will add to its luster, Countess."

With some difficulty, Maggie extricated her hand and she and Rafe departed. They chatted with several more guests so that they would not appear to have lost interest after talking to Varenne, but within half an hour they were on their way back to the Boulevard des Capucines.

As soon as they were alone, Rafe asked, "What is your judgment on the count?"

"I'm glad that the choice of targets rules him out as our conspirator, because he seemed utterly ruthless, as dangerous as his reputation." Remembering that black gaze, she repressed a shiver. "Who will be at Orkov's ball?"

"General Roussaye, our Bonapartist suspect." Rafe gave her a lazy smile. "Wear that green gown unless it would ruin your reputation to be seen in it again too soon."

"I think my credit will stand it," she replied. "I am only a poor Magyar widow. People will make allowances."

Rafe accompanied her into her house, this time without dismissing his carriage. For a moment there was uncertainty in the air, as if he were considering a kiss.

Not daring to find out, Maggie hastily turned away and led him to the chessboard, where they continued the game in progress. She wondered if anyone in Paris would believe that she spent private moments with Rafe playing chess. She had trouble believing it herself.

The game devolved into long pauses and steely contemplation, and ended in stalemate. She thought the symbolism was appropriate, since it was the story of their relationship.

When the game was finished, Rafe got to his feet. "I'm off to the Palais Royal to see if I can find the mysterious conspirator. The conversation was heard at the Café Mazarin?"

Maggie nodded and followed him to the front door. Rafe towered over her, strong, confident, and utterly in control. He would undoubtedly feel insulted if she betrayed a lack of faith in his abilities. Nonetheless, she had the most absurd desire to tell him to be careful.

Uncannily, Rafe seemed to be aware of her thoughts. "Never fear, I shan't stir the hornets up." He lifted her right hand and kissed it, not with a light, formal brush of his mouth, but seriously, his lips warm and sensuous against her fingers.

Then he was gone. Maggie involuntarily curled her hand into a fist, as if to ward off the tingles of pleasure his kiss had sent up her arm. Just that light caress revived the desire that had almost overwhelmed her earlier in the carriage.

Acidly she reminded herself that he probably had to cut notches in his bedposts in order to keep track of the women he had bedded. By now the posts must be whittled away to nothing.

Face tight, she headed upstairs to her chamber.

Where Rafe was concerned, her sense of humor wasn't giving her any perspective or amusement at all.

The Palais Royal had a long and checkered past. Cardinal Richelieu had built part of it, and sundry royal relatives had lived there. Shortly before the Revolution, the Duc de Chartres had built a huge addition around the gardens, renting out the lower levels as shops and the upper as apartments.

These days, the Palais Royal was the very heart of French dissipation, with every manner of vice available to the hopeful bucks who swarmed there. Externally it was the only really well-lit place in Paris, and idlers of every nation could be seen drifting under the arcades and clustering by the columns.

The only females visible were of the more public sort, and one of those approached Rafe as he alighted from his carriage. He wondered with some interest what kept her low-cut gown from falling off. A fortunate thing that the evening was mild, or she would be courting pneumonia.

She had plied her trade long enough to size up a man's nationality and wealth quickly. "Is the English milord here for pleasure?" she asked in a husky voice with a provincial accent. Her heavy mask of makeup couldn't conceal the lines in her face.

None of Rafe's distaste showed in his face. She was a coarse, unattractive creature and any man sampling her charms risked the pox, but she was no better or worse than half a hundred other women wandering the arcades and gardens. For that matter, she was little different from many of the great ladies of society except for her price, which was lower and more honest. Courteously he said, "I feel in luck this evening. I understand the gaming is good at the Café Mazarin."

"The café is that way." Tossing her head coquettishly, the prostitute added, "Perhaps later you will wish a companion to celebrate or commiserate with?"

"Perhaps." Making his way through a crowd of Allied officers, Rafe soon found a sign for the Café Mazarin. On the ground floor was a jeweler's shop, still open at this late hour in the hope that a lucky gambler might wish to buy some bauble to bestow upon his lady.

Beside the shop a dim staircase led up to the café. A flamboyantly dressed woman presided over the counter, her dark eyes shrewdly assessing new customers. Liking what she saw of Rafe, she came around her counter to greet him in person. "Good evening, milord. Are you here for dining or gaming, or perhaps to go upstairs?"

Upstairs would mean ladies of a higher grade than the streetwalkers outside. With luck, they would be pox-free and not steal the customers' wallets. "I've been told that the play is good here, madame. Perhaps later I will dine as well."

The woman nodded and led him through the dining room to the gambling salon. It looked like any number of other gambling hells Rafe had been in. In one corner was a *rouge-et-noir* table, in another a roulette wheel. A scattering of tables contained card games such as faro and whist.

The patrons ran the full range from innocent young pigeons to the Captain Sharps who preyed on them, and the smoky atmosphere was dense with the desperate excitement of serious gamesters. The low murmur of voices was punctuated by the rattle of dice at the hazard table and the soft slap of cards on green baize. All in all, a typical den of iniquity, and not the sort of place that Rafe had ever found attractive.

Still, he was here for information, not pleasure, so he spent the next two hours playing at different tables. Whist was the only game he would have enjoyed, because it was more a test of skill than chance, so he avoided the whist table lest it prove too absorbing. Over dice, cards, and wheel, he exchanged casual comments with other gamesters, listening more than he spoke.

Not surprisingly, much of the conversation was political. However, he heard only the talk that could be heard anywhere in Paris. This particular establishment was patronized by a mixture of Frenchmen and foreigners, but if any were extremists, they kept their mouths discreetly shut.

An hour past midnight Rafe was preparing to call it an evening and find some fresh air when his attention was drawn by a thin, dark-haired man at the *rouge-et-noir* table. The man had been winning earlier, but luck had turned against him and the bank had taken all his money. A wide scar across his cheek shone livid in the candlelight as he reached into an inside pocket to draw out his final stake. Defiantly he slapped a pile of notes on the red diamond.

In the hush that sometimes falls on a crowded room, it seemed that everyone was watching. Rafe was too far away to see the cards dealt, but when the scar-faced man whooped a moment later, it was obvious that he had won.

It would have meant nothing, except that the Frenchman next to Rafe said, "It looks like Lemercier is in the money again. The man has the devil's own luck."

The name was familiar, and after a moment Rafe remembered why. There was a Lemercier on the list of secondary suspects that Maggie had given him, a Bonapartist officer if he recalled correctly. Rafe studied the scar-faced man as he rose from the *rouge-et-noir* table. The fellow had a military bearing; now to see if he was Captain Henri Lemercier.

As the man crossed the room, Rafe casually intercepted him. "May I buy you a drink to celebrate your beating the bank?"

His quarry smiled jovially. "You may. Lost a few to the bank yourself, eh?"

The hostess set them up with a bottle of bad port in the café section of the establishment. Rafe discovered that the man was indeed Captain Henri Lemercier, and the port was obviously not his first drink of the evening.

As the level of the bottle dropped, Rafe learned that the captain despised all Germans, Russians, and Englishmen, present company excepted, and that he was a devil of a fellow. Soon he was boasting of the numerous times that his iron nerve had caused him to win when lesser men would have withdrawn from the game.

It was not an enlightening conversation, though Rafe was interested to learn that Lemercier was a regular patron of the Café Mazarin. ("At least the tables are usually honest, my English friend.")

Lemercier had the nervous gestures and darting eyes of a ferret. Rafe guessed that he was an addicted gambler, the kind of man who would do anything for money. If the captain had political convictions, they would easily be subordinated to personal gain. There was an excellent chance that he was the Frenchman Maggie's contact had overheard here the night before. If so, who was the foreigner the captain had spoken with?

After half an hour of listening to the man's ramblings, Rafe decided that he was unlikely to learn anything more. He took his leave with mutual assurances of esteem and hopes of meeting at the Café Mazarin in the future. If he did seek Lemercier out again, Rafe made a note to do so earlier in the evening, when the man was more likely to be sober. He was not an interesting drunk.

Rafe paid the bejeweled woman behind the counter for the port. Before going downstairs, he cast one last glance across the room. His eyes narrowed when he saw a blond man taking the empty chair opposite Lemercier. In spite of the dark smokiness of the room and the man's distinctly French way of dressing, Rafe had no trouble identifying the newcomer who was talking so earnestly to Lemercier.

It was Robert Anderson, the ubiquitous underling from the British delegation. Maggie's lover.

The Englishman was tense even though he had made this blindfolded journey once before. The summons from Le Serpent had been curt, with no explanation of why his presence was needed. Once again a hackney circled through Paris and the silent escort refused all conversational overtures. However, this time when he was brought into Le Serpent's presence, the sibilant voice instructed him to remove his blindfold.

The Englishman felt a stab of fear that the order meant he would not be leaving, but a hoarse chuckle allayed that. "Don't worry, *mon Anglais,* you will not recognize me. You will need your eyes for what you must tell me tonight."

Pulling off the blindfold, he found himself in a dark room lit by the feeble glow of a single candle and furnished only with a desk and two chairs. Le Serpent sat behind the desk, his face masked and a black cloak disguising his body so thoroughly that it was impossible to tell if he was tall or short, fat or thin.

Disdaining preliminaries, the dark figure said, "Draw me a detailed sketch of the British embassy stables. There have been changes since the Princess Borghese sold it to Wellington, and I need to know about them. I am particularly interested in where Castlereagh's horses are kept. I want you to describe his beasts exactly, in both looks and temper."

The Englishman's eyes widened. "You're plotting against Castlereagh? If anything happens to him, there will be hell to pay. Wellington is his best friend, and he would set the whole British Army to searching for assassins if necessary."

And a diligent investigation might uncover matters to the Englishman's detriment. Only a complete lack of suspicion had made it possible for him to pass so much information.

Reading his mind again, Le Serpent smiled nastily. "You needn't fear for your worthless neck. Whatever happens to Castlereagh will seem like an accident. Soon the illustrious duke himself will be in no position to investigate anything."

As the Englishman started sketching floorplans of the stable and its yard, his mind was racing. It sounded like his repellent host wished to eliminate both of the top British officials, a fact that had interesting ramifications. Clumsy attempts had been made on Wellington's life before, but there would be nothing clumsy about an attempt by Le Serpent. The question was, how could this information be turned to account?

Le Serpent asked a number of questions about the routine of the stables and the grooms, curtly demanding that his visitor find the answers to anything he couldn't answer immediately. After discussing the stables, he made exhaustive queries about the daily routines and habits of Castlereagh and Wellington.

Tiring under the interrogation, the Englishman said irritably, "Surely you know that the duke prefers low company—he doesn't even live at the embassy. How am I supposed to know about all his movements?"

"I am quite aware that Wellington lives at Ouvrard's Hotel," Le Serpent replied. "Nonetheless, he is often at the embassy, and if you have the brains of a rodent you should be able to learn what I require. I will expect a report with the answers you could not supply tonight within forty-eight hours."

"And if I decide I no longer wish to be in your employ?" It was an ill-chosen time for defiance, but the Englishman was too tired and irritated to be wise.

In a voice heavy with menace, Le Serpent hissed, "Then you are ruined, *mon Anglais.* I can have you assassinated, or I can let Castlereagh know of your duplicity and your own people will destroy you. Publicly, so that every one of your relatives and friends, if you have any, will know of your humiliation. Do not think you can buy your life by informing against me, because you know nothing."

He slapped his hand on the desk and pushed himself to his feet. "You live on my sufferance, you dunghill cock. I *own* you, and you are fortunate that I am a man of honor. If you serve me well you will prosper, unless you are caught through your own stupidity. If you try to betray me, you are a dead man. Those are the only choices you have."

The Englishman's eyes fell as he tried to hide his fear. That was what led to his stroke of luck; the hand his adversary had braced on the desk bore a heavy gold ring with a complicated crest on it. He knew better than to stare, but his quick glance showed that the central coat of arms was twined by a three-headed serpent.

It would take time to identify the owner, but at least the Englishman had a clue. Slumping in pretend defeat, he muttered, "I will serve you well."

Inside, his heart sang with inner exaltation. He'd find out who Le Serpent was, by God, and then the bastard would be sorry for his insults. If he played his cards right, he would be able to come out of this a hero—a *rich* hero.

Chapter 9

The next morning Maggie received a note from Hélène Sorel reporting that a discontented French officer had asked a group of café idlers if anyone wanted to earn some money by shooting the Duke of Wellington. Since the idiot had made his offer before a dozen witnesses, he had been arrested within minutes.

Maggie smiled wryly as she set the note aside. There was plenty of dissatisfied grumbling in the city, but most of it was as harmless as this. Men like the foolish French officer were not the problem.

Her amusement faded as she considered her own lack of progress. Robin had stopped by the night before and they had stayed up late talking, but without reaching any new conclusions. It was vastly frustrating. Too many possibilities, too little time . . .

She spent the day pushing harder, looking at the information she had and trying to see some pattern, but without success. She could only continue as she was doing, and hope that General Roussaye might hold the key.

As she dressed for Prince Orkov's ball, even her favorite green satin gown failed to improve her mood. She was silent as Inge styled her hair into a tumble of golden curls. Privately she wondered how much Rafe was adding to her tension.

Though she trusted his good intentions about their mission, that was all she trusted. As a spy, he was an untested amateur. On a personal level, he was like a loose cannon on the deck of a ship: uncontrolled and dangerous. Maggie could pretend to a sophistication that played at love without being burned, but she knew how perilously thin her facade was. For her, lack of deep feeling was an act. For Rafe Whitbourne, it was the real thing.

When Inge announced that the duke had arrived, Maggie schooled her face to pleasantness and went to join him. When she entered the salon, her attention was distracted from the concerns of spying by Rafe's admiring expression.

"You look splendid tonight, Countess. Thank you for wearing that dress. It will go very well."

"Go very well with what?"

He held out a velvet-covered box. "With these."

Maggie opened the box, then caught her breath at the sight of an emerald necklace and earrings of dazzling beauty. Delicate gold settings entwined with flawless stones to create jewelry that looked light and airy while at the same being indecently sumptuous. "For heaven's sake, Rafe, what are these for?"

"For you, of course."

"I can't possibly accept anything this valuable. People would think . . ." She stopped.

"That you were my mistress? That is the point, my dear."

His voice was deep and caressing, and for one perilous moment she considered what it would like be to be his mistress in fact as well as fiction. Then her jaw hardened.

Even though he was the most attractive man she'd ever known, she'd be damned if she would let this unreliable nobleman conquer her, no matter how much they would both enjoy it. Conquest was still conquest, and she was no man's trophy.

She snapped the box shut and handed it back. "A

queen's ransom in gems is not necessary to our charade, your grace."

Undeterred, Rafe said, "But it is necessary. Half of London society is in Paris now, and my habits are not exactly a secret. I've always given bits of trumpery to my ladyfriends. People would think it strange if I didn't do the same with you."

"Bits of trumpery!" she said with exasperation. "You could buy half an English county with the value of these."

"You exaggerate, my dear. No more than a quarter, and it would have to be a small county at that."

His smile invited her to be amused, and Maggie could not resist laughing with him. "Very well, if you insist, I will accept the *loan* of these until our masquerade is done. Then you can store them away for your next genuine mistress."

Taking the box from her hand, Rafe steered her over to a pier glass hanging between two of the windows. He stood behind her and deftly unhooked her simple jade necklace.

"But these emeralds wouldn't be appropriate for just any woman. They will look best on one whose eyes will turn green to match." He lifted the necklace from the box. "Someone with the style and countenance to wear what you call a queen's ransom without being overpowered by it. I can't think of another woman they would suit as well."

Rafe placed the necklace around her neck, his warm hands contrasting with the cool touch of the gems. Her ball gown was cut very low, exposing her neck, shoulders, and a dramatic expanse of bosom, and she felt suddenly naked as his fingers brushed her bare skin. Desire coiled inside her, tense and demanding. When she was eighteen, she had first explored the nearer edges of sexuality with this same impossible, attractive man, and time had only deepened her yearning.

Her gaze met Rafe's in the mirror. His hands came to rest on her exposed, sensitive shoulders and when he spoke there was no teasing undertone in his voice.

"Margot, why can't we forget all the complications of our past and be ourselves? You are the most irresistible woman I have ever known. Being so close to you without touching is in a fair way to driving me mad." He began gently massaging the back of her neck with his thumbs. "I want you, and I think you want me, too. Why can't we be lovers in truth?"

He was no longer the polished, sardonic duke who set her nerves on edge, but the direct young man she had fallen in love with. Her heart ached for what they had once had, and lost. Struggling for sanity, she said weakly, "It would be a mistake."

Bending over, he kissed the edge of her ear where it showed beneath her golden hair, then nibbled down her neck. His hands skimmed down her bare arms with feather lightness, then wrapped around her waist to pull her back against him. She gasped and tried to ignore the fiery reaction his touch aroused.

"We are both adults, old enough to know what we want," he whispered in his deep, velvet-rich voice. "No one would be hurt, and I know we would find a rare pleasure together." His hands brushed upward to cup her breasts. Slowly he moved them in a circle, and she felt her nipples harden against his palms.

Involuntarily she rolled her hips into his groin. When a hard ridge of flesh pressed against her, she forced herself to be still. "No, blast you!" she said breathlessly. "Nothing is that simple."

His right hand slipped into her bodice and he began teasing her nipple. At the same time, his left hand stroked down her torso to the jointure of her thighs. "Do you really mean no?" he asked as his knowing hands found her most sensitive places. "Your words say one thing, but your body says another."

There was too much truth in what he said, and the fire in her body was no fiercer than the torrent of confusion in her mind. Of course she wanted him. She was weak with longing, and dared not admit how perilously close she was to consigning past and future to the devil and letting him make love to her in the intoxicating present.

But she had learned self-control in the hardest of schools, and even now she knew that he was wrong to claim that no one would be hurt by what they did. She would be more than hurt; she would be devastated if she fell in love with Rafe again. Losing him once had nearly destroyed her, and no handful of days as his mistress could be worth the agony that intimacy would bring.

As she tried to find the strength she needed to break away, he murmured, "I promise that you won't be the poorer for it, Margot. The emeralds are only the beginning."

He wanted her to be his whore.

The knowledge gave her the fury she needed to resist. She jerked away, unconsciously raising one arm defensively. "No means *No*! If I'd meant yes, I would have said yes!"

As she whirled around, her elbow clubbed his solar plexus with a force that knocked all the wind out of him. Rafe gasped and staggered back.

Appalled, Maggie stared at him, backing up until she was pressed against the pier table under the mirror. In a stifled voice, she said, "I'm sorry, I didn't mean to hit you."

He straightened up, fighting for breath. His gray eyes weren't cool now; they blazed with anger, and something more. Maggie had never felt physically afraid of Rafe, but now she was acutely aware of the height and breadth and sheer athletic strength of him.

She had wounded his pride, and that was a far graver blow than an accidental elbow.

The moments it took for Rafe to regain his breath gave him time to grab the last shreds of his temper. "It's fortunate for you that I was taught never to strike a woman," he said with icy fury. "If you were a man, I would teach you a lesson you would never forget."

"Surely if I were a man, this situation would not have arisen," she said tremulously.

Rafe's anger began to fade. "No, I suppose it wouldn't have. I'm rather conventional in my preferences."

She gave him an uncertain smile. "Will you forgive me if I promise not to hit you again unless I mean it?"

He had to smile. "Forgiven."

Her gaze dropped and she busied herself with putting on her evening gloves. He guessed that she had been deeply affected to lash out like that, and that was promising. Yet he felt a stirring of guilt at having caused her unhappiness.

Cool strategy and analysis disappeared when she raised her beautiful gray-green eyes to his. There was infinite courage and vulnerability in those smoky depths, and with a surge of emotion that left him shaken, Rafe realized that it wasn't the maddening, elusive countess he desired. What he really wanted was to have Margot Ashton back.

At that moment, he would have given his title and half his fortune to turn back the clock to the uncomplicated love they had shared when they were young. Though that was impossible, clearly the girl he had loved still lived somewhere inside the lady spy. If it were humanly possible, he would call Margot forth again.

With mild surprise, he recognized that in his mind, she was always Margot when he was thinking of her as she was—or as he wanted her to be. He asked, "Why don't you like to be called Margot?"

She gazed at him for a long, long time, her changeable eyes unfathomable. Speaking as if the words were being torn out of her, she said, "Being Margot hurt too much."

It said everything and nothing, but intuition told him that it was not the time to ask for a clearer explanation. After a pause, he said, "It's time we left for Prince Orkov's ball. We have a general to hunt."

"Very true." Maggie turned to the mirror and replaced her jade earrings with the emeralds. "The day our mission is completed, you will have your 'bits of trumpery' back." After wrapping her long cashmere shawl around her bare shoulders with casual artistry, she turned to face him, the Countess Janos once more. "Shall we be off?"

Rafe offered her his arm, pleased that he did not give in to the nearly overpowering desire to embrace her again. Still, as he helped her into his coach, he found himself reaching out to touch her golden hair. The silky strands flowed over his fingers like gossamer, and he wished he dared bury his hands in them.

More than ever he wanted her, but she was proving to be a far more difficult challenge than he had expected. He had thought she would yield to the passion of the moment, like the society beauties he had known, and he had been wrong.

But Rafael Whitbourne was unaccustomed to failure, and he would not accept it now. There had to be a way to win her, and by God, he would find it.

Prince Orkov's ballroom was decorated with barbaric Mid-Eastern splendor, including footmen dressed as Turkish harem guards and an Egyptian belly dancer performing in a side room. Even the jaundiced tastes of Paris society admitted that it was out of the ordinary.

In spite of frustration with their lack of progress in uncovering the plot, Maggie was enjoying herself. Their host held her hand and gazed into her eyes with Slavic soulfulness, but fortunately he was too busy to seek her out.

For the first part of the evening, Rafe stayed close to Maggie's side, playing the part of the devoted lover, as if there had been no traumatic scene earlier. But for him it would not have been traumatic. There were plenty of women available to relieve his physical frustrations later this night.

Fleetingly she toyed with the idea of letting him have his way with her so she would no longer have the cachet of being unavailable. After a night or two, surely he would grow bored and try his luck elsewhere.

As soon as the thought surfaced, she squashed it, recognizing it for an outrageous rationalization. No matter what reasons she concocted to allow him into her bed, the emotional repercussions would be disastrous. He was upsetting her enough as it was. Whenever she looked at Rafe, she felt his lips moving sensuously down her neck, and her knees started to weaken. It was hard to keep her mind on the business of the evening.

Though General Roussaye was supposed to be present, they couldn't locate him in the crush, and Maggie was beginning to fear that they would be unsuccessful. After an hour, she and Rafe decided to separate and hope for the best.

Midnight came and went, supper was served, the dancing resumed, and still she hadn't found her quarry. Exasperated, she wandered into the room where the belly dancer was performing for a handful of guests.

The woman undulated in veils and bangles while three musicians on the low dias behind her played minor-key music that sounded strange to European ears. As her eyes adjusted to the dimmer light, Maggie realized that she had found her man. While she had never been introduced to the general, he had been pointed out to her once, and she recognized him immediately.

Michel Roussaye was below medium height and wiry in build, but at first glance he reminded her of Colonel von Fehrenbach. The blond Prussian was an aristocrat who had been bred to the trade of war, while the dark-haired Frenchman was a commoner who had achieved his rank by merit. Nonetheless, even in this dim light it was clear that they were brothers under the skin, with the tough watchfulness of the professional man of war.

Would Roussaye have as much anger in him as von Fehrenbach did? Of their three suspects, the Bonapartist had the best motive for creating disruptions.

Maggie crossed the room to take a seat near Roussaye, wondering how she might strike up a conversation since there was no one to introduce them. The general was intent on the dancer and her eyes followed his.

She had never seen a belly dancer before, since the few places where they might be seen were off-limits for females. The sight made her blink with astonishment. Was it really possible for a woman to make her breasts twirl in opposite directions? Improbable as it was, the evidence was before her eyes. The spinning tassels heightened the effect. The dancer was heavy by European standards, but there was a large amount of her visible, all of it superbly trained.

Maggie must have made some sound of surprise, because a soft tenor voice said, "A very talented performer, do you not agree?"

She turned and saw that Roussaye was watching her with amusement. She replied, "Indeed, monsieur, I had no idea that it was possible for a human body to do such things."

He gestured at the stage. "Though Orkov hired her as a curiosity, she is an artist of great skill."

"Is artistry what a man sees when he looks at a belly dancer?"

"That may not be the first thought in most men's minds," he admitted with a hint of smile, "but I have spent time in Egypt, and have some appreciation of the fine points of the art."

She remembered that Roussaye's first military experience had been in Napoleon's Egyptian campaign of 1798, when he had been scarcely more than a boy. A formidable man. Keeping her tone light, Maggie agreed, "She does have rather fine points."

The music ended and the sweat-drenched dancer took a bow and retired for a break. The rest of the audience also left, leaving Maggie alone with Roussaye. She asked, "What was Egypt like?"

This time his smile was warmer. "Remarkable. The temples are almost impossible to believe, even when they are right before you. We look at a cathedral five hundred years old and think it ancient. *Their* temples are many times that age. And the Pyramids . . ."

The general was lost in memory for a moment. "Bonaparte spent the night in the largest. The next morning when he was asked what he had seen, he said only that no one would believe him." With an undertone of sadness he added, "In the history of Egypt, the brief French occupation is less than the blink of an eye. In the history of France, Napoleon may be of no more importance than that."

Maggie said dryly, "A thousand years from now, people may be that detached. In our time, Napoleon appears as the greatest and wickedest man of our age."

Roussaye stiffened, and she wondered if she had gone too far. While she wanted to stimulate responses from him, it would be a mistake to alienate him entirely.

"You are not French, madame," he said coldly. "It is not to be expected that you would see him as we do."

Wanting to know what motivated him, she asked, "How *do* the French see Bonaparte? I am one of many who paid a high price for his ambition. Can you convince me there was any value to it?"

The general's dark eyes held hers. "You were right to say that he is the greatest man of our age. In his younger years, to be around him was to feel . . . to feel as if a strong wind was blowing. The emperor had more force and vitality than any man I have ever seen, more strength and more vision. We will never see his equal again."

"Thank God," she said, unable to repress her bitterness.

Leaning forward, he said intensely, "After the Revolution, the hands of every nation in Europe were raised against us. France should have been destroyed, but we weren't. Bonaparte gave us back our power and pride. We were everywhere victorious."

"And in his later years, your emperor lost whole armies. Hundreds of thousands of soldiers, countless civilians, died for France's glory. He once said that the lives of a million men were nothing to him," Maggie retorted. "When Bonaparte came back from Elba, were you one of those who forgot his vows to Louis and followed your emperor?"

After a long silence, the general said quietly, "I was."

She took a deep breath, reminding herself that she must be controlled. "Do you think it was right to rally to him?"

He surprised her by saying, "No, I can't say that it was right, but that didn't matter. Napoleon was my emperor, and I would have followed him to hell itself."

"Then you got your wish. They say that Waterloo was a close approximation of hell."

"The emperor was not the man he once was, and fifty thousand soldiers paid the price. Perhaps I should have been one of them, but God had other plans for me." Roussaye's expression eased. "Though it is a salvation I do not deserve, I have learned that there is life beyond war."

An odd, mystical statement for a warrior. Maggie was saved from further comment when two people entered the room. Glancing up, she saw Rafe accompanied by a tiny, exquisite woman with raven black hair and the swelling figure of midpregnancy. Roussaye rose, a smile transforming his serious expression.

Rafe said, "Magda, my love, permit me to introduce you to Madame Roussaye. She has been showing me our host's paintings. We are cousins of some sort, for she is from Florence and her family is connected to that of my Italian grandmother."

The raven-haired woman greeted Maggie warmly. Judging by the way the Roussayes looked at each other, it was easy to guess that his wife was the salvation he had referred to; the bond between them was almost tangible. Was the general an ardent enough Bonapartist to risk his personal happiness in a treacherous plot?

Unfortunately, Maggie feared that he was.

The intensity of the earlier discussion disappeared in a general conversation. All four of them shared a serious interest in art, and before the couples parted they made an engagement to visit the Louvre together three days hence.

Back in the main ballroom, a waltz was playing. Rafe swept Maggie into it without asking her permission. As they whirled across the floor, she decided ruefully that conservative opinion was right. Even though he held her at a perfectly proper distance, the waltz was still altogether too erotic to be decent. With her awareness of him heightened by their encounter earlier in the evening, it was all too easy to notice how much the closeness and rhythms of the dance were like making love.

It was not entirely a relief to discover that his purpose was strictly business. He asked, "What is your judgment of General Roussaye?"

She hesitated for three complete circles before saying, "He is devoted to France and the emperor, and I think he is quite capable of participating in a plot to restore Bonaparte to the throne. He has the best motive of all our suspects, coupled with the intelligence and conviction to achieve his ends."

"But you have reservations," Rafe said, reading the undercurrents of her speech.

Maggie sighed. "Only that I liked the man. Starting with very little, he has achieved his rank on pure merit. Beyond his military skills, he has taste and sensitivity. I wish that Varenne was our villain, but Roussaye is more likely."

"If so, my newfound cousin may be a widow in short order," Rafe said, his eyes grave. "Since Roussaye has already broken his oath to Louis once, the slightest hint of evidence that he is involved in a plot will put him in a cell next to Marshal Ney, waiting for execution."

"Men are such fools!" Maggie said with exasperation. "He has a beautiful wife who adores him, he has earned enough legitimate wealth to live a comfortable life, yet he would throw that all away."

"I liked him, too. Are you sure that he is our man?"

She shook her head regretfully, her eyes unfocused. "I can't be sure, but I sense that all is not aboveboard with the general. Perhaps he isn't involved in our particular plot—but I fear that he is."

At times like this, she hated being a spy. If she was wrong, she might contribute to the ruin of an innocent man. All the important Bonapartists were on dangerously thin ice, and a hint of suspicion could ruin a man, perhaps even send him to the firing squad.

Grimly she reminded herself that the stakes were higher than one person's life; the successful assassination of an Allied leader could hurl Europe into another war. "We should pass our speculations on as soon as possible. Lord Strathmore may know something that will corroborate them."

"I'll send a courier to Lucien tonight, but I think the time has come to talk to Lord Castlereagh."

Used to working indirectly, Maggie was momentarily startled. However, the foreign minister knew of her work and had reason to trust her speculations. If she and Rafe talked to him in person, they might be able to impress on him the seriousness of the situation. "We would have to meet with him in a way that would not arouse comment."

"Easily done," Rafe replied. "Lord and Lady Castlereagh often entertain distinguished British visitors, which, in all modesty, I can claim to be. As my companion, a woman already known to them, you would be equally welcome. I will contact him and ask that a private breakfast or lunch be arranged."

"You'd better make it as soon as possible," she said darkly. "I feel in my bones that something will happen soon."

The music stopped and they moved toward the edge of the ballroom. She was about to suggest they leave when the orchestra struck up another waltz and Robin approached them. He greeted Rafe amiably, then bowed before Maggie.

"Countess Janos, would you honor me with this dance?"

In spite of the steely glint in Rafe's eyes, it never occurred to Maggie to refuse. Publicly she and Robin were only the most casual of acquaintances, and he would not ask her to dance if there wasn't something he needed to discuss with her. She smiled and extended one hand. "It would be my pleasure, Mr. Anderson."

She blew a kiss to Rafe as Robin took her in his arms and carried her away in the rapid turns of the waltz.

For all the years they had known each other, and as intimate as they had been, they had never waltzed together. She was not surprised to discover that he was an excellent dancer, nor that they knew each other so well that there was no need to concentrate on footwork. A carefree smile on her face, she asked, "Is something wrong, Robin?"

"I heard something that I wanted to pass on in the hope that you might be able to make something of it." His grave blue eyes contrasted with his frivolous mien. "One of my underworld informants has given me a name to put behind the conspiracy. Not a real name, unfortunately, but it's a start. The man is called Le Serpent."

"Le Serpent?" Her brow wrinkled in concentration. "It's unfamiliar to me."

"And to me. There is no one in the Parisian underworld by that name. My informant couldn't even say if the man is French or a foreigner. Apparently Le Serpent has been recruiting criminals to carry out a plot against some of the Allied leaders."

She thought about what he had said, but the information rang no bells. "I'll ask if any of my women have heard of such a man. Were there any other clues?"

"Not as such. But I have wondered ..." Robin's voice trailed off as he deftly removed them from the path of a drunken Russian officer whose enthusiasm for waltzing exceeded his skill.

When they were safely clear, Robin continued, "Is it possible that the name might come from a family crest or some such? The man we are after is certainly someone of power and position, and would likely have a family coat of arms."

She felt a tingle at the words. In his own way, Robin was as intuitive as Maggie herself, and it would not be the first time that a small fact triggered a mental leap to something quite different. When inspiration struck, he was usually right.

"That's very plausible," she agreed. "I'll ask around to discover whose arms involve any kind of snake. There can't be many. It will be good to have something concrete to investigate after so many days of frustration."

During the latter part of the dance, she described her meeting with General Roussaye and her suspicions of him.

Robin listened intently. When she had finished, he said, "I'll see if I can find any snakes in his background. I think we're on the edge of a breakthrough. But for God's sake, Maggie, be careful. My informant seemed to think Le Serpent is a direct representative of Satan. Whoever he is, the man is dangerous."

The music ended. Robin had maneuvered so that the last bars brought them to the Duke of Candover. Gracefully handing Maggie back to Rafe's keeping, he bid them good night, then disappeared.

Maggie's worried gaze followed him. Robin must be as tired as she was, but if she knew him, he would spend half of the remaining night in Parisian stews and gaming hells looking for further traces of Le Serpent. And he told *her* to be careful!

Intent on her friend, she didn't see the black look on Rafe's face as he observed her preoccupation.

Chapter 10

The first thing the next morning, Maggie began her inquiries about snakes and related heraldic creatures by calling on a fragile old lady in Faubourg St. Germain. Madame Daudet had lost all her male descendants in Napoleon's wars, and she longed for peace. She also knew the history, marriages, and arms of every important family in France. After listening to Maggie's request, she promised that within forty-eight hours she would have a detailed list of possibilities among both the old and the new French aristocracy. With luck, it would provide some clues.

Around noon, a note was delivered from Rafe saying they would join the Castlereaghs for luncheon the next day. Maggie nodded with satisfaction, then prepared to call on a gossipy woman who was an expert on the upper levels of Bonapartist society. Perhaps she would also be well informed about serpents.

Maggie's departure was delayed when the butler brought in the card of an unexpected visitor. Mrs. Oliver Northwood.

Curious what Cynthia Northwood might have to say, she ordered her butler to admit the visitor. The young woman was tense when she entered, her pretty face pale against the dark curls.

"I'm glad to find you at home, Countess," she said in labored French. "I wish to discuss something with you."

Responding in English, Maggie said, "But of course, my dear. Would you care for some coffee?"

At her visitor's nod, Maggie gave orders to the butler, then seated herself, gesturing Cynthia to a sofa near the window where it would be easy to read her expression. Maggie made general remarks and received monosyllabic replies until coffee and delicate pastries were served. When they were alone, she said, "If you have something to ask me, perhaps you should simply come out with it."

Cynthia's wide brown eyes slid away. "It's harder to say than I thought it would be. You scarcely know me, and have no reason to listen to my troubles. But . . . but I needed another woman to talk to."

"And you chose me because of our mutual relationship with Candover?"

Cynthia looked startled, then smiled faintly. "Perhaps that is it. Since we have a . . . mutual friend, and you listened kindly once, I thought I could talk to you." She drew herself up with visible effort. "When we spoke before, I told you that I was unhappy in my marriage."

"When I met your husband later that evening, I understood why," Maggie said encouragingly. "Why did you marry him?"

Cynthia spread her hands in a despairing gesture. "I fancied myself in love, of course. Oliver was handsome and dashing and lived such an exciting life compared to mine in Lincolnshire, where I grew up. The aunt who presented me was impressed that he was the son of a lord, and told me what a splendid conquest I had made. I didn't look beyond his lineage and tailoring.

"He was handsome seven years ago, before his indulgences caught up with him. I was only eighteen, dazzled that such a man of the world should court me. It never occurred to me to consider his character." She

shrugged. "I got what I deserved. It's incredible that
we choose our life's companions after a handful of
meetings, usually under the most artificial of circumstances. Since Oliver came from a noble family, my father saw no reason to deny his suit. I was so pleased by
my good fortune that I never asked what he saw in
me."

"You are too hard on yourself. You are a very attractive woman, one any man might fall in love with."

"Perhaps," Cynthia said, unmollified. "But it was
more to the point that I had a fine dowry. As a younger
son, Oliver would have needed to marry well in any
case, but his gambling debts made the situation urgent." She sighed. "It took very little time for me to realize what a poor bargain I had made. I come from
simple country folk who believe in old-fashioned
things like fidelity. I won't bore you with how I discovered about his women, but it shattered all my illusions. When I confronted him, he mocked me for being
a provincial little fool."

Cynthia's voice broke, and she stopped speaking.
Ever practical, Maggie poured her more coffee. The
girl choked when she sipped it, then continued her depressing tale.

"I decided to pay him back in his own coin." She
flushed and stared into the depths of her cup. "It was
foolish. Women are not the same as men, and it was a
poor form of revenge. Except for Rafe, I have few
good memories of that time. He was always kind, and
he told me to put a higher price on myself."

She glanced up again. "I didn't know what he meant
at first, but I did eventually. I started behaving in a
way that would not shame my father if he knew of it,
and I found it much easier to live with myself."

"Yet something has gone wrong to bring you here."

"I fell in love, and was happier than I had ever been,
and now everything is much, much worse." Cynthia's

eyes were bleakly unhappy. "Michael Brewer is everything I should have sought in a husband, but was too foolish to appreciate. He is kind, reliable, and honorable. Most of all, he loves me, in spite of all the mistakes I have made."

Maggie looked at her with compassion. No wonder the poor girl looked so miserable. She was in a situation where there was little prospect of a happy resolution.

Cynthia put her cup down and toyed nervously with her wedding ring. "I want to marry and settle down somewhere in the country with Michael and raise lots of babies and get plump and warm my feet on his back in the winter. That is what he wants, too. He hates the dishonesty of what we are doing."

"But as long as you and your husband live, that is impossible. In England divorces are virtually unobtainable. Even if you had the money and influence to get a bill of divorcement through Parliament, you would be an outcast."

"There is no time for that," Cynthia said grimly. "I am with child."

Maggie inhaled sharply. "And it is not your husband's?"

"We have not been man and wife for years. Unfortunately, while he doesn't want me for himself, he doesn't want anyone else to have me, either." Cynthia shuddered. "I am frightened about what he will do when he learns I am increasing."

"And it is not the sort of thing one can conceal very long," Maggie observed. "What does your major think?"

Cynthia started twisting her hands together. "I haven't told him yet. When I do, I know he will insist that I leave Oliver and live with him."

"It will be a scandal, but hardly unique. Perhaps that would be the best solution."

For the first time, Cynthia's voice became uneven. "You don't know my husband. Oliver is horribly vindicative, and he would sue Michael for criminal conversation. Michael is not a rich man—he would be ruined. His military career would be over, and both our families would be disgraced."

In a whisper, she finished, "And it would break my father's heart." She buried her face in her hands as sobs overcame her. Between gulps for breath, she managed to say, "Worst of all, I fear that Michael would come to hate me for ruining his life."

Maggie crossed quickly to sit next to her guest on the sofa, putting one arm around her to give what comfort she could. Fiercely she cursed the inflexible marriage laws that kept husband and wife tied together no matter how wretched they were.

When Cynthia's sobs abated, Maggie handed over a fresh handkerchief and said, "Your choices are limited. You can stay with your husband or leave. If you leave, you can return to your father, live with your major, or perhaps set up an independent establishment."

Cynthia straightened, wiping her eyes with the handkerchief. "It sounds simple when you put it that way. I do want to leave, but it will be very difficult. Oliver would be injured in his purse as well as his pride, for my father's money supports us. My dowry is long gone, of course, but Papa sends an allowance that I use for household expenses. That would stop if I left. With the amount that Oliver loses gambling, he might be unable to maintain an establishment if I wasn't there." She lifted a nervous hand to brush back a loose strand of hair. "Though perhaps he could manage. He always seems to have money."

An alarm bell went off in Maggie's mind. Northwood was an inveterate gambler with unexpected financial resources? They had concentrated on investigating the assassination plot since that was most urgent, but there was also the matter of a possible spy in the British delegation. If there was such a person, the mysterious Le Serpent might be using his services. Since Maggie heartily disliked Oliver Northwood, she was quite willing to believe him a villain. And if he was in contact with the master conspirator . . .

Controlling her excitement, she said casually, "His salary from the Foreign Office must help."

"It is a mere pittance, only two hundred pounds a year." Cynthia shrugged indifferently. "Perhaps he has become a cleverer gambler. If he didn't pay his debts, I suppose no one would continue to gamble with him."

"Is it possible that your husband might be involved in something he shouldn't?"

"What do you mean?"

Maggie put on her innocent face. "It's just a hope. If Northwood has some secret, he might be more easily persuaded to let you leave without causing trouble." She smiled wickedly. "I assume that part of the reason you wished to talk with me was to get the ideas of a wily European who was not raised with your English sense of fair play."

Cynthia's momentary shock swiftly turned to embarrassment. "Perhaps it was, without my being aware of it." Her expression became withdrawn as she thought about what her hostess had said. "Perhaps he *is* concealing something. He seemed to change when he joined the Foreign Office, and it has become more pronounced since we came to Paris. He has had more money since then, too. More than can be accounted for by his salary, I mean."

"Do you suppose he could be taking bribes?"

"He hasn't much influence to sell," Cynthia said doubtfully.

"He might pretend to more than he has," Maggie said. Bribery was common, and many people would accept bribes who would never consider spying against their country. Northwood might be one of those. None-theless, the possibility was worth further investigation.

Cynthia said slowly, "Several weeks ago when I was writing letters, I ran out of paper and looked in Oliver's desk for more. He happened to come in then, and became outraged when he saw what I was doing. In fact, he struck me. At the time I didn't think much about it since he is often unpredictable, but ever since then he has made a point of locking up all his papers. Do you think that's significant?"

"Possibly, possibly not. Some men are naturally furtive. But if he has some guilty secret that you could discover, it might give you ammunition to defend yourself." Maggie caught Cynthia's gaze and said soberly, "It is not a nice thing that we are talking about. Are you willing to behave so dishonorably?"

Cynthia took a deep breath, but her gaze was unwavering. "Yes. We women have few weapons at our disposal, and I would be foolish to waste one. Perhaps I can stop some greater tragedy, like a duel. I don't think Oliver would dare challenge Michael, but I could be wrong." She trembled as if a cold draft had touched her. "I couldn't bear to be the cause of Michael risking his life."

Satisfied, Maggie said, "If you are sure. Do you think you could unlock your husband's desk and study his private papers?"

Cynthia bit her lip, but nodded her head.

"You must be extremely cautious, not only in acting when he is away, but in leaving no traces of your search. Your husband has a violent temper, and if he suspects you, he could do you a serious injury. You have not only your own life to consider." Maggie put as much earnestness in her voice as she could. Though she was not particularly proud of herself for setting a wife to spy on her husband, the opportunity was too good to pass up. Moreover, if Oliver Northwood really

was a spy, that fact might make it easier for Cynthia to
escape him.

"I promise I will be careful." Her mouth twisted. "I
know better than anyone what Oliver might do."

"If you discover anything suspicious, bring it to me
first," Maggie said. "I have considerable experience of
the world, and I might better understand what you have
found."

Cynthia nodded again as she stood. "I can't thank
you enough, Countess. Talking to you has helped enormously."

Maggie rose also. "Perhaps you should call me Magda
since we are going to be conspirators. Or Maggie, if you
prefer."

"Thank you, Maggie. And please, call me Cynthia."
Leaning forward, she gave the older woman a heartfelt
hug.

After again cautioning Cynthia to be extremely careful, Maggie showed her guest out. Then she sat back to
think about what she had learned.

Quite apart from her dislike of Oliver Northwood,
her instinct said that he was capable of treachery. She
did not rule out the possibility that he was innocent, or
guilty of no more than minor corruption. However,
given the volatile situation in Paris, information was
tremendously valuable. A weak man might easily succumb to temptation.

The next question was whether to tell Rafe. She
frowned. While Rafe and Northwood were not close
friends, they had known each other forever, and had
been part of the same circle when they were young
men about town. Rafe would have trouble believing
that someone from that group of bluff, honest Englishmen was a traitor. It was much easier to suspect a
stranger than an acquaintance.

Maggie decided that she would not tell Rafe of her
suspicions unless Cynthia discovered some concrete

proof. For all of their sakes, she hoped that would happen, and soon.

That evening Rafe went to the Salon des Étrangers, the closest thing to a gentlemen's club in Paris. It was a rendezvous for confirmed gamblers, and many of the richest and most influential men in Paris were regular customers. Though he had visited several times in the hope of hearing something useful, so far he had had no success. Still, it felt better to be doing something than nothing.

Standing at the entrance to the main gambling room, he surveyed the crowd for familiar faces. The Salon was larger and far grander than the modest Café Mazarin, but the signs of gambling fever were the same.

The proprietor, the Marquis de Livry, came forward. The marquis bore a remarkable resemblance to the Prince Regent, both in girth and grandeur of manner. Smiling graciously, he said, "How delightful to see you this evening, your grace. What is your preference?"

"I'll wait to see what table calls me," Rafe said.

The marquis nodded, accustomed to gamblers who looked for magical signs that fortune favored them. After urging Rafe to enjoy himself, Livry left to greet a party of Austrians.

Taking a glass of excellent burgundy from a footman, Rafe strolled through the crowd. With a feeling of inevitability, he saw Robert Anderson sitting at a faro table. The blond man had a talent for turning up in unexpected places. It seemed highly probable that Anderson was also involved in the murky shadows of intelligence gathering.

But if so, for whom did he work? The logical answer was that he kept his ears open on behalf of the British delegation. Yet Rafe had his doubts.

Shielded by a Corinthian column, he sipped his wine

and studied the younger man. Again he felt that tantalizing sense of near-recognition, but could not identify it.

His attempts to remember were interrupted by a jovial greeting. "Evening, Candover. Good to see you again."

Rafe turned without enthusiasm to greet Oliver Northwood. He was surprised to find his old acquaintance at a place where the play was so deep, for men of much greater fortune than Northwood had been ruined in the Salon des Étrangers.

As the men exchanged idle talk, Rafe watched Anderson push half the counters in front of him across the table after losing a bet, as imperturbable in defeat as in victory. The man looked as blond and angelic as a choirboy. Was that what Maggie saw in him, that handsome face? Or did she fancy herself in love with him? *What the hell did Anderson have that he himself didn't?*

Rafe was shocked by the violent jealousy that surged through him. It was an unfamiliar emotion, and not one that he liked. He had always been willing to bid a graceful farewell to women who developed other preferences—except where Margot was concerned. Even thirteen years later, he bitterly resented Northwood's intimacy with her, and the anger he felt at the memory of Anderson slipping in Maggie's back door was a serious blow to his view of himself as a civilized man.

In an effort to control his primitive emotions, Rafe reminded himself that Anderson was just one of the men in Maggie's life. There was no point in being jealous merely because the bastard was the only one of her lovers Rafe knew.

The reflection was a singular failure at calming him.

Deciding that he might as well take advantage of the opportunity to learn more about his rival, Rafe said,

"Your colleague Anderson reminds me of someone, but I can't remember who. What's his background?"

"Hasn't any." Northwood drained his glass of wine. "Fellow just appeared in Paris in July, and Castlereagh took him into the delegation. Must have had letters of recommendation, but I don't know from whom. Says he isn't related to any Andersons I know." He hailed a footman and exchanged his empty glass for a full one. "Comes here often."

"Really? Then whatever Andersons he comes from must be well off."

Northwood frowned, giving the appearance of a man coming to a decision. "Perhaps I shouldn't say this, Candover, but there's something dashed smoky about Anderson. Sprang from nowhere, always poking into things that don't concern him, then disappears like a bloody alley cat. And he has more money than he should."

"Interesting." Rafe tried to suppress his unworthy excitement. "Have you spoken to Castlereagh about your suspicions?"

After looking around to assure that no one was within listening distance, Northwood said quietly, "I've talked to Castlereagh, all right. That's why I'm here—the foreign minister asked me to keep an eye on Anderson. Informally, you know." At Rafe's questioning look, he added, "To see if he talks to anyone suspicious. Shouldn't be telling you this, but I know you can be trusted, and want to put you on your guard. You know what the situation is here in Paris. Can't be too careful."

Northwood looked as if he were weighing whether to continue, then added in an almost inaudible voice, "Confidential information has been getting out of the British delegation. Don't want to slander an innocent man—but we're watching Anderson very closely."

Rafe had never seen Northwood so serious, and he

wondered if he had misjudged his old schoolmate. Perhaps the hail-fellow-well-met demeanor was a disguise. He studied the other man, trying to be objective.

Though Rafe could not like Northwood's vulgarity of manner, he had no reason to distrust the man. Had jealousy been coloring Rafe's judgment? Undoubtedly.

The same jealousy made it all too easy to believe the worst of Anderson. Rafe reminded himself that he was in Paris to help his country, not to pursue personal intrigues. But if the blond man was a traitor to England, it would be pure pleasure to see him caught and punished.

Rafe said, "I'll keep my eyes open, and perhaps I'll remember why Anderson looks familiar. It might be significant."

After a nod of complicity, he drifted from Northwood, ending at the *rouge-et-noir* table. It was a game that involved more luck than skill, so Rafe was able to monitor what was happening elsewhere in the room. He noticed when General Michel Roussaye took an empty chair at the faro table next to Anderson, noticed the intense words the two men exchanged, which might or might not have anything to do with faro.

Noticed, and frowned.

Chapter 11

The next day, Maggie and Rafe were both silent as they went to the British embassy to visit the Castlereaghs. She briefly considered telling him of her suspicions of Oliver Northwood, but he was too much the cool, remote aristocrat today, his dark face handsome and detached.

They ate in a private dining room, and the excellent luncheon was served on Pauline Bonaparte's own plate, which Wellington had bought along with the house the previous year. Looking every inch a duke's mistress, Maggie wore a sky blue gown with matching ostrich plumes in her hair. Lord Castlereagh was relaxed and witty, and the meal was an enjoyable one.

The talk did not turn serious until a silver pot of coffee was placed on the table and Lady Castlereagh signaled for the servants to withdraw. The foreign minister started the discussion by saying, "Have you heard the latest news from the Tuileries?"

Both of his guests shook their heads. The French king's court at the Tuileries was a whirlpool of rumor and gossip as factions of royalists struggled for ascendancy, but there hadn't been any serious news from that quarter recently.

Castlereagh said, "Fouché has been forced out of the government, and Talleyrand will also be gone in a few days." A spark of humor showed in his eyes. "Whenever Prince Talleyrand comes under heavy criticism, he loftily offers his resignation. Much to his surprise, this time the king decided to accept it."

Maggie bit her lip as she considered the implications, then glanced at Rafe. His eyes were grave. Though Talleyrand was difficult and unpredictable, he had also been brilliant and a force for moderation. His departure might increase the danger for other moderates. She asked, "Has a new prime minister been chosen yet?"

"The tsar suggested that the king choose one of the French royalists who governed for him in Russia, either the Duc de Richelieu or the Count de Varenne. Louis agreed to accept Richelieu," the foreign minister answered. "The consensus in the diplomatic corps is that he will last only a few weeks."

"Don't be too sure of that, your lordship," Maggie said. "I've met the man, and I think he will provide some surprises."

Castlereagh regarded her shrewdly; he must have hoped for such information. "What is your evaluation of Richelieu?"

"Absolute integrity, capable of being forceful if necessary," she said without hesitation. "He will be a strong advocate for France, but I think you will deal well together."

Castlereagh nodded slowly. "That confirms my own impressions. The negotiations are going well, and the monarchs should be returning to their own countries in another fortnight or so." He gave his wife a reassuring glance. "There are a number of details to be worked out over the next several months, but I think that the worst is over."

"I hope you're right," Rafe said, "but we're afraid that the next two weeks will be very dangerous for you personally, Lord Castlereagh." Briefly he described the rumors that he and Maggie had been pursuing, and their suspicions.

The foreign minister took the threats calmly. "Lord Strathmore has informed me of what you say. I realize that there is some danger, but it's not the first time I have been threatened, and I don't suppose that it will be the last."

Maggie thought with exasperation that stoicism was all very well, but a little fear could be a useful thing. She glanced at her hostess and saw that Lady Castlereagh's round face was tense and her fingers had tightened around a silver spoon. While her husband was being heroic, Emily was dying inside. However, she had been a political wife too long to make a fuss in front of anyone, and only Maggie noticed her anxiety.

They talked a few minutes longer, until the dining room clock struck two. Lord Castlereagh said, "I must leave now for a meeting with the French and the tsar at the Tuileries. I expect it will be rather lively."

He and Rafe talked about the tsar's Holy Alliance as they headed to the stables where the duke's carriage waited with the embassy horses. Lady Castlereagh accompanied her guests to the rear door, and Maggie lagged behind for a moment to say, "There is some danger, Emily, but I'm sure he will come through safely."

"I can only pray that my husband has the same magical ability to avoid bullets that Wellington does," Emily said in a brittle attempt at humor. "We have discussed putting guards on all the embassy doors. Now I will insist on it." She gazed after her handsome husband. "I'll be glad when this is over and we are back in London. Sometimes I wish that Robert would have been content to stay in Ireland and raise sheep. It would have been much easier on my nerves."

"No doubt," Maggie admitted, "but he wouldn't have been the man that he is if he had done that."

"True. I remind myself of that." With visible effort,

Lady Castlereagh schooled her face to that of a calm hostess. "So pleasant to see you and Candover, Lady Janos. We must get together again soon." Then she reentered the embassy.

Going down the steps into the yard between the embassy and the stables, Maggie was some distance behind the two men. Candover's carriage had been called, along with a restless bay gelding for Castlereagh to ride to his meeting.

Maggie frowned, her instinct for danger tugging at her. She scanned the yard and the windows that overlooked it, but saw nothing suspicious.

Her gaze returned to the stable yard, and she saw Castlereagh's mount fidget and toss its head, eyes rolling. The beast seemed too wild for city riding, and she wondered that the groom was not holding it in better.

Rafe and Castlereagh had reached the horse's side, but they were so absorbed in their discussion that they didn't notice the animal's behavior. Maggie's gaze went next to the groom, who stood on the opposite side of the horse. He was a dark man with a scarred face, and something about him was subtly wrong.

While she was trying to decide why the groom seemed out of place, the horse suddenly neighed, a furious sound that echoed harshly between the stone buildings. Neighing again, the gelding reared and jerked free of the groom, then put its head between its front legs and kicked back.

Rafe and Lord Castlereagh were standing too close to escape, and the wild, iron-shod hooves smashed into the foreign minister. As Maggie watched with horror, Castlereagh was hurled into Rafe and both men crashed to the ground.

She instantly raced down the steps, shouting for help. Trapped in a corner of the yard, the horse couldn't easily bolt, so it continued stamping and bucking over the foreign minister's unconscious body.

Rafe scrambled to his feet and grabbed Castlereagh under the arms. As he tried to pull the minister out of danger, the horse kicked again. This time one of the lethal hooves almost struck Rafe's head. He managed to dodge, but the hoof clipped his shoulder, knocking him off balance. After a moment, he got a new grip on Castlereagh and resumed the retreat.

Maggie swore out loud as she reached them. Where the devil had the groom gone? The man had disappeared as soon as the horse went out of control. Pulling her ostrich plume headdress from her hair, she waved it at the maddened gelding in an attempt to drive it away from Rafe and Castlereagh.

The horse neighed violently again, its eyes rolling wildly and flecks of foam around its mouth. Maggie stood her ground, the tall, fluttering headdress causing the bay to shy away from her. As it backed along the wall of the stables, frantic shouts came from the embassy.

When the horse was clear of the humans, it whirled and thundered across the yard. A young redheaded groom ran out of the stables and tried to corner the frantic animal.

Tossing aside her headdress, Maggie turned back to Rafe, who was kneeling by the foreign minister's side.

"How is he?" she asked breathlessly as she dropped to her knees on the cobbles. Castlereagh was unconscious, a bleeding gash on the side of his head, but he was breathing.

"I'm not sure," Rafe said grimly. "The first kick caught him full in the ribs, and another hoof grazed his head." As he spoke, he expertly checked the damage.

People were pouring out of the embassy, including a white-faced Lady Castlereagh. Rafe automatically took command, ordering a litter and sending a footman for a physician.

Maggie got to her feet and put an arm around Emily. "That was a nasty accident, but I'm sure he'll be all right."

Though Lady Castlereagh nodded, her eyes were terrified. Two footmen returned with a hastily improvised litter and gently lifted the foreign minister onto it, then carried him into the embassy. His wife followed, and Maggie went with her to offer support while they waited for a physician.

As the procession entered the embassy, Rafe turned and went into the stables. The young redheaded groom had caught the gelding and taken it inside to a box stall. The horse danced fretfully, still wearing its saddle and bridle, while the groom waited warily outside the stall.

Rafe said, "I'm Candover. Has Lord Castlereagh's horse always been this wild?"

The young groom gave him a worried glance. Like all of the embassy staff, he was British, and he answered in a broad West Country accent. "Nay, your grace. Samson is spirited, but a better-tempered beast you never saw. Is his lordship hurt bad?"

"We won't know until the physician has examined him, but I think the chances are good that he'll recover."

"Will . . . will they destroy Samson, your grace?"

"I don't know." Rafe saw that there was blood in the foam around the gelding's mouth. Swinging open the door of the stall, he entered and quietly approached the beast. "I'll look at him more closely."

Remembering all the Gypsy lore he had learned from his friend Nicholas, Rafe made himself utterly calm, from the inside out. As Samson jerked his head back and flattened his ears, Rafe murmured a string of nonsense words. The horse began to relax, and soon allowed its neck to be stroked.

After several minutes of stroking, Rafe breathed into Samson's nostrils, another Gypsy trick. The horse's rough breathing slowed and it stood still. Rafe had brought a handful of oats into the stall, and soon Samson was literally eating out of his hand.

After the horse finished the oats, Rafe cautiously removed the bridle. He found what he had suspected: the bridle had a cruel cutting bit, and the least pressure against Samson's tender mouth would have caused the horse considerable pain.

The young groom looked at the bit, then at Rafe, his eyes wide with questions. "Why would anyone do that to a good-tempered horse, your grace? A cutting bit is a nasty thing to use even with a rogue."

"I can guess, but I won't." Rafe studied the gelding again. "The bit explains why Samson reared in the first place, but something more must have been required to make him kick like that. Let's see what else we can find."

Cautiously he uncinched the girth, then lifted off the saddle and cloth. Samson stirred fretfully, so Rafe ran one hand down the sweaty neck until the horse relaxed again.

Rafe examined the area that had been under the saddlecloth, and was unsurprised to find a small metal object lodged in Samson's hide. The horse jerked when it was removed, and a line of blood trickled sluggishly down the brown flank.

The object Rafe pulled from the wound had four spikes joined in the center, rather like a miniature version of the caltrops that were used to cripple horses in warfare. He showed it to the groom, who had gone beyond surprise to anger.

"Someone wanted to hurt his lordship." The boy's mouth was hard. The lad was no fool, and he must know something of the tense political situation in Paris.

"Who usually handles Lord Castlereagh's horse?"

"The head groom, Mr. Anthony, but he's not here now. He had to go to Saint Denis this morning."

"Do you know who would have saddled Samson today?"

The groom thought, then shook his head again. "Not exactly, sir. I was cleaning tack and didn't see who it was. Didn't know nothing was wrong until I heard Samson screaming."

"Could you make a guess? Has there been anyone suspicious about the stables?"

"I can't swear it was him for sure, but there's been a Frenchy groom working here 'cause we're short-handed," the boy replied. "One of the regular grooms had to go back to England 'cause his father died, and another was beat up in a street fight and can't work for a few days. Probably it was the Frenchy that saddled up Samson and took him out."

"What does he look like?"

"Medium height, dark, a scar on his face." The lad thought again. "Brown eyes, I think. He kept to hisself, and I never really talked to him. His name was Jean Blanc."

The description fit Captain Henri Lemercier. Rafe looked hard at the young groom to impress him with his seriousness. "Don't be surprised if you don't see Jean Blanc again. Also, don't tell anybody what we have found. I'll talk to Lord Castlereagh myself. Is that clear?"

The boy nodded, and Rafe left the stables and joined Maggie and Lady Castlereagh.

It took an hour to get the physician's verdict on the foreign minister, but the news was good. Though Castlereagh had several cracked ribs and a mild concussion, he was conscious, and already planning to hold meetings in his bedchamber, to his wife's exasperation.

Lady Castlereagh gave Maggie and Rafe her heartfelt thanks for their part in preventing the accident from being more serious. Then Rafe took his dusty and bedraggled ladybird back to his carriage.

Maggie didn't speak at first; she simply lay back against the cushioned seat with her eyes closed. They were halfway home before she opened her eyes and said, "He could have been killed right in front of us."

"I know," Rafe said bleakly. "It speaks poorly for our abilities as spies and bodyguards."

"What did you discover in the stables?"

Rafe described the cutting bit, the spike in Samson's side, and the mysterious French groom, Jean Blanc.

"I suppose Blanc jerked on the bridle, cutting Samson's mouth," Maggie said. "When the horse reared, Blanc slammed his hand onto the saddlecloth, driving the spike in. Then he ran away."

"He might have run because we were there and things weren't going according to plan," Rafe said. "If Castlereagh had been trampled, he could have been killed outright. There would have been such an uproar that Blanc could have stayed around long enough to remove the cutting bit and the spike, and the death would have seemed like an accident."

"I thought something looked wrong about that groom." Maggie tried to remember her brief glimpse of the man. "He didn't have the look of a servant. He carried himself like a soldier, though that may not mean much since so many Frenchmen served in the emperor's army."

"I didn't see him myself, but from the description I was given, he could be one of your secondary suspects, Captain Henri Lemercier. I met Lemercier the night I went to the Café Mazarin."

Maggie said icily, "And you didn't mention that to

me, even though we had a report of an assassination being discussed there?"

Rafe hadn't mentioned the meeting because Lemercier had ended the evening with Robert Anderson, but that was a topic he wanted to avoid. Unless Rafe had undisputable evidence of Anderson's guilt, there was no point in confronting Maggie about the man. He said mildly, "I didn't tell you because Lemercier was drunk and said nothing of interest."

Maggie was regarding him suspiciously, but she did not pursue the point. Rafe wished he knew what thoughts were passing behind those wide, smoky gray eyes. Her golden hair was tangled after the incident in the stable yard, and her low-cut gown caressed the sensual body that was so incredibly good at distorting a man's judgment. If she were really his mistress, he would take her right here in the carriage.

Instead, he forced himself to reevaluate what he knew. The near-disaster had shaken Rafe badly, and brought home to him the dangers of this business as nothing else had.

It was time to question his assumptions about Maggie's professional loyalties, for her association with Anderson was damning evidence against her. The blond, bland Anderson, who looked like a choirboy or Lucifer fallen, was almost certainly an agent of Britain's enemies. Had Anderson been arranging Castlereagh's "accident" that night he met Lemercier at the Café Mazarin? And what had he and General Roussaye discussed when they met in the Salon des Étrangers?

Most important of all, was Maggie Anderson's dupe, or his accomplice? Though she had helped save Castlereagh this afternoon, that didn't mean she wasn't selling information or plotting against her country. There were too many hidden years lying between Margot Ashton and Magda Janos to take her on trust any longer. She might be a mercenary, working for whomever would pay her, or Anderson may have persuaded her to work against Britain's interests.

Yet in one sense, it didn't matter. Rafe wanted her, no matter what she was or what she was doing. If he exposed the conspiracy and Maggie proved to be a traitor, she might have to choose between accepting him or going to the gallows. He would prefer that she came to him willingly, but if necessary, he would take her by any means short of violence.

It was not a thought he was proud of.

The Englishman was becoming accustomed to these trips to Le Serpent and no longer worried as he had the first time. Still, on entering the darkened room where his master waited, he reflected that his blond hair would make him a clear target even in this dimness. Had he known the shadowy paths he would be treading, he would have had the foresight to be born dark.

The failure of Le Serpent's attempt on Lord Castlereagh had made the masked man seem less fearsome. The Englishman couldn't help thinking that there were surer ways of killing a man than with a horse. He made the mistake of saying that to his dark host.

"You presume to criticize me? You, who have no idea who I am or what my objectives are? You're a fool." The sibilant voice hissed like wind over ice. With a ghost of cool humor, he continued, "You should be pleased, *mon Anglais*, to learn that the next plan will have less element of chance.

"As of tomorrow, the important diplomatic sessions will be held in Castlereagh's bedchamber because of his injury. I will need complete floor plans of that part of the embassy. Every room, every corridor, every closet, with accurate measurements of each. Plus, information on the staff and their movements."

"Is that all?" the Englishman asked with veiled sarcasm.

Taking the question at face value, Le Serpent said, "I also need to know who will be attending each session. I *must* know that, without fail, no later than the evening before." He stood, a looming figure in the half-light. "And you will tell me, *mon petit Anglais*. Every evening, without fail."

The Englishman nodded reluctantly. He was already in too deeply to withdraw. But he needed time, time to trace the crest he had seen on Le Serpent's hand, and to allay any suspicions of himself. He decided to offer a piece of information that he had been keeping in reserve.

"You heard about Countess Janos, who drove the horse away from Lord Castlereagh before the job was finished?"

"I heard. A pity that she and her lover were there, but one cannot plan for everything." Le Serpent gave a slight, worldly shrug, implying that minor impediments might delay but never defeat him. "Quite a beautiful woman. There is no one like a Hungarian in bed."

The Englishman said, "She isn't a Hungarian. She's an Englishwoman named Margot Ashton, an impostor, a whore, and a spy."

"Indeed?" The breathy voice held menace, but not directed against his visitor. "You interest me, *mon Anglais*. Tell me what you know about the woman. If she is working for the British, it may be necessary to . . . deal with her."

Succinctly the Englishman told everything he knew about Magda, Countess Janos, who had once been known as Margot Ashton. It would be a great pity if such a ravishing female must be sacrificed, but one's own interests must come first.

Chapter 12

The next morning Maggie and Hélène Sorel went to the home of Madame Daudet, who had compiled a list of all the French family crests that included serpents. After an obligatory half hour over the teacups, the guests were presented with the listing, written in script as fragile as the old lady herself. Then they were given the freedom of the library.

The two women looked up the names in massive, gilt-stamped volumes that contained hand-colored plates of heraldic devices and family arms. They traced the most promising crests on sheets of translucent parchment that Maggie had brought. Though they rejected dragons and medieval creatures of dubious ancestry, they examined anything that was clearly snakelike, including three-headed Hydras like that featured in the d'Aguste crest.

It took four hours to complete the search, and by then they were tired and a little sleepy from the library's stuffiness. However, as they prepared to leave, Hélène noticed a book on the Prussian aristocracy.

Turning to "von Fehrenbach," the Frenchwoman became so still that Maggie came to look over her shoulder. What she saw brought her instantly alert. The von Fehrenbach crest was a lion holding a spear with a snake twined along the shaft.

Unemotionally Hélène translated the Latin motto. "The cunning of a serpent, the courage of a lion."

Maggie was shaken. "Of all our prospects, I thought Colonel von Fehrenbach the least probable."

"This proves nothing," Hélène said, an edge in her voice. "We copied a dozen other crests as likely."

"But none of them belonged to suspects." Maggie paused, then said, "Hélène, I asked this before, and I will ask again. Is there something between you and Colonel von Fehrenbach?"

Hélène slipped back into one of the leather-upholstered chairs, her eyes not meeting Maggie's. "There is nothing except . . . an attraction. We have met several times, always in public, and have said nothing that anyone might not hear."

Maggie sat also, brushing her hair back with fingers dusty from old books. Like herself, Hélène acted on instinct, usually a more reliable guide than logic. "Do you think the colonel could be involved in a plot against France?"

"No," Hélène said flatly. She raised her gaze to Maggie's. "I will investigate him more closely for you."

Maggie sat forward in her chair with misgivings. "Hélène, what do you have in mind? If the colonel is really Le Serpent, he is a dangerous man. In fact, he probably is anyhow."

Hélène smiled faintly. "I will do nothing that will endanger either myself or your investigation." Seeing the mutinous expression on her friend's face, she added, "You can't stop me, you know. I am not your employee, but a free agent who works with you because we share the same goals."

Maggie sighed, eyeing Hélène's soft features and gentle face. Though her friend looked as innocent as a newborn lamb, Hélène was both tough and intelligent. If she was determined to approach von Fehrenbach, Maggie could only wait and hope that something worthwhile would come of it.

* * *

Summoned by Maggie, Robin came late that night to her house. The moon was only half full, but bright enough so that the man watching from a window across the alley had no trouble making an identification. Blond and handsome as Lucifer, just as the duke had described him.

The watcher settled back in his chair philosophically, glad that his post was comfortable. It wasn't likely that a midnight visitor to the delectable countess would be in a hurry to leave.

He had no idea that another pair of hidden eyes was also watching the same house.

Maggie slept badly after Robin left. He had found the sketches of crests promising, and intended to show them to members of the Parisian underworld in the hopes that tongues might be loosened.

Robin had little to say in return, which made Maggie nervous since she guessed that he was withholding something. There could be any number of good reasons for that, but most likely he was trying to protect her, which reinforced the idea that this was a dangerous business. Fervently she wished that the treaty was settled so she could return to England—to peace and quiet and safety.

Her eyes opened and she stared unseeing into the darkness. The idea of a little cottage in England was less appealing than it had been a few weeks before. While she would welcome the peace, the days stretched empty and uneventful. She could walk and read, make friends and pay morning calls on them—day after day, month after month, year after year. . . .

The prospect was not an exciting one. She would be very much alone in that life of blameless respectability that she had yearned for. There would be no men like

Rafe to verbally fence with her, or make disgraceful proposals.

At that thought, she laughed softly. Based on history, there would be no shortage of men to proposition her. There just wouldn't be any that she would want to accept. And that, finally, was the core of her restlessness.

Rafe Whitbourne was still the most fascinating man she had ever met, intelligent, more than a little arrogant, alternately tender and enigmatic. And damnably, maddeningly attractive. He had been charming women since he was in leading strings, so it was hardly surprising that she was among his legions of admirers.

From the vantage point of thirty-one, she could see how fortunate it was that they hadn't married. They had both been children then. She had been so in love with Rafe that it had never occurred to her that he would have mistresses, like most men of his station. The first time that had happened, she would have been shattered, just as Cynthia Northwood had been.

Rather than embrace promiscuity herself, Maggie knew that she would have turned into a rampaging virago, as unwilling to let Rafe go as she was to accept his infidelities. Rafe would have reacted with incredulity and embarrassment, regretting that he hadn't taken a more sophisticated wife who understood the way of the world.

The harder Maggie fought, the more distant he would have become. Love would have died, and they would have made each other miserable. It was all tragically clear.

Since she had just proved how lucky she was that Rafe had broken their engagement, why didn't that conclusion make her happy?

Despairingly Maggie laid her forearm over her eyes in a vain attempt to block out images of Rafe, and the memory of how his touch dissolved her common sense and self-control.

It was feeble comfort to know that her greatest significance in his life was to be the one woman he had propositioned who hadn't accepted. But was that really better than nothing?

Maggie and Rafe's visit to the Louvre with the Roussayes turned out to be educational in unexpected ways. Napoleon had looted art treasures wherever he went, then installed them in the old palace. It had been named the Musée Napoleon and state receptions had been held in the magnificent galleries.

Art had become a major point of contention during the treaty negotiations. The conquered nations understandably wanted their paintings and sculptures back, while the French royalists and Bonapartists were united in their desire to retain the fruits of conquest. The issue was still unresolved, though the Allies were bound to win in the end; the only sovereign who favored letting the French keep their spoils was the Russian tsar, who had lost no art himself.

When the two couples stopped in front of a magnificent Titian, Roussaye made an oblique reference to the ongoing dispute, saying, "We must admire these while we can. Never has such a collection been seen before, and perhaps the world will never see its equal again."

They were regarding the superb canvas respectfully when an unexpected voice came from behind them. "You are quite correct, General Rosssaye. This museum is one of the finest fruits of the empire."

The dark, whispery voice made the hair on Maggie's neck prickle. She turned to see the Count de Varenne.

Michel Roussaye said coolly, "I am surprised to hear a royalist approve any of Bonaparte's acts."

The count smiled. "I am a royalist, not a fool, General Roussaye. The emperor was the colossus of our age, and only a fool would attempt to deny that."

His words produced a noticeable thawing in the general's expression.

Varenne continued, "Like you, I am here to say good-bye to some of my favorite paintings."

The words were hardly out of his mouth when a commotion sounded farther down the gallery. Amid French shouts, the stamp of marching feet heralded the entrance of a company of soldiers. Maggie recognized the uniforms as Prussian. As museumgoers watched in disbelief, the soldiers started unhooking paintings from the wall.

General Roussaye swiftly crossed to the Prussians and demanded furiously, "By what authority do you do this?"

The Prussian commander turned, and Maggie recognized Colonel von Fehrenbach. Expression coldly satisfied, the colonel said, "By the authority of ownership. Since the negotiators are no closer to a just settlement now than they were in July, Prussia takes what is hers."

Intent on observing every word and nuance of the confrontation, Maggie started to follow Roussaye across the gallery. Rafe stopped her in her tracks by clamping his hand around her wrist.

"Keep out of it," he said in a voice that allowed no argument.

Maggie considered defying him on general principles, but common sense made her concede the point and stay at his side.

Count de Varenne had gone to stand by his countryman. Though his tone was less fierce, he sounded equally hostile when he said, "The Congress of Vienna allowed France to keep her treasures, and it is by no means certain that that decision will be reversed. What you are doing is theft."

The tall Prussian was unmoved. "Say what you will,

I am here by my king's orders. We have both might and right on our side, and will brook no interference."

The soldiers began packing paintings in wooden cases that they had brought. A crowd of sullen-faced French citizens had gathered around the disputing men. Briefly Maggie wondered if they might rush the soldiers, but the moment passed and the bystanders remained passive.

Varenne's sibilant voice said, "Do not be so righteous, Colonel. Many of the artworks that the Allies are so virtuously reclaiming were stolen in the first place. The bronze horses of St. Mark's, for example, which the Venetians plundered from Constantinople."

Von Fehrenbach looked cynically amused. "I don't deny it, but the nature of loot defies easy moralizing."

Roussaye said tightly, "All nations may be looters, but only France has made such beauty available to all. Even the poorest of the poor can come here to glory in the sight."

"Quite right, the French are the most efficient thieves in history," the colonel agreed. "You studied guidebooks and sent artists to ensure that you missed none of the best pieces. The emperor even made the Vatican pay the cost of shipping his spoils to Paris. But don't forget what Wellington himself said—loot is what you can get your bloody hands on and keep."

Von Fehrenbach turned back to his men, but said over his shoulder, "And France bloody well can't keep these."

It was fortunate that the colonel had brought such a sizable troop of soldiers, because his words caused a rumble of impotent rage to rise from the watchers.

After a frozen moment, General Roussaye spun on his heel and returned to his companions. "I think it best that we leave now." He took his wife's arm, leading her down the gallery away from the soldiers as Maggie, Rafe, and Varenne silently followed.

Word of the assault on the Louvre had spread

quickly, and outside a crowd was gathering in the Place du Carrousel. Under the shadow of the great victory arch that carried the bronze horses of St. Mark's, Maggie and her companions were privileged to see the Venus de Medici being carried out feet first, followed by the Apollo Belvedere.

Nearby, a young man in a paint-smudged smock gave a howl of anguish. "Oh, if only Wellington had ordered the removal to take place at night, so we should be spared the horror of seeing them torn away from us!"

Though the artist's anguish was vivid, Maggie could not help thinking tartly that the Venetians and Prussians and other victims of Napoleon's greed had felt equal pain.

Behind her, Rafe said softly, "Wellington is being blamed for this, more's the pity. His popularity with the French will vanish quickly."

Roussaye turned to face them, his wife clinging to his arm with distress in her huge black eyes. "I fear that I will not be good company for some time," the general said with admirable composure. "Pray forgive us for taking our leave now."

Ever urbane, Rafe said, "Of course, General Roussaye, Cousin Filomena. Perhaps we can meet again for a less controversial engagement."

The general smiled humorlessly. "Nothing in France is without controversy."

Varenne spoke up for the first time since they had left the Prussians. "All France shares your outrage, General."

As she saw the two dangerous, capable Frenchmen share a sympathetic glance, Maggie had the disquieting thought that France would again be the most dangerous country in Europe if the royalists and Bonapartists ever united. Thank God that there was too much hatred between the factions for that to happen any time soon.

After the Roussayes departed, Varenne said to Maggie and Rafe, "I'm sorry you were subjected to such a scene. I had heard rumors that the Prussians were growing restive over the pace of the negotiations, but no one expected them to move so quickly."

"I'm afraid that matters will be worse before they get better," Rafe said. "The art controversy is becoming a symbol of all the conflicts of the peace conference."

"The situation is very volatile," Varenne agreed. "As I'm sure you know, the king's government is in disarray, and I fear that Richelieu is not strong enough to maintain order." Putting aside his dark mood, he smiled at Maggie. "I should not talk of such things before a lady."

Maggie supposed he meant that she was too much of a lackwit to understand politics. Still, the less intelligent he thought her, the better. Fluttering her eyelashes, she cooed, "It's all so dreadful. Since the wars are over, one would think there would be no more problems."

"I'm afraid matters aren't quite so simple," Varenne said, a satiric glint in his dark eyes. "I look forward to the day when I can retire to my estate and concentrate on my own affairs, but it will not be soon."

"Is your estate near Paris?" Maggie asked, though she knew the answer from her research.

"Yes, not far from the emperor's house at Malmaison. Chantueil is perhaps the finest medieval chateau in France."

"It sounds wonderfully romantic."

"It is." Varenne gave her a smile that would have been charming were it not for the calculation in his eyes. "I would be delighted to show it to you. Perhaps next week?"

Maggie's answer was forestalled when Rafe put his

arm around her waist. "Perhaps later. The countess and I are much engaged for the near future."

Seeming amused by Rafe's show of possessiveness, Varenne took Maggie's hand and sketched a kiss above it. "You and the enchanting countess would be welcome at Chantueil at any time, Monsieur le Duc."

Then he disappeared into the seething mass of angry Parisians. Maggie watched his broad back retreat with disquiet. The count had behaved flirtatiously, yet she sensed that he wasn't really interested in her.

Before she could analyze her unease, Rafe said brusquely, "Time to leave, Countess. This crowd could turn ugly."

His words made her aware of the angry mutterings, and she felt the clenching fear that crowds always produced in her. As people fell away from Rafe, she was grateful for his presence. Anyone would think twice or thrice before accosting the Duke of Candover, not only because of his obvious wealth, but because of his air of gentlemanly menace.

When they were free of the crowd, Rafe summoned a cab to take them to the Boulevard des Capucines. In the privacy of the cab, he remarked, "It was interesting to see all three suspects together, but I can't say that I have any better idea of who is guilty of what. Do you have any thoughts on the subject?"

She frowned as she reviewed her impressions of the confrontation in the museum. "The same thoughts I had before, only more so. Colonel von Fehrenbach despises the French and enjoys their humiliation. While I still don't see him masterminding a plot, it's possible that he could be used by someone of more devious temperament."

"And General Roussaye?"

"He behaved with unusual restraint," she said slowly. "He was so furious with the invasion of the

Louvre that I wouldn't have been surprised if he had rallied the French mob to attack the Prussians."

"Surely he wouldn't have risked that with his wife there."

"I'm sure that was a factor," she agreed. "Also, he's an intelligent man and must realize that driving the Prussians out would do no real good. But he is a warrior, and I had the feeling that it was very difficult for him not to fight back. Remember that I suspected that he might be involved in something secret? Perhaps he left rather than act in a way that might jeopardize another project. I would go long odds that some parts of his life wouldn't bear the light of day."

"What about Varenne and his so-romantic chateau?" Rafe inquired, a sardonic note in his voice.

She smiled a little. "I wouldn't trust that man further than I could throw his drawbridge. I suspect that he is so devious by nature that it would be impossible to determine if he is conspiring, or merely obfuscating on general principles."

Not responding to her light tone, Rafe said somberly, "I feel the way one does before a storm, when the clouds are gathering. I wish to God that I knew from which direction the winds will come."

Speaking from her own hard-won wisdom, she said, "Knowledge is not what saves one in a storm, but flexibility. It is those who won't bend who are broken."

His dark brows lifted. "Is that an oblique comment on rigid souls like me? Remember that flowers bend before a storm, yet still they are torn apart, their petals scattered to the four winds."

"Don't push the analogy too far, your grace," she said dryly. "I may look like an overblown rose, but I have survived fiercer storms than you will ever know of."

The cab pulled up in front of Maggie's house and

they alighted. Since the premature end to the expedition had gotten them back hours early, he followed her inside.

Rafe's mood seemed odd, so she suggested, "We haven't played chess lately. Shall we finish our current game?"

He agreed, but both of them were so abstracted that it was an open question who played more carelessly. Maggie scarcely noticed what moves she made until he said, "Check."

Seeing that a black bishop was threatening her king, she moved a white knight into the bishop's path. Rafe could capture her knight, but then Maggie would be able to take his bishop, restoring the balance of power as well as saving her king.

"I like knights," she said idly. "They move in such a deceptive manner."

"Like you do, Countess?"

Surprised by the sharp edge to Rafe's voice, she said, "I suppose so. Spying is the art of deception, after all."

"Will the white queen sacrifice herself for the white king?"

Rafe's gray eyes bored into her, and she realized that he was no longer talking about chess. The lean planes of his face were hard, and his whole body radiated tension.

Her mouth tightened. She had suspected that at some point he would become difficult, and apparently the time had arrived. "Rafe, what are you trying to say?"

Instead of answering, he swept his black king across the board to capture the white queen.

"You know perfectly well that that isn't a legitimate move," she said with exasperation. "What obscure point are you trying to make?"

Rafe scooped up the white queen and the black king

and lifted them from the board. "Only this, Maggie—I won't let you sacrifice yourself for the white king. With or without your consent, I am going to take you out of the game."

Chapter 13

Maggie stared at Rafe, wondering what idiocy was possessing him. "'Take me out of the game?' " she said coldly. "You'll have to speak a good deal more clearly."

With a furious sweep of his arm, Rafe knocked the antique chess pieces from the board. The enameled figures fell to the Oriental carpet and bounced in all directions, thudding and clicking against each other.

"We're talking about Robert Anderson," he snapped. "Your lover, who is a spy and a traitor."

Maggie stood so abruptly that her chair skidded backward. "You don't know what you're talking about!"

Rafe stood also, towering over her. The urbane, uninvolved man of the world was gone, and he blazed with angry emotion. "Oh, yes, I do, my lady trollop. I know that he comes here late at night, even though Lucien told you not to communicate with anyone in the British delegation."

Refusing to turn away from his scorching gaze, Maggie said softly, "I have been playing dangerous games far longer than you have, your grace. I work with those I trust."

"Even if they are traitors? Your lover has been seen surreptitiously meeting General Roussaye. I myself saw him meeting Henri Lemercier at the Café Mazarin, perhaps planning the attempt on Castlereagh's life."

For the first time she felt apprehension, but she said stubbornly, "That proves nothing. Spies must talk to everyone, not only respectable citizens."

Rafe stepped around the table until he was only inches away from Maggie. "You admit that he's a spy?"

"Of course he is! We've worked together for years."

"So you've been his mistress for years," Rafe repeated, his eyes like ice. "Do you know who he works for?"

"The British, of course. Robin is as English as I am."

"Even if that's true, nationality means nothing to a mercenary. He probably sells to the highest bidder, and has been using you as a dupe." Rafe's eyes narrowed. "Are you sure that he is English?"

Maggie exploded. "You ignorant fool! Your accusations are absurd, and I won't listen to them."

She spun away, but Rafe grabbed her by the arm. "Absurd? Where does your money come from? Who pays for the silk gowns and the carriage and the town house?"

She jerked her arm free. "I do, with what I earn from the British government."

"Are you paid directly?"

After a pause, Maggie said, "The money comes through Robin."

It was exactly as Rafe expected. "I wrote Lucien and asked how much the government has paid you over the last dozen years. It came to about five thousand pounds, not enough to keep you for a year in the style you live in."

Her eyes widened, but she refused to back down. "Perhaps that is all Lord Strathmore has paid, but there must be other British agencies that need information. Robin probably deals with several of them."

Though her words were defiant, he saw that she was

shaken by what he had revealed. Pressing his advantage, he said, "I admire your loyalty. Nonetheless, the odds are that Anderson is the spy within the British delegation, and that he is almost certainly involved in the conspiracy against Castlereagh. The only question is, are you his knowing accomplice, or his pawn?"

"I won't believe it!" she said furiously. "Robin is the best friend I've ever had, and if I must choose between believing him and believing you, I choose *him*. Get out of here!"

Until now Rafe had restricted himself to telling his suspicions of Anderson's loyalty, but Maggie's refusal to believe ill of her lover shattered his control. Grabbing her by the shoulders, he demanded, "Why him, Margot—why him and not me? Is he a matchless bedmate? Do you think you love him, or is it because he has supported you in such elegance?" His fingers tightened on her arms. "If it's money you want, I'll pay your price, no matter how high it is. If it's sex, give me one night, then decide who is better."

He drew in a raw, unsteady breath. "And if you're defending him from blind loyalty, think hard about whether a traitor is worthy of such allegiance."

She laughed in his face. "You *dare* ask why I prefer Robin? It was he who saved my life and gave me a reason to go on living. As God is my witness, I'd rather be the pawn of a traitor than the mistress of a man who accused and judged me without proof, a man whose insane jealousy drove my father to take me away from England."

Her voice dropped, and he saw bone-chilling rage in her face. "My father would not have been murdered by the French if it hadn't been for what you did, Rafe. For that alone, I can never forgive you.

"As for your vain, masculine egotism—I don't care if you've learned your skills in the bed of every slut in Europe. I'd never give myself to a man without love, and you're incapable of loving anyone. You're a selfish, arrogant, conceited rakehell, and I don't ever want to see you again. Now let go of me!"

She raised her arms and tried to break his grip, but Rafe was too strong for her. He slid one hand behind her head and turned her face up to his. Hoarsely he said, "Oh, God, Margot, don't fight me. I just want to keep you safe."

He kissed her fiercely, hoping that passion would dissolve her opposition. As always when they embraced, heat flared between them, swift and impossible to deny.

She struggled violently at first, but as he held her steadfast, she softened and began to respond with an intensity that matched his own. Her tongue entered his mouth and her hand slid down his body between them, seeking.

When she touched him, he groaned and hardened under her caress. This was how they were meant to be—loving each other, not fighting. He eased his grip and began running his hands down the swell of her hips.

She took advantage of his relaxation to jerk her knee up in a savage street fighter's trick. Sickeningly aware that her passion had been a ruse, he twisted away barely in time. Her blow landed on his thigh instead of smashing his genitals, but he saved himself at the cost of losing his hold on her.

As soon as Maggie freed herself from his embrace, she dashed across the room to the pier table and yanked a pistol from the drawer. Then she whirled to face Rafe. "Get out of here, and don't ever come near me again! If you make any move to hurt Robin, I will have you killed." Though her voice trembled, the gun she held with both hands was lethally steady.

Rafe stared unbelievingly at the pistol. "Maggie . . ."

"Stay where you are!" She cocked the hammer. "I

warn you, if you injure Robin, you will die even if I
am dead myself. I know how to arrange an assassination, and there will be nowhere on earth distant enough
for you to hide. Now take your clumsy amateur spying
and your jealousy and your absurd accusations and go
back to England!"

She was bluffing, he was sure of it. The gun probably wasn't even loaded.

He took a step toward her, and she pulled the trigger.

The roar of the gun was numbing in the enclosed
space. He felt the vibration of the ball as it struck near
him, and debris struck his calf.

At first he thought Maggie's shot had gone wild.
Then he blinked the stinging smoke from his eyes and
saw that she had fired into the black king, which had
been lying on the carpet near his foot. The ball had
splintered the antique chess piece into a thousand frag-
ments. An admirable bit of marksmanship; it was obvious that she could just as easily have put the bullet into
his eye.

By the time he raised his gaze, she had expertly reloaded and trained her weapon on him again. "As you
can see, I haven't forgotten my marksmanship," she
said grimly. "If you try anything, the next ball will go
into you."

He weighed the odds of trying to take the pistol
away from her, but there was a wide expanse of salon
between them, and murder in Maggie's eyes. He
damned himself for the idiotic folly of attacking
Anderson as he had. It would have been difficult to
convince her of her lover's duplicity under the best of
circumstances. By muddying the evidence with his
jealousy, he had lost any chance of changing Maggie's
mind.

Nonetheless, with as much calm and conviction as
he could muster, he tried. "For your own sake, Maggie,
don't trust Anderson. Though I may be a jealous fool,

I told you the truth about him. Do you want Castlereagh, and perhaps others, to die because you're too stubborn to see Anderson for what he is? He's the only lead to the conspiracy that we have, and we should get Wellington to detain him for questioning."

"You haven't convinced me, your grace," she said, her smoky gray eyes as hostile as her words. "As I said, spies must talk to everyone, especially suspects like Lemercier and Roussaye. As for the money—you may be too rich to realize it, but most of the world must be practical about such sordid things. Selling the same information to more than one of Napoleon's enemies might be simply good business, not treason."

"But you're not sure, are you?" Rafe said softly, sensing the bravado that fueled Maggie's defense of Anderson.

At his words, she tensed, and he wondered how light the trigger was on her pistol. He felt a flicker of cool amusement at the thought that the noble Duke of Candover might be killed in a vulgar lover's quarrel— with the added irony that they were not even lovers.

Breasts rising and falling with agitation, she said, "You could produce iron-clad evidence and a dozen unimpeachable witnesses that Robin was a traitor and I might possibly—just possibly—believe you, but I would still not come to your bed. Will you leave on your own, or shall I ring for my servants to throw you out?"

Despairingly, Rafe saw that he had failed, and his failure had made everything worse. Though Maggie was wrongheaded in her loyalty to Anderson, it was still impossible to believe she would condone an assassination plot. Now that Rafe had challenged her, she would be even more hell-bent on exposing the conspiracy, if only to prove that he was wrong about Anderson. That might put her into grave danger, and he wouldn't be there to protect her.

The pistol tracked him without wavering as he crossed the room to the door. Pausing with one hand on the knob, he looked back. Even the fact that she had a gun aimed at his heart did not alter his desire. "I'm not leaving Paris until this is over," he said quietly. "If you need help at any time, for any reason, you know where to find me."

Then he left, the paneled door swinging silently shut behind him.

Maggie set her gun on the pier table, then sank to the floor when her knees gave way beneath her. As the horrible scene replayed in her mind, she wrapped her arms around her midriff and fought her nausea.

She had often wondered what lay beneath Rafe's cool detachment. Now she knew, and wished that she didn't. While he had always made it clear that he desired her, she had not suspected that he felt such violent jealousy. Of course, he had behaved much the same way thirteen years earlier. At the time she had thought it was from love, but apparently the real source had been pride and possessiveness.

Could he have been lying about Robin? Though Rafe's information was disconcerting, it was hardly evidence of double-dealing. Admittedly Robin hadn't mentioned meeting with either Roussaye or Lemercier, but that meant nothing, for he seldom discussed his activities in detail. By the same token, she didn't inform him of all that she did.

It was much harder to shrug off Rafe's revelations about the money. While Maggie had not lived lavishly for most of these last years, Robin had given her thousands of pounds more than the amount Strathmore said she had been paid. Some had gone to her informants, some for living expenses, and the rest was invested in Zurich, where it drew enough interest to allow her to retire to England.

She had never questioned the amount of money that

she received, assuming that it was the normal rate for spying. Could Robin really have been serving more than one master? He had always implied that all of the money was British.

She forced herself to consider the question of Robin's nationality. When they first met, he had said that he was English, but he had never spoken of his early life. Uneasily she realized that he could have grown up anywhere, for he had the same unerring talent for languages that she did. In fact, it was Robin who had taught her the tricks of listening that enabled her to perfect an accent.

Though much of his life was a mystery, Maggie had never once doubted that he was honest with her about things that mattered. Now she could no longer be sure. A bare fortnight earlier he had told her never to trust anyone, not even him. At the time she had dismissed his comment as teasing, but now it haunted her.

Shakily she pulled herself to her feet, then went to the cabinet for the decanter of brandy. After pouring a glass, she downed half of it at a gulp. It warmed her, but gave no clues about what to believe.

Rafe might be mad with frustrated lust or wounded pride, but she would wager that he believed what he had told her. Yet how could she mistrust Robin, her best friend, who had saved her life and sanity?

Blindly she finished the brandy, oblivious to the way it burned her throat. Strange how much Rafe could affect her, in spite of past crimes and betrayals. He could arouse depths of emotion in her quite different from the solid, warm friendship she shared with Robin.

What a pity that Rafe used that power only to hurt her.

The Englishman provided Le Serpent with the requested information about the British embassy, acquired at no small risk. Twice he had nearly been

caught by other members of the staff, and he thought
he had seen suspicion at his presence in places where
he didn't belong. Still, no one had asked awkward
questions, and he had been paid a handsome price for
his risks.

The light was a little brighter this time so that Le
Serpent could review the sketched floor plans. After
several minutes, he gave a grunt of triumph. "Perfect,
absolutely perfect. *Le bon Dieu* must have designed it
for my purposes."

Having no desire to know more of the plan, the Englishman straightened up to leave. "If you have no
more need for me . . ."

Le Serpent straightened also, his eyes a hard gleam
behind his mask. "I have not dismissed you, *mon petit
Anglais*. My plan requires your willing participation.
Do you see that closet there?" A blunt finger tapped
the floor plans.

The Englishman glanced down. "Yes. What of it?"

"It is directly underneath Castlereagh's bedchamber.
You told me that it is seldom used, and always kept
locked. If it is packed with gunpowder and ignited, it
will blow that end of the embassy to rubble."

"You're mad!" the Englishman gasped, understanding why Le Serpent had wanted to know who was attending the different meetings. If the right day was
chosen, Wellington and all the chief Allied ministers
could be destroyed along with Castlereagh.

"Not in the least," the hooded man said calmly. "My
plan is audacious, but wholly workable. The most difficult part will be getting the gunpowder into the embassy, but since you are on the staff, that presents no
insurmountable problems."

"How do you intend to set the explosion?" the Englishman asked, horribly sure that he knew the answer.

"A candle will do the trick nicely. A slow-burning,
hard wax candle will take hours to melt down. You

will have plenty of time to get safely out of the way, and no one will suspect you."

"I want no part of this madness! If the Allied leaders are killed, there will be a manhunt such as France has never seen."

"Oh, there will be an uproar, but the Allies will be like beheaded chickens with their leaders gone. By the time the dust settles"—Le Serpent paused dramatically before finishing—"there will be a new order in France."

"What do I care about France? I'll not put my neck in the noose for it!"

The Englishman tried to move away, but Le Serpent reached out and seized his wrist with an iron grip. In a voice from a nightmare, he hissed, "I will tell you once more, *mon ami,* you have no choice. To defy me means death. On the other hand, your cooperation is vital for this particular project, and I reward my underlings very generously."

He let those words sink in, then continued softly, "Notice I make no attempt to buy your loyalty, because I know you have none. Greed is the best lever with creatures such as you, so I make you a promise: help me to success, and you will be rich and powerful beyond your wildest dreams."

The Englishman was unsure whether it was better to work with Le Serpent, expose the bastard, or fly from France. He was uneasily aware that he would have to choose sides within the next few days, and if he chose wrong he was dead.

Of course, he would die anyway if he betrayed Le Serpent, or if the British discovered his treachery. Co-operation was his best, and most profitable course. Harshly he said, "Once more I find the brilliance of your logic convincing."

"Very good." Le Serpent released his grip. "I like a man who learns quickly. Now sit, I have more questions for you. There are several British agents sniffing at my heels, and it will be necessary to remove them from my path. Tell me everything you know about the people in question."

Two of the names Le Serpent gave were expected, but one was a surprise. A most pleasant surprise, and quite logical when he thought about it.

The Englishman suppressed a smirk of satisfaction; he could think of no one he would rather see removed.

Chapter 14

The staff had long since retired and Maggie had been sitting in her kitchen for hours, with only a candle and the kitchen cat for company. Robin had said he would stop by if he had something new to report, but he would not come this late.

She was desperate to talk to him, to hear his explanation of the points Candover had raised. There was surely a reasonable explanation. . . .

And if he lied to her, she would know it.

She could not sleep with so much unresolved—with treacherous doubts about Robin, with the echoes of the horrible fight with Rafe. Impulsively she decided that if Robin wasn't coming to her, she would go to him. He had rooms near the Place du Carrousel, adjacent to the Louvre and the Tuileries. If he wasn't there, she would wait until he returned. It would not be the first time she had walked the streets of Paris after dark.

Upstairs she swiftly changed to men's clothes, glad that the September night was cool enough to justify the dark, form-concealing cloak. As always when she traveled alone, she carried her pistol and a knife. While she preferred to avoid trouble, Robin had seen to it that she knew how to fight.

Robin. Always Robin. She needed most desperately to believe in him.

If she didn't have him, who did she have?

* * *

*"It's always been you, Rafe," Margot said softly, her
eyes misty with desire. "For all these years, I've
waited for you to find me. Why didn't you come
sooner?"*

*She kissed him, unbuttoning his shirt to press her
heated lips to the hollow at the base of his throat. His
clothing seemed to melt away, allowing her wheat gold
hair to flow tantalizingly over his skin. Her clever
hands slid down his torso, teasing, arousing him to
madness. . . .*

Heart pounding and body throbbing, Rafe awoke to
unpleasant reality. He had not slept long; just enough
for his fevered dreams to tie him in knots. He had returned to his hotel after his fight with Maggie, written
a report for Lucien, and gone to bed. Yet even in sleep,
she haunted him.

Wearily he decided that he might as well make the
final descent into absurdity. After changing to his
plainest clothing, he returned to the Boulevard des
Capucines, where one of his men was watching
Maggie's house from a room rented on the other side
of the back alley.

Rafe had instituted the watch several nights earlier.
Apart from visits by Anderson on two different occasions, the watcher had seen nothing of interest, and
probably tonight would be no different. Nonetheless,
because Rafe could not stay away, he dismissed his
man and took the post himself.

He should have turned around and headed back to
London as soon as he had learned that Lucien's
damned spy was Margot Ashton. Certainly his sojourn
in Paris had been of no help to his country, and it had
wreaked havoc on his orderly life.

With bitter resentment, he acknowledged that the
simple schoolboy love he had felt for Margot had been
replaced by the dark strains of obsession. She was the
only living creature who could destroy his prized de-

tachment, and he hated her for it, even as he compulsively imagined what it would be like to make love to her. He already knew the taste of her mouth, and his imagination supplied vivid images of how she would look, of how it would feel to be inside her, of how she would respond . . .

Once more he jerked his thoughts from their unhealthy circle. The force of his desire was so intense that for the first time in his life, he wondered whether he would be capable of rape if the opportunity presented itself.

Wondered, then shied away from the question because he feared the answer.

Maggie had accused him of wanting her because she was unavailable, and he knew that there was some justice to that. After all, she was only a woman, and all females were made much the same. He also knew from experience that the most beautiful women were seldom the best mistresses; females who were less blessed by nature usually tried harder. If he could just once make love to Maggie, it would free him of his obsession, which was rooted in his youthful memories.

But there was no chance of that happening. She would put a bullet in him if he came within fifty feet of her.

It was fortunate that Anderson hadn't called on Maggie tonight. Rafe would have been tempted to kill him out of hand, and the blond man was much more useful alive. Tomorrow Rafe would notify Wellington of his suspicions and urge that Anderson be questioned, but tonight he kept his morbid watch.

The town house was dark except for a light in the kitchen. He wondered if Maggie was sleeping, or whether she was as restless as he. The accusations against Anderson had upset her, and perhaps she was suffering doubts. Savagely, he hoped so.

It was very late when he saw a dark figure slip from

the house, moving with catlike stealth and grace. He knew instantly that it was Maggie. Curious about her mission, he left his post and swiftly went outside.

No sooner had he reached the alley when he saw another figure exit the building to his left and go after Maggie.

Bloody hell, who else was watching her? Had his own men missed the competition, or was this a new development? He was abruptly glad for the impulse that had made him take tonight's watch. If she were to run into danger, at least he would be there. He trusted his own ability to protect her more than that of his hirelings.

Maggie led them a merry chase. Rafe admired the speed she made while managing to be almost invisible. Avoiding the well-lit boulevards, she was one more shadow in the narrow back streets. Occasionally she glanced back, but she had no reason to suppose anyone was behind her, and the same darkness that shielded her passage concealed the followers.

Mindful of the farcical aspects of several people trailing each other, Rafe checked his own back to be sure that no one was behind him, but he seemed to be the last of the parade.

When they neared the Place du Carrousel, he realized with dismay that she must be heading for Anderson's nearby lodgings. A planned assignation, or was she going to challenge the man with what Rafe had told her? It was something else that he wasn't sure he wanted to know.

Ahead of him, he saw Maggie pause at the end of the street where it led into the plaza. Looking beyond her, Rafe saw the great victory arch that Napoleon had built in the middle of the plaza and crowned with the four bronze horses taken from St. Mark's in Venice. Torches burned around the monument, and their flickering light illuminated workmen standing on top of the

arch. As the clink of chisels and hammers echoed
around the plaza, he saw a supervisor in the uniform of
a British officer. Apparently Wellington had decided to
spare French feelings by removing these most visible
examples of loot by night. Rafe hoped that old Louis
would sleep through it. The work was taking place literally under the king's windows in the Tuileries.

Maggie was hesitating, as if wondering whether to
cross the plaza or to go around.

Then a clatter sounded behind Rafe. He looked back
and saw a detachment of the French National Guard
surge from a cross street and charge toward the Place
du Carrousel. He realized that there had been shouting
audible for some time, but the jumbled medieval
streets had made the noise seem distant.

Rafe darted up a nearby set of stone steps into the
shelter of a deep doorway. The Guardsmen ran by, followed by an angry throng of Parisians. All mobs
sounded the same: like a ravening beast that was all
teeth and belly and claws. No one paid any attention to
Rafe in his safe spot above the swirling bodies.

Seeing the Guards and the mob, the men on the arch
abandoned their tools and beat a hasty retreat. After
reaching the ground, they dashed for the Tuileries
where a door opened to allow the workers inside. Wise
of Louis' people not to let the workers be torn to
pieces; Wellington would take an exceedingly dim
view if the king let British soldiers and citizens be
murdered.

In the moments that his attention was on the plaza,
Rafe lost sight of Maggie. Fearful of her being caught
in the turmoil, he ran down the steps and forced his
way through the crowd to where he had last sighted
her. He kept a wary eye out for the man who had been
following her, but made no attempt to conceal himself.
In his modest clothing, he was just another member of
the churning throng.

Shouts rose near the mouth of a small alley to the left, followed by the bellow of a familiar French voice. "Here's an English spy—one of Wellington's thieves!"

Frustrated by the escape of the workmen, those members of the mob close enough to hear started moving toward the fracas in search of new prey. Then a woman's scream of terror cut through the general rumble.

Maggie.

Galvanized by panic, Rafe plunged toward her, ruthlessly using his size and boxing skills to elbow, kick, and shove his way through as quickly as possible. Though he was followed by curses and blows, he scarcely noticed them.

As he neared the center of the disturbance, there was a sharp sound of ripping fabric. The familiar voice yelled excitedly, "Ai, it's a woman!"

The animal voice of the mob took on a dark new tone.

Rafe shoved aside two drunken youths, and found his nightmare image from the theater riot, made horribly real.

Maggie had been knocked to the ground, but she still fought furiously, twisting and kicking and slashing with a knife. Her shoulder and part of her chest showed white against the torn fabric of her clothing, and in the uncertain light her face was distorted by fear such as Rafe had never seen before.

A raggedly dressed laborer tried to grab her wrist. She put the point of her blade through the back of his hand. The laborer shrieked as blood gushed from the wound.

With shocking abruptness, a heavy boot caught the side of Maggie's head and her struggle ended. She slumped into unconsciousness, the knife falling from her nerveless fingers.

The man who had kicked her hauled her upright and

held her against his chest, one hand cruelly squeezing her exposed breast. Rafe looked into his face, and recognized the scarred, triumphant visage of Henri Lemercier.

"You'll have to wait in line, *mes amis*," the captain said genially, "I saw her first, but don't worry, there's plenty to go around."

He began dragging her backward toward the alley. Acknowledging the practical difficulties of more than one man raping a woman at a time, the surrounding rioters fell back a little, opening the space around Maggie and her captor.

Audacity was the only hope. Rafe bolted from the crowd, chopped the side of his hand across Lemercier's throat, and grabbed Maggie as the Frenchman's grasp loosened.

As Rafe raised her, he felt the unmistakable shape of a pistol in her cloak pocket. One bullet would not have helped her against the mob, but it might be of use to him. As he slung her limp body over his left shoulder, he transferred the pistol to his own pocket. Then he sprinted down the alley away from the plaza, praying that the crowd would react slowly.

Before he had gone ten yards, a roar rose behind him. "Another of Wellington's spies!" Lemercier shouted in a strangled voice. "Kill them both!"

A stone struck Rafe's shoulder, knocking him off-stride. As he recovered, he spared a quick glance back, and saw that Lemercier had rallied the crowd and was pounding in pursuit.

Slowed by Maggie's weight, Rafe would never be able to outrun the mob. There was only one possible hope. He pulled the pistol from his pocket and cocked the hammer one-handed. For a bare instant, he saw again that horrifying vision of her being ravished by the mob, and considered putting the single bullet into her heart.

The thought left as quickly as it had come; he could not hurt Margot, even to save her from a ghastly death. He raised the pistol and held it out at arm's length, aiming with the same deliberation he used when shooting wafers at a gallery.

The priming fizzled oddly, and for a heart-searing moment he thought the pistol had misfired.

Then the weapon kicked in his hand. Time seemed to slow, and he could almost see the ball spinning, spinning through the air—until it struck Lemercier dead between the eyes.

Still in eerie slow motion, the Frenchman's expression changed from vicious lust to disbelieving shock. There was a small spurt of blood and bone as the force of the ball drove Lemercier back into the arms of the rioters. At the loss of their leader, the mob's cohesion disintegrated into confusion.

Rafe wasted no more time in observation. Holding Maggie again, he turned and escaped into the maze of alleys that surrounded the plaza, dodging left, then right, then left again. The unexpected shooting slowed the mob down long enough for him to get out of their sight.

After five minutes of running full speed with no sign of pursuit, he staggered to a halt. There wasn't an ounce of Maggie that he didn't like exactly the way it was, but she was no featherweight and his lungs burned with exertion.

Gasping for breath, he laid her on the pavement and made a quick examination. It was too dark to tell much, but her breathing and heartbeat seemed strong.

In the distance, he could still hear shouts from the Place du Carrousel. As soon as he regained his breath, he lifted her in both arms and started walking. Eventually he emerged into one of the boulevards and flagged down a cab, then curtly ordered the driver to take them to the Hôtel de la Paix.

In the dank privacy of the cab, he held her in his lap, her black cloak spilling over them both. Though her hat had been lost in the plaza, her bright hair was still concealed under a black scarf. He untied it, then carefully probed the area where the kick had landed, praying that the heavy boot hadn't hit her squarely. To his relief, it seemed that her heavy coils of hair had cushioned the effect of the blow.

For the rest of the ride, he cradled her in his arms, trying to warm her chilled body. A lingering trace of exotic scent was in her hair, a reminder of the glamorous countess. Yet with a vague sense of wonder, he realized that for the moment, tenderness had overpowered his lust.

When they reached the Hôtel de la Paix, he climbed from the carriage, tossed a gold piece to the cabby, and carried Maggie up the steps without looking back. The doorman looked startled, but said nothing. One didn't question a duke, even one with a ragged, unconscious female in his arms.

A kick at the door of his apartments brought his valet on the run. Carrying Maggie inside, Rafe snapped, "Have the concierge wake a maid and get her down here with a clean nightgown. Then go for a doctor. I want one here within half an hour even if you have to bring him at gun point."

The suite was small, with no guest room, so Rafe took her into his own bedchamber. Her black-clad figure was dwarfed in the huge four-poster. The irony did not escape him; he had dreamed of having her in his bed, but not like this. Dear God, never like this.

He lit a branch of candles and set it on the bedside table. Maggie's pale, smudged face was oddly peaceful as he pulled the torn shirt over her exposed breast.

A yawning maid entered in her dressing gown, a white garment over her arm.

Rafe glanced up at her. "I'll buy the nightgown from you. Undress this lady and put it on her."

The maid blinked. When gentlemen brought women here, they were usually interested in doing the undressing themselves. With a very French shrug, she set to work.

Rafe left the room. Acquaintances who knew him as a consummate ladies' man would have laughed at the idea, but after what Maggie had gone through, it would have seemed like an unforgivable violation of her privacy to watch, or to undress her himself.

A few minutes later the maid went back to bed, her sleepy eyes widened by the size of the tip Rafe gave her.

When he reentered his chamber, Maggie lay beneath the covers as if she were asleep, the only sign of her ordeal a graze on her left cheekbone. The maid had combed her hair out so that it lay around her shoulders in a fine-spun golden mist. Delicate embroidery surrounded the neckline of the soft muslin nightgown, and she looked like a schoolgirl, except that schoolgirls didn't have figures like hers.

The doctor arrived quickly, a tribute to the persuasions or threats of Rafe's valet. Told only that the patient had been caught in a riot, the physician examined her while Rafe paced restlessly in the overfurnished drawing room.

After an endless time, the doctor emerged to say, "The young lady was very lucky. Apart from some bruises and a headache, she'll be fine. No broken bones or signs of internal injuries."

Examining his disheveled patron, the doctor added, "Should I examine you also? You don't appear to have escaped unscathed."

Rafe made an impatient gesture with one hand. "There's nothing wrong with me. Or at least, nothing to signify," he qualified. Now that his anxiety was allayed, he became aware of aches and bruises all over. It was like the time he had been thrown from his horse during a steeplechase race, and half the field had galloped over him.

Sending his valet back to bed, Rafe built a fire in the small hearth, then took off his coat and boots and settled down with a glass of brandy in a chair by the bed. He didn't want Maggie waking in a strange place with no familiar faces, so he would sit with her until she was conscious again. As he stretched his long legs out before him, he thought humorlessly that she might hate him, but at least he was familiar.

He sipped his brandy, wishing he could obliterate the image of his bullet smashing into Lemercier's skull. Since he couldn't, he forced himself to look directly at the fact that he had killed a man. Would shooting the Frenchman in a less lethal place have been equally effective? At the time, he had acted from pure instinct, and obviously his instincts were savage. At least, they were where Margot was concerned. If he had had a cannon, he would have fired it into that mob in order to save her.

Wearily he rubbed his temples. The shooting had been necessary, and in the same circumstances he would not hesitate to do it again. Yet taking a human life was not an act that could be dismissed as if it had no significance. Perhaps some day he would ask his friend Michael Kenyon, who had been a soldier, if one ever became used to killing.

Or perhaps he would not ask. There seemed to be a large number of questions he didn't really want answered.

He was dozing when faint, restless movements woke him. Sitting up, he saw that Maggie was writhing back and forth, fear rippling across her face and her breath coming in gasps. As he watched, she twisted violently and began to scream, the same blood-chilling cry of panic that she had made in the plaza.

Coming instantly awake, he propelled himself from his chair to sit on the edge of the bed. "Maggie, it's all right!" he said sharply. "You're safe here."

Her eyes opened, but they were dazed, without recognition. As she drew her breath for another scream, he shook her shoulder. "Wake up, Maggie. There's nothing to fear."

Slowly her gaze focused on him. "Rafe?" she said uncertainly. Feebly she pushed herself to a sitting position.

"Yes, my dear. Don't worry, apart from a bang on the head nothing happened to you." He spoke softly, but his words must have brought back memories of the riot. She began to cry, crumpling forward as racking sobs shook her.

Rafe drew her into his arms, and she clung to him like a drowning woman. In a remote corner of his mind he was mildly surprised by the degree of her distress. The tough-as-leather countess had seemed equal to anything.

But this wasn't the countess, it was Margot, and she was hurting terribly. He held her shivering body close, murmuring a soothing flow of platitudes and reassurances. When her sobs abated, he said, "Lemercier was the one that turned the mob on you. Did you see him?"

She nodded, her face hidden.

"If it's any comfort, justice was visited on him rather quickly."

Startled, she looked up. "Did you . . . ?"

"With your pistol," he said. "Pure poetic justice." Succinctly he described what had happened, and how he had managed to get them away.

Satisfaction flickered across her face, but it quickly vanished. "I keep seeing them," she said unsteadily. "The faces and the hands, all reaching for me. . . . No matter how hard I try, I can't escape. And then, and then . . ." She buried her face against him again.

Stroking her hair, Rafe said forcefully, "Maggie, it's over, and you're safe. I won't let anything happen to you."

She lifted her head and looked at him, her pupils so distended that her eyes looked black. In a wavering voice, she said, "Rafe, I . . . I want you to make love to me."

Chapter 15

In a day full of drama, nothing had been as stunning as Maggie's words. Incredulously Rafe said, "Do you know what you are saying?"

Though her long fair lashes were clumped with tears, her eyes were bleakly aware. "I know what I am asking, and I know it isn't fair to you, but I want to—need to—forget."

Her voice trailed off and she shuddered, closing her eyes for a moment before opening them to renew her plea. "Rafe, if you have ever cared for me at all . . ."

Still he held back. Despite his vivid fantasies, he found that he didn't want to take her like this, when she was injured and terrified. He wanted her to desire him as he desired her, not see him only as a way to block out unbearable memory.

She reached out and brushed his cheek with her fingertips, her expression desolate. "Please, I beg you . . ."

Rafe couldn't bear to see her fierce pride broken. Turning into her hand, he kissed her palm and whispered, "Oh, God, Margot, I've waited so long. So very, very long . . ."

The desire that had been consuming him for days flared to white heat, and for an instant his vision blurred. More than anything on earth, he wanted to bury himself inside her—to lose himself in passion. Yet this was not the time for a wild, heedless coupling; if he was to help her, he must be stronger and calmer than she.

He took hold of her shoulders to draw her into a kiss. As soon as he touched her, she began shaking.

He became absolutely still. "Is that desire or fear?"

Not meeting his eyes, she replied, "A little of both."

How strange to think that the evening before, he had wondered if he might be capable of rape; the mere thought that Margot could fear him was like a red-hot poker in his belly.

While he was trying to decide what to say, she raised her hand to brush nervously at her hair. The sleeve of her gown slipped a little, revealing an ugly bruise on her forearm.

When he saw the purple-blue splotch, he dropped his hands from her shoulders. The knowledge that strangers had hurt her made him want to do murder. "This isn't a good idea," he said tightly. "I don't want to do anything that you'll regret later."

"I won't regret this." She took his hand and clasped it to her heart. "I need to remember that . . . that not all men are vicious brutes."

Unable to keep an edge from his voice, he said, "Given that I'm a selfish, arrogant, conceited rakehell, are you sure that I'm a good choice for restoring your faith in men?"

Her face flooded with color. "I'm sorry for what I said. I . . . I didn't mean to hurt you."

"Yes, you did, and with some justice. I'm certainly selfish, definitely arrogant, and quite possibly conceited." He made a show of pondering. "I'm not sure I'll admit to being a rakehell—I like to think that I practice my vices in a civilized fashion."

"Then I'll retract that particular insult." She offered a tremulous smile. "Truce?"

He had wanted to amuse her, but when he looked into her smoky eyes, he saw devastation. Chilled, he realized that the only thing holding her together was willpower, and even the steeliest will had its limits. If she was not brought back from the precipice of fear, she might fall into the abyss.

"Truce, my dear." Again he drew her into his arms and bent his head to hers. When their lips touched there was a small shock, like the spark that sometimes occurred in cold weather. Part of that was the attraction that always vibrated between them, but this time there were disquieting undercurrents.

As she responded to the kiss, her rigidity lessened, but the improvement was short-lived. Her eyes drifted shut, and she suddenly stiffened again. Then she began tugging clumsily at his shirt to free it from his breeches.

He caught and immobilized her hands. "We have hours until dawn, and I intend to use every moment well," he said soothingly. "Relax, accept, enjoy. I promise that when we are done, what happened in the Place du Carrousel will seem like no more than a distant nightmare."

She bit her lip. "I'm sorry, Rafe. Whenever I close my eyes, I see the hands and faces again. It's . . . it's like being set on by wolves." She drew an unsteady breath. "I can't control the terror, and the only thing I know that is stronger than fear is passion."

"It's true that passion has a way of obliterating everything else, at least for a while," he agreed. But he also knew that it would be hard for her to lose herself in desire when she was emotionally so close to the breaking point.

Then he saw how he must proceed. Not once had she called him "your grace" with her razor sarcasm. By the same token, for him the formidable countess had vanished, replaced by Margot Ashton. Quietly he said, "We need more than a truce, Margot. Let's try to go back to our earlier selves—to a time before life became so painful and complicated. Forget tonight's riot, and every other episode that has left scars and cynicism. Pretend that you're eighteen, and I'm twenty-one, and the world is a place of infinite promise."

"I don't know if I can," she said, her voice aching. "If only it were really possible to go back."

"I would take you to the past if I could, but I'm afraid that's beyond my power." Tenderly he brushed a shining strand of hair from her grazed cheek. "Still, for a few hours, we can recreate what might have been if the world were a simpler—or kinder—place."

"The world is neither simple nor kind," she said bitterly.

"Tonight it is." He lifted her hands and kissed them as if she were made of egg-shell porcelain. "Believe, Margot, if only for the next few hours.

Her tense fingers slowly uncurled. "I'll try, Rafe."

He resumed their kiss, deliberately focusing all of his attention on the sensual merging of their mouths. Tonight was the wedding night he had dreamed of when they were betrothed. Nothing in the world mattered beyond the softness of her lips on his, the rough, moist texture of her tongue, the warmth of her breasts compressing against his chest.

At eighteen Margot had been innocent, but also impetuous and eager for new experience. Though Rafe at twenty-one had been experienced enough to insure that all would go smoothly, he had still had enough youthful optimism to believe in happy endings.

For a moment the ugly reality of what had destroyed that optimism intruded on his imaginings, but he pushed it away. Tonight was for what might have been, and silently he vowed that all the subtle skills of love that he had ever learned would be his gift to her.

As when he had been calming Castlereagh's frightened horse, he created tranquility within himself so that his mood could be transmitted to Margot. Her fear gradually diminished, the tension flowing from her like sand from an hourglass.

When her body had become malleable, he began trailing kisses across her high cheekbones. He reached her ear and licked the dainty, complex shapes with his tongue.

She gave a breathy sigh of pleasure, and her head fell back. With humility, he thought of what trust it took to offer one's vulnerable throat to another being. Strange, that in spite of all the suspicion and conflict there had been between them, she could trust him when she was at her most defenseless.

He pressed his mouth to the fragile skin below her jaw, feeling the beat of her blood and the whispery vibration of her breath. Spreading one hand behind her back for support, he began unfastening the small round buttons that secured the front of her nightgown.

As her pale skin was revealed, his lips drifted, slow and thorough. Pretending that tonight was an earlier, simpler time gave him a delicious sense of naughtiness as he delved lower and lower. When he blew lightly into the shadowed valley formed by her breasts, she trembled, then began kneading his back with restless fingertips.

After six buttons the nightgown would open no further, so he reached for the hem of the garment to remove it entirely. But when he had raised the hem to the middle of her thighs, he paused. For a clothed man to make love to a naked female implied things about power and dominance that were not what he wanted Margot to feel. They should be equally exposed.

He slid from the bed and swiftly removed his clothing, then joined her again as her dazed eyes opened to see where he had gone. Her high cheekbones were dramatically sculpted by candlelight, and the shadow of fear was still on her.

"I haven't forsaken you, Margot," he said quietly.

"I'm here for as long as you want me to be, and no longer." Though if she wanted him to stop, he didn't know how he would be able to endure it.

This time she moved to him, wrapping her slim, strong arms around his bare waist before touching her full lips to his mouth. He guessed that tonight she would speak little, so it was up to him to sense what she needed.

During the deep, unhurried kiss that followed, he drew her nightgown up over the tantalizing curves of her body. The flimsy fabric stayed crumpled around her shoulders for several minutes because neither of them could bear to separate long enough to allow the garment to be pulled over her head.

Finally he broke away and tugged the gown off, then tossed it aside. As his gaze went over her, he drew an involuntary breath. What a fool he had been to think that all women were made much the same. For him, Margot was the essence of female mystery, and she aroused him as no other woman ever had.

A tremor in his voice, he said, "You're as beautiful as I've always known you would be."

She gave a fleeting smile, then hid her face against his shoulder like the shy virgin bride of his imagination. "It's nice to pretend. To begin again," she whispered, her breath caressing his neck.

"More than nice. Marvelous." He stroked her hair, and the lustrous strands twined around his fingers. "Magical."

When she exhaled with delight, the movement caused her nipples to swing teasingly across his chest. His body tightened painfully, less willing to accept patience than his mind.

For a moment he teetered perilously between lust and restraint. Perhaps she was ready. . . .

No. It was too soon. Over the years, his feverish

dreams of her had been a product of his own eternal desire, but tonight his needs must be secondary.

After mastering himself, he gently pressed her back into the pillows. She was as pliant as willow, like the trusting girl she had been. He found it remarkable that for tonight, at least, she had managed to put aside her stubborn independence in favor of a sweetly feminine yielding.

Numerous bruises, obscene and ugly, marred the creamy perfection of her body. Instinctively he touched his lips to a purple-black patch on her forearm before remembering that he should be more careful. "Did that hurt you?"

"No." Her fingers curled into the counterpane. "Oh, no."

Taking that as encouragement, he gave each mark a feather-light caress with his tongue. Shoulder, elbow, hip; ribs, abdomen, and thigh. Ragged changes in her breathing tracked his progress like musical counterpoint.

When each bruise had been acknowledged, he cupped her lush breasts in his hands and buried his face in the tender cleft between. Her heart beat against his cheek, powerful and warmly alive.

If matters had gone differently—if the pistol had misfired—that indomitable heart might have been forever silenced.

Needing to obliterate the unthinkable, he turned his head and began suckling her breast. She whimpered and arched upward, her nipple going taut against the roof of his mouth.

Her hips began shifting with restless eagerness, so he drew both hands downward, his palms shaping the rich swell from waist to thigh. The tawny thatch between her thighs was a shade darker than the hair on her head, autumn oak rather than summer gold.

As he licked the warm convex surface of her belly,

he slipped his palm between her knees. She gave a sudden gasp that was not pleasure, and her legs locked together.

"Trust me, Margot," he murmured, "It's natural to be nervous the first time, but I swear that I won't harm you."

She made a sound that seemed wrenched from deep inside her. Then, with obvious effort, she forced herself to relax again.

He caressed her tense limbs until her relaxation was genuine. At the same time, and moving with the same rhythm, he nuzzled and kissed her breasts and belly. By the time his hand had progressed to the top of her inner thighs, she radiated heat and yearning. He wove his fingers through the soft tawny curls to the hidden mysteries below.

When he touched her, she gave a small cry. Her hips shifted spasmodically, pressing into his hand. He probed more deeply, finding folds of delicate flesh that pulsed against his fingertips, lavishly moist.

As he expertly petted and probed, her nails bit painfully deep into his shoulders. "N-now?" she quavered.

"Soon, my dear. Soon." He continued until he judged that she was on the verge of culmination. Then, throbbing with painful desire, he positioned himself over her. He entered slowly, and the tight, welcoming clasp of her body was everything he had ever dreamed of, and more. Knowing he was on the verge of explosion, he held still, his whole being hammering with an insistence that drowned out all the world but her.

Maggie had expected that there would be awkwardness at joining their strangers' bodies for the first time, but there was none. They might have been designed by nature as ideal mates, and she felt completed as never before. Without conscious volition, her pelvis curled demandingly against Rafe's.

He gasped. "S-steady now." He was braced above

her, his broad shoulders rimmed by light, his strong
features enigmatic in the shadows. He had as many
bruises as she, and again she was awestruck by the
courage and strength he had displayed in saving a
woman he despised.

He was magnificent, all power and masculine grace,
and she would savor every instant of their mating. In a
distant corner of her mind, she knew that she would
pay a bitterly high price for this joy, but she refused to
think about that now. Wanting more of him, she
wrapped her arms around his torso and pulled him
down, relishing the hard weight of his body pressing
her into the feather mattress.

Stormclouds had been gathering around them ever
since Rafe had arrived in Paris, and as he thrust into
her, the storm struck. Furiously it swept her along, racing through her blood, driving all fear and doubt away.
Then lightning blazed through every cell of her body.
Moaning, she clung to him as the one certainty in the
tempest.

The tumult died away, leaving her body quivering
and her consciousness fractured. Only gradually did
she realize that he was still hard within her. She ran her
hands over his sweat-slicked back. "You haven't . . ."

"Don't worry about me," he said before she could
finish. "The night is young."

Though that wasn't true, she did not bother to disagree.
It was enough simply to be joined with him. Safe.

Yet desire still simmered within her. Rafe understood her body better than she did, for he knew when
to begin moving again. His first strokes were infinites-
imal, yet they generated an astonishing amount of heat.
She matched his movements, and as the tempo increased, they ignited each other. The intimacy between
them was scorching, a baring of mind and body that
was frightening in its intensity.

Frantically she twisted her head back and forth as

their bodies melded with stunning force. What had gone before was prologue, mere overture to a more urgent hunger than any she had ever known. This time the rising storm was not wind, but fire, burning away her awareness until there was only flame within her. Gone were fear and prudence, anger and hate, leaving only the searing knowledge that the man she loved was enfolding her with passion and exquisite tenderness.

She reached shattering fulfillment, and was consumed by fire. Unable to suppress the words, she gasped, "I love you."

Storm and fire. Disintegration and rebirth. Through the conflagration, she heard him groan, "Oh, God ... God help me."

With shocking suddenness he withdrew, crushing her in his arms as he thrust hotly against her belly. After a handful of violent movements, his seed spurted between them.

She held him with all her strength, tears seeping between her eyelids. Once again Rafe was protecting her from potential disaster.

During the years she and Robin had been lovers, they had taken great care not to start a child, for there was no place in their perilous lives for a family. In her mind, she knew that was still true.

Yet some of her tears were for the loss of what might have been—the children she and Rafe might have had in the last dozen years if they had married; the baby that might have been conceived in tenderness tonight. Gone like the wind, like all her other dreams.

Rafe shifted his weight from her and used the discarded nightgown to dry them both. Then he drew her into his arms and they both dozed off without speaking.

The words did not exist that could describe how she felt.

* * *

With a terrified gasp, Maggie awoke from nightmare. Panic, pain, destruction—all of the familiar, ghastly fears that had been triggered by the incident in the Plaza du Carrousel crowded into her mind.

Shivering, she burrowed closer to Rafe. Even in sleep he radiated safety. Almost compulsively, she stroked his chest, smoothing the dark hair that felt so sensual against her breasts.

When his breathing changed, she stopped, not wanting to wake him. Yet she found that she couldn't keep her hands away. She loved the smooth warmth of his skin, the candlelit contrast between his darkness and her paleness.

A stirring under the sheet indicated that part of him, at least, was waking. As if it had a life of its own, her hand pulled the sheet down and touched him. Heated male flesh unfurled into her palm.

His eyes remained closed, but his hand lifted and he started massaging the nape of her neck. Warmth spread through her, and she wanted to purr like a kitten. Even more, she wanted to roar like a lioness.

She began kissing him, bypassing his mouth in favor of other sensitive places. The junction between jaw and throat; the hollow above his collarbones; his flat, dusky nipples; the supple indentations between muscular thighs and flat abdomen.

Though he didn't move from his supine position, his breathing quickened and his right hand caressed whatever parts of her came within reach. Vowing that this time she would drive him to madness, she bent forward and kissed him in the most sensitive place of all, using her mouth and tongue to demonstrate what she could not speak aloud.

He sucked in his breath, and his limbs began to tremble. She redoubled her efforts, reveling in her power to move him. This time he would be swept into the storm as thoroughly as she.

He made a guttural exclamation and ground his fist into the mattress. Yet before she could bring him to culmination, he abruptly abandoned passivity and rolled her onto her back, reversing their positions. He pleasured her expertly, his heated mouth enflaming her, holding her at the brink of ecstasy, until she panted with frantic need.

Finally they came together like clashing cymbals. This was not the remembered innocence of youth, but the ardent sensuality of experience—skilled and knowing and unashamed.

Yet in spite of the mind-drugging pleasure, she knew that only his body was fully engaged. His mind and spirit held back, leaving a shadow of emptiness at the heart of intimacy.

Even as she shuddered with convulsive release, she mourned. He was as superb as a lover as one could imagine—except that he did what he did without love.

Margot slept in his arms, utterly still in the depths of exhaustion, her tangled hair adrift on his bare chest. Rafe was so tired that he could barely find the strength to raise his hand and brush the dark gold strands from her eyes, to trace the fine bones of her face. Yet he could not sleep.

One might say that he had been lucky, for fate had given him the opportunity to free himself of his obsession by allowing this passionate interlude with the woman who held him in thrall.

One would have been wrong. Though he had succeeded in his goal of briefly severing her awareness from her tortured memories, for him it had been an empty victory.

For years, he had dreamed of Margot coming to him with sweet words of longing and an intoxicating invitation. Tonight part of his dream had come true, yet he had discovered the bitter truth that the invitation was hollow without the sweet words.

If there had been only silence between them, he would have been able to maintain the illusion that they were lovers in truth. Instead, Margot had been so lost to her circumstances that words of love had escaped her. The declaration had hurt more deeply than he would have dreamed possible, because he knew that it was meant for another man. It was Anderson who held her heart. Only chance had brought her to his own bed tonight, when she desperately needed oblivion.

Yet in spite of the pain, he wished the night would never end. He had wanted Margot Ashton back, and with the bittersweet treachery that marked the gods' answers to human prayers, he had gotten what he wanted. What Rafe hadn't realized was that if he found Margot again, he would once more be as blindly, helplessly in love with her as he had been at twenty-one.

The obsession he had felt for Countess Janos was only another name for that love, but he had been too cynical to name his emotions truly. In the dark, with the palest of dawn light etching the windows, he recognized starkly that he had never stopped loving Margot. No matter what her betrayals and lies, no matter how many beds she had passed through, he loved her—more than wisdom, more than pride, more than life itself.

And in the morning, she would leave him. Tomorrow all the barriers would be firmly in place again, perhaps with an additional layer of shame on her part, for what she had done so shamelessly.

The irony was crushing. Rafael Whitbourne, fifth Duke of Candover, had been beloved of the gods—blessed with health, intelligence, charm, and wealth beyond imagining. Those who crossed his path gave him admiration and respect.

Yet he damned his fate with dark, despairing anger

that this one woman, who mattered more than all else, could not love him. She had cared for him when she was young, surely, but not enough to be faithful through the short months of their betrothal. He had never come first with her, not then, and not now, when a traitor and spy held her first allegiance.

Staring upward into the softening dark, Rafe wondered what deep, crippling flaw made him unable to love any woman except one who could not love him back.

Tomorrow would be time enough to ponder that. For now, he would savor this handful of moments with the only woman he had ever loved.

With the bleakness that lies beyond hope, he knew that it was all the time he would ever have.

Chapter 16

Maggie felt deeply rested when she awoke, though the angle of the sun showed that it was still early. In the clear light of day, it was hard to believe that she had had the audacity to ask Rafe to make love to her. Yet the warm length of his body lying beside her was irrefutable proof of what had happened.

As a woman of the world, she had thought it likely that he would oblige her; though females needed a reason for intimacy, men usually needed only a place. She had had a reason, and Rafe had supplied the place.... Yet what had passed between them had gone far beyond anything she had been able to imagine, and it would stay etched in her brain forever.

Turning her head slightly, she studied Rafe's sleeping form. His numerous bruises had matured to melodramatic purple-black. God only knew how he had gotten her away from that mob. Take away his title and his wealth and his influence, and he would still be a man among men—strong and brave and heartstoppingly beautiful, in an utterly male fashion.

Maggie closed her eyes in anguish. She had always known that if they became intimate, she would be helplessly in love with Rafe again, and it had happened. The love had always been there, since she had first met him thirteen years ago. Perhaps that was why she had never been able to love Robin as completely as he deserved.

No, the problem was not how *much* she loved Robin, but *how* she loved him. She cared for both men more deeply than words could ever express, yet Rafe she loved with conflict as well as harmony, challenge as well as understanding.

Strange to think that it was the harsher elements between them that gave her feelings for him such depth and intensity. With Robin there was always harmony, and their love was that of friends, almost siblings. Rafe she wanted as a mate, the archetypal male who made her feel most deeply female.

She swallowed hard and slid away from Rafe's arm, careful not to wake him. Though she would like nothing better than to spend the rest of her life in his bed, that was impossible. Conspiracy and death still surrounded them, and there were the charges against Robin.

One way or another, the business would be resolved, and then she would never see Rafe again. Considering the sexual fire between them, he might still want her for a mistress, if his pride wasn't too deeply injured by the way she had used him. But she would never dare accept. The memory of the previous night's passion made it almost impossible to imagine life without him. If they became lovers in truth, she would never survive the end of the affair.

When the end came, Rafe would be perfectly charming, of course, kind and a trifle bored. She could imagine it already.

Laying the back of her hand against his cheek, Maggie said a silent farewell to their brief hours of intimacy, resisting the temptation to kiss him one last time.

Since her clothes were neatly folded on a chair, she dressed, wincing over the incredible range of aches and bruises she discovered. A little crude mending disguised the worst of the rips in her garments so that she was more or less decent. Apart from being dressed as a man, that is.

Then she went to the window seat and curled up, hugging her knees to her chest as she waited for Rafe to awaken.

It was perhaps a quarter of an hour until he stirred. His first movement was toward the side of the bed Maggie had occupied. The emptiness woke him, and he pushed himself up on one elbow, his gaze scanning the room until he found her on the window seat.

Relaxing fractionally, he stared across the intervening space, his face unreadable. Maggie found herself distracted by the elegant patterns of dark hair on his bare chest. Last night she had experienced them as a texture, but now sight provided a different kind of pleasure.

Hoping that some of the previous night's intimacy would survive the light of day, she said tentatively, "Good morning."

He watched her with damnably cool gray eyes. "Is it a good morning?"

He was going to make this difficult for her. Maggie swung her feet to the floor and forced herself to meet his gaze. "Well, I'm alive, for which I am profoundly grateful. There wouldn't have been much left of me after the mob was done." After a brief struggle with the panic that flared at the thought, she continued, "There are no words strong enough to thank you for saving my life."

"Don't bother trying," he snapped, his gray eyes like ice chips. "I didn't do it because I wanted gratitude."

With dread, she knew that she must refer to what had happened in the heat of the night. If she didn't, he would, and she feared what he might say. "I also owe you an apology," she said unevenly. "You saved my life, and I used you in an unforgivable manner. Asking you what I did was ... an offense against honor and good taste. You helped me survive a nightmare—I hope you can also find it in your heart to forgive me."

A caustic edge in his voice, Rafe said, "Think nothing of it, Countess. I'm sure that a woman of your experience knows that men don't usually mind servicing distraught females. And you're remarkably skilled. It was a privilege to have the opportunity to sample your wares."

Maggie felt as if she had been slapped. Though she had guessed that he would be angry, this was far worse than she had imagined. No man would like the idea of being used as an anodyne against pain, and this one would like it less than most. Pride was undoubtedly the deepest of his emotions, and she had gravely wounded that.

At least he didn't taunt her with the words of love that had escaped when all her defenses were down and her heart spoke uncensored. If he had mocked her unguarded declaration, the hurt would have been unendurable.

Yet in her secret heart, Maggie could not regret what had happened, even though she knew how much it would cost her in the future. Quietly she repeated, "I'm sorry," as she stood and turned to leave.

His voice lashed across the bedchamber. "Where the hell do you think you are going?"

She stopped, but wouldn't look at him. "To Robin's, of course. I must talk to him."

"Do you mean I actually managed to raise a few doubts about him in your irrational female mind?"

Turning to face Rafe, she retorted, "Yes, damn you, you did. Now I must give him the chance to explain himself."

He sat upright, the covers spilling across his lap as his gaze bored into hers. "What if he has no satisfactory explanation?"

"I don't know." Her shoulders sagged. "I just do not know."

"Ring for breakfast when you reach the drawing room. I'll join you in fifteen minutes."

When Maggie started to protest, he cut her off. "You're not leaving here without some food in you. Afterward, I'll take you to Anderson's myself."

She started to sputter, unsure whether to be amused, alarmed, or outraged at his high-handedness.

Fixing her with a gimlet eye, Rafe said, "If you think I will let you walk the streets alone looking like that, the kick in the head did more damage than the physician thought. Every night men are killed in the streets of Paris—two bodies were found near the Place du Carrousel just the night before last.

"Speaking of physicians . . ." he picked up a small bottle and tossed it to her. "The doctor left this for what he assured me would be the devil of a headache. Now kindly get out of the way while I dress."

Not waiting for her to leave, he swung from the bed, magnificently naked. Knowing that if she didn't leave instantly, she would be tempted to drag him back among the covers, she hastily averted her face and headed for the door.

As soon as Rafe had mentioned the probability of a headache, she realized that her head was throbbing. Once she was safely in the drawing room, she swallowed one of the doctor's pills.

What a pity that heartaches could not be treated as easily as headaches.

Too foul-tempered to wait for his valet, Rafe started to shave himself, his mind seething. Apologies and gratitude were not what he wanted from Margot. In the ultimate idiocy, he wanted her to have magically fallen in love with him. But as soon as he awoke and saw her curled on the window seat, as bristly as a hedgehog, he had known that there had been no miraculous transformation in her feelings.

As his hand clenched involuntarily on the handle of his razor, he felt a stinging pain on the edge of his jaw. He swore as blood dripped messily into the china basin. Christ, if he wasn't more careful, he was going to accidentally slit his own throat. He pressed a towel to the cut to stop the bleeding, wondering what the devil was happening to him.

Margot was what was happening. He had always prided himself on rational, civilized behavior. In the House of Lords and among his friends, he was known for his ability to coax opposing factions into finding common ground.

Yet the moment he had walked into that small room in the Austrian embassy and recognized Margot, he had started to fall apart. He had lost his temper and his sense more often in the last fortnight than in the previous decade. It was becoming obvious that the only reason he had a reputation for an even disposition was because there hadn't been anything in his life that he cared enough about to make him lose control.

He couldn't face Margot in such a state, so he forced himself to take slow, deep breaths. She had been completely honest about why she wanted him to make love to her, and he had no right to be furious with her. For the sake of his own pride, he must stop acting like a spoiled schoolboy.

He lifted the towel from the razor cut and found that the bleeding had stopped. Margot had managed to master herself after her terror of the night before, and he could do no less. He supposed that he should feel proud of the fact that his exertions on her behalf had had such a beneficial effect.

And he was. Bloody proud.

* * *

By the time Rafe finished dressing and joined Margot for breakfast, The Duke was once more in control. After a wary glance at him, she relaxed. He was glad that he could still maintain the appearance of being a civilized man.

There was little discussion over the excellent coffee and croissants, or on the first part of the ride to Anderson's lodgings. Then their carriage reached the edge of the Place du Carrousel and was forced to stop by a milling crowd.

As the driver carefully turned the carriage around, Rafe and Maggie saw that the plaza was sealed off by thousands of Austro-Hungarian troops, the sunlight dazzling on their white uniforms and brass artillery. With such protection, the task of removing the bronze horses of St. Mark's was proceeding without incident.

As the first horse was lifted from the arch, the Austro-Hungarian troops cheered and the French crowd howled in anguish. This time, Napoleon's loot was leaving for good.

Rafe smiled grimly. "Wellington must have been furious when he heard about last night and decided on a show of force. Paris might not love him now, but, by God, she will respect him!"

Maggie's flat voice drew him back to the implications. "Let us hope that increased unpopularity won't increase his chances of being assassinated."

The rest of the journey was made in silence. They detoured around the Place du Carrousel and the Louvre to reach the small hotel where Robin had rooms. Rafe waited in the carriage while Maggie went in, warning that he would follow her if she was gone more than ten minutes.

No such action was required, for she returned quickly, her face drawn. "There was no answer when I knocked on Robin's door," she said as she climbed into the carriage. "The concierge told me that Robin hasn't been home in two days."

Rafe frowned. "Could he be staying overnight at the embassy because of the amount of work to be done?"

She shook her head. "The British delegation doesn't know where he is, either. Yesterday they sent a groom to ask if Robin was in his rooms."

She settled back into the luxurious seat, her stomach twisted into an agonized knot. If Robin had learned that there were suspicions about him and run away, he was guilty. If he was innocent, he never would have left Paris without notifying her.

Therefore, since he had disappeared without a trace, he was either guilty or dead.

Rafe was silent as he returned Maggie to her town house, his brows drawn like thunderclouds. She could only be glad that he refrained from saying "I told you so."

As soon as she reached home, she sent a message to Hélène Sorel, asking her friend to join her for a light luncheon. With matters reaching a crisis, she needed a confederate who might be able to see things she herself had missed.

Then she withdrew into her bedroom for two hours of pacing and tortured thought. She cared too much for Robin to hope that he was a dead patriot rather than a live traitor—but if he had betrayed his country, she never wanted to see him again.

Hélène appeared promptly, mild inquiry on her face. As soon as they had taken the edge from their appetites, Maggie filled her in on recent events, including Robin's disappearance.

Hélène listened gravely, her brown hair drawn back in a modest chignon. She looked like any other pretty young French matron, except for her precise, intelligent questions.

When Maggie ran out of words, Hélène said, "The picture is larger and darker than I knew. With Talleyrand out of power and Castlereagh confined to his bed, it would seem that Wellington is the most likely target for assassins, *n'est-ce pas?*"

"I'm afraid so. Candover has gone to speak to Wellington, to warn him to take special care. They know each other, so Wellington may listen, but he is notorious for ignoring danger. A warning might not make much difference."

"It is time we reduced the number of suspects," Hélène said. "I have finished my inquiries about Colonel von Fehrenbach, and this evening I will call on him. When I am done, I think he will no longer be a suspect."

"I can't afford to lose any more friends," Maggie said soberly. "Candover is asking Wellington for the use of some soldiers, so please take him and an escort, for safety's sake."

"I will if you insist, but they must wait outside and not come unless summoned." Hélène's brown eyes showed amusement as she selected a pastry from the tray between them on the dining table. "They will not be needed."

Maggie wished that she shared her friend's faith. If she could be disastrously wrong about Robin, Hélène could certainly be wrong about a man she barely knew.

"If von Fehrenbach is eliminated, that will leave General Roussaye as the most likely prospect." Maggie sighed. She wanted to retire to her room and sleep forever, and not have to face a world where she had lost Robin, where Rafe despised her, and the fate of European peace might be resting on her weary shoulders. Planting her elbows on the polished mahogany table, she buried her face in her hands and rubbed her aching head, telling herself not to be melodramatic.

A knock sounded, followed by her butler and a female caller. The butler said apologetically, "I know you didn't wish to be disturbed, my lady, but Mrs. Northwood said it was most urgent."

Pulling herself together, Maggie got to her feet. "Very good, Laneuve."

The butler stepped clear of her guest, and Maggie gasped at the sight of Cynthia's violently bruised face. In a shaky voice, the girl said, "I didn't know where else to go."

"My dear child!" Appalled, Maggie walked over and put her arms around her guest.

Cynthia sagged against her for a few moments, then resolutely pushed herself away. "I'm sorry, I didn't mean to do that. I must talk to you." She looked doubtfully at Hélène, who had poured a glass of brandy and now offered it.

Maggie said, "Don't worry, you can speak freely before Madame Sorel. She and I are close friends, and she can be trusted with anything. Now, what has happened to you?"

Accepting both the assurance and the brandy, Cynthia sank into a chair and set down the small portmanteau she carried. "I was able to search my husband's desk."

"Did he catch you and beat you?" Maggie exclaimed, feeling horribly guilty for having put Cynthia up to it.

"No, he beat me for quite different reasons," her guest said bitterly. "When I searched the desk yesterday, I had ample time to find a secret drawer, copy everything inside, and leave the papers as I found them." She pulled half a dozen sheets of writing paper from her portmanteau and handed them to Maggie. "I didn't dare bring the originals, but I thought you might be able to make sense of these."

Maggie set the papers down for later examination.

"If Northwood didn't know of your search, why did he beat you?"

"I had finally decided to leave him. To stay was insupportable, and Michael swears that he is willing to face the consequences, no matter what Oliver might do. However, Michael was sent to the fortress at Huninguen and won't be back for several more days, so I had to wait. Unfortunately, reaching a decision made me almost giddy with relief, and I think that Oliver guessed that something was in the wind."

She looked down at her hands, with their short-bitten nails. "This morning Oliver came into my room unexpectedly when I was dressing, and immediately saw that I was increasing. He knew the baby couldn't be his, and he was enraged. He made my maid leave and began to beat me, calling me horrible names and saying that he hoped I'd lose the filthy brat, and if he was lucky, I'd die, too. Then he locked me in my room."

She began weeping, but managed to say through her tears, "I can't go back there, he'll kill me! Please, Maggie, can I stay with you until Michael returns?"

"Of course you can," Maggie said warmly. "He'll never find you here. How did you escape from the locked room?"

Cynthia smiled with a touch of pride. "I was quite the tomboy when I was a girl. After he left for work, I tied the bedsheets together and climbed down, then came here in a cab."

"That was resourceful," Maggie said with genuine respect. "But now it's time for you to rest—you must be exhausted."

Maggie installed Cynthia in a guest room and sent for a physician to check the girl's injuries. Then she settled down with Hélène in the dining room to study the papers Cynthia had brought. Most consisted of cryptic phrases, the kind of jottings a person doodles while thinking, and which are almost impossible for another person to decipher. There was one list of gambling vowels, and another that detailed sums of money in francs, possibly from winnings or losses.

Though Maggie was disappointed, she supposed that even a dolt like Northwood was unlikely to leave anything too incriminating around—always assuming that the man was guilty of anything more than ordinary beastliness. Secret compartments were common in desks, and one of the first places that would be searched. Maggie's own desk had a secret drawer; she had filled it with scorching but synthetic love letters that would support her reputation as a brainless doxy if anyone discovered them. She and Robin had gotten helpless with laughter when they had composed them. . . .

The memory made her ache, so she turned to the next page. A phrase scrawled in the middle jumped out at her: "Anderson—spy? Possible danger."

She and Hélène saw it at the same time. Voice tight, Maggie said, "This doesn't prove anything about Robin."

"No, it doesn't," Hélène agreed. "You still believe in his innocence, don't you, *mon amie*?"

"Yes," Maggie said bleakly. "I think that he disappeared because he got too close to the fire once too often." Eyes stinging, she laid out the last sheet of paper.

The drawing on it caught both women by surprise, for it was one of the crests that Maggie had traced at Madame Daudet's: the three-headed serpent of the d'Auguste family. Underneath was written, Le Serpent, and a triumphant Eureka!

After a long moment, Maggie said, "Obviously Northwood is involved in some secret work. The question is, for whom?"

"And what did this crest mean to him? If this is indeed the crest of Le Serpent, the puzzle is solved once we understand who it is connected to," Hélène said thoughtfully.

"Perhaps we are finally making some progress," Maggie replied. "But I feel more as if we are opening Chinese boxes, and that each contains another that is even more complicated."

At that moment, the butler entered to announce the arrival of the physician. Hélène rose to take her leave, promising to return that evening after her confrontation with Colonel von Fehrenbach.

Maggie prayed that her friend's initiative would bring them closer to their goal before another disaster struck.

Chapter 17

Hélène dressed carefully for her confrontation with Colonel von Fehrenbach, choosing a blue dress that was feminine but unprovocative. Though she had two reasons for visiting him, neither was seduction in the usual sense.

Candover took her to von Fehrenbach's in his own carriage. He had also arranged for four British soldiers to meet him at the colonel's building, where they would wait on the back stairs in case she needed assistance.

On the carriage ride, Rafe offered Hélène a pistol small enough to fit into her reticule. She rejected the offer with distaste. To appease him, she agreed to take a whistle whose shriek could penetrate several walls if necessary.

Her mind drifted to thoughts of Maggie and Rafe. She could feel the tension between them and wondered if it was because they desired each other and had done nothing about it, or because they had. . . .

Thinking about them made a refreshing change from worrying about her own concerns, because in spite of her surface confidence, the prospect of this interview with the Prussian officer terrified her.

The carriage halted in front of a mansion in the Marais district, not far from Madame Daudet's. The building was divided into flats, and the colonel lived in one with only a manservant, who should have the evening off. Since von Fehrenbach avoided the temptations of Parisian nightlife, going out only when his duties required it, Hélène should find him alone.

Candover got out and went around to the back to meet his soldiers and enter the building from the rear. After touching a nervous hand to her hair, Hélène also stepped down from the carriage. Inside, the concierge directed her to the second floor, front apartment.

The mansion had been built in the early eighteenth century, and it retained much of its grandeur. As she stood in front of von Fehrenbach's door, Hélène glanced down the hall to the door which concealed her bodyguard. Then she knocked.

After a delay of some moments, the colonel answered the door himself, confirming that the servant was out. Though von Fehrenbach was not in uniform, his unyielding posture marked him as unmistakably a soldier. His pale blond hair shone silver in the lamplight; he was a very handsome man, in the fashion of an ice prince.

They regarded each other in silence while fierce, primal attraction thrummed between them. It had been that way since the first time they had met, though neither had ever acknowledged it.

His face reflecting shock, and a complex mixture of other emotions, he said coldly, "Madame Sorel. What an unlikely pleasure. What brings you here this evening?"

"A matter of some urgency." Meeting his gaze required her to tilt her head rather far back. "If I promise not to compromise you, will you let me come in so that I may discuss it?"

A hint of color touched his cheeks, and he stood aside so she could enter. Inclining her head in thanks, she stepped into the drawing room and accepted an offered chair.

The rooms were well proportioned and impeccably

neat, but apart from the well-filled bookcase, there was an unwelcoming austerity. It was as Hélène expected; a person's interior state was mirrored in his surroundings, and the colonel had winter in his soul.

Not bothering to offer refreshments, von Fehrenbach seated himself some distance away and said forbiddingly, "Yes, madame?"

Before answering, Hélène spent a moment studying his face, feeling the tension that lay beneath his impassive expression. In a stab of self-doubt, she wondered if she might be wrong about the nature of that tension. Perhaps he really did make dark and dangerous plans to injure others. She was suddenly glad of the whistle in her reticule.

Not bothering with social niceties, she said bluntly, "There is a conspiracy to disrupt the peace conference by assassination. The accident that sent Castlereagh to his bed was in fact an attempt on his life, and Wellington may be the next target."

Von Fehrenbach's pale brows rose marginally. "Paris is rife with plots. What has that to do with me?"

Her hands locked in her lap, for what she was about to do was outrageous. "There is some reason to believe that you might be behind the conspiracy."

"What?" His calm shattered, the colonel bounded furiously to his feet. "How dare you accuse me of such a thing! What perversion of logic could lead anyone to suspect me?" With a flash of blue fire in his eyes, he added in a low, menacing whisper, "And why do I hear it from you, of all people?"

Hélène remained still. "That is three questions, none of them simple to answer. If you will sit and listen for a few minutes, I will explain." As he hesitated, she added, "It is in your best interest to hear."

His eyes narrowed. "Are you threatening me, madame?"

"Not at all, Colonel. What threat could I possibly

pose to you? You are one of the victors, a man of
wealth and position, while I am only a widow from a
defeated nation. If you are threatened, it is not by me."
As he stood uncertainly, she added impatiently,
"Come, surely you do not fear me. It will cost you
nothing to listen."

He took a chair closer to Hélène, saying so softly
that she might have imagined the words, "In that you
are wrong, Madame Sorel. I do fear you."

With dizzying relief she knew that she was right—
that every exchange between them took place on more
than one level. But before pursuing her own ends, she
must attend to the business that had brought her here.
"Considerable effort has gone into investigating this
plot, and it was determined that you were one of a
handful of possibilities who had the intelligence, skill,
and motive to organize it."

"I am flattered by your assessment of my ability," he
said dryly. "Now explain to me why I would do such
a thing."

"You are known to hate France and everything
French. Twice you have killed French officers in duels.
You have also said repeatedly that the proposed settlement is too moderate. If Wellington or Castlereagh is
killed, what will happen to the treaty that is so close to
acceptance?"

The colonel's brows arched with surprise. "I begin
to understand. If either of them is assassinated, the
voices of moderation would be stilled and all Europe
would demand reprisals. France would be dismem-
bered and impoverished."

"Does that thought please you, Colonel von
Fehrenbach?"

"It might please me, but I am a soldier, not an assassin," he said curtly. "I killed two predatory French officers who preyed on junior Allied officers. That is a
long way from plotting against your country. My duty

is to follow my sovereign's orders, not to make policy."

"I believe you, and that is one of the reasons I am here." She sat without flinching as he examined her with new thoroughness. He was beginning to really hear what she was saying, and that was what she had hoped for.

"Are there other reasons I am under suspicion?" he asked. "I am hardly the only Allied officer who hates France."

"There is another reason, circumstantial but strong. We have learned that the man behind the plot is called Le Serpent."

"Again, what has that to do with me?"

"'The cunning of a serpent, the courage of a lion,'" she quoted, watching his reaction closely.

He sucked in his breath. "Of course, my family motto. Interesting, but as you said, entirely circumstantial. Many family arms carry serpents. In fact," he added after a moment's thought, "it needn't refer to family arms. There is a French general who was nicknamed Le Serpent, and for all I know the Parisian king of thieves is called that as well."

Ignoring his later words, Hélène asked with sudden excitement, "What general is that?"

The colonel gave her a hard look. "Michel Roussaye. A friend of mine tried to capture him and a small force of French soldiers after the Battle of Leipzig. Roussaye slithered away time and again, very much like a serpent. He's a fine soldier."

"General Roussaye is another leading suspect."

"How would he benefit if France is crippled by the peace settlement?" von Fehrenbach said with exasperation. "You are guilty of massive illogic."

"A revolutionary might welcome a settlement that would anger France to the point where she would once more take arms."

The effect of Hélène's words on the colonel was immediate. His face closed and he seemed to forget that she was there. Eventually he returned his gaze to her. "Why have you come here to tell me this? If I am truly under suspicion, why didn't Wellington simply have me arrested?"

"There are political realities," she replied. "Marshal Blücher would be furious if a valued aide was arrested on such flimsy evidence. Indeed, there is no evidence to speak of, merely probabilities. That is one reason why this business is being handled with as much discretion as possible. If the story of the plot became well known, the effect would be almost as disruptive as an actual assassination."

"Perhaps," the colonel agreed. "But as you say, there is no real evidence—which is not surprising since I have done nothing. What makes you think that there is a plot at all?"

Hélène shrugged. "Rumors and small inconsistencies that would never stand up in a court of law. The only truly solid evidence is the attack on Lord Castlereagh, which was designed to look like an accident. Also, a British agent may have been murdered because he was getting too close to Le Serpent."

"Or else because he got into a fight over a woman— I've never heard that spies were a very honorable lot." Von Fehrenbach's gaze bored into her. "Which brings us to you, Madame Sorel. You have answered my other questions, but not why you, of all the men and women in France, have come to accuse me."

Now the conversation was going to become really difficult. Palms damp, Hélène said, "I have an unofficial connection with British intelligence, and have been involved in the investigation."

"So the lady is a spy," he said with disgust. "Or is that a contradiction in terms? Spying is just another form of whoring, and I understand that female spies sell themselves in many ways."

She had known that something like this would be said, but it still stung. "I have never sold myself in any way, Colonel, and I accept no money for what I do," she said sharply. "Someone else could have come to question you, but I wanted to."

"Why?" He leaned forward in his chair, his face hostile. "Once again, why you?"

"You know why, Colonel." She gazed at him with all the warmth and honesty she possessed.

Though his eyes might be the cold blue of northern ice, in their depths she saw raw, blazing pain. Muttering a German curse, he wrenched his gaze away from her and stood, turning toward his bookcase. She could see some of the titles from where she sat. Philosophy and history, mostly, with a number of Latin and Greek texts. The colonel was a man of broad interests.

Not looking at her, he said, "You speak in riddles, Madame Sorel."

"I am speaking very clearly, though it might not be a language you wish to acknowledge." She rose and crossed the room, stopping several feet away from him. "Even if you will not admit it, there has been something between us since the first time we met."

He spun around and faced her, anger melting his calm. "Very well, I admit it. You arouse me, like a mare in heat inflames a stallion. You feel it, too, or you would not be flaunting yourself here. Have so many Frenchmen died that you must seek farther afield for a stud? Shall I take you here on the carpet, do to you what I want the Allies to do to France?"

Hélène's face whitened. She had expected him to fight her, and recognized that his cruelty was a measure of how much she affected him. Even so, his words cut too close to the bone to ignore. "If casual fornication was all I wanted, I could find it easily enough without coming to a man who insults me."

"Then why are you here, madame?" His words were bleak, yet not so bleak as his haunted eyes.

Steel in her soft voice, Hélène said, "I want you to look at me, just once, without remembering that I am French and you are Prussian."

The colonel looked down at her for a long moment, a blood vessel throbbing visibly under his fair Nordic skin. Then he spun away from her. "That, madame, is quite impossible."

When there was a safe distance between them, he turned to hurl bitter words at her. "I look at you and see my burned home, my murdered wife and son and sister. Murdered by the French, madame, by your people, perhaps by your brother or husband. I can never forget that we are enemies."

"I am not your enemy," she said softly.

He stared at her, his face working. "Yes, you are. The only worse enemy I have is myself, for being attracted to a woman of a race I hate and despise. You have given me many sleepless nights, madame. Does it please you to know how much you have made me despise myself?"

Hélène made no attempt to close the distance between them. Standing before the bookcase, she was a small, gently rounded figure. Soft, yet unyielding. "I can never be pleased at another's pain. I became involved in spying to make what small contribution I could to peace. I did have brothers, Colonel. One died in the retreat from Moscow, the other under torture by Spanish partisans. I was told it took him two days to die. That was my younger brother, Pierre, who wished to be a painter.

"And I had a husband, too, killed at Wagram two months before my younger daughter was born. You fought at Wagram, Colonel. It might have been your troops that killed him."

"Splendid, Madame Sorel, we have both suffered." His voice was a lash of bitterness. "You have my permission to hate the Prussians as much as I hate the French. Will that satisfy you?"

"No!" she cried, her pain finally overcoming the hard-won serenity she had learned in a lifetime of loss. 'I want to see an end to hating. If Prussia had been the aggressor rather than France, would my husband be any less dead? I want my daughters to live in a world where their husbands will grow old with them, where boys like my brother can paint flowers and pretty girls and write silly love poetry, instead of dying screaming."

She looked at him pleadingly, wondering how to melt the ice around his heart. "As a Christian, I have been taught to hate the sin but love the sinner. I hate war and the unspeakable evil it brings—and if we cannot learn to love one another, we are doomed to fight and die again and again."

"And you think that if I could love you, that would put an end to war?" Though his voice held scorn, there was also a thread of yearning to believe.

"I don't know if we can love one another, perhaps there is nothing between us but physical attraction," Hélène said, tears flowing down her face. Though she saw that her words affected him, she feared that it was not enough. He had lived in his agony for too long to risk life again. Voice breaking, she continued, "If two individuals cannot even try, there is no hope for mankind. We will be condemned to suffer our mistakes forever."

Von Fehrenbach began pacing about the room, his broad shoulders rigid. He stopped by a table where a miniature portrait in a silver frame stood next to a closed Bible. The painting was of a lovely blond woman holding a child in her arms.

Looking down at the portrait, he said huskily, "You are a brave woman. Perhaps women have more courage than men. If a body is injured badly enough it dies, but with an injured heart one survives to suffer pain without end."

Gently he touched the face of the woman in the portrait, then looked up at Hélène, his face deeply sad. "You ask too much, Madame Sorel. My strength is not equal to the task."

She had failed. Blinking back her tears, she said sorrowfully, "It is not that women are braver, Colonel, but that we are more foolish."

Turning away, she fumbled in her reticule until she found a handkerchief. The mundane business of blotting her tears and blowing her nose gave her a chance to establish a fragile self-control. Then she crossed the drawing room to the vestibule.

His words followed her. "What will you tell your masters about me?"

"I will say that I think you are not involved in any way. You will be closely watched until the conference is over, so even if I am wrong, your opportunities for villainy will be reduced." She put her hand on the doorknob. "Farewell, Colonel von Fehrenbach. I don't think that we shall meet again."

To her surprise, he crossed the room and looked searchingly into her face, as if trying to memorize her appearance. "You are a very brave woman indeed." Then he lifted her hand and kissed it, not romantically, but with a kind of sad respect.

As the colonel held the door, Hélène managed to walk out with her head high, but after it closed she leaned against the paneled wall. She was so incredibly weary. . . .

Finally she straightened and walked to the door at

the end of the hall and opened it. Four soldiers were engaged in a friendly card game on the floor. They scrambled hastily to their feet as Hélène appeared. They seemed so very young. She smiled at them, and the gangling young lieutenant blushed and bobbed his head.

His dark face registering relief that she was safe, Rafe asked, "Did your meeting go well, Madame Sorel?"

Sighing, she said, "As well as can be expected."

Inside the austere apartment, Karl von Fehrenbach moved around restlessly, picking objects up and setting them down, pulling out a book by Fichte and replacing it unread, then opening a volume of Virgil at random. Looking down, he read, *"Omnia vincit Amor: et nos cedamus Amori."* Love conquers all: let us too surrender to Love.

He slammed the book shut and reshelved it so violently that he dented the leather binding.

Leaning his head against the books, he thought with anguish of Hélène Sorel standing where he stood now, small and sweetly feminine. Was she an angel come from heaven to redeem him, or a demon from hell sent to seduce him out of what was left of his immortal soul? Whatever else the woman might be, she had courage, to expose herself to such rejection.

He went to the portrait of Elke and Erik and lifted it to study their beloved faces. His wife, who had had the gift of laughter, and his son, who had inherited his father's height and his mother's sunny nature. Elke had sent the picture three months before she and Erik were killed. The house had been burned around them. Von Fehrenbach prayed they had died of the smoke rather than the flames.

Unbearable grief welled up in him, dissolving all the defenses he had built to dam the pain. In desperation he flipped open his Bible and glanced in, hoping for guidance.

The verse that leaped out at him read, "'Her sins, which are many, are forgiven, for she has loved much.'"

If it was a message from God, it was one too painful to be borne. He sank onto his knees by the brocade-covered Louis Quinze armchair, burying his head in his arms and giving way to the gut-wrenching sobs of a man who had never learned to cry.

Chapter 18

This visit to Le Serpent was a short one. The Englishman no longer cared that his dread host was masked; he knew now whom he served, and at the right time he would reveal that knowledge.

Le Serpent said curtly, "The gunpowder is now secured in the closet?"

"Yes, I brought it in over several days, and it's unlikely anyone will discover it by chance. Even if someone looks in the closet, the powder is in boxes that should arouse no suspicion."

"Very good." The masked man nodded with satisfaction. "Thursday is the day."

"The day after tomorrow?" The Englishman was startled; all of a sudden, it seemed too close.

"Exactly. The gunpowder must go off as close to four o'clock as possible. The candle I gave you should burn for eight hours, so light it at eight in the morning. I trust that will present no problems."

The Englishman considered. "It could be difficult. I've been playing least-in-sight the last few days, and it might seem suspicious if I'm at the embassy, and so early."

"I am not interested in the complications that your personal life is causing you," Le Serpent said coldly. "I pay you for results. Once the candle is lit you can run as far as you wish, but the explosion *must* take place on Thursday. That's the only day the king himself will join the other ministers in Castlereagh's bedchamber. Castlereagh will be on his feet again soon, and there may never be another time when everyone is gathered in one accessible place."

"Don't worry, I'll manage." The Englishman was awed at the scope of the destruction that would be caused. Yes, he must certainly cast his lot in with Le Serpent. The conspirator's boldness of vision and strength of will could take him to the very top during the chaos that would follow the explosion, and those who had assisted would go with him.

It was an intoxicating prospect. But he wished to inquire about another subject, not vital in the long run, but of great personal interest. "About the British spies . . ."

Le Serpent looked up impatiently from his desk. "They are being dealt with. Do not concern yourself."

"I'm interested in the woman, Countess Janos."

The masked man leaned back and laced his fingers across his ribs. "Do you want her for yourself, *mon petit Anglais?*" he said with amusement. "She's a handsome wench, I admit."

"Yes, I want her—at least, for a while."

"Since you have done your job well, I will let you have her as a bonus. Now, leave me, there is much to be done."

The Englishman was seething with anticipation as he left. He had never forgiven Margot Ashton for scorning him. Now she would pay for that and every other humiliation a woman had ever given him. She would pay, and pay, and pay.

Hélène and Rafe returned to Maggie's house, and the three of them talked for hours. After discussing the Frenchwoman's meeting with the Prussian colonel, they tried to decide what needed to be done next. All of them felt that the situation was critical, and that they must behave more brashly than spies usually did.

During the course of the evening, Maggie sent a note to an informant, and received quick confirmation that Roussaye had been nicknamed Le Serpent. She bit her lip when she read the reply, for she had half hoped that von Fehrenbach had fabricated the story. If Robin had been paying surreptitious visits to Roussaye, it seemed likely that both men were conspirators. The general might be considered a patriot, albeit a misguided one, but it was hard to judge Robin's collaboration as anything other than treason. Maggie's emotions fought that conclusion, but her mind could not deny the mounting evidence against him.

Clearly the next order of business was to confront General Roussaye. In pursuit of that end, Rafe sent a note to the general asking permission to call at Roussaye's earliest convenience. Roussaye had returned a courteous reply suggesting eleven o'clock the next morning.

When the general's message arrived, Hélène rose wearily to go home. Rafe instantly got to his feet and said that he would escort her, but his expression made it clear to Maggie that he didn't want to be left alone in her contemptible company.

Sorrowfully she accepted that whatever warmth there had been between them was gone. She could only hope that the plot would be neutralized as soon as possible so they need never see each other again.

Maggie started her next day by visiting the British embassy. Though it was ostensibly a courtesy call on Lady Castlereagh, her real purpose was to deliver a report on her suspicions of Oliver Northwood. She explained her doubts to Emily, urging that the information be passed to her husband as soon as possible.

A worried Lady Castlereagh promised to do so immediately, then offered the information that Northwood hadn't been at work for the last two days. A note had been received saying that he had food poisoning and would be back as soon as possible.

Maggie thought hard during her ride home. Northwood's "food poisoning" had coincided with his attack on his wife. Fearful of what Cynthia might say about him, had he decided to run when he discovered that she had escaped her prison? Or was he seeking her himself, intent on forcing her to return to him? Thank heaven Cynthia had come to Maggie; as long as the girl stayed hidden, she would be safe.

The carriage dropped Maggie off in front of her house, then continued around to the mews in back. In less than half an hour, Rafe was due to pick her up for the visit to General Roussaye, and her thoughts were on the upcoming interview as she started up her marble steps.

When a carriage pulled up behind her she turned, thinking Rafe had come early, but the luxurious dark blue berlin was unfamiliar. However, she recognized the man who climbed out. "Good morning, Count de Varenne," she said with her brightest smile. "If you are calling on me, I fear that I must disappoint you—I will be going out again almost immediately."

Varenne's broad figure was garbed with his usual discreet elegance, but the coldness of his eyes caused Maggie to take an involuntary step back. He said, "When I saw you here, on impulse I decided to take you to see my estate at Chanteuil. The gardens will not be at their best much longer."

"I'm sorry, my lord, but . . ."

The count interrupted her to say jovially, "Really, my dear, I will accept no excuses. It is scarcely an hour's drive from here, and I can guarantee you an interesting visit." He laid a casual hand on her waist, as if to help her to his carriage.

Maggie froze. Varenne had a knife in his hand, and he held it against her with such force that the point penetrated her green muslin dress and stabbed into her flesh.

Softly he said, "I really must insist."

If she tried to call her servants, the knife would be between her ribs before the first sound escaped. Stony-faced, Maggie climbed into the carriage, where a wizened man dressed like a clerk sat with his back to the horses.

Still holding the knife to her side, the count took the seat next to her as the door was closed and the carriage began moving again. The whole episode was over in less than a minute.

Even the woman watching from the window above noticed nothing amiss.

The count withdrew the knife once the carriage was under way. "You're a prudent woman, Countess Janos—it would have done you no good to attempt a scene." He gave her a menacing smile. "Or should I call you Miss Ashton?"

"Call me whatever you like." Maggie said, furious at having been so easily taken. "I see that my instincts were correct. It was obvious from the first that you were despicable, but I was unable to imagine any possible reason for an Ultra-Royalist to plot against the British leadership."

"Lack of imagination is a dangerous failing, as you are about to find out." Varenne nodded to the clerk, who poured a few drops of sickly sweet liquid from a bottle onto a scarf. "Pray forgive my rudeness, Miss Ashton, but I have a great respect for your abilities and don't wish you to be damaged prematurely. You acquitted yourself well in the Place du Carrousel, though your efforts would have done no good if your muscle-bound lover hadn't been on the scene."

The clerk leaned forward and pressed the rag over Maggie's nose and mouth, his other hand clamped behind her head so that she couldn't turn away. When she struggled, Varenne held her down with terrifying force.

As her consciousness faded, she heard the count say, "Candover cost me the services of Lemercier, which I cannot easily forgive. Still, I am a flexible man. Since you survived that little altercation, I have found a good use for you. I will give you to an associate of mine. He admires that lovely flesh, and doesn't care whether it is willing or not."

His last words produced a wave of horror in Maggie, but her muscles were no longer responding to her will. Accompanied by terror, she fell into blackness.

Rafe was on edge when he arrived at the Boulevard des Capucines town house, uncertain whether he was more upset at the thought of confronting General Roussaye, or at having to spend time with Margot. He could no longer think of her as Maggie; that name belonged to the elusive, maddening countess. During their intimacy she had become fully Margot Ashton to him again, and he refused to let go of that.

Already the memory of the night they had spent together seemed incredibly distant, as if it had happened years earlier rather than a scant day ago. He wondered if there was any chance that Margot might come to want him if Anderson was permanently out of her life. It might take a long time, but he was prepared to wait. God knew, he'd waited thirteen years already.

Frowning at the butler's statement that the countess had not yet returned, Rafe waited for fifteen restless minutes before summoning Cynthia Northwood. Though Margot had told him why the girl was staying there, Rafe was still shocked by the extent of her injuries. "How do you feel, Cynthia?"

"Better than I have in a long, long time, Rafe," she said ruefully. "I only wish I had dared leave sooner."

"It must have taken a great deal of courage to leave at all," Rafe said, glad that her state of mind seemed healthy. Though their affair had been over for years, he was still fond of Cynthia and her sometimes reckless spirit. She would need all her courage in the scandal to come; he hoped that Major Brewer would prove equally strong. He continued, "I'm sorry to disturb you, but I wondered if the countess said whether she was going anywhere besides the embassy. We have an urgent appointment, and it surprises me that she is not here."

"Maggie returned from the embassy about half an hour ago, but left again without coming into the house," Cynthia replied. "I happened to be looking out the window, and I saw a man pull up in a carriage. They talked a bit, then went off together."

Rafe felt sick to his stomach. "You know Robert Anderson from the delegation. Was he the man?"

"No, it was a dark fellow not much taller than Maggie," she said without hesitation. "A Frenchman, I think."

Rafe forced himself to quell his rising jealousy and think clearly. It was conceivable that Margot might have gone off with Anderson like that, but it seemed unlikely that anyone else could persuade her to break the engagement to visit Roussaye. Therefore, she might not have gone willingly. "Tell me exactly what you saw, Cynthia—every detail you can remember."

She could add little beyond the color of the coach, for the sheer window curtains had obscured details. Her description of the man would have fit half the men in France.

First Anderson had disappeared, and now Margot.

Rafe felt the beginnings of fear, and the best antidote for that was action. It was more important than ever that he talk to Roussaye. If the general turned out to have kidnapped Margot . . .

He stood and said crisply, "I must keep our appointment by myself. Send a note to Madame Sorel and ask her to meet me here. I should be back in an hour or so, and it is urgent that we talk."

Then he left, leaving a worried Cynthia Northwood.

On the drive to Roussaye's house, Rafe decided that the best strategy was to shock the general with accusations and hope the man would give something away if he was guilty. In his present mood, it would be very easy for Rafe to sound accusing.

Roussaye received him affably from behind the desk in his study, standing and offering his hand. "Good day, your grace. Kind of you to call, though I am sorry Countess Janos isn't with you. My wife was hoping to visit with her."

"This isn't a social call, Roussaye," Rafe said harshly. "I have been conducting a secret investigation for the British government, and I am here to tell you that the game is up. Even Le Serpent cannot escape this time."

The general's face paled and he sank back into his chair. After a stunned moment, he reached toward a drawer.

Swiftly Rafe produced a loaded pistol from under his coat. His hand rock-steady, he snapped, "Don't do it, Roussaye. You're under arrest. I have British soldiers waiting outside. Even if you could shoot me, you'd never escape."

"Such fierceness," the general said with a hint of bitter amusement. "I was reaching for a cigar. If I am under arrest, this may be my last opportunity to partake of civilized pleasures. Care to join me?"

Moving with exaggerated care, he produced an inlaid walnut humidor and placed it on the desk, then took out a cigar. He clipped the end and lit it with leisurely grace, as if he had all the time in the world. It was an impressive display of savoir faire for a man facing the wreckage of his plans and the likely loss of his life.

Refusing the offered cigar, Rafe took a seat in front of the desk, the pistol still trained on Roussaye. There would be time enough to call the soldiers later. Before that happened, the general had some questions to answer.

Roussaye drew in a mouthful of smoke, then released it with a sigh. "There is one thing I would ask of you, Candover, as one gentlemen to another. I swear my wife knows nothing of this. Please do what you can to see that she does not suffer for my sins." Scanning his visitor's hard face, the general added, "Filomena is your kinswoman. That should mean something, even if someone of your distinguished lineage cannot accept a man of my birth as a gentleman."

Rafe's lips thinned at the gibe. "I will use what influence I have. Unlike you, I do not make war on women."

"That was uncalled for, Candover," Roussaye said, an edge to his voice. "While no officer can always restrain his troops, I did my best to minimize the atrocities that occur too often in war."

"I'm not talking about war, I'm talking about today, and Countess Janos." Rafe stood and leaned over the desk, his tall frame taut with menace. "She's disappeared, probably kidnapped. If anything happens to her and you are behind it, I swear you will not live long enough for the firing squad."

The general removed the cigar from his mouth and looked at his visitor with astonishment. "I haven't the remotest idea what you are talking about. Why should I have any desire to injure the countess? Quite apart from the fact that she is a delightful woman, my interest now is in preserving life, not destroying it."

"Fine words, General," Rafe said bitterly. "After you tell me what you have done to Margot, perhaps you can explain how you rationalize assassination as preserving life."

Roussaye studied his visitor intently. "I am beginning to think that we are speaking at cross purposes. What exactly are you accusing me of, and why should your lady be involved?"

Rafe was beginning to loathe the calm he had admired. Fleetingly he wondered if his own imperturbable control had maddened others as much over the years.

Throwing discretion to the winds, he said, "The countess is a British agent and has been instrumental in uncovering your conspiracy. I assume that you realized what she was doing and decided to remove her, but it's too late. We already know about the attempt on Castlereagh's life, and that Wellington was your next target. After you tell me what you have done to her, I want to know what your future plans were. I shot your confederate Lemercier, and by God, I'll put a bullet in you if I have to!"

Roussaye threw his head back and laughed. "This would be hilarious, except that I will probably end up just as dead as if I were really guilty of what you accuse me of." He took another pull on his cigar. "My villainy, of which it now appears you were ignorant, was an attempt to help some of my distinguished colleagues who are on King Louis' death list."

As Rafe stared at him, the general elaborated. "Come, Candover, surely you know about the death list—the names of many of the chief imperial military men are on it. It is only a matter of time until Marshal Ney and a score of others are executed. They are considered 'traitors.' It is the sheerest chance that I am not in prison with them."

He stared at the coal on the end of his cigar, his expression brooding. "Treason is so often a matter of dates. The condemned men were all honorable soldiers—their only crime lies in serving the losing side. I had hoped I might help a few of them escape. Even some of your countrymen agree that the king's reprisals are outrageous. Indeed, a Briton has been aiding me."

He exhaled a thin wreath of smoke. "I won't give you his name, so don't waste your time with threats. Though I suppose that your government would not execute a British national for participating in a foiled escape plot."

Mouth dry, Rafe asked, "Was it Robert Anderson?"

Roussaye paused, then said slowly, "You are well informed."

Stunned, Rafe rapidly rearranged everything he knew. If Roussaye was telling the truth, it removed a major piece of the evidence of Anderson's treachery. Many men, Rafe included, disagreed with the vindictiveness of the royalists. Anderson's money might be suspect, but as Margot had defensively suggested, her lover might have been selling the same information in several places without actually betraying his own country.

As for the general, his nickname of Le Serpent could be a coincidence; after all, the three-headed serpent crest found among Northwood's papers was still unexplained, and it might be the symbol of the true Serpent. The only other possible link was from Lemercier to Roussaye, and the fact that both were Bonapartist officers didn't mean that they were conspirators.

Rafe asked, "Was Henri Lemercier also working with you?"

The general wrinkled his nose as if a bad odor had

forced its way through the cigar smoke. "You insult me. Lemercier is a jackal, the worst kind of officer. He would never lift a finger to help anyone unless he was well paid. If the price was right, he'd strangle his own grandmother and cook her in a fricassee."

Numbly Rafe uncocked the gun and thrust it beneath his coat. Perhaps Roussaye was simply a brilliant liar, but Margot had always doubted that he had the temperament of an assassin, even though she had suspected that he was involved in something secret. Her instincts were proving to be remarkably sound.

Rafe said woodenly, "I owe you an apology. I hope you will forgive my accusations."

"Wait." The general raised his hand. "Why did you think I would want to murder Castlereagh or Wellington? Without them, France would be forced to accept a much more punitive peace."

"Exactly. It seemed possible that a true revolutionary might want to see France humiliated, to the point where she would be willing to take up arms again. Now if you will excuse me, I must leave and start looking for Margot."

Roussaye shook his head. "Ingenious thinking, but I assure you, I would do nothing to prolong my country's suffering—France can afford no more Waterloos. If there is a conspiracy that threatens the peace, I am as interested in uncovering it as you are. If you will tell me what you know, perhaps I can help."

Rafe hesitated, then sat down, cursing himself for being so bewitched by Margot that he hadn't asked more questions when he had the chance. Now it was too late; with both Anderson and Margot out of the picture, he was crippled by his own ignorance. Without access to their information sources, he had no idea where to turn, so any assistance was welcome. Briefly he outlined what they knew or guessed, then listed all of the primary and secondary suspects they had been investigating.

The general listened attentively, his face darkening at the news of Robert Anderson's disappearance, but he interrupted only when Rafe mentioned that Count de Varenne had been a suspect. "Why Varenne? The Ultra-Royalists have the greatest stake in the status quo."

Rafe had to think back to remember. "At the beginning, there was some thought that the Ultra-Royalists might want to assassinate the king so that the Count d'Artois could succeed him. Once it became clear that the attack was aimed at the British leaders, we eliminated Varenne from our list."

Roussaye nodded. "I had never met him before our encounter at the Louvre, so I made a few inquiries. Varenne was heavily involved in royalist intelligence work during his exile, but his activities are now legitimate. Pray continue."

When Rafe was finished, the general pondered while the air became blue-gray with smoke. Eventually he said, "I am familiar with most of those men, and of them all, Lemercier was the most likely to be involved in a conspiracy. However, he wasn't intelligent or ambitious enough to be the mastermind. We need to know who he was working for."

After more thought, he said, "I might be able to discover that. If we know the identity of Lemercier's employer, you may have your Serpent. I'll begin inquiries this afternoon and notify you if I learn anything significant. What will you do—ask Wellington for men to search for the countess?"

"No, without some idea of where to look, we could set all of the Allied troops in France searching and not find her. Still, you have given me an idea. If Varenne was involved in royalist information gathering, he might still have some sources. Perhaps I can convince him to help me, for the countess's sake. He seemed to admire her."

"What man wouldn't?" Roussaye said with his first smile since the duke had made his accusations. Then seriousness returned, and his fingers tightened on his cigar stub. "Will you tell the royalist government about my interest in freeing prisoners?"

"I will not turn in a man for being loyal to his friends," Rafe said as he got to his feet. "But have a care, General, your wife deserves your loyalty, too."

"I know." Roussaye was silent for a long moment. "When you told me I was under arrest, I had a vision of my wife a widow, my unborn child an orphan. I will not subject them to that. Besides," he added with self-mockery, "I would be a liar if I did not admit that life is sweet to me, now more than ever."

Rafe offered his hand. "There is nothing wrong with enjoying life. God knows there is enough misery in the world."

After shaking hands, he left, wondering what on God's earth he could do next.

Chapter 19

Consciousness returned slowly to Maggie, accompanied by a feeling of nausea that she guessed was caused by the drug they had given her. She was lying on a bed, but her vision was so blurred and the light level so low that she saw only vague shapes when she opened her eyes. From the silence, she guessed that she was alone, so she lifted her right hand in a gingerly exploration of her surroundings.

The side of her hand brushed a round, hairy object, and a bolt to sheer panic blazed through her. She jerked upright, even as her mind said that the shape and texture were wrong for a man's head.

She turned to the right, which triggered more vertigo, and blinked her eyes clear. Then she blinked again as two reflective gold circles materialized in the blackness. As she teetered on the verge of hysteria, the gold circles were joined by a yawning pink mouth with small, gleaming fangs.

The relief was so great that she almost laughed. She was not sharing a bed with a rapist, but a cat. Curled in a ball on her pillow, it was very large, very shaggy, and very black, with the pushed-in face of a true Persian. The silly creature must have slipped in when Maggie was deposited here.

Cautiously pushing herself upright, she croaked, "If you're Varenne's cat, you keep low company, Rex. Or are you imprisoned for spying, too?"

She scratched the silky black head, and was rewarded with a purr so vibrant that she felt it through the mattress. "By the way, your name *is* Rex, isn't it?"

Since the cat didn't disagree, she considered the matter settled. Swinging her legs over the edge, she cautiously stood and took inventory. Aside from light-headedness and a dry mouth, she felt reasonably well. Though her green muslin dress was rumpled, she hadn't been ravished while she was unconscious, and that had been her greatest fear.

Holding the corner post of the bed for support, she surveyed the sparsely furnished bedchamber. Once, a very long time ago, it must have been attractive, but now the wallcoverings were dingy and the gold bedhangings threadbare.

The darkness was caused by equally shabby draperies that had been drawn across the window, so she crossed the room and pulled them apart. Blessed, blessed sunshine poured in, completing the job of clearing her mind. From the position of the sun, she guessed it was early afternoon, so she had been unconscious for two or three hours.

The window overlooked a sheer, two-hundred-foot drop to a river, and looking down brought back her vertigo. There would be no escape that way. Apparently Varenne had brought her to Chanteuil, his estate on the Seine.

Maggie spent some time exploring her surroundings. As expected, the heavy door was locked, and there was nothing in the room that could be used as a weapon. With a sigh, she settled on the bed again.

Rex immediately flopped across her lap, his furry weight threatening to cut off her circulation as he purred thunderously. She scratched his head, thinking that it was foolish to take comfort from the cat's presence. Nonetheless, she did. She had always liked cats, and Rex was a splendid example of his kind.

Leaning back against the headboard, she evaluated the situation. Though his motives were obscure, obviously Varenne was Le Serpent. She cursed herself for letting logic overrule instinct. Varenne's lack of apparent motive was less important than her distrust of the man, and she should have been more suspicious of him.

Still, there was one silver lining; if Varenne had kidnapped her, he might have done the same to Robin. In fact, Robin might be under this same roof, alive and not a traitor. The possibility made her feel better.

Since she and Rafe had been engaged to visit Roussaye, her absence would already have been discovered. However, that would do her no good since it was unlikely that Varenne would be suspected of kidnapping her. She had better prepare herself for a long stay.

The only excitement that occurred in the next hour was when Rex jerked his head up, then hurled himself across the room with a speed surprising in a creature so somnolent. A squeal, sharply cut off, made it clear that he had caught lunch. Maggie shuddered as he settled down with the limp little body and proceeded to eat. While she couldn't blame the cat for being a predator, she identified more with the mouse.

The rays of the sun had shifted to midafternoon when a grating in the lock announced the appearance of Count de Varenne. He was accompanied by a ruffian carrying a shotgun and an elderly manservant who placed a tray of covered dishes on the single table, then left the room.

At least they weren't planning to starve her, she thought wryly. In another few hours Rex's mouse might have started to look good. At the count's entrance, Rex himself immediately jumped to the floor and slithered under the bed, thereby proving that he had good sense.

While the guard trained his shotgun on Maggie, Varenne stopped a dozen feet away. His half-open eyes had a reptilian look; perhaps that was the origin of his nickname. "I hope you won't feel offended if I keep my distance, Miss Ashton," he said, as polite as if they were meeting for tea. "You see what respect I have for you."

Maggie arched her brows. "I can't imagine why—I certainly haven't shown any great brilliance on this case. I don't even understand why you are behind this particular plot."

"The usual reasons, Miss Ashton: power and wealth." His chilly gaze went over her. "I must confess that you had me convinced that you were only a Hungarian doxy looking for a rich protector. It was a surprise to discover who and what you are."

"I pride myself on being full of surprises," she said dryly.

Ignoring her comment, he went on, "However, my information about you is incomplete. Is Miss Ashton still the correct designation or have you acquired some husbands over the years?"

"Not legal ones," she said tartly.

The count smiled knowingly. "I'm sure there have been many of the left-hand kind, like your blond friend."

Maggie's pulse quickened. "I suppose you mean Robert Anderson. Do you have him, too?"

To her intense relief, the count nodded. "Yes, though his quarters are less comfortable than yours. He is almost directly below you, five levels down. Castles have certain drawbacks as living quarters, but they do have excellent dungeons."

"What are you going to do with us?"

Varenne gave a faint, chilling smile. "One of my associates yearns to further his acquaintance with you, so I shall give him the opportunity to do so. After that, it depends on how cooperative you are. You could be quite an asset, my dear."

Nausea returned, and it was all Maggie could do to keep her revulsion from her face. "What about Robin?"

"I had hoped that he might prove useful, but he's a remarkably stubborn young man. There isn't much point in keeping him around indefinitely." The count shook his head with spurious regret. "But I fear I bore you by thinking out loud. If there is anything you would like to make your visit more comfortable . . ."

Though she doubted that he expected her to take his ironic comment seriously, she said, "A hairbrush, comb, and mirror would be nice. Also a washbasin, soap, water, and something to read."

He smiled with genuine amusement. "You are a most adaptable woman, Miss Ashton. Do you wish to make yourself presentable for your new paramour?"

She wanted to spit at him. Instead, she smiled sweetly. "Of course. One must make the best of circumstances."

Varenne glanced at the guard. "See that she gets what she asked for." Then the two men left.

As soon as she heard the key turn in the lock, Maggie doubled over on the bed and buried her face in her hands. Her stomach heaved, and she struggled to prevent herself from being violently sick. Dear God, she had tried so hard not to be a victim, and for a dozen years she had been successful.

But now she was caught in events that showed how powerless she really was. She was merely fodder for a mob, or a helpless prize for a conspirator. And this time there was no Rafe or Robin to save her.

The first small victory was controlling her nausea. When she had managed that, she got shakily to her feet and walked to the window, where she inhaled deeply of the cool air. Far below, rocks were visible at the base of the cliff. With a sense of relief, she realized that she could always jump.

Her mouth firmed. That was a coward's way out, and she had not survived as much as she had to die without a fight. Still, it was a comfort to know that the cliff was available as a last resort.

Turning from the window, she went to the tray and found a bowl of savory stew, a small bottle of wine, half a loaf of bread, and several pieces of fruit. Determinedly she sat down to eat, for she would need all her strength.

A soft 'Mroowp' by her chair announced that Rex had come to join her, clearly desirous of sharing her meal. She smiled a little as she watched his enormous tail switch back and forth hopefully. Then she spooned several lumps of meat onto the floor. He was the only ally she was likely to find here.

Hélène Sorel was waiting when Rafe returned from seeing Roussaye. As he had feared, there was still no word from Maggie. Hélène had questioned Cynthia exhaustively about what she had seen, but without learning anything more about Maggie's kidnapper. Her face taut with anxiety, Hélène asked, "Is Roussaye our man?"

Unable to sit, Rafe prowled about the room. "No, he convinced me that his desire for peace is as great as ours. He is going to try to discover who Lemercier was working for."

"I pray that he is successful," Hélène said grimly. "We have no other leads, do we?"

Succumbing to morbid curiosity about how Margot did her work, Rafe asked, "Not unless you can utilize the same sources that Maggie did. Is that possible?"

"Not really. She knows hundreds of women throughout the city—laundresses, maids, street peddlers. All across Europe, actually. I was merely one of them, except that we became friends. We each needed a friend."

Rafe stopped and stared in astonishment. "She got all her information from women?"

Hélène clicked her tongue in disgust. "You're as bad as Colonel von Fehrenbach. Why do men always assume that the only way a female spy can work is on her back? Think about it, your grace. Women are everywhere, yet they are often treated as if they are invisible. Men speak of secret plans in front of maids, throw vital papers in the trash, boast of their achievements to prostitutes. Maggie's genius was in collecting so many pieces of information, then making sense of them."

She bit her lip for a moment before continuing. "I suppose that somewhere there might be a list of Maggie's informants, but it would be well hidden, and certainly in some kind of code. Even if we could find and decipher such a list, most of her women would not talk to a stranger. Our loyalty is to Maggie's cause, and to her personally. Money was secondary."

Rafe drummed his fingers on the mantelpiece while he thought about Hélène's revelation. In his jealousy, he had assumed that Margot traded her body for information, with the cynical connivance of Anderson. Bloody hell, had he been right about anything?

Interrupting his thoughts, Hélène asked, "What will you do now, go to Wellington?"

"No, as I told Roussaye, all Wellington could do is lend some troops, and without knowing where to search, that would do no good. I've sent an urgent message to the man in London who sent me here. I'm sure he'll have some useful suggestions, but it will be several days before I can expect to hear from him."

"And in the meantime?"

Rafe grimaced. "If Roussaye is successful at discovering Lemercier's employer, we may be able to go right to the source of the conspiracy. Apart from that, damned if I know. I'll go back to the Hôtel de la Paix and rack my brains. Write down your direction, and I'll contact you if I come up with anything."

Hélène went to the escritoire for pen and paper and ink. After writing her address, she said, "I, too, shall see if I can think of anything else. There must be someone who could help, if I can only think who it would be."

The two exchanged a bleak look, then Rafe left.

It was on the carriage ride home that he decided that it was worth talking to Count de Varenne. If, as Roussaye had said, the count had been active in royalist spy work during his exile, he might still have useful information sources.

Rafe stopped at his hotel only long enough to change to riding clothes and to ask the concierge for directions to Chanteuil. Then he set off on the bay gelding he had bought the first week in Paris. Not only would riding be faster than his carriage, but he desperately needed the physical release of being on horseback.

His route led west past the imperial palace of Malmaison, which Josephine Bonaparte had bought as a quiet country retreat. Josephine had retired and died there after the emperor divorced her for failing to produce an heir. It was said that Malmaison was where Bonaparte had spent his last free hours on French soil, for he had wanted to be near the spirit of the woman he had never stopped loving.

It was a romantic story, and as Rafe passed the estate he felt a twinge of sympathy for the Butcher of Corsica, who had continued to love where it was neither wise nor expedient. It was perhaps the only thing they had in common.

It took Rafe less than an hour to reach Chanteuil. The iron gates were rusted but solid enough, as was the gray stone wall that protected the estate. An ancient gatekeeper examined Rafe with deep suspicion before allowing him entrance.

Once inside the grounds, Rafe saw that the castle was as dramatic as Varenne had claimed. The original fortress had been on a rocky upthrust that towered above the surrounding countryside. Since it lay within a bend of the Seine, there was water on three sides. Over the centuries, new buildings and wide formal gardens had spread below the turreted keep, but the overall effect was still menacingly medieval.

As he cantered up the long gravel drive, Rafe had the fleeting thought that Chanteuil looked like a setting for one of Mrs. Radcliffe's lurid melodramas. The estate showed the effects of years of neglect. The gardens were jungles of unkempt vegetation, and most of the outbuildings were in a poor state of repair. Though attempts were being made to return Chanteuil to its former grandeur, it would take Varenne several years and a substantial fortune to finish the task.

When Rafe reined in before the main entrance and dismounted, a servant appeared to take his horse. Impatient with the sense of valuable time slipping away, Rafe took the steps two at a time and wielded the massive knocker vigorously while he prayed that the visit would produce something of value.

After subjecting Rafe to another scrutiny, the elderly butler who admitted him consented to take a card to the master. At least, thank God, Varenne was at home. It was about time something went right.

The Count de Varenne was working in his library amidst the musty odor of ancient books when the card was presented to him. The sight made him smile with deep satisfaction. Surely the gods were on his side. Who would have dreamed that the next fly would walk right into the web and offer the spider a card? And this fly was solid gold. He asked the butler, "Is the duke alone?"

"Yes, milord."

Varenne glanced at the wizened clerk who was his companion in the library. "Grimod, go up to the gun room in the west turret and bring down another shotgun and ammunition." Turning back to the butler, he said, "Fetch Lavisse, then wait ten minutes and bring up Candover."

The vast hall where Rafe waited was cold and drafty even in the last days of summer. As he watched a mouse scamper across the uneven flagstones, he wondered what it would be like in winter, with cold wind and river damp. Damned uncomfortable was his guess. Varenne would have his hands full making this dank medieval fortress habitable.

Eventually the old butler shuffled back and gestured for the visitor to follow. After a long, slow journey through uneven stone passages and up narrow stairs, the butler opened a door and waved Rafe through. "The library, milord," he wheezed.

As soon as Rafe stepped into the room, hard metallic objects were jammed into his sides. "Put your hands up in the air, Candover," an amiable voice said. "Those are fowling pieces. At point blank range, the shot will rip you to shreds."

Rafe saw that two men had been waiting by the door with shotguns. Knowing that it would be suicidal to reach for his pistol, he slowly raised his hands. What a damned fool he had been; what a bloody damned fool.

He stood still while a servant searched him, removing the pistol. When the servant was finished, Rafe said dryly, "I assume that one could say that I've found Countess Janos, in a manner of speaking."

"So you have," Varenne replied, "and I assure you that she is quite well. Adjusting to her captivity with remarkable speed, in fact." The count gestured for Rafe to take one of the chairs in front of the desk. The guards remained near the door, their shotguns trained on the duke.

Varenne continued, "Your fraudulent countess is quite the little survivor. Did you know that she is as English as you are, without an aristocratic bone in her delightful body?"

Taking Rafe's stony face for shock, the count gave a malicious chuckle. "Don't be too hard on yourself, Candover, I didn't guess either. But that's enough about that little doxy—I'm more interested in you. Does anyone know that you're here?"

Rafe considered lying and saying yes, but he hesitated too long. Varenne seized on the pause and interpreted it correctly. "Good, you didn't tell anyone you were coming. This close to the critical hour, I would not like to waste my men's time in hunting down whomever you told."

So the plot was on the verge of execution, and Rafe and Margot couldn't do a blasted thing about it. "Satisfy my curiosity, Varenne. What are you up to? If I'm going to die, I'd like to know why."

The count looked shocked. "Going to die? Whatever made you think that I would unnecessarily eliminate a man of your wealth? That would be profligate, and I did not get where I am by wasting my opportunities. That brings me to another question. You are said to be worth about eighty thousand pounds a year. Is that correct?"

Rafe shrugged. "Near enough. It varies some depending on how different business interests are doing."

"Splendid!" The count positively beamed, his dark eyes sparkling like agates. "Since I have a few minutes to spare, I will satisfy your curiosity, or at least part of it. Care to join me in a glass of burgundy? This is a rather fine vintage."

Rafe felt as if he had wandered into Bedlam, but he nodded his agreement; he could use a drink. A few minutes were spent in ordering glasses and pouring the wine. Rafe took a sip, and conceded that the vintage was excellent.

After a sip of his own wine, the count said pensively, "You wondered what I am about. It is quite simple—France needs strong leadership, and she will not get it from the decadent dregs of the House of Bourbon. After my plan is executed, there will be chaos, and I am prepared to step in to sort it out. I have royal blood in my veins—some of it even legitimate. The royalists will greet me with open arms. After all, I have served my time in exile, I am one of them."

"Given the quality of the Bourbons, it should be possible to convince the royalists," Rafe admitted with reluctant interest, "but what about the Bonapartists? They will never accept a member of the old order who wants to turn back the clock."

"But I do not wish to turn back the clock, my dear duke, that is what makes me unique," Varenne said complacently. "I am a flexible man, I can prate of the rights of man, of 'liberty, equality, fraternity,' as well as any revolutionary. I already have Bonapartists working for me. Remember, Napoleon spoke of liberty and created the greatest tyranny Europe has ever known. If one tells a great lie boldly, one can do almost anything."

"That's very clever, Count." Rafe lifted the bottle of wine and topped up both of their glasses. He didn't know whether Varenne was insane or a genius, or if there was a difference between the two. "But I would think it will be difficult to get the factions to agree on anything."

The count shook his head. "Under Napoleon, France became the greatest power since Rome. No true

Frenchman wants to give that up, and that includes the royalists."

"So you will rally the nation together *'pour la gloire'* one more time," Rafe said. "But there is one group that you have forgotten. What of those people who are tired of fighting, who want to live in peace?"

"The wolf will eat the lamb every time, Candover."

There was no doubt that Varenne believed his own words. Yet when Rafe thought of Margot and her army of women, of Hélène Sorel, of the tough pragmatism of Michel Roussaye, who had seen enough of war, he was not sure that he agreed. Enough brave lambs might overwhelm even the most ruthless of wolves.

However, this was not the time for a philosophical discussion. He asked, "If you aren't going to kill me, what do you intend?"

"You are insurance, Candover. Though my plan is excellent, it is possible that I might fail. Chaos is inherently hard to control, even when one is expecting it. If someone else rises to the top, I will need a great deal of money."

"Aren't you already a wealthy man?"

"I try to convey that impression. However, you see the condition of my estate, and conspiracies are expensive. At the moment I am almost penniless. If my coup d'état succeeds, I will have all the wealth I need, and you will be returned to England unharmed. If I fail"—he shrugged—"I assume that you would be willing to pay a substantial price for your life and freedom."

"For mine, and the countess's as well."

"You are so fond of the little trollop?" Varenne said with surprise. "I really should find out what she does that is so special. She's only a woman, after all."

Rafe discovered that the expression "to see red" was not a metaphor. His blood roared, and if a small fragment of common sense hadn't reminded him of the armed men at the door, he would have tried to take Varenne apart with his bare hands.

Some of that must have showed in his face, because the count said, "If you feel that strongly, I'm sure something can be arranged. Of course I would not free you without your word as an English gentleman not to retaliate in any way. It is one of the delightfully amusing things about Englishmen—they take such promises seriously."

A knock sounded at the door, and a courier entered with a message. Varenne looked at it and frowned. "Sorry, Candover, I can't chat any longer. Matters require my attention. I apologize for the quality of the accommodations, but if you became too comfortable, you would be in no hurry to pay your ransom and leave." He glanced at the guards. "Please escort our guest to the dungeon."

Rafe's thoughts were racing as the gunmen herded him out of the library and down the corridor. Varenne might be mad, but there was no denying that his scheme was diabolically clever. Given the precarious political state of France, a well-chosen blow might indeed take the count to ultimate power. Louis' throne stood on sand, and a strong leader who could unite the factions would be welcome.

It was also likely that once the deed was done, the rest of Europe would accept any French leader who had a fig leaf of respectability. Yes, Varenne's plan might very well work, and France would find herself in the hands of a new Napoleon. It was a terrifying prospect.

After descending several flights of winding stone stairs, they reached the lowest level of the castle. Though the upper section was dank and unpleasant, the cellars were far worse, stinking of death and ancient evil.

Eventually they reached a dismal antechamber containing a massive iron-bound door. Lavisse took a key ring from a hook on the wall and inserted the single heavy key into the old lock. As his companion kept Rafe covered with the shotgun, Lavisse struggled with the ancient mechanism until it turned.

Swinging the door out just enough to admit a man, the guard said with heavy sarcasm, "Enjoy your visit, your bloody grace." Then he gave Rafe a shove in the middle of the back that propelled him headfirst into the cell.

Even before he hit the stone floor, Rafe knew that he was not alone.

Chapter 20

Rafe automatically stayed down in a wary crouch while he scanned his surroundings. The cell was roughly cubical, about a dozen feet in each dimension, with walls of coarse stonework. The only furnishings were a slop bucket in one corner and a pile of straw with a couple of blankets.

Light came from a narrow, barred window high in the wall. Though the cell was dim, it was bright enough for Rafe to identify the blond man sprawled on the straw.

Bloody hell, it only needed this. Rafe took a deep breath before getting to his feet. Though he supposed he should be glad that Robert Anderson was alive and apparently no friend to Count de Varenne, Margot's lover was the last man on earth Rafe would have chosen as a cellmate.

Not bothering to rise, Anderson said, "I'm sorry that they got you, too, Candover. What has been happening?"

"Riots, kidnappings, conspiracy—the usual sort of thing." Rafe brushed the dirt from his breeches, then straightened and said soberly, "Varenne has the countess."

A black expression on his face, Anderson sat up, wincing at the sudden movement. "Damnation, I was afraid of that. Do you know if she's all right?"

"For what it's worth, Varenne says so." As his eyes

adjusted to the light, Rafe realized that his companion looked considerably worse for wear, with his left arm cradled awkwardly in his lap and his face badly bruised. Forgetting his jealousy, he exclaimed, "Good God, man, what did they do to you?"

Anderson smiled humorlessly. "In a tribute to my legendary ferocity, Varenne sent four ruffians to invite me here. I attempted to decline, but they insisted."

Something clicked in Rafe's memory. "The morning after you disappeared, the bodies of two unidentified Frenchmen were found near your lodgings. Did you have anything do with that?"

Anderson's smile became more genuine. "I was *very* reluctant to accept their hospitality."

Surveying the slight build and almost feminine good looks of his companion, Rafe realized that he had been guilty of still another misjudgment. With a half smile, he said, "Remind me not to get into any arguments with you."

"I doubt I'd be a danger to a husky sparrow at the moment."

Anderson's pallor was extreme even for someone of such fair coloring, so Rafe crossed the cell and knelt by him in the straw. "Better let me take a look at that arm."

He whistled softly at the sight of the ugly swelling that had completely engulfed Anderson's left hand and wrist. As he began a careful examination of the injured area, he said, "Did you hit someone too hard?"

"No, I was fairly intact when I arrived here. However, Varenne was interested in chatting and I wasn't."

The sheen of sweat on Anderson's face showed how much his studied casualness was costing him. Rafe's reluctant admiration for his rival increased. "It looks like one of the bones in the wrist is broken, and three fingers," he said. "Luckily, the fractures look clean.

Let me help you take your coat off so I can bandage
the area. That should help some."

Rafe took off his waistcoat and tore it into strips,
then undertook the basic medical work learned in the
hunting field. As he did, he was struck by a gut-
wrenching image of that same elegant hand caressing
Margot. He froze, fighting sick jealousy, while he told
himself furiously that it was neither the time nor the
place for such self-indulgence. After a long moment,
he managed to resume his ministrations.

For his own self-respect, he took special care to
make his efforts as painless as possible. Even so, the
procedure nearly broke the younger man's stoicism. By
the time Rafe had finished the bandaging and rigged a
sling for the arm, Anderson was lying full-length in the
straw, sweat matting the edge of his hair. Rafe guessed
that he must be half unconscious from pain.

After his ragged breathing had steadied, Anderson
said, "Since Varenne ended up capturing Maggie anyhow, maybe I should have just written the damned
note."

In answer to Rafe's questioning glance, the blond
man explained, "The count wanted me to write Maggie
and lure her out here. Said he'd break bones until I
agreed. I didn't mention that I was left-handed until
he'd already neatly fractured three fingers, and by then
he'd wrecked any chance of my handwriting being normal. He should have been working on the right hand."

As he settled down on the straw at Anderson's feet,
Rafe found himself chuckling at the dark humor of it.
"I'd like to have seen Varenne's face when you told
him that."

"You wouldn't have enjoyed it—he broke my wrist
from sheer irritation," Anderson said dryly. "Still, I've
been in worse prisons. The straw is fresh, the blankets
clean, and since this is France, they serve quite a toler-

able wine with the meals. At this season, the temperature is reasonable, though I'd rather not winter here."

Rafe tried to repress his shudder at the prospect. Surely Varenne would not keep them for so long.

Anderson said, "Professional curiosity dies hard. Did Varenne give you any idea what he's up to?"

Rafe brought his companion up-to-date on the interviews with von Fehrenbach and Roussaye, mentioned the death of Lemercier without elaborating, then repeated what Varenne had said about his motives.

After asking several probing questions, Anderson sighed and closed his eyes briefly. "Missed by a mile. I feel like a damned fool."

"You have plenty of company in not deducing what was going on," Rafe said bleakly. "Everyone was wrong." Rafe most of all.

After that, there was little to say. The two men sat in the gradually fading light without talking. Though there were many things Rafe would have liked to ask Anderson, none of them seemed appropriate.

As the hours passed, Rafe concluded that the worst part of imprisonment must be boredom. The cell was too small to stretch one's legs, the stone walls were singularly unstimulating, and if he had to spend any length of time here, he'd soon be raving.

He envied Anderson's tranquility. Worn down by pain, the other man slept for much of the time. But even awake, he had a philosophical relaxation Rafe doubted he could ever match. Of course, Anderson claimed prior experiences with incarceration; perhaps practice perfected one's skills.

At dusk, dinner was delivered with the usual caution, one man setting a tray inside while another stood guard with a shotgun. The meal was a very decent beef stew with bread and fruit, accompanied by a jug that held about a gallon of red wine. Besides pewter bowls and mugs, the only utensils were soft, easily bent spoons that wouldn't make effective weapons. Though the tray, bowls and spoons were collected later, the prisoners were allowed to keep the wine and drinking vessels.

There wasn't enough to make a man drunk, but it was sufficient to loosen tongues. The two men were talking in a desultory fashion about what Varenne might be planning when Rafe found himself asking, "Why is Margot the way she is?"

After a long pause, Anderson said, "Why didn't you ask her?"

Rafe laughed harshly. "I didn't think she would tell me."

"If she won't, why do you think I will?"

Rafe hesitated, trying to think of a compelling argument. Instead of a direct answer, he said, "I know I have no right to ask, but I want—rather badly—to understand her. I knew her very well once, or thought I did, and now she's a mystery to me."

After an even longer pause, Anderson said, hostility in his voice, "Ever since Maggie heard you were coming to Paris, she's been different—moody and unhappy. I met her when she was nineteen and I know very little about her earlier life. However, I do know that someone started a job of wrecking her that the French bloody near finished. If you're the one who did that, I'll be damned if I'll tell you anything."

The darkness was nearly total now, only a faint glow of moonlight illuminating the cell. Anderson's figure was barely visible, black against black to Rafe's right. In the dark, the pain of thirteen years ago was very close. Reaching out to find the jug by touch, Rafe poured them both more wine. "She never told you what happened?"

"No."

Anderson's voice was flat, but Rafe heard an undertone of unwilling curiosity. If the other man was in love with Margot, he must also be interested in her past.

In the anonymity of the dark, it was easy to make a suggestion that never would have occurred to him by the light of day. "Each of us holds a key to part of Margot's past. Why don't we exchange information?" Anticipating objections, Rafe added, "I know it's ungentlemanly, but I swear I don't mean her any harm."

Rafe could almost hear the factors weighing in Anderson's mind. Finally the other man said ruefully, "My father always said that I didn't have a gentlemanly bone in my body, and he was right. But I warn you, it's not a pretty story."

Knowing that it was his place to begin, Rafe said, "Margot Ashton made her come-out during the 1802 Season. Her birth was no more than respectable, her fortune negligible, it was generally agreed that she was not a classic beauty—yet she could have had any eligible man in London."

He stopped, remembering his first sight of Margot, when she was entering a ballroom. One look and Rafe had walked away from the group he was with and gone directly to her, cutting through the crowd like a hot knife through butter.

Margot's chaperone recognized the heir to Candover and made an introduction, but Rafe was barely aware of that. Only Margot mattered. At first she had been gently amused by the expression on his face. Then her smoky eyes met his and changed as an echo of his own feelings flared in her. At least, that was what he had thought at the time. Only later did he question the fact that her response had come after she had learned who he was.

Aloud he said, "It appeared to be a perfect fairy tale, love at first sight and all that nonsense. Colonel Ashton wouldn't let us become formally betrothed until after the Season, but we had a firm understanding.

I have never been so happy as I was that spring. Then ..." He halted, unable to continue.

"Don't stop now, just when we're getting to the crux of the matter, Candover," Anderson prodded. "What happened to love's young dream?"

Rafe swallowed hard. "It was simple enough. I was out with a group of friends one evening, and someone who had drunk enough to be indiscreet described how ... how Margot had given herself to him a few days before. In a garden during a ball."

He swallowed a mouthful of wine, needing it to lubricate his dry throat. "In retrospect, I can see how badly I overreacted. I was young and idealistic and completely unbalanced by love. Instead of accepting her actions as curiosity, or experiment or whatever, I acted as if she had committed the greatest crime since Judas when I confronted her the next morning. I would have been happy to accept any defense, or even a show of remorse, but she made no attempt to deny it. She simply threw my ring at me and walked out."

After another swallow of wine, Rafe gave a heavy sigh. "I decided that the people who had told me she was a fortune hunter were right and she was only sorry to be balked of her quarry. But a few days later, she and her father left England to travel on the Continent. I don't think that would have happened if she weren't as miserable as I, so I suppose you could say we wrecked each other."

With a rustle of straw, Anderson shifted position. "Let me see if I have this correctly. You asked if she had been carrying on with this friend of yours and she didn't deny it?"

In the interests of accuracy, Rafe said, "Actually, I didn't ask her. I told her what I knew."

Anderson clambered to his feet, uttering an impressive stream of profanity as he paced around the cell. At length, he said with disgust, "Given the stupidity of the

British nobility, I can't understand why the whole lot hasn't died out. If you took a drunken sot's word without questioning it, you never knew the first thing about Maggie. You deserved what you got, though God knows that she didn't."

Rafe flushed, angry but not quite able to dismiss Anderson's words. "You obviously don't know much about the nobility, or you wouldn't make such a sweeping statement. No man of honor would ever lie about such a serious matter. Even dead drunk, it was surprising that anything was said. Probably even that wouldn't have happened if Northwood had known that I was betrothed to Margot."

Anderson stopped in his tracks. "Northwood? Would that have been Oliver Northwood?"

"Yes. That's right, I forgot that you work with him."

A new burst of profanity put the former one to shame. "If you aren't stupid, you are too naive and honorable to live in this highly imperfect world," Anderson snapped. "I can't believe that you would accept the word of a man like Northwood against Maggie but maybe he was more believable in those days than he is now. Obviously he was no more honest."

"Don't be absurd," Rafe said heatedly. "Why would Northwood slander an innocent girl?"

"Use your imagination, Candover," Anderson said with exasperation. "Maybe he was jealous of you. It doesn't sound like it would have required a very discerning eye to observe that you and Maggie were thick as inkle weavers. Or perhaps it was spitefulness because she had scorned him, or immature male boasting. Maybe you never had to invent exploits, but plenty of young men do. Hell, knowing Northwood, he might have lied from sheer bloodymindedness."

Feeling compelled to offer some rebuttal, Rafe said, "Why are you so hard on Northwood? Granted, he's always been a boor, and he's treated his wife badly, but that still doesn't make him a liar. A gentleman is always assumed to be honest until proven otherwise."

"What a wonderful standard. Why didn't you apply it to Maggie?" Anderson said caustically as he flopped down on the straw again. "This *boor* you are so anxious to defend has been selling information about his country for years to anyone who will buy it. From what I know of him, I doubt that he has an honest bone in his pudgy body."

"What . . .?" Rafe stammered, feeling as if he had been poleaxed. Though he had never been close to Northwood, he had known the man for more than twenty years. They had gone to the same schools, been raised by the same rules. He had never had a reason to doubt Northwood's honesty.

And yet, it explained so much. Margot's white face when Rafe had accused her of infidelity swam before him. How would he have felt if the person who should have most trusted him had accepted slander without question?

He would have felt exactly as she had: furious, and hurt beyond words. What had she said then, something about how fortunate it was that they had discovered each other's true characters before it was too late?

At the time, he had taken her words as an admission of guilt, and that admission had confirmed his belief in Northwood's accusations. Now her answer took on a whole new meaning.

Burying his face in his hands, Rafe groaned, "Bloody, bloody hell . . ." His rasping breath filled the cell, and only the other man's presence kept him from a total, shattering breakdown.

Even when Rafe had felt the most desperate pain at her imagined betrayal, he had been soothed by his belief that he was the injured party. Now that comfort was gone, and he saw his actions as Margot must have seen them.

Whatever she had become could be traced back to his betrayal of her, to his jealousy and lack of trust. The dim hope he had of regaining her love crumbled among the ruins of his pride.

How could she ever trust him again when he had utterly failed her? By his own actions Rafe had lost what was most important to him, and there were no words strong enough for the bitterness of his guilt.

As Robin's anger faded, he felt reluctant sympathy for the other man. The poor devil—it must hurt like hell to be knocked off the moral high ground by the realization that he had caused his own suffering, and Maggie's as well. A man like Candover, who was obviously honest to the backbone, had been easy prey for Northwood's sly malice.

In spite of Candover's accusation, Robin was very familiar with the world of aristocratic Englishmen, with their infernal games and clubs and gentleman's codes. It would have been natural to believe a companion, and Northwood would have seemed bluff and honest.

On the other hand, a young woman would have been a mysterious, almost magical creature to a romantic young man. It took maturity to learn that the similarities between men and women were greater than the differences.

Given the passion and possessiveness of first love, it was easy to understand how Candover had blundered, his emotions swamping his judgment. Who wasn't a fool when he was young? Robin certainly had been, though his foolishness had taken a different form from that of Candover.

Robin also knew Maggie well enough to be sure that her temper had contributed to the problem. If she had had the sense to burst into tears and deny the accusation, the breach could have been patched up in half an hour, and the two of them might have been happily married these last dozen years. In that case Robin would never have met Maggie, which would have been his loss but her gain.

Robin located Rafe's mug and pressed it into the other man's hand. "It's a little late to be suicidal, if that is the direction your guilt is taking you," he said dryly.

Still shaking, Rafe straightened up enough to drink, wishing that he had something stronger. Over the years he had prided himself on his civilized attitude, thinking that he should have accepted Margot's infidelities in return for her charm and companionship. He had even felt regret that she had been more in tune with the morals of their order than he, and had attributed his violent emotional reaction to immaturity.

Instead, he had been closer to the truth with his youthful idealism than with all the fashionable cynicism he had cultivated over the years. Margot Ashton had been as true and loving as he had believed her. It was Rafael Whitbourne, heir to the dukedom of Candover, universally respected scion of the aristocracy, who had been unworthy of such love.

Anderson said acerbically, "No wonder Maggie didn't want to have anything to do with you when you came to Paris. If she had told me about your past relationship, I would never have suggested that she get within seven leagues of you."

He fumbled one-handed with the heavy wine jug. Rafe helped him pour another mugful. The jug was much lighter than it had been; the last of the wine emptied into Anderson's mug. They must have put away the equivalent of two or three bottles each. Rafe wished there was more, though there wasn't enough alcohol in France to drown the way he felt.

"I gather that you are still in love with Maggie," Anderson remarked, as if the matter were of only minor importance.

"I'm as unbalanced about her now as I was when I was twenty-one." Rafe drew a shuddering breath. "I had always rather prided myself on my balance." He finished the last of his wine with a gulp. "She's too good for me."

"I wouldn't argue the point."

"What has happened in the years since then, and how did Margot come to be a spy? You said that you'd explain." Now that Rafe saw how her journey had begun, he could better understand the wary, slightly brittle woman she had become, with her toughness and suspicion, her flashes of humor and vulnerability. But there was still much that he wanted—*needed*—to know.

"There's been enough raging emotion in this cell for one night," Anderson said as he rolled up in one of the blankets. "I'll tell you the rest of the story in the morning, by which time I may have slept off my desire to kick you in the teeth."

As he burrowed into the straw, he added, "If you're going to spend the night flagellating yourself, kindly be quiet about it."

Anderson was right, enough had been said for one night. Rafe wrapped himself in the other blanket against the increasing chill, then settled in the straw.

Unlike his companion, he doubted that he would sleep.

Chapter 21

Considering how much wine he had drunk the night before, Rafe felt fairly well the next morning. He had even slept a little. By the time Anderson stirred, Rafe had come to terms with his new knowledge. There was no chance that Margot would ever forgive him, but he hoped that he would have a chance to beg her pardon for his criminal misjudgment. It seemed very important that he do so.

Breakfast proved to be fresh bread, sweet butter, strawberry preserves, and a large quantity of excellent hot coffee. As Rafe spread preserves on the bread, he said, "I have eaten a good deal worse at respectable English country inns."

"A pity Varenne's ambitions aren't aimed at the restaurant trade rather than at dictatorship," Anderson commented.

Rafe studied his companion. Though Anderson claimed that his arm was feeling better, he was probably lying; his face was flushed and he seemed feverish. Again Rafe was struck with a fleeting sense of recognition. The more he saw of Anderson, the more familiar the man seemed, yet the memory still eluded him.

They were just finishing breakfast when the door creaked open. Rafe expected that it would be a servant to remove the tray, but Varenne himself entered, the usual shotgun-carrying guards behind him.

Not bothering with amenities, he said tersely to

Anderson, "I suppose Candover has explained what I am about?"

Anderson drained his coffee mug before answering. "He did. I was curious where I went wrong."

"Good." Reaching under his black coat, Varenne drew out a pistol. Aiming it at the precise center of Anderson's forehead, he said, "I would be reluctant to kill a man who doesn't know why he is dying. Though I regret the necessity of this, I have been unable to imagine any circumstances where you might be useful to me, and as long as you are alive you are a danger. A pity you could not be brought over to my side, but even if you pretended to do so now, I would not trust your promises."

As Rafe watched with frozen horror, Varenne added, "Do you have any last prayers or messages, Anderson? If so, be quick about it. This will be a busy day for me."

His face pale, Anderson glanced at Rafe. "Please . . . give Maggie my love."

In the silence that followed his words, the sound of the hammer being cocked rang like the anvil of doom.

Though the hour was very early, the British embassy buzzed with activity and Oliver Northwood was greeted with relief by several of his colleagues who had worked all night. Even bedridden, Lord Castlereagh generated enough letters, proposals, memos, and draft treaties to keep a dozen men fully occupied, and being short-handed was taking its toll on the staff.

He heard several men express concern about Robert Anderson, who had been missing for several days. No surprises there; Northwood had a very good idea what had happened to him. Served the supercilious puppy right.

Shortly before eight o'clock, Northwood excused

himself and made his way to the passage that ran beneath Castlereagh's bedroom. After nervously checking that the corridor was deserted, he unlocked the closet door and entered, closing it behind him. He hadn't considered how he would feel carrying a candle into an enclosure filled with gunpowder, and his hands were sweaty as he made the necessary preparations.

First he used his regular candle to create a pool of melted wax on the floor. Then he set the special candle of dense beeswax firmly into the puddle. When the wax had cooled and the candle was secure, he used his penknife to gouge a hole in the corner of a box of gunpowder. Finally he took a small bag of gunpowder from his pocket and laid a careful trail from the box to the candle, ending with a mound of powder around the base.

With exquisite care, he lit the beeswax candle. Then he cautiously let himself out of the closet, making sure that no draft would bring flame and gunpowder together prematurely.

Le Serpent had said it would take about eight hours for the candle to burn down. Except for the remote chance that someone would notice the scent of a burning candle in this seldom-used part of the embassy, the explosion would go off about four in the afternoon. By then, Northwood would be long gone.

When he was safely upstairs, he dug out his handkerchief and wiped his brow. He deserved every bloody franc he had been paid, and then some. In the last couple of days security had gotten very tight at the embassy, with British soldiers at every entrance checking the credentials of strangers. As a regular employee Northwood had gotten in easily; Le Serpent could never have done this without him. Maybe he should ask for more money.

After returning to the clerks' copying room, Northwood settled down to make a fair copy of one of the interminable letters. The only other person present was a senior aide called Morier, who looked up with a tired smile. "Glad to see you, Northwood. Are you sure you're well enough to work? You look a little gray."

He couldn't look half as bad as Morier would after the explosion. The other man would attend the meeting this afternoon and he would be blown up, a minnow dying with the big fish. Northwood suppressed the thought uneasily; Morier had always been pleasant to him, and it was too bad that he would be caught in the conflagration. Well, it couldn't be helped. Smiling bravely, he said, "I still feel pretty beastly, but I thought I could manage a couple of hours. I know how overworked the rest of you are. A rotten time to be ill."

Morier murmured, "Good show," and returned to his document.

Northwood worked for two hours, the back of his neck prickling with knowledge of the candle burning toward that lethal trail of gunpowder. He excused himself when he could bear no more, and had no trouble looking sick. Morier and the other clerks who had come in commiserated about his illness and thanked him for making the effort.

As he left, Oliver reflected that it was enough to make even a man without a conscience squeamish, but he repressed his disquiet. In spite of casual friendliness, he knew the other members of the delegation looked down on him, thought they were more intelligent than he was. Well, they were wrong; he would have more power and wealth than any of them.

He hailed a cab in the Rue de Faubourg St. Honoré and returned to his house, then changed into riding dress. The time had come to call on the Count de Varenne and let him see what a knowing one Oliver Northwood was.

With luck Le Serpent would also have the promised

bonus waiting: the gorgeous, unobtainable Margot Ashton would finally be in Oliver Northwood's power.

As early as was decent, Hélène Sorel sent a messenger to Candover's lodgings to see if he had learned anything. Less than three-quarters of an hour later her footman returned with the unwelcome news that the duke had not been seen since the previous afternoon.

Though the day was pleasantly warm, the implications of the news chilled Hélène to the bone. Perhaps the duke's absence was not significant, but given the disappearances of Maggie and Robert Anderson, she must assume the worse.

If the unknown Le Serpent had seized the other three, was Hélène also on his list?

Briefly she was tempted to flee back to the country, to her two daughters and safety. With the conspiracy so close to culmination, Le Serpent would never bother to follow her there. What could she do alone, without help?

Her hands curled into fists and she rejected that solution. If worse came to worse, and she, too, disappeared, Hélène's own mother would take care of her granddaughters faithfully and well. But if there was any action Hélène could take, she would do it rather than live a craven.

But *was* there anything she could do? Hélène was too unimportant to convince any government officials that danger was imminent even if she knew what form the plot would take, which she didn't.

Her hands unclenched and she got determinedly to her feet. There was something she should have thought of sooner, and she would see to it right now.

The sound of the hammer being cocked freed Rafe from his momentary paralysis. The stark resignation on Anderson's face had caused an elusive memory to click into place, and Rafe was reasonably sure he knew who the blond man was.

His voice crackling with authority, Rafe said, "Varenne, shooting Anderson would be a serious mistake. Remember that you said you were never profligate?"

The finger that had been tightening on the trigger paused, but the count was annoyed as he glanced over. "Don't interfere, Candover. You are worth keeping for your potential value, but a spy is not the same category."

"If he were only a spy, that might be true," Rafe agreed, his gaze steady on the count. "But the man you are so wastefully about to kill is Lord Robert Andreville, brother of the Marquess of Wolverton, one of the richest men in Britain."

"What!" Varenne's gaze snapped back to his intended victim. "Is that true?"

"Yes," Anderson admitted. "Does it make a difference?"

For a long, tense moment Varenne weighed the potential benefits against the risks. Then he uncocked the pistol and thrust it back under his coat. "Yes, it does. Though if you're lying, I can always eliminate you later."

"It's the truth," Rafe said tersely. "I went to school with his older brother."

Varenne nodded absently, his mind already on other matters, then left with his gunmen. Rafe felt a shudder of distaste as he wondered how many of the brute's other chores were going to be casual, efficient murder. Probably he had put the two men in the same cell so that Rafe would be properly intimidated by witnessing Anderson's execution. It would have been a very effective demonstration.

As the sound of steps disappeared from the anteroom, the blond man let out an explosive breath and slumped back against the stone wall, his eyes closed from reaction. After several moments, he opened his eyes and said with commendable calm, "I thought my sins had caught up with me that time. I owe you a considerable debt, Candover. How long have you known who I was? For that matter, how did you recognize me? My brother and I don't look much alike."

"I wasn't certain—it was an educated guess that struck me when Varenne cocked the hammer of his pistol." Feeling a little weak-kneed himself, Rafe folded down into the straw. "Your expression reminded me of how your brother Giles looked after his wife died. Even if I was wrong about your identity, it was obviously worth a try."

"I'm glad your mind worked faster than mine did," Anderson, or rather Andreville, said fervently. "It never occurred to me that my connections would make any difference."

"I had the advantage of knowing that Varenne was interested in holding me for ransom if his other plans fell through. He also agreed to let me ransom Margot." Rafe studied the other man's face. Now that the relationship had been confirmed, it was easier to see subtle traces of family resemblance. "I know Giles from Eton, where he was a couple of years ahead of me. Though he doesn't come to London often, when he does we always try to get together for an evening. Occasionally he has mentioned his scapegrace younger brother Robin."

"That must make for lively dinner conversation," Andreville said dryly.

Rafe grinned. "To say the least. Did you really manage to get expelled from Eton your very first day?"

Andreville gave a rueful smile. "It's true. I wanted to go to Winchester, but my father insisted that I follow in the footsteps of countless Andrevilles to Eton. It was a busy year. The old boy didn't want to be defeated by an eight-year-old child, so I had to get myself expelled from three public schools before he let me go where I wanted."

"What made you so set on Winchester?"

"I had a friend going there, and my father was against it. Either reason would have sufficed," he said wryly. "Though you were stretching a point by assuming my brother would be willing to ransom me. Given my checkered past, he might be relieved if I vanished without a trace before I can embarrass the family any further."

"Giles would never do that." Rafe thought for a moment. "Even if he had trouble meeting a ransom demand, I thought that you had inherited considerable property from someone else."

Andreville nodded. "My great-uncle. The Andrevilles produce a black sheep every generation or so. Uncle Rawson was the last one before me, so of course we got along splendidly. But if I were a common, garden variety spy, I would be in no position to ransom myself—this is not a lucrative profession."

Rafe shrugged. "The Candover estate could have stretched to another twenty or thirty thousand pounds if necessary."

Andreville looked at him with surprise. "You would have done that for someone you hardly know, and don't much like?"

Uncomfortable that his companion had picked up that concealed resentment, Rafe said shortly, "Margot wouldn't like it if you were killed. It would have been convenient if you'd gone to Eton or Oxford, though. If you had, I'd have known you already, and been spared considerable confusion."

Andreville looked scandalized. "Attend those hellholes when I could be experiencing the joys of Winchester and Cambridge?"

Rafe laughed. "I assume that you work for Lord Strathmore. How did you come to know him?"

"There is some vague family connection between the Andrevilles and the Fairchilds. Lucien and I always got on well, but since we went to different schools, we seldom saw each other," Andreville replied. "I heard about the famous Fallen Angels, of course. In fact, I once met Lord Michael Kenyon when he was serving on the Peninsula, though he didn't know me by my real name. But that's another story."

He pushed himself to a sitting position. "I'd finished my first year at Cambridge when the Treaty of Amiens went into effect, so I decided to take a year off and do the Grand Tour. As I traveled through France, it became obvious that it was only a matter of time until war broke out again. When I came across some information that I thought might interest the British government, I sent it to Lucien, because I knew that he had taken a position in Whitehall.

"Lucien immediately came to Paris to tell me that he was working in intelligence and to ask me if I would be willing to stay on the continent as a British agent." Andreville shrugged. "Being young and stupid, I thought it sounded like quite an adventure, so here I am."

Thinking out loud, Rafe said, "Why the devil didn't Lucien tell me about you before I came to Paris?"

"In this business, it becomes second nature never to say more than is absolutely necessary. Lucien sent you over to work with Maggie—there was no need for you to know that I was also an agent."

Rafe digested that for a bit. "Yet Lucien didn't know Margot well enough to be sure that she was English."

"That's because he knew her through me, and I said only that she was English—there was no need for him to know her real name and background."

Rafe made a face. "I can't help thinking that matters

would have been greatly simplified if there had been less secretiveness."

"In this case, that's true." Andreville's expression darkened. "But there are times when men have died because their names were tortured out of imprisoned colleagues."

Deciding that it was time to return to the subject closest to his heart, Rafe said, "You were going to tell me about Margot's life in the years since you met her."

"If you're really sure you want to know. It's a hard story to hear."

"If it's difficult to listen to, it must have been a damned sight worse for Margot to live through," Rafe said grimly. "I want to know it all."

"As you wish." Restively Andreville pushed himself to his feet and went to lean against the wall under the window. "I believe you know how Maggie and her father and his servant were assaulted by a gang of former soldiers who were heading to Paris?"

"Yes, it was quite a scandal in England. However, no details were known, which is why Margot was thought to have died."

His voice flat, Andreville said, "Maggie and her father and Willis were eating in a country auberge when a half dozen or so ex-soldiers arrived, already drunk and bullying everyone in sight. Colonel Ashton tried to get his party away quietly, but someone recognized his accent as English, they were accused of being spies, and the soldiers attacked them.

"Ashton and his man fought, of course, but they never had a chance against so many. At the end, the colonel threw himself across his daughter to protect her, hoping that her life might be spared." Andreville's fair skin drew tightly over the fine bones of his face. "Maggie's father died sprawled on top of her, Candover, bleeding from a dozen knife and bullet wounds."

"Dear God," Rafe whispered. Margot had adored he father. To see him die like that ... The thought mad him ill. Well, Andreville had warned him. Steeling himself for what he feared was coming, he asked "What then?"

"What the hell do you think happened, Candover? Andreville said with barely controlled rage. "A gir who looks like Maggie, in the hands of a drunken gan of ex-soldiers?"

Rafe pushed himself to his feet and began pacing, n more able to sit quietly in the face of such an atrocity than Andreville was. With anguish, he thought of Mar got's near-hysteria in the Place du Carrousel and after Dear God, no wonder she had nightmares of clawin hands and beastly faces; no wonder she needed to b reminded that not all men were savages.

Andreville began speaking again, his face averted "Since they had a beautiful girl and a cellar full o wine, they were in no hurry to move on, so they settle down and enjoyed themselves. For the next day and half, they stayed continuously drunk, raping her when ever one of them was in the mood.

"Then I happened by, traveling in the uniform of French grenadier captain. When the villagers saw me the mayor came out and begged me to get the soldier pigs to move on before they destroyed the whole vil lage.

"I was going to pass on by. After all, I was alone. and not even a genuine officer. But when the mayor said they had an English girl. . . ." The fingers o Andreville's right hand splayed flat out on the wall be side him. "I had to see if I could help. So I went into the inn, praised the soldiers for their patriotism and cleverness in catching spies, chided them for overzeal ousness, and inspired them to get moving to Paris be cause the emperor needed them."

Rafe imagined that slight, elegant figure facing

down a gang of armed drunks, and understood why Margot had fallen in love with him. Lord Robert would have been hardly more than a boy himself. "How did you get them to release Margot instead of taking her with them?"

"Sheer force of personality." Andreville said with even greater dryness. "I said that I would take the English spy to Paris for questioning myself. Her horse and luggage were in the stable, so I got her mounted and both of us the hell away from there.

"It didn't take long to realize what kind of girl I'd rescued. She was half dead from what they'd done to her, and wearing a ragged dress covered with her father's blood. Any other woman would have been raving mad or unconscious. But Maggie ..." His drawn face eased a little.

"When I stopped the horses a mile down the road to introduce myself and assure her that she was safe, she pulled a pistol on me. It had been hidden in her saddlebag. I'll never forget the sight: her hands were shaking, her face was so bruised that her own mother wouldn't have recognized her, and she'd been through an ordeal that I wouldn't have wished on Napoleon himself. Yet she was unbroken." After a long silence, he added softly, "She's the strongest person I've ever know."

Rafe realized that he was pacing around his end of the cell, hands clenched, his eyes unseeing. Never in his life had he had a stronger desire to be alone, to assimilate the horror of what had happened to Margot.

To see her father murdered in front of her eyes; to have had her sexual initiation as the victim of a gang of brutes ... How had she kept her sanity? Yet she had not only survived, but developed into an extraordinary woman. The thought of the strength and resilience that required staggered him.

On top of the helpless pain he felt on her behalf was the crushing knowledge of his own guilt. If he hadn't hurt Margot so badly, she would not have been in France. No wonder she had accused him of being responsible for her father's death. It was true, and there was no way on God's earth that he could ever make amends for the catastrophe which he had indirectly caused.

The frantic energy churning inside him was unbearable. Rafe, the quintessential civilized man, burned with the need to do something physically violent—preferably kill Margot's assailants with his bare hands.

Accurately reading Rafe's expression, Andreville said, "If it's any comfort, most of the men who joined the Grand Armée that long ago are probably long since dead. One can only hope that each of them died slowly and painfully."

"One can only hope," Rafe said thickly. He pictured one of those anonymous men being flayed alive by Spanish partisans; another dying of gangrene after ten days with a bullet in his belly; a third slowly freezing to death on the plains of Russia.

The visions didn't help much.

Muscle by muscle, he forced himself to relax. If he didn't, he'd go mad.

Andreville had returned to his corner and sunken into the straw. The emotions of his story were etched on his face and shadows showed under the blue eyes. Since he also loved Margot, this must be harrowing for him to speak of.

When he had reestablished a fragile control, Rafe said, "I suppose that after that, things had to get better."

"Yes, though it was a bit of a quandary for me. I could hardly abandon Maggie in the middle of France, but I was engaged in some vital business. When I explained, she said that she had no reason to return to England, so why didn't I take her with me? So I did.

"I took a flat in Paris. Because of our similar coloring, we claimed to be a brother and his widowed sister. She became Marguerite to the world in general, and Maggie to me, because she no longer wanted to be Margot Ashton." Forgetting his injured arm, Andreville started to make a gesture with his left hand, then winced. "Even before we reached Paris, I asked her to marry me so that she would have the protection of my name. Also, of course, if something happened to me she would be a considerable heiress."

Rafe swallowed, then said woodenly, "So you are actually husband and wife."

"No, she refused, saying that we shouldn't marry merely because of some unlucky circumstances. Instead, she offered to become my mistress if I wished."

So that was how it had begun. Rafe said, "I'm amazed that she could bear to let a man touch her."

"I was amazed, too, but she said that she wanted some happier memories to replace the bad ones," Andreville explained. "I had some doubts about the arrangement—remnants of a proper upbringing, no doubt—but I agreed. I was only twenty years old myself and didn't really want to be married, yet only an absolute fool would reject such an offer from a woman like her."

Though Andreville was glossing over what he had done, Rafe knew that it must have taken infinite kindness and patience to help Margot overcome such a shattering experience and become the passionate woman she was now. Rafe was profoundly grateful that she had had such a man to help her. With equal intensity, he resented the fact that he himself had not been the one; when she had needed him most, he had not been there.

Needing to acknowledge what the other man had done, he said, "She was fortunate to have you."

"We were fortunate to have each other." Andreville turned his uninjured hand palm up. "We've worked together ever since. I would move around Europe as necessary, often for months at a time. I've traveled with armies, crossed the Channel with smugglers, and generally did a lot of other harebrained, uncomfortable things that seem like great adventures when one is young and foolish." He smiled wryly. "As a child I rebelled against staid English respectability, but I must say that rebellion has lost its appeal since I turned thirty.

"Anyhow, home was wherever Maggie was living. Usually that was Paris. She led a quiet life, not like now when she's playing the countess and moving in society. She developed her own network of informants, and turned out to have a really spectacular talent for gathering information. The rest I think you know."

Rafe sighed. "To think that I had decided that you must be the spy in the delegation."

"Oh?" Andreville's eyebrows arched.

Rafe explained how he set up his own watchers, and how he had discovered that Andreville visited Margot, Roussaye, and Lemercier. He also mentioned the inferences he had drawn from the amount of money that Margot had received from her partner in spying.

"Even though your conclusions were wrong, you do have talent for this work." Andreville observed. "In retrospect, it would have been better if you'd known about me from the beginning, but as I said, secrecy becomes a habit. You know why I was communicating with Roussaye. As for Lemercier, I was trying to find out what he was up to, since I was sure that he was involved with the conspiracy."

"What about the money? It was the strongest evidence against you."

"Maggie didn't know how much Whitehall paid for information, so she accepted whatever I gave her without questioning," Andreville explained. "I never told her that most of the money came from me because she might have gotten all prickly and independent if she knew that I was supporting the household, even though it was my home, too. Also, since she wouldn't marry me, I wanted to insure that she had enough to live on comfortably if my luck ran out."

"You could have made her your heir even though you weren't married."

"I did, actually, but there was a good chance that I might simply disappear, with no one knowing how or when I died. In that case, my estate could have been tied up indefinitely. And of course my English executor would never have been able to communicate with Maggie while the war was on." He gave Rafe a curious glance. "Did you ever mention your suspicions of me to Maggie?"

When Rafe nodded, Andreville asked, "How did she react when you tried to convince her that I was a traitor? She knows almost nothing about my background, and there was strong circumstantial evidence against me."

Rafe said ruefully, "She flatly refused to believe it, and threw me out of her house at gunpoint. And if you are thinking of pointing out that she could teach me a few lessons in loyalty, don't bother—I already know." He ran his fingers distractedly through his hair. "Thank you for telling me so much. I needed to know."

Rafe settled down on the straw and tried again to master the grief, guilt, and anger that threatened to overwhelm him. Now that he understood the strength of the bond between Andreville and Margot, he realized that he had never had a chance of winning her.

It was amazing—and humiliating—to remember how he had arrogantly assumed that he could use seduction to bend her to his will. The only reason she had turned to him for a night was because of the horrific memories aroused by the mob in the Place de Carrousel. Now that he thought about it, the unusually

passionate embrace in the carriage after the theater riot
must have had the same cause.

He had wreaked havoc in her life, and he could think
of only one small thing that he could do to atone: make
damned sure that Andreville never learned of the night
Margot had spent in Rafe's bed. Even the most tolerant
of men would not be happy to learn that his mistress
had lain with another man, and Rafe did not want to be
a source of discord between Margot and the man of her
choice. He had already hurt her too much.

Though the restraint had half killed him at the time,
he was profoundly glad that he had done what he could
to prevent her from conceiving. Now that the wars
were over she might want to start a family, but a black-
haired baby would have been hard for her to explain to
Andreville.

Rafe closed his eyes and tilted his head back against
the wall. It was bitterly ironic that in helping Margot
forget, he had found a magic and a memory that would
always torment him. If she had ever wanted vengeance, she had achieved it. Wearily he said, "If we all
get out of his alive, are you going to marry her, Lord
Robert?"

After a long pause, Andreville said, "I certainly intend to ask her again. Incidentally, I'd rather you didn't
call me Lord Robert. That name belongs to another
life, just as the woman who is Margot to you will always be Maggie to me."

"What do you prefer to be called?"

"My friends call me Robin."

Were they friends, then? Rafe wasn't quite sure, but
there was certainly a bond between them composed of
respect, shared danger, and love for the same incompa-
rable woman.

"I'm usually called Rafe." He smiled a little. "The
actual name is Rafael, but as Margot said when I met

er, naming me after an archangel was singularly inappropriate."

His cellmate laughed, and the silence that followed was a comfortable one.

Chapter 22

"The Count de Varenne will want to see me," Oliver Northwood assured the decrepit Chanteuil butler.

The servant looked doubtful, but turned and hobbled into the depths of the castle. Not wanting to give the count time for too much thought, Northwood quietly followed. When the butler entered the library to inform his master of the visitor, the Englishman stepped inside also.

The count was seated at a desk covered with stacks of papers full of figures. He narrowed his eyes at Northwood's entrance. "Do we know each other, monsieur?"

"Of course we do, Comte le Serpent. Or shouldn't I call you that in front of your servants?" Northwood said boldly. He intended to be accepted as a valuable associate, not the lowly pair of hired hands that he had been in the past.

The coldness of Varenne's dark gaze confirmed his identity. Yet after a moment, he gave a slow smile and dismissed the butler. "No need to worry about the servants. Every man on the estate, from the cook to my little army, is personally loyal to me, and all look forward to a better day for France." He waved toward a chair. "Pray take a seat, monsieur. I see that I underestimated you. How did you discover my identity?"

"Your signet ring. I traced the crest." Deciding that he should put his insurance policy into effect,

Northwood added, "Incidentally, a sealed envelope with what I know is with someone who will take it to the authorities if I should disappear."

"There is no such need for such precautions, just as there will be no need for secrecy soon." His gaze sharpened. "You *have* done as we had discussed at your embassy, I assume?"

"Everything went according to plan. In about four hours, half the diplomats in Paris will be only a memory."

"You've done well, *mon petit Anglais,* very well." He glanced at his watch. "I regret that I have no time to socialize, but this is a most busy day. My soldiers must be prepared for whatever comes, I am considering matters that must be attended to after the explosion . . . a thousand things." He tucked the watch away. "Have you come for your bonus?"

"Partly that, partly to make sure that I am not forgotten in your rise to power." Northwood relaxed. Though there had been a menacing flash in Varenne's eyes when Northwood had first arrived, this affable aristocrat was turning out to be much less threatening than the masked Le Serpent had been.

"I promise that you will not be forgotten." The count smiled smoothly. "But as I said, I am very busy just now. Perhaps you would like to spend the next few hours amusing yourself with Countess Janos?"

Northwood ran an eager tongue over his lower lip. "I was hoping you had her. I can see her now?"

"If you wish. As I said, you have done well, so it is right that you enjoy a reward for your labors. Follow me."

Varenne led his guest up the stairs and along a dusty corridor to a door with worn gilding. He pulled a key from an inside pocket and handed it to Northwood. "Be sure to keep the door locked. She's a tricksome wench, and I don't want her loose in the castle."

Northwood's fingers tightened greedily on the key. He had waited a long time for this. "I'll keep her too busy to cause trouble."

"Enjoy yourself, but don't damage her too badly, Monsieur Northwood. I want to try her myself when I'm not so busy."

Nodding in acknowledgment, Northwood put the key in the lock and turned it.

It had been maddening to wait two hours at Madame Daudet's for the old lady to wake up, but the maid had been adamant about not disturbing her mistress. Hélène had scarcely been able to contain her impatience. Apart from finding the book that contained the three-headed serpent crest of the d'Aguste family, she had nothing to do but worry. A pity that they hadn't asked about the crest earlier, but at the time, it had merely been one of many possibilities.

In time, Madame Daudet emerged to greet her visitor. The old lady seemed scarcely more than black lace and delicate bones, but there was still strength and the ghost of beauty in her face. "What can I do for you today, child? Is your pretty blond friend here, too?"

"No, madame, I am here because I am worried about her," Hélène replied. "Countess Janos and some other friends have disappeared, and the only clue I have is that a d'Aguste might be involved. Can you tell me anything about the family?"

The old lady pursed her lips. "There is little to say, because the direct line is extinct. There have been no noble d'Agustes for the last fifty years or so."

Hélène's disappointment was so bitter she could taste it. Grasping at straws, she asked, "What happened fifty years ago?"

"Let's see . . .," Madame Daudet murmured as she cast her mind back over the years. "The last of the d'Agustes was an only daughter named Pauline. She married the

Count de Varenne and the d'Aguste name died out. Pauline was the mother of the present count. A strange girl. There's bad blood in the d'Agustes."

"Varenne!" Hélène exclaimed. After thanking Madame Daudet, she flew out of the apartment and down to the street. She still didn't know what to do about it, but at least she now knew who Le Serpent was.

Michel Roussaye frowned over the notes he had made after visiting a dozen clubs and cafés where Bonapartist officers gathered to drink and gamble and reminisce about the glorious days of the empire. Mention of Captain Henri Lemercier had produced blank looks, expressions of distaste, or occasionally a hard stare followed by a curt disclaimer of any knowledge of the man.

The lack of information was not surprising, since discretion was wise these days, but Roussaye had noticed something else that was disquieting. In every café, there had been fragmentary rumors of change in the wind. Several times he had heard whispers about Le Serpent, a man who would lead France once more to the glory she deserved. Two or three men who remembered Roussaye's army nickname had even asked obliquely if the general was the coming leader.

Roussaye had vehemently disclaimed any such role, but the hints were worrisome. Though most officers were like him, tired and willing to give peace a chance, there were still a few hotheads whose truest happiness had been in the days of the great victories. Such men refused to see what a high price their country had paid for a fleeting taste of *la gloire*.

Even more alarming was the news his servant received when he tried to deliver a message to the Duke of Candover: the duke had gone out the previous afternoon and had not returned. Roussaye swore to himself.

First Robert Anderson, then Countess Janos, and now
Candover; the crisis must be near.

Impatiently he got his feet and decided to go to
Silves's, another popular Bonapartist café. More and
more, it was necessary to learn who had employed
Henri Lemercier.

While Maggie sat in a shabby wing chair attempting
to read a lurid French novel, Rex sprawled on the floor
beside her. He lay on his back, curled sideways like a
comma, his massive furry feet in the air. She gave him
an affectionate smile. If he wasn't snoring she would
have wondered if he was alive. A pity that she couldn't
relax so thoroughly.

In the past twenty-four hours she had made what
plans she could, and now there was nothing to do but
wait. With a sigh, she laid the novel on the table next
to her and leaned over to scratch Rex's neck.

The cat was much better entertainment than the
book, since the servant who had filled her requests
seemed to think that females enjoyed reading the most
appalling tripe. Besides having characters too absurd to
believe, the novel had a spy subplot that was pure idiocy. The author had no idea what an unglamorous
business spying was.

At the moment, Maggie would have been delighted to
embrace the most boring spy work in existence. Being
kidnapped might be exciting in a book, but it was a combination of terrifying and tedious in real life. After making what meager preparations she could, there was
nothing left to do but wait.

A key grated in the lock. Since lunch had already
been served, a visitor must mean either Varenne or,
much worse, the associate he had promised her to. She
straightened in her chair and dried her damp palms on
her skirt while Rex scuttled under the bed.

When Oliver Northwood came through the door, she

was almost relieved. The man was a coarse brute, a wife abuser, and a traitor to his country, but at least he was a known quantity, with neither the intelligence nor the calculated wickedness of Varenne. Against him, she would have a chance.

As he relocked the door, she ordered herself to forget the horror of rape; forget the open window that promised an end to panic and pain; forget everything but the role she had decided on. If she didn't play it well, her nightmares would become brutal reality.

Northwood turned to face her, his broad, fleshy face openly gloating. He would expect her to be frightened. In fact, he was probably looking forward to it, and would be on her in an instant if she cowered or begged.

There was a good chance, however, that being treated with the social amenities would make him respond in kind. Rising to her feet, she offered her most gracious smile. "Mr. Northwood, what a pleasure! I did so hope it would be you, but the count wouldn't tell me, naughty man. Do sit down." She gestured to the brocade chair that she had set by the table. "Would you care for some wine?"

Taken aback, Northwood took the seat indicated.

With the air of a hostess in her own drawing room, Maggie poured part of her lunchtime carafe of wine into her glass, then handed it to her visitor. "Here you are. I'm sorry that it's only vin ordinaire, but I have nothing better to offer you."

Expression baffled, he accepted the glass. "You're glad to see me?"

"But of course! I've always fancied you, you know."

"You picked a damned funny way of showing it, Margot Ashton," he said belligerently. "You always treated me like dirt."

She took the chair opposite him, soft folds of green muslin settling in a way that exposed a hint of ankle.

That morning she had spent considerable time combing her hair into a loose style designed for the boudoir, and she had also made some adjustments to her neckline. Judging by Northwood's expression, her appearance was having the desired effect.

With a delicate sigh, she said, "Oh, dear, I had always hoped that you would understand. We are kindred spirits, you know—I have always sensed that."

Obviously enjoying her flirtatious manner, Northwood leaned back in his chair. Nonetheless, he would not let himself be appeased too easily. "If we're such bloody kindred spirits, why were you always so rude to me, both when you made your come-out and these last weeks? You never treated Candover like that."

"Of course not." She put a hint of exasperation in her voice. "The man's insanely jealous, and it wouldn't be safe to flirt with anyone else when he's around. You're much cleverer than he is, though. He mentioned that I looked like a girl he had known once, but even though we had been engaged, he has never recognized me! The gullible fool actually believes that I'm a Hungarian countess."

Gulping a third of the wine, Northwood said, "Oh, I'm clever all right, though I never let that lot at the embassy know. They all think they're so bloody superior." He brooded for a moment. "So why did Candover get the royal treatment, not me?"

"Because he's rich, of course," Maggie said, making her eyes wide and innocent. "Surely you don't think women would waste time on the man for any other reason?"

"You're talking nonsense," Northwood said viciously. "The bastard has always had any woman he wanted—including my wife."

"Well, he's always been very, very rich, hasn't he?" Maggie said reasonably. "Oh, he's not bad-looking, but he's also a bore, both in and out of bed." She gave a bawdy chuckle, then asked silent forgiveness for the enormous lie she was about to utter. "Really, Oliver—do you mind if I call you Oliver? I always think of you that way—if Candover had to rely on his physical attributes to keep a mistress, no woman would go back for a second round."

It was what Northwood wanted to hear. Leaning forward greedily, he asked, "How much of a man is he, then?"

"Well, a lady really shouldn't talk of such things. Let's just say that where she would hope to find the most, she would have to be content with the least." She giggled and undulated in her chair a little, her posture signaling availability. "He's also a thirty-second wonder with absolutely no imagination. Why, he won't even . . ."

She listed several exotic variations on the common theme, and had the satisfaction of seeing Northwood's eyes nearly bulge from their sockets with fascinated lust.

Tilting her head to one side, she said reflectively, "In spite of losing all that lovely money, I was rather relieved that I didn't marry him. Besides being tedious and madly jealous, he's dreadfully stuffy. But when I was eighteen, I was so proud to have attached the heir to a dukedom that I didn't care what he was like."

"You have me to thank for his breaking the engagement."

Maggie felt a cold chill on the back of her neck, but she managed to purr, "How did that happen?"

"It was easy. You're right, Candover isn't very clever. Anyone could see that he was head over heels for you even without an announcement."

"He did follow me around like a stag in rut," she agreed.

Northwood sipped more wine, his expression dark.

"I always despised him. We were in school together, my birth is as good as his—and a damned sight better than that Gypsy friend of his—but Candover was always too high in the instep to associate with the likes of me. Just because he had a fortune and was heir to a grand title, he acted as if that made him better than me. But I watch people, you know, I know what their weaknesses are."

Cutting off the flow of self-congratulation, Maggie coaxed him back to the original topic. "What was his weakness?"

"Why, his weakness was you, of course. He thought you were so pure and perfect. I decided to let him find out that you weren't." Northwood looked at her challengingly. "Even though you had him flummoxed, I knew you were too good to be true. It was obvious that you were a hot-tailed wench."

She had to swallow before she could say admiringly, "That was very perceptive of you, Oliver. What did you do about it?"

"A group of us had been out one night, drinking and carrying on. When I knew that Candover was within earshot, I described how you had spread your legs for me in the back garden of one of those balls. I pretended that I was too drunk to know that I was being indiscreet, but I knew exactly what I was saying." Northwood gave a smile of pure malice. "Candover acted as if he'd been kicked in the stomach. He got up and left right away, and the next I knew, you had left London."

She stared at the florid, self-satisfied face, feeling ice in her veins. Though her opinion of Northwood had never been high, it was still a numbing shock to hear him boast of performing the vicious, cold-blooded act that had had such catastrophic repercussions. He had a genius for low cunning; something said by a man in his cups was far more convincing than a direct slander would have been. No wonder Rafe had come to her that morning half mad with pain and jealousy. His lack of trust was still a betrayal, but a far more understandable one.

Though she felt ill, she daren't give in to it. If she lost her self-possession now, she would be at the mercy of this beast. She shaped her mouth into a pout. "Really, Oliver, that wasn't at all nice of you. It injured him—and believe me, he took it *very* badly—but you caused all kinds of problems for me, too. If you'd wanted me for yourself, all you would have had to do was wait a decent interval after the wedding."

"You would have been interested in an affair?" Northwood said, skeptical but willing to be convinced.

"Of course I would have." She looked wistful. "Once I had the ring on my finger, I could have done anything I wanted. Candover is far too proud to sully his name with divorce, no matter what his wife did. Oh, I would have given him an heir, of course, fair is fair. But after that . . ." Her smile was infinitely suggestive.

She stood and poured the rest of the wine into Northwood's glass, careful to give him a good look down the low-cut bodice of her dress. Then she sat again and crossed her legs, exposing a fair amount of shapely calf.

"Before we get down to pleasure, could you satisfy my curiosity? I've been wondering what you and Varenne are up to."

Northwood reached over and roughly squeezed her breast. If she had flinched, it might have roused his doubts, so she gave him a sultry smile instead.

Willing to boast of his cleverness again, he said, "We're blowing up the British embassy this afternoon."

Her eyes widened involuntarily. "Is that possible?

Surely it would require an enormous amount of gun-powder."

"Actually we're only blowing up one section, but that is where everyone important will be." He slid his hand down the front of her bodice and pinched her nipple.

It took every hard-won shred of control Maggie had not to hit him. Reminding herself how many lives were at stake, she squeezed his knee, as if being mauled by a swine aroused her. "I've heard that all the important meetings are being held in Castlereagh's bedchamber," she said throatily.

"Exactly, and there is a closet directly below. I filled it with gunpowder, and it will explode this afternoon at four o'clock. Nobody will find it, either. I have the key to the closet right here." He patted his jacket pocket smugly.

"Oh, then you'll have to leave soon! I was hoping you could stay." Then, as if the thought had just struck her, she asked, "Won't it be dangerous for you to set off the powder?"

"That's where cleverness was called for," North-wood boasted. 'I set a candle in the closet. When it burns down, it will hit a trail of gunpowder, ignite the boxes and, *Boom!* Everyone in Castlereagh's bedchamber will be blown to bloody shreds."

Maggie shuddered, then tried to make it appear that she was excited by the idea. "How splendid! I wish that I could have been involved in something as important."

Northwood's eyes raked her. "Oh, really? I thought that you were quite the loyal little British spy."

"Whatever gave you that idea? If you're a girl of no fortune like me, you have to take what money comes. And I've taken it from everyone."

Now that she had learned what was planned, it was time to act, because if she didn't move quickly she would lose the initiative. She got to her feet and stretched provocatively, her arms over her head. His heated gaze followed the sway of her breasts.

"I've done what's needful for money, Oliver." With a rich bedroom chuckle, she gave him her hand. He took it and tugged her onto his lap, exactly as she had expected.

"But some things I do for myself . . ."

Breathing heavily, he pulled her gown from one shoulder and grabbed her bare breast. She looked deep into his eyes, and finished, ". . . and this will be pure pleasure." Bending her head for a kiss, she murmured, "Oh, Oliver . . ."

Then, as his lips crushed into hers, she lifted the china pitcher that she had carefully positioned on the table and smashed it into his head with all her strength.

The impact made a ghastly sound, pulpiness mixed with shattering china, and water cascaded over both of them. Northwood's eyes showed a flash of incredulity before he pitched over sideways, taking the chair and Maggie with him.

The fall knocked the breath from her, but she scrambled up quickly, equally fearful of having killed him and of not having hit hard enough. To her relief, he was unconscious but alive.

Earlier she had disconnected the drapery cords, and she used them to tie his wrists and ankles. Another length secured him to the legs of the heavy table. She also tore a length of fabric from the drapery lining and gagged him.

Then she searched his pockets. Besides the key to her room, he had a ring with several other keys in his coat. Not knowing which was for the closet in the embassy, she took them all.

After unlocking the door, she peered cautiously into the corridor. It was deserted. She gave the black cat pressing against her ankle a quick glance. "Come on, Rexie darling. We're gong to find Robin."

At Silves' café, Roussaye settled at the table of a man he had served with in Italy, Raoul Fortrand. As soon as he could, he raised the subject of Henri Lemercier.

Fortrand spat on the floor. "The swine. He was always a swine, and before his death he proved it."

His pulse speeding up, the general leaned forward. "What was he doing? And for whom?"

Fortrand shrugged. "God knows—something illegal, no doubt. I heard that he was working for Count de Varenne. They say Varenne expected to be prime minister after Talleyrand, and that he was furious when the king picked Richelieu. Maybe Varenne wanted Lemercier to assassinate the new prime minister."

Roussaye thought for a moment. Varenne's estate lay scarcely an hour outside Paris, convenient for plots and prisoners. Perhaps Roussaye was wrong, but his soldier's instinct demanded he investigate, and do it in force.

Rising to his feet, he looked around the café at the two dozen men there, many former comrades-in-arms. In a battlefield voice he called, *"Mes amis!"*

Quiet settled on the room as everyone turned to him.

Roussaye climbed onto his chair so that he could be seen by all. "My friends, I have evil news of a royalist plot against the Duke of Wellington, a soldier second only to Bonaparte himself. They say the Iron Duke will be assassinated, and the Bonapartists will be blamed. Men like us who have faithfully served our country will be persecuted, and France herself may be driven to the brink of civil war."

The silence was absolute. Roussaye looked at the familiar faces: at Moreau, who had lost his arm at Waterloo; at Chabrier, one of the handful of survivors of the disastrous Moscow campaign; at Chamfort, with whom he had shared a billet in Egypt. His voice soft, he said, "We may find the answers, and perhaps even a beautiful lady to rescue, at Chanteuil, the estate of the Count de Varenne. Will you come with me?"

Men began to rise to their feet, coming to him and offering their arms. Pitching his voice above the babble, Roussaye said, "All of you who have horses and weapons, follow me. Together we will make one last ride for France."

Hélène Sorel had run two blocks before fatigue and common sense made her slow down. She was sure that Varenne was Le Serpent, and his lack of obvious motive had shielded his activities. But merciful heaven, what should she do now?

As she stood on a corner of Faubourg St. Germain, agonized indecision on her face, the clattering hooves of a passing horse suddenly stopped beside her. She looked up to see Karl von Fehrenbach swinging down from his mount, an uncertain expression on his face.

"Madame Sorel, I'm glad to see you. I have been thinking . . ." Then he registered her distraught face and said sharply, "What's wrong?"

Logically Hélène knew the colonel lived nearby, and it was mere chance that he was passing by. Yet when she looked at his broad, capable shoulders, it was hard not to think that he had been sent by heaven. The colonel was an influential man, and since he knew of her spy work he might believe her story.

After pausing a moment to organize her thoughts, she poured out the story of the conspiracy: the disappearance of the three British agents, her realization that Varenne must be the master plotter, and her belief that Chanteuil contained the answers.

The colonel listened without interrupting, his light blue eyes intent. When Hélène came to the end of her story, he swung onto his horse, then extended his hand to her. "There is a Prussian barracks near the St. Cloud road. I will be able to get some men there to search Varenne's estate."

As Hélène hesitated, he said impatiently. "To save time, you must come with me and show us the way to Chanteuil. If you are right, there is no time to be wasted."

Hélène took his hand, and he lifted her easily onto the horse. As she settled sideways in front of him, she said anxiously, "But if I am wrong?"

'If you are wrong, there are compensations." The grave Prussian colonel did not quite smile, but he had a mischievous glint in his eyes. For the first time since they had met, it was possible to believe that he was really only thirty-four years old, the same age as she.

Hélène became abruptly conscious of how close she was to his lean, athletic body, and how warm was the arm that held her steady. For a moment, the serene and worldly widow disappeared, and she blushed like a girl.

This time von Fehrenbach actually did smile. Then he put his heels to the horse, and they were away.

Chapter 23

Though they knew the odds were poor, Rafe and Robin decided that they would attempt to break out the next time anyone entered their cell. Not long after the midday meal, the key rattled in the lock. Immediately they took the positions previously agreed on. Since Robin was in poor shape to fight, he lounged innocently in the straw while Rafe concealed himself in the corner behind the door so that he could attack whoever entered.

The door swung open with a squeal, and Rafe prepared to jump. Then Margot hurtled into the cell, saying urgently, "Robin, are you here?"

Barely in time Rafe checked his leap. Not seeing him, Margot darted across the cell and dropped beside Robin, enfolding him in a heartfelt hug. "Thank God you're all right! I was so frightened ..."

Though he winced as she jarred his injured arm, Robin hugged her back. "I'm well enough, Maggie. We have reinforcements, too." He glanced at his fellow prisoner.

Margot turned to follow his gaze. "Rafe!"

They stared at each other for an eternity that lasted for perhaps two heartbeats. With her golden hair loose around her shoulders, she looked like a Valkyrie. Rafe took an involuntary step toward her, then forced himself to stop when he saw alarm flash across her face.

He wondered if she feared that he would do something that would embarrass her in front of Robin. Kiss her, perhaps, or start babbling about how much he loved her. Swiftly he said, "I'm glad to see that you're uninjured, Countess. I'm even gladder that the dungeon key was hanging outside." It was an inane comment, but he hoped that it would convey the message that he didn't intend to cause her any problems.

She must have understood, for her expression smoothed out. "I'm not sure whether I should be glad to see you, or sorry that you're a prisoner, too."

Looking back at Robin, she frowned at the sling. "You aren't looking your best, love. What happened to your arm?"

Though they were all impatient to be away, the next few minutes were spent exchanging vital information. When Margot described how the gunpowder was set to explode that afternoon, Rafe exclaimed, "Damnation! Robin, is there any chance that someone will smell the candle smoke and find the gunpowder before it's too late?"

Face grim, Robin replied, "Virtually none. That closet is on a corridor that's almost never used. Even if someone became suspicious, time would probably be wasted searching for a key, and Margot may have the only one."

Rafe took a quick look at his watch. As he shoved it back in his pocket, he said, "We have about two hours to get out of here and reach the embassy." He thought for a moment. "I have a general idea of the layout of the grounds. Have either of you seen enough of the castle to know the best way to escape?"

Robin shook his head. "Sorry. Since I was brought here unconscious and dumped in this cell immediately, my ignorance is total."

"I learned a few things about the interior when I was finding my way down here," Margot said. "Even though Varenne said that Robin was being held directly under the room I was in, it took forever to find this cell—the lower levels of the castle are a labyrinth of service stairs and passages. Luckily, there are very few people about—I didn't see a single servant, though I heard voices once."

"I guess the only possible plan is to try to steal horses, then ride like hell and hope we get to the embassy in time," Robin said. "If we're discovered, we'll have to scatter and hope that one of us can get through alone."

As Rafe opened the cell door, he felt a pressure on his ankle. He looked down to see a fluffy black cat brush against him coquettishly. "Where the devil did this beast come from?"

"This is Rex." Margot leaned over and scooped the cat up. As it settled, purring, into her arms, she said, "He kept me company upstairs. Since I fed him, we're friends for life. I think I'll take him with me for luck." She eyed Rafe warily, as if expecting him to disagree.

The idea was absurd, of course, but the way she held the cat made Rafe think that she derived some kind of comfort from it. "I'm not sure whether this is melodrama or farce," he said with wry amusement. "Bring him if you must, but be prepared to release him if he slows you down. He's in a lot less danger than we are."

Holding the door for his companions, he said, "Time to be off. And if anyone knows any good prayers, please say them."

Oliver Northwood regained consciousness to find himself wet, bound, and gagged. Rage cleared his mind. As he tugged at his bonds, he swore mentally at the little slut who had done this to him. He should have raped her immediately rather than falling victim to her lying tongue.

The water-softened drapery cords stretched as he strained at them. He swore again, this time in gratitude that his luck had turned. After ten minutes of struggle, he was free of his bonds.

He lurched to his feet and searched his pockets. As expected, the room key was gone, so he pounded on the door and shouted for help. Again he was in luck. A servant was in the vicinity, and soon Northwood was out of his prison.

He hastened to Varenne's library and burst into the room without knocking. The count was still seated behind his desk working at his infernal plans.

When Varenne glanced up, Northwood gasped, "She's gotten away! The little bitch is loose somewhere in the castle!"

The count examined his bloody, disheveled visitor. "You let a female half your size do that to you? I have overestimated your abilities."

Northwood flushed angrily. "There's no need to be insulting. That brazen-faced hussy could bamboozle a saint. She's dangerous."

"Quite deliciously so," Varenne murmured, more amused than alarmed. As he rang for a servant, he said, "She won't get far. Besides, how much trouble can one woman cause?"

Uneasily Northwood said, "She knows what's going to happen at the embassy this afternoon."

"What! You fool, why did you tell her that?" The count's lip curled in disgust. 'You needn't answer. Obviously you were boasting. My respect for Miss Ashton grows hourly greater."

When a footman entered, Varenne said, "The woman has escaped. Set all the servants searching for her." He gave Northwood's bloody head an ironic glance. "Tell them to carry shotguns and travel in pairs. She's quite a ferocious wench."

As soon as the count stopped speaking the footman said urgently, "Milord, I was just coming to inform you that the lady has freed the two Englishmen. They are loose somewhere on the lower levels."

The count's air of calm disintegrated and he bounded to his feet. "Jesu! Alone she was a minor threat, but the three together are dangerous. Tell the searchers that while I would prefer to have the spies captured alive, they should shoot if necessary. The English cannot be allowed to leave Chanteuil."

The footman nodded and left. When Northwood started to follow, Varenne stopped him. "Where are you going?"

"To help search. I want to be the one to find her."

"I need you elsewhere," the count said, voice controlled again. "The lower castle is a maze of passages, and the prisoners might conceal themselves indefinitely. That would be a nuisance, but not a disaster. The real danger is that they might reach the stables and steal horses. If they managed that, they could reach Paris in time to undo my plan. Therefore you and I shall wait for them in the stables until it is too late for the explosion to be stopped."

"Very well—as long as that treacherous slut is punished," Northwood growled.

"Never fear, she will be." Varenne reached into his desk and brought out a mahogany box containing two dueling pistols. He loaded both and offered one to Northwood. "I trust that you know how to use this?"

The Englishman glowered. "Don't worry, I'm a crack shot."

As they went downstairs, the distant boom of a shotgun blast was heard from somewhere below. The count gave a nod of satisfaction. "Perhaps our vigil in the stables will be unnecessary. Nonetheless, we cannot afford to take a chance."

Before they went outside, he gave orders for his small troop of soldiers to surround the stables and conceal themselves. Even if the three Britons got that far, they would go no farther.

Varenne took a footpath down to the stables, which were built on the lower slope of the hill. Inside the stone building, the main room stretched back with box stalls on each side of a wide central area. Most of the stalls were occupied, and the earthy scents of animals and sweet hay were heavy in the air.

A couple of horses whickered greetings, but Varenne ignored them, turning to the right to enter a long, narrow harness room. As Northwood followed, he asked, "Why are we going to wait in here?"

"Because I still hope to capture them alive, imbecile," the count said with exasperation. He walked to the window at the far end of the room and stared out. "Come look at this."

The Englishman joined him at the window, but saw nothing. "What do you want me to see?"

"This." Behind Northwood came the unmistakable sound of a pistol being cocked. Startled, Northwood spun around and found himself facing the barrel of Varenne's pistol.

"You have ceased to be an asset, *mon petit Anglais*," the count said coldly. "You are too stupid to know your place, and I greatly disliked your attempts to coerce me. As a last gesture for services rendered, I was willing to grant you a fling with the countess, but you have bungled even that. I cannot waste any more time on you."

"You bloody French bastard!" Desperately Northwood reached for his own pistol, but he never had a chance. Calmly Varenne squeezed his trigger. The gun bucked in his hand, the report shatteringly loud in the enclosed space.

The impact of the bullet knocked Northwood back against the wall. He made a breathy sound like a sudden exhalation and clapped a hand to his chest. Then, an expression of disbelief on his face, he slowly slid down the wall and fell forward in an ungainly sprawl, his pistol beneath him.

Varenne walked over to his victim and prodded Northwood's ribs with the toe of his boot. The only response was the slow spread of blood from under the body.

In general the count was not involved with death directly; it was such a messy business. With a grimace of distaste, he turned away. The servants could retrieve the gun later. He disliked the necessity of sharing the tackroom with a corpse. However, shooting the imbecile here had saved the library carpet from being ruined by blood, which had been Varenne's objective.

He reloaded his own weapon with meticulous care. One pistol and the element of surprise were all that would be necessary to capture the escaped prisoners. All he need do was threaten the fraudulent countess, and her lovers would fall into line immediately. The fools.

Maggie kept a watchful eye on Robin as they made their way swiftly through the shadowy passages. Though he was keeping up with the others, his drawn face showed the amount of effort it was taking. She had great faith in his formidable willpower; nonetheless, she uttered a silent prayer that his strength would last long enough for them to escape Chanteuil.

Worrying about Robin's condition had the advantage of preventing her from brooding about Rafe. Her first reaction to seeing him had been pure, uncomplicated joy in spite of their dangerous circumstances. However, his cool detachment had quickly put her in her place. He obviously couldn't wait until this mission was over, so he wouldn't ever have to see her again.

But this was not the time or place to think about her personal problems. Sharply tamping down her grief, she turned her attention to the present. To escape the castle, they would have to go up at least two levels, then find a side exit.

In the flagstoned passageways, their footsteps made little sound. The castle seemed almost deserted, and they went up one flight of stairs and turned right into another passage without seeing anyone.

Then their luck ran out. They had almost reached the end of the corridor when two hulking men with shot-guns appeared around the corner just ahead of them.

"You two run for it!" Rafe barked as he threw himself forward in a flat dive, barreling into the man in the lead.

Maggie froze, terrified to leave Rafe behind. Robin snapped, "Come on, Maggie!" and grabbed her arm, pulling her back the way they had come.

She resisted for an agonized moment, but the pressure on her arm left her no choice. With Rex draped over her shoulder, she raced along beside Robin as the hideous blast of a shotgun echoed through the stone halls.

Because the Prussian barracks lay off the main St. Cloud road, Colonel von Fehrenbach's Hussars didn't intersect the French party until they were a bare half mile from Chanteuil. The Prussians entered the main road at a right angle from a lane they had taken as a shortcut.

With a squealing of horses, both groups pulled to a chaotic halt to prevent a collision. As the uniformed Prussian cavalrymen faced the armed French officers, mutual suspicion and hostility throbbed between them. A single spark would set off a full-scale conflagration. A Frenchman uttered an angry oath, and a nervous young Hussar started to raise his musket.

Before catastrophe could strike, von Fehrenbach threw his hand up imperiously. "No!"

Hélène was beside the colonel on a mount supplied by the Prussian barracks. Recognizing Michel Roussaye, she urged her horse into the open ground, crying, "Don't shoot, we're friends!"

Having an attractive woman intervene released the tension, particularly since lack of a proper riding habit allowed an indecent amount of leg to show. Von Fehrenbach cantered after her, meeting Roussaye in the space between the groups.

After a terse discussion of where each group was going, and why, the colonel frowned for a moment. Then he suggested, "Perhaps we should join forces, General Roussaye."

Roussaye raised his brows, his dark face skeptical. "Frenchmen and Prussians riding together?"

The colonel's gaze touched Hélène, who was tensely waiting at the third corner of their triangle. "Such a thing should not be impossible when men share the same goal." He offered his hand. "Shall we try to go forward together?"

Roussaye gave a slow smile and took the Prussian's hand. "Very well, Colonel. Instead of looking back, we shall go forward—together."

Chapter 24

Though Rafe's charge took the two searchers by surprise, the taller one whipped up his shotgun and fired both barrels. Rafe managed to knock the weapon upward so that the shot discharged into the ceiling, but the blast was deafening and a ricocheting pellet grazed his wrist.

Undaunted, the tall man swung the empty shotgun above his head to use it as a club. Before he could bring it down, Rafe kicked him viciously in the groin. The gunman shrieked and doubled over.

Glad to see that he hadn't forgotten the lessons of distant college tavern brawls, Rafe turned his attention to his other foe, a broad, balding fellow who was clumsily trying to aim his weapon. Before he succeeded, Rafe hit him in the jaw with a right jab that could have felled a small ox.

The tall man lurched toward Rafe in a feeble attempt to rejoin the fight. Rafe stepped aside, then chopped the edge of his hand down on the back of the man's neck. The servant promptly joined his companion on the floor.

Rafe snatched up the two shotguns and the ammunition pouches. Not stopping to reload the gun that had been discharged, he raced down the hall after Margot and Robin. The whole encounter had taken less than a minute, and he caught up with the others around the next corner.

Rafe looked so rakishly handsome that Maggie would have stopped to admire him if there had been time, which there wasn't. With a glance at the two shotguns, she panted, "I'm impressed, your grace. I didn't know that rough and tumble fighting was taught at Jackson's salon."

"It isn't, but I did have a liberal university education," Rafe retorted, laughter in his voice.

The passage ended with a door. Robin swung it open, revealing another pair of searchers literally face-to-face with them. Since Maggie was already halfway through the doorway, she collided full force with one of Varenne's men.

The impact knocked her breathless, but it bore much harder on Rex, who had been letting himself be carried with amazing passivity. The cat erupted straight up in the air with a blood-curdling shriek of feline fury.

He came down on the man who had collided with Maggie, and his flailing claws and powerful hindquarters ripped and slashed with gory effect. Using the man's face as a launching ramp to safety, Rex left the gunman screaming as blood poured from his face. The cat vanished down the passage behind the servants, his black tail a feathery plume of rage.

Rafe dragged Maggie back, then slammed the door on the demoralized searchers. As they ran back the way they had come, he said, "You are *not* going after that damned cat!"

Maggie was too out of breath to say anything other than a sarcastic, "Yes, your grace."

"Amazing," Rafe said as they swung into another passage. "That's the first docile remark I've ever heard from you, Countess."

"Savor it," she said tartly. "It's the first *and* the last."

The fleeting humor disappeared when they reached an intersection where two corridors crossed. Another pair of armed men appeared in front of them, drawn by the sound of the earlier shotgun blast. Maggie glanced back, and saw that the cat-struck duo had recovered and were coming after them.

"Go to the right!" Rafe ordered. "And take this." He handed her one of the shotguns and an ammunition pouch.

While she and Robin dashed down the right-hand cross passage, Rafe raised the other gun and cocked both hammers. After discharging one barrel ahead of them, he spun around and blasted the other one behind. He didn't bother to aim, relying on the scattering effect of the shot to discourage the searchers. Then he followed his companions.

Seeing that Robin was near collapse, Maggie halted by a door in the middle of the corridor. It was locked. With a silent prayer, she fumbled for the key to her bedchamber, which she had kept after locking Northwood in. To her acute relief, the key worked and the door opened to reveal an ascending staircase.

When Rafe pelted up, she said, "Thank God that the locks in this place are so old and crude. The same key probably works on all of them. Come on!"

Instead of following, Robin slumped against the wall, his face white. "I can't . . . keep up. You'll never escape with me slowing you down," he gasped. "Leave me with a loaded shotgun—maybe I can buy you some time."

Before Maggie could speak, Rafe snapped, "Don't be a damned fool." He looped his free arm around Robin, then started up the steps.

Maggie relocked the door, then followed the men upward. With luck, the hunters wouldn't be able to guess that their quarry had gone this way.

They climbed for what she estimated was two floors before reaching another door. It opened into a hall that was wider and better kept than the service passages below; they had reached the section of the castle where the masters lived. After the hubbub below, it was eerily silent.

Rafe eased Robin into a sitting position against the wall, then reloaded the shotguns. "From the direction of the light, I think that the river face is to the left, so we have to go right to get out of the castle."

Worriedly Maggie said to Robin, "Can you keep going for a little longer?"

Robin was chalk-pale and perspiration beaded his face, but he struggled to his feet again. "Now that I've caught my breath, I'm fine. Don't worry, I've ridden a hundred miles with worse."

"Liar." Tenderly she brushed sweaty hair from his forehead. "Luckily, we don't have to go a hundred miles."

Observing the intimacy between his companions, Rafe felt very much the outsider. Mentally he vowed that if they survived this, he would go away as silently as possible; they would never even notice he was gone. "Time to go," he said, his voice clipped. "Varenne claimed to have a small army, and they're probably all outside between here and the stable. Margot, be prepared to use that shotgun."

She nodded soberly, and he gave thanks for the unladylike skills her father had taught her. He was also grateful for the fact that Robin had a coolheaded recognition of his own limitations. With luck, they might actually make it out alive.

A few minutes of exploration brought them to a stairway to the ground floor. In a low voice, Rafe said, "Since the doors are probably guarded, let's find a room on the east side and go out through a window."

Stealthily they went downstairs and soon located a shabby morning room with windows only about five feet about the ground. Rafe opened the casements and helped Margot and Robin out, then dropped lightly beside them. "Shall we see if the stables are being guarded by Varenne's army?"

"They had better not be." Margot hoisted her shotgun again. "We're running out of time."

It was a sobering remark. While saving their own lives had high priority, it was far from their only concern.

When the combined French and Prussian forces reached the gates of Chanteuil, there was no one in sight and the gate was locked. Hélène watched tensely as von Fehrenbach dismounted and rattled the gate. Eventually an ancient gatekeeper emerged.

Sharply the colonel said, "Open this gate in the name of Marshal Blücher and the Allied Army of Occupation."

Since the gatekeeper seemed rooted to the ground, Roussaye called out, "You will not be harmed as long as you obey orders."

The Frenchman's reassurance succeeded where the Prussian order hadn't, and after a minute of fumbling the gate was opened. Riders began streaming through. As the Hussars entered the grounds, the flat, deadly rattle of gunfire came from the castle that crowned the hill. Von Fehrenbach wheeled his mount to face Hélène. "Wait here, Madame Sorel, until we have dealt with whatever rabble Varenne has."

She nodded, her tired hands clutching her horse's reins. "Just . . . please be careful."

He nodded and touched one hand to his forehead. Then he spurred his mount toward the sounds of firing.

As Hélène watched the men gallop up the driveway, she prayed that they were in time.

Maggie and company saw no one on the shrubbed path between castle and stable. The open yard felt horribly exposed, and it was a relief to reach the stable door. Rafe unfastened the latch, then stood to one side as he kicked the door open, his shotgun ready for any danger within.

His precautions were unnecessary; the stables appeared to be empty of everything but horses. Probably the grooms had been pressed into the search at the castle.

After scanning the interior, Rafe said, "Robin, pick the best horses. Margot, find some harness. I'll stand guard."

The other two nodded and moved off, meshing together into a smoothly working team. As she turned right to look for the harness room, Maggie thought it was remarkable how well they were getting on considering that all three people were by nature leaders, more accustomed to giving orders than receiving them.

Her thoughts were abruptly cut off when she entered the tack room and was seized in an iron grip. Before she could scream a warning to her companions, an iron hand clamped over her mouth. She fought fiercely to free herself, but she was no match for her assailant's strength. Viciously he twisted her arm until she was forced to drop the shotgun. Then he pulled her head around so that she could see him.

She found herself looking into the black eyes of the Count de Varenne. He smiled, his usual congenial social smile, and jammed a cocked dueling pistol against her temple. There would be bruises, if she lived long enough.

"Congratulations on escaping my men in the castle," he said, a little breathless from the exertion of subduing her. "I am not entirely surprised—you and your lovers are formidable adversaries. Have the three of you ever shared a bed? I would think that would account for the harmony among you."

Not bothering to wait for an answer, he forced her ahead of him into the main stable block. Once there, he slipped his left hand from her mouth and locked his arm around her midriff, pinning her arms to her sides. "Now you may scream all you like, Countess."

Hearing Varenne's voice, Robin swung around. His furious oath caused Rafe to turn, then stop dead, frozen with horror.

"I'm sure that neither of you gentlemen wishes any harm to come to your lovely fraudulent countess," Varenne snapped. "Drop the gun, Candover. Then both of you raise your hands above your heads and move into the center of the room."

Instantly Rafe tossed the shotgun aside and went to stand by Robin.

Margot's face was white, and there was fear in her eyes, but she said evenly, "Don't let him stop you. It's only a single-shot dueling pistol, so he can't get all three of us."

"While the countess shows an admirable willingness for martyrdom, I wouldn't advise you to try anything, gentlemen." Varenne began backing toward the door, still holding Maggie firmly against him. "My men are concealed outside, and you would never escape. I have gone to this effort because I prefer to capture you alive, but I warn you, at the least move from either of you, I will blow the lady's head off."

When Oliver Northwood swam dimly back to consciousness, he knew that he was dying. There was too much blood puddling below him, and the final chill was reaching into his bones. At first he thought the voices were in his head. Then he realized that the people he hated most were talking only a few feet away, in the main stable.

Knowledge that his enemies were near galvanized him. Though the smallest effort exhausted him, he still had a little strength left, and by God, he would use it well.

An eternity was required to struggle to his knees, another to gain his feet. Northwood was gratified to discover that he still had Varenne's pistol. He cocked it, a time-consuming act since his fingers had no sensation.

The wound in his chest wasn't bleeding much—he must be running out of blood—but he was very clear about what must be done. Blinking to clear his eyes, he lurched the length of the harness room, one hand on the wall to steady his faltering step. He didn't have much time left, but he vowed that it would be enough to kill the one he hated the most.

To Rafe, the scene was a tableau from hell—he and Robin motionless with their hands up, Varenne inching back to the door, Margot's golden hair falling about her shoulders, the high cheekbones stark in her rigidly calm face. Though almost consumed by his fury, Rafe remained absolutely still, unwilling to risk angering the count.

Then, eerily silent, a blood-soaked figure staggered from the harness room behind Varenne. His face contorted with an ugly blend of hate and rage, Oliver Northwood raised a pistol that was a mate to the count's. The barrel wavered feebly as he tried to center the weapon between Varenne's shoulder blades.

For an instant Rafe was paralyzed, not knowing whether Northwood's intervention was more likely to help or harm Margot. Then he realized that if Varenne was shot, his hand would spasm and pull the light trigger of the dueling pistol. "Look out, Varenne! Northwood is behind you."

"I thought you were cleverer than that, Candover," the count sneered. "You won't trick me into turning away from you to look for a dead man."

Varenne wasn't quick enough to realize the significance of the fact that Rafe had called Northwood by name, but the flash in Margot's eyes showed that she understood.

Beyond hearing, beyond knowledge of anything but his goal, Northwood lifted his other hand to steady the pistol. Then, expression gloating, he squeezed the trigger.

The blast shattered the tableau. Varenne was knocked forward by the impact, his weight carrying Maggie with him. Alerted by Rafe's warning, she was already twisting frantically when Northwood's gun went off.

As she tried to duck away from the muzzle of Varenne's weapon, it fired, scorching her cheek with gunpowder. She hit the floor hard and lay stunned, pinned beneath the count's heavy body. There was warm blood on her face; perhaps she had been mortally wounded and was too numb to feel pain.

Then the count's body was wrenched away and Rafe lifted her to a sitting position. "Oh, God, Margot, are you all right?" Cradling her against his chest, he gently examined the side of her head, alternately swearing and praying under his breath.

She managed to say through dry lips, "I—I think the blood is Varenne's."

Rafe embraced Maggie so tightly that she thought her ribs would crack. She was shaking violently, and it was hard to breathe with her face buried against the scratchy wool of his coat. Yet despite the discomforts of her position, she wanted to stop the world and stay in his arms forever, safe and warm.

Robin's voice pulled her back to reality. "Any moment now, Varenne's men are going to come in here to investigate the gunshots. Though the count preferred us alive, his loyal followers will probably be less generous."

He retrieved Rafe's shotgun and cradled it awkwardly against his chest with his good arm. "How much ammunition do we have?"

As abruptly as it had begun, the embrace ended. Rafe released Maggie, a stark, unreadable expression in his eyes. As he helped her to her feet, he answered, "Not much. Margot, get the other shotgun while I saddle the horses. If we ride out together at full speed, at least one of us may get through."

Rafe's heart was hammering as he saddled the horses. If they didn't break out immediately and ride like fury, they would never make it to the embassy in time. He was glad to see that one of the horses was Rafe's own mount. It was an exceptionally mannerly beast and would be a good choice for Robin.

A shot crackled outside, followed instantly by a whole barrage of gunfire. A bullet came through the upper part of the door and Rafe instinctively ducked, swearing under his breath. Varenne hadn't been lying about having an army out there!

Then the sounds of firing diminished, as if the combatants were moving away from the stables. Puzzled, Rafe led two of the horses forward into the front of the barn. Before he could go for the third, the door eased open. A voice called in French, "Surrender! Resistance is futile."

Margot raised her shotgun and Rafe grabbed the other, but they held their fire. Whoever was entering was moving with the same kind of caution Rafe had exercised earlier. It was a tall man, silhouetted against the bright yard, the unmistakable shape of a pistol drawn and ready in his hand. . . .

Maggie was the first to identify the uniform and fair hair of Colonel von Fehrenbach. She lowered her weapon, almost dizzy with relief. "I hope you are here to rescue us, Colonel," she said unsteadily, "because we certainly need it."

Recognizing her voice, he lowered his gun and

swung the door open, revealing that General Roussaye was right behind him. With a slight smile, the Prussian said, "Then we came in time. Madame Sorel will be pleased."

"You're in time for us, but if we can't reach Paris in the next hour, the foreign ministers meeting at the British embassy will be blown to kingdom come." Rafe gave a staccato summary of the situation as the three of them led the horses outside.

The sound of firing still came from the right, away from the main road out of the estate. Roussaye said, "Our men are herding Varenne's back to the river. They won't last long without a leader. Some have already surrendered."

Maggie mounted, then watched with concern the effort that it took Robin to get into the saddle of his horse. "Will you be able to manage, love?"

"The horse will be doing most of the work." He closed his eyes for a moment, his face as pale as parchment. Then he opened them again and managed a reassuring smile. "I might be useful at the other end, since I know the embassy better than you or Rafe."

That was undeniable, so she said no more. If Robin wasn't up to the whole trip, she and Rafe would manage on their own.

None of the horses carried sidesaddles and Maggie was astride, her long legs visible. The animals pranced nervously as the acrid scent of gunsmoke curled through the air.

Von Fehrenbach asked, "Should I send an escort with you?"

Rafe shook his head. "We have fresh horses, and three of us can travel faster than a larger group. Wish us luck. I'll send word if we're successful."

Then the three Britons put heels to their horses and galloped out of the stable yard.

Chapter 25

The details of the ride were never clear in Maggie's mind afterward. She had waved reassuringly at Hélène as they dashed by the gatehouse, but hadn't stopped for explanations. There was a mad exhilaration in racing toward Paris with the two men she loved most in the world. They had survived one set of horrors, and for the moment she felt invincible, as if no amount of gunpowder on earth could harm them.

Though they made excellent time through the countryside, the heavy afternoon traffic around the city slowed them down. Rafe was in the lead, setting the fastest possible pace. Maggie kept a concerned eye on Robin. He rode with grim determination, never slowing the other two.

As they got closer, Maggie's earlier exultation faded, leaving exhaustion, and a fear that tightened her nerves like steel wires. When they finally cantered down the Rue du Faubourg St. Honoré, their horses sweaty and shaking with fatigue, she heard a church tower clock striking four times, proclaiming that the fatal hour had arrived.

They jolted to a halt in front of the embassy and swung off their horses, leaving the reins for any street boys close enough to grab them. They raced up the steps, Rafe helping Robin with a hand on his good arm. He ordered, "Margot, when we get inside, you go up to Castlereagh's chamber and get them to evacuate.

Give me Northwood's keys so Robin and I can reach the gunpowder."

She nodded and tossed him the keys. Wryly she recognized that his gentlemanly instincts were still functioning—upstairs, she would have a better chance of surviving an explosion than he and Robin. If they died, she wasn't sure she would want to go on living, but this was no time to argue the point.

The guards at the door recognized them in spite of their dishevelment. As the corporal in charge saluted, Rafe snapped, "There's a plot to blow up the embassy, and the explosion will go off at any moment. Go with Countess Janos and help her clear people from the area of the bomb."

Maggie ran through the foyer, the befuddled corporal gamely following.

"To the left," Robin panted. With a superhuman effort that showed on his face, he began to run at a speed that nearly equaled Rafe's. They bolted past startled embassy servants, not stopping for more explanations.

Down a stairwell. Left, right along a passage, through a door, left again. Without Robin's guidance, Rafe would never have been able to find his way.

"Here," Robin said tersely, stopping beside a door.

Rafe had studied the keys as he ran, and he shoved the most promising one in the lock. Precious seconds were wasted while he tried to make the key turn, but it was the wrong one. He tried another. The pungent scent of a guttering candle was noticeable. How much longer—minutes? Seconds?

Damnation! Another wrong key. At least if the flame reached the gunpowder before the closet was open, they would be dead before they knew they had failed.

Eureka! The third key was the correct one. Rafe twisted it savagely, then yanked at the doorknob. As the door moved toward him, the tendril of flame fluttered in the draft from the door, then lazily dipped toward the mound of gunpowder only a fraction of an inch below.

Moving as smoothly as if they had rehearsed, Robin dived into the closet the instant that Rafe wrenched the door open. As he hit the floor, he swept his right arm across the line of gunpowder. The flame touched the explosive and flared down the powder trail faster than the eye could follow, scattering into burning particles when it hit his arm.

For a minute both men slapped furiously at the red-hot sparks that flew around the closet. The odor of sulfur permeated the air, and clouds of eye-stinging smoke billowed around them.

Then, with startling anticlimax, there was no more fire. It was over.

Robin crumpled to the floor, struggling for breath, while Rafe leaned heavily against the door frame. He could scarcely believe they had made it in time, and that they were alive and reasonably well.

Several members of the embassy staff had followed them and were drawing near, their voices murmuring in confusion. Rafe said to one who looked as if he had authority, "You can tell the ministers that the evacuation isn't necessary." The man nodded and turned to go upstairs.

Robin looked up, a wry smile on his drawn face. "I'm ready for a new career. I'm getting too old for this kind of excitement."

Rafe returned the smile tiredly. "I think I was born too old." He felt an intense sense of comradeship with this man who was both friend and rival.

No, not his rival, for that implied the issue was in doubt; Robin was not a rival, but the victor. Well, Rafe would try to live up to his own standards of sportsmanship. He helped Robin up, steadying the other man when he swayed. Now that the crisis was over, Robin was half dead on his feet.

Margot forced her way through the onlookers. The wheat gold hair was disastrously snarled from their ride, her green dress had taken such a beating that it was barely decent, and her face showed the same exhaustion that the two men were experiencing. Rafe thought that she had never looked more beautiful.

She mutely put her arms around both men, burying her face between them. Rafe wrapped his free arm around her waist, desperate for the feel of her.

All too soon, Margot raised her head and stepped away from Rafe. He was painfully aware that she kept an arm around Robin. Needing to say something, he said, "Did you manage to clear Castlereagh's chamber?"

She made a face. "It's a good thing you got to the closet in time—I hadn't even persuaded the guard to let me in, much less gotten any of the august personages to move. Considering how long it's taking them to agree on a treaty, they would have been debating whether to evacuate from now until Twelfth Night."

The onlookers parted and another man joined them. The Duke of Wellington was of only average height and the famous hooked nose was more striking than handsome, but even the dullest of mortals would know immediately that this was a man to be reckoned with. "I understand that you uncovered the conspiracy in the nick of time, Candover."

"I deserve very little of the credit," Rafe replied. "My companions here were the ones who managed it."

"We could never have gotten here in time without the Duke of Candover," Robin said. "If not for him, the day would have ended in disaster."

Rafe considered introducing his companions to Wellington, but he had no idea what names they would prefer, or even if introductions were necessary. Wellington solved the problem by offering his hand to

obin. "You must be Lord Robert Andreville. I've
eard of you, sir."

Robin looked startled, but nowhere as much so as
Margot, who shot an incredulous glance at her partner.

Wellington turned to her. "And surely you are
Countess Janos.'"

Margot smiled. "I have been called that."

Wellington bowed, then said, "Lord Strathmore was
ight."

"About what, your grace?"

"He said that you were the most beautiful spy in Eu-
ope," the duke responded, a twinkle in his light blue
yes.

Margot Ashton, dauntless in the face of death and
lisaster, blushed a most becoming shade of rose.

Wellington's tone turned serious. "There is no way
o overestimate the importance of what you have done.
3esides Castlereagh, Richelieu, and myself, all of the
Allied foreign ministers were upstairs, plus," he low-
red his voice, "King Louis and his brother, the Count
l'Artois."

They all gasped. If the explosion had killed the king,
is heir, and the chief ministers, France would have
een ripe for chaos indeed. Varenne might well have
merged a victor in a struggle in which all Europe
would be the loser.

Wellington continued, "None of our visitors know
hat anything was amiss, and perhaps it's best that way.
We wouldn't want anyone to feel unsafe in the British
embassy, would we?"

"We spoke to several soldiers and staff members on
our way in," Rafe said.

"I'll talk with them myself," the Iron Duke said.
"When I get through, they'll understand the importance of keeping their tongues between their teeth."

Rafe didn't doubt it.

Wellington surveyed the three of them. "Castlereagh

will want to see you, but tomorrow will be soon enough. Get some rest—you all look rather the worse for wear."

He started to turn away, then stopped as another thought struck him. "I must return to the conference, but there is one other thing. The foreign minister was concerned that one of his aides, Oliver Northwood, might have been involved in this affair. Is that true?"

Rafe hesitated and glanced at his companions. Robin's face was noncommittal while Margot's smoky eyes were trying to convey some message. Picking his words with care, he said, "Northwood apparently had suspicions that something was amiss and came out to Chanteuil to investigate. His timely intervention was instrumental in foiling the plot, and his was the hand that felled Count de Varenne, the man behind the conspiracy. Unfortunately, Northwood died of wounds inflicted by the count."

Wellington's keen eyes studied him. "That's the story?"

"It is," Rafe said firmly.

Wellington nodded, then left.

"Getting some rest is the best suggestion I've heard in quite some time," Robin said wearily. "A month or so of sleep would be a nice start."

"You, my lad, are not going back to that dismal little hole you call home," Margot said forcefully. "I'm taking you to my house so you can be waited on hand and foot."

Robin gave her a lopsided smile. "I defer to your superior will."

With sudden, searing pain, Rafe felt the bond that had connected the three of them shiver and dissolve. Once more he was on the outside.

Her expression uncertain, Margot asked if Rafe wished to come back to her house with them. He declined, saying that he must send a message to

Chanteuil, write a report for Lucien, and a thousand other things.

As he had promised himself, he didn't say a single word, or make a single gesture, that could alert Robin to the fact that Rafe and Margot had been more than friends. He had shattered her life once; he would not do it again.

Margot looked at him for a moment with some indefinable emotion in her eyes. Surely it couldn't have been pain. Then she turned and left, her arm around Robin.

Watching them walk away together was the hardest thing Rafe had ever done.

An embassy carriage was detailed to take Rafe back to the Hôtel de la Paix. As he rumbled through the streets, he felt a curious kind of numbness, except for his heart, which seemed to have been hacked into small pieces with a dull knife.

Yet even though he had discovered Margot again only to lose her, he had been left with something of great value: learning the truth about the past had given him back his faith in love. For that, at least, he was profoundly grateful.

At his hotel, he walked unseeing through the foyer, wanting only to get to the privacy of his apartment. He didn't even notice the tall blond man talking to the concierge, until a familiar voice said, "Rafe, what the devil has been going on?"

Rafe's eyes snapped into focus, and he saw a travel-stained Lucien standing in front of him. "What are you doing in Paris?" he asked stupidly.

"Your reports got me so worried that I asked St. Aubyn to take care of my work while I came here myself." His friend raised his brows at Rafe's disheveled appearance. "If you're a Fallen Angel, you must have hit the ground hard and bounced a few times."

Rafe closed his eyes for an instant; it was immensely good to see a friend. Gesturing for Lucien to accompany him to his rooms, he said succinctly, "Plot foiled, the wicked destroyed, while the virtuous, including your agents Maggie and Andreville, have survived. Beyond that . . ."

As they entered his drawing room, Rafe drew a shuddering breath. "Don't ask me to explain anything more before tomorrow. Care to join me while I become exceedingly drunk?"

Lucien studied Rafe with shrewd, compassionate eyes, then briefly laid a hand on his shoulder. "Where do you keep the brandy?"

As soon as she returned home, Maggie settled Robin and called a physician to properly set his injured hand.

Before she could rest herself, she had to break the news of Northwood's death to Cynthia. Besides giving the official story they had tacitly agreed to, Maggie also recounted the facts. Oliver Northwood could be a hero to the rest of the world, but Cynthia knew better, and deserved the truth.

After Maggie had finished speaking, Cynthia bowed her head, her fingers restlessly twisting the fringe of her shawl. "I didn't want it to be like this. I never wanted to see him again, but I didn't want him dead." She looked up at Maggie. "That may be hard for you to believe after the way he treated me."

"I think I understand," Maggie said quietly. "He was part of your life for many years. Surely there are some good memories."

Cynthia closed her eyes for a moment, a spasm of grief crossing her features. "There are some—only a handful, perhaps, but yes, there were some genuinely good times. For all the things he did wrong, Oliver was not really an evil man, was he?"

Maggie thought of Northwood's act of casual malice

that had brought so much pain to her and Rafe. It had changed her life forever and it was done from the meanest of motives.

Was that evil? By Northwood's actions she had lost Rafe and gained Robin, and she would rather not judge if her life was better or worse for the path Northwood had forced her to take. "His intervention helped bring off a fortunate result. Perhaps, at the end, he was trying to make amends for what he had done."

"Perhaps." Cynthia smiled sadly. "It was generous of you and your friends to give him the benefit of the doubt. It will make things easier for his family, especially his father."

"Blackening his reputation would have done no good, and saving it does no harm." Maggie gave Cynthia a sympathetic hug, then withdrew.

Alone in her own chamber, she wearily fell back onto her bed without changing from her ragged dress. She thought of Rafe, then closed her eyes against the sharp sting of tears. The way he had embraced her when he thought she had been shot by Varenne implied that he still cared for her a little.

But it wasn't love. The brief moment of time when they had loved each other was as dead as the flowers that had bloomed in that long ago spring. It was mere unlucky chance that those feelings had never really died in her.

The future stretched ahead of her, achingly lonely. Perhaps she should ask Robin if he would marry her; though he hadn't really wanted a wife at twenty, the idea might be more appealing now. If she asked him, she knew that he would agree from the same sense of responsibility that had made him offer when she was nineteen.

Yet even as the thought passed through her mind, she knew that she could not ask. Robin deserved a woman who would love him heart and soul. After all he had done for Maggie, she could not deprive him of the chance for that kind of love.

With a sob, she rolled over and buried her face in the pillows. In the future she would not let herself weep over the injustice of it all. She had learned to live without Rafe Whitbourne once before, and she would again.

But for this one hour, she would allow her tears to flow unchecked. She had earned the right to that much self-indulgence.

Chapter 26

Hélène Sorel sat in her drawing room sipping a late morning cup of coffee and going through her correspondence. With the shafts of early autumn sunlight illuminating the graceful room, the high drama of the day before seemed no more than a fever dream. Roussaye and von Fehrenbach had dispersed Varenne's little army with only a handful of minor casualties on the part of their men. The estate that might have been the center of a new empire was now deserted except for the Prussian guards. The threat to peace was gone, and she had done her part.

She told herself that her feeling of depression was merely the sense of letdown that came at the end of a great enterprise. It was time to think about the future. In a few weeks it should be safe to bring her daughters back to Paris. The thought lightened her heart a little. Yet still Hélène stared at the coffee grounds, wondering why she didn't feel happier.

Then the parlormaid entered to say that Madame had a caller. A Prussian gentleman, very tall.

After a frantic thought for her hair and the fact that this was only her second best morning gown, Hélène touched tongue to dry lips and told the maid bring in her visitor. The colonel had brought her home yesterday with a respectful bow, but had said nothing about calling. No doubt he was here only to ask if she had suffered any ill effects from that frantic ride.

Karl von Fehrenbach looked very tall and very handsome, his fair hair gleaming in the morning light. He
was also very grave as he bowed over the hand Hélène
offered.

After an awkward moment of silence, the colonel
said slowly, "I have thought about what you said, that
day you called on me."

Hélène's pulse quickened. "Yes?"

His light blue eyes clouded by his attempt to express
his emotions, he continued, "You said that someone
must stop the hating, and that you wanted me to look
at you without remembering that you are French and I
am Prussian."

Hélène remained silent, waiting, her expression as
warm and encouraging as she knew how to make it.

After another long pause, the colonel said with difficulty, "I have tried to cut myself off from all feeling,
but I was unsuccessful. The pain was still there. Yet
surely if a heart can feel pain, it can feel happier emotions."

There was a question in his tone, and Hélène suggested softly, "Emotions such as love?"

"Exactly." His earnest gaze met hers. "If you are
willing to forgive my coldness, perhaps . . . perhaps we
can try."

Hélène gave him a brilliant smile. "I should like that
above all things."

The tension went out of his face. Looking years
younger, he said, "Would you be free to take a drive
out to Longchamps now? My carriage is outside."

Hélène blinked in surprise; the colonel certainly didn't
waste any time! But then, why should he? Enough time
had been wasted already. Getting to her feet, she said, "It
will be my great pleasure to go with you."

"There is one thing . . . with your permission?" He
stepped forward, then drew Hélène to him, giving her
ample time to pull away.

She stood firm, almost quivering with hope and fear.

His lips were warmly masculine, not at all what she had expected of an ice prince. With a soft sigh, she settled against him, tilting her head back to make it easier for him to taste the depths of her mouth. What started as gentle exploration rapidly escalated to full-scale passion. Life surged through her, and she tingled right down to her toes.

Their arms tightened around each other as each sought to fill years of emptiness. She was dizzied by taste and touch—by the pressure of his hard body against hers—by the hungry way he caressed her, shaping the curves of her small body. After an eternity that was only a beginning, she became vaguely aware that her back was against the wall, and that without the colonel's strong arms she would melt into a happy puddle on the floor.

He lifted his head, as breathless as she. "I have wanted to do that since the moment I met you." Tenderly he touched her cheek. "Now I shall take you for a drive, then for a luncheon at the finest café in Paris, and at various times along the way, there will be more kisses. Yes?"

"Yes!" Bubbling with laughter, Hélène took his arm and they went out to his carriage. The colonel would always be a reserved man, grave rather than effervescent, but that was all right. She was emotional enough for both of them.

Lucien was an excellent drinking partner. Not only did he not ask questions, but he packed his host off to bed at a fairly early hour, so that Rafe awoke the next morning with only a mild headache. He found Lucien sleeping peacefully on the drawing room sofa.

Over a breakfast of croissants and coffee, Rafe gave a full report of what had happened. Or almost full; there were several omissions, all of them relating to

Margot. He suspected that Lucien noticed, but once more his friend knew what not to ask.

After the meal, Lucien left for the embassy. Rafe was finishing the last of the coffee when a messenger arrived with a small package for the Duke of Candover. He regarded it unenthusiastically, certain that he knew what it contained.

Sure enough, inside was the velvet box containing the ill-fated emeralds. A brief note said, "The masquerade is over. Thank you for the loan. Always, Margot."

He wondered if there was any significance to the fact that she had signed it Margot. Doubtless it was only an acknowledgment that he no longer called her Maggie.

He lifted the emerald necklace from the box and let the cool stones slide through his fingers as he remembered how lovely she had looked wearing it. And the earrings, the perfect adornment for her delectable ears . . .

He had spent some time choosing the gems, and could not imagine them on anyone else. On impulse he decided to go to her house and return them. Perhaps she would accept the set as a wedding gift. He wanted Margot to have something that had come from him. He also wanted to say a civilized good-bye, since the day before he had been more than a little crazed.

But it seemed that even that simple ambition was to be frustrated. When he arrived at Margot's house a short time later and was shown into the drawing room, the only occupant was Lord Robert Andreville, who greeted Rafe with apparent pleasure.

Bathed and shaved and impeccably dressed, Robin looked almost normal except for the sling supporting his left arm. Apparently his recuperative abilities were as remarkable as his stamina. He and Margot were well matched.

After returning the greeting and accepting a seat, Rafe asked, "Is Margot in?"

"No, she's gone out to Chanteuil." Robin grinned. "Something about a cat."

"Good Lord, is she going to bring that mangy beast back here?" Rafe said, unable to resist an answering smile.

"No doubt. The Prussians will not neglect the horses, but she was afraid that since the servants had all fled, the cat had been left to starve."

Rafe shook his head admiringly. In spite of all that had happened, trust Margot not to forget the cat, which, to be fair, was not at all mangy.

His amusement faded, leaving emptiness in its wake. He wouldn't even have the chance to say good-bye.

He got to his feet. "I'm sorry to have missed Margot. Since I'm returning to London tomorrow, will you give her these? I'd like her to have them. That is, if you don't object," he added after Robin accepted the velvet box.

Robin looked at him appraisingly. "Why should I object?"

Rafe felt a flash of irritation at the other man's willful obtuseness. "As her future husband, you might not like her accepting jewelry from another man."

"As her future husband . . . ?" Robin tossed the box lightly in his right hand, then set it on a piecrust table. "What makes you assume that we are getting married?"

"If you recall," Rafe said shortly, "you said that you were going to ask her to marry you."

Robin gave him a long, level look, his face for once serious. "I said that I was going to ask her. I didn't say that she would accept. Frankly, I doubt that she will."

Rafe felt as if he had been clubbed in the midriff: numb, confused, and unsure what the blow meant. "Why would she refuse? You've been lovers for the last dozen years or so, and from what I can see, you're on the best of terms."

Robin stood and walked to a window, then gazed out, deep in thought. Coming to some decision, he turned to Rafe, leaning against the windowsill so that his face and body were dark against the outside light. "That is not precisely accurate. We have not been lovers for over three years. Three years, two months, and"—he thought a moment—"five days, to be exact."

"But I saw you calling at her house late myself." And kissing her, as Rafe recalled with painful clarity.

Robin shrugged. "Professionally we have continued to be partners, and friends as well."

"Then why . . . ?" Rafe stopped, aware of how shockingly intimate was the question he had almost asked.

Unfazed, Robin said, "Why are we no longer lovers? Because Maggie no longer felt right about it. She wouldn't marry me in the beginning because she wasn't in love with me. Many things changed over the years, but not that."

"Didn't you mind when Margot no longer . . . ?"

Robin's face shuttered. "Oh, I minded, but if you understand anything at all about Maggie, you will know that one does not compel her. Except for sharing a bed, our friendship stayed the same, which was what mattered most—though one can always find women for physical relationships, there is only one Maggie. Until this last year, when she took on the role of Countess Janos, we continued living together when I wasn't out risking my neck. It wasn't until I joined the British delegation that we pretended to be mere acquaintances."

Needing desperately to make sense of what he was hearing, Rafe said, "Surely you think there is some chance that she will marry you, or you wouldn't be planning on offering again."

After a slight hesitation, Robin said coolly, "Once I

was rather optimistic. Maggie intended to go back to England for a quiet life in some genteel place like Bath. I thought I would wait about three months, then show up and offer again. By then, she would have been ready to accept from sheer boredom." He looked down and made a minute adjustment to the bandage on his wrist. "It could have worked very well. I'm rich, she's beautiful, and we are the best of friends. Most marriages have much less. But the situation has changed, and I no longer think that she would accept an offer from me."

It was time for the ultimate question in this extraordinary conversation. Rafe asked, "Are you in love with her?"

Silhouetted against the bright window, Robin's lean body was very still. "In love? I don't really know what that means. Perhaps I lack the temperament for grand passions. Certainly I am not in love as Maggie would define it." He stopped, then said in a voice meant more for himself than Rafe, "I would go through fire for her, but that's not quite the same thing."

Feeling as if he were being torn in half, Rafe crossed the room and stood close enough to see the other man's face. Quietly he asked, "Why are you telling me this?"

"Because I think Maggie is in love with you. I knew she had loved someone before we met, and I have seen how she has been since you came to Paris." Robin's tone became sardonic. "While there's no guarantee that she would be willing to overlook the past and marry you, from the way you've been acting, I assume that you would at least like to make the offer."

Rafe's aching confusion began to disappear, washed away by an almost unbearable hope. "I was on the verge of going back to England without seeing her again."

"I know. That is why I spoke."

After a shaken pause, Rafe said, "You're a generous man."

"I want Maggie to be happy." Robin's expression changed as he allowed the underlying steel to show through. "But if you marry her and make her miserable, you'll answer to me."

"I'll have to answer to myself first, and I guarantee that I will be harsher even than you would be." Rafe drew an unsteady breath. "It's shockingly inadequate, but—thank you." After scooping up the jewelry box, he left at a near run.

Robin held aside the sheer drapery and watched the duke emerge from the house, leap into his curricle and set off for Chanteuil at a reckless pace.

He dropped the drapery and turned away, his mouth tight. He was indeed a very generous man.

He was also a damned fool.

Chapter 27

Though ordinarily Maggie would not have wanted to return to Chanteuil, going for Rex provided a convenient excuse to be out of the house if Rafe called to see how she and Robin were faring. The day was as sunny and warm as high summer, which made the drive enjoyable.

When she reached the castle, the Prussian guards at the gatehouse told her that all of Varenne's servants had fled, leaving the estate empty. The sergeant in charge recognized her from the day before, so he was easily persuaded to allow her in when she explained that she had come for a cat, and perhaps to view the gardens.

It didn't take long to achieve her first objective; whoever said that cats were aloof had obviously never met Rex. Within five minutes of entering the castle and starting to call his name, he trotted out to greet her, ready for food and adoration.

Being no fool, Maggie had brought some sliced chicken with her. After Rex dined, he was quite happy to sleep off his meal while draped over her shoulder.

The lush, overgrown gardens were very lovely, the flowers bright with the flamboyant splendor of the last days before frost. She sensed no lingering trace of Varenne's evil, and for that she was grateful.

When Rex began to feel heavy, Maggie decided to sit and enjoy the sunshine. In a small rose garden completely surrounded by high hedges, she found a stone bench under a blossom-covered arbor. She sank down on it, grateful for the shade. The scene was extraordinarily peaceful, the silence broken only by the fluting of birdsongs and the gentle splashing of a small fountain in the center of the garden.

Rex slept with his head on her lap, the rest of him sprawled along the bench, one back paw in the air. The cat would be a fine tutor as she learned to live a normal, quiet life, for he had a truly remarkable talent for relaxation.

The tranquility soothed her strained nerves. Though the last weeks had been harrowing, the experience had been worthwhile, for she and Rafe had made a kind of peace. She also had an unforgettable night to cherish for the rest of her life.

Her musings were interrupted by the crunching of footsteps on gravel. She looked up to see Rafe walking swiftly along the path. Seeing her, he paused, then proceeded toward her at a slower pace, his expression reserved. Though his hair was uncharacteristically windblown, he was dressed with his usual damn-your-eyes elegance, and was so handsome that she realized she was forgetting to breathe.

Though this meeting would mean another night of tears, she couldn't help but respond to his presence. "Good afternoon, your grace," she said with a carefully casual smile. "What brings you to Chanteuil?"

"You. May I sit down?" At her nod, he settled on the other side of Rex. "It's rather eerie. Apart from the Prussian guards at the gatehouse who said you might be in the garden, the place seems deserted."

"Not so much as a cook or a scullery maid left," she agreed. "It's fortunate that I came for Rex. Perhaps he could have survived on castle mice, but he would have been lonesome. He's a sociable creature."

Instead of answering, Rafe studied her face, his expression intent. There was something subtly different about him this morning. Perhaps it was only imagination, but to her eyes he looked less like a duke and more like the young man she had fallen in love with.

Before the silence could become too uncomfortable, he said, "One reason I came out here was to offer you an apology. Northwood was the one who claimed that you had lain with him. Looking back, it's hard to understand how I was fool enough to believe him."

She would much rather discuss weather or the gardens, but there were some things that should probably be said, since they were unlikely to meet again. "I learned that it was Northwood yesterday, when he boasted of what he had done. It was clever of him to pretend drunkenness—it's easier to believe a whisper than a shout."

Rafe grimaced. "Lord knows that I have been punished for my unreasonable jealousy. I'm profoundly sorry, Margot. Not trusting you was the worst mistake of my life."

He hesitated, as if seeking the right words, then said haltingly, "My parents had a fashionable marriage. After they did their duty and produced me, they were seldom under the same roof, much less in the same bed. I wanted a different kind of marriage. When I met you, I thought I had found what I was looking for. Yet I don't think I truly believed that it was possible for me to attain such happiness, which may be why I was susceptible to Northwood's slander."

"I don't remember you ever talking about your parents before," she said quietly.

He shrugged. "There was very little to say. My mother died when I was ten—her demise made so little difference in my life that I scarcely noticed she was gone. My father believed in Lord Chesterfield's maxim that there was nothing so vulgar as audible laughter. He was quite punctilious about his responsibilities to his heir, just as he was conscientious about caring for his tenants and taking his seat in the Lords. A true English gentleman." Rafe glanced down and began stroking the cat's silky belly. "Having Colonel Ashton for a father-in-law was a . . . refreshing prospect."

His uninflected words made Maggie's heart ache. At eighteen, it had not occurred to her that tall, confident Rafe had not only desired her, but needed her. She wondered why he revealed that. Not for sympathy, she was sure.

Deciding to ask a question that had often occurred to her, usually late in a lonely night, she said, "If I had denied Northwood's charge, would you have believed me?"

"I think so. I wanted—rather desperately—for you to throw my words back in my face." He stopped, then added painfully, "The fact that you made no attempt to deny it seemed like proof of your infidelity."

"My wretched, wretched temper," she said sadly, feeling the ache of old anguish. "I was so angry and hurt that I had to escape before I fell apart in front of you. I should have stayed and fought."

"My lack of trust was far more reprehensible than your justifiable anger," Rafe said, his voice tight with self-condemnation. "If your father hadn't felt that he needed to get you away from London, he never would have died in France."

She shook her head. "It's my turn to apologize. In spite of what I said when we had that horrible fight, I never blamed you for his death. It's true that we originally left England because of my broken betrothal, but we overstayed our time in France because my father was sending reports to army headquarters. He was sure that the peace wouldn't last, so he used our travels as a cover for observing French troops and armaments." She gave Rafe a wry glance. "As you see, I came by my spying abilities naturally."

Rafe sighed. "Thank you for telling me that. It helps a little."

"Life is a tapestry of interwoven events," she said slowly. "If we hadn't come to France—if Father hadn't been killed—if I hadn't gone to work with Robin—who knows what would have happened in Paris this week? Varenne might have been successful, and Europe would be sliding toward war again. So perhaps my father's death wasn't as meaningless as it seemed at the time."

"I hope you're right. There is comfort in believing that some good has come from the tragedies of the past." He pulled a velvet box from his pocket and handed it to her. "Another reason I came out here was because I wanted you to have these."

Recognizing the box, she tried to give it back. "I can't possibly keep the emeralds. They're too valuable."

His brows lifted. "If I gave you flowers, you would accept them. What is the difference?"

"At least five thousand pounds," she said tartly. "Probably a good bit more."

He laid his hand over hers where it rested on the velvet box. "The cost is unimportant. What matters is that they are from the heart, no more, and no less, than flowers would be."

The warmth that spread through their joined hands weakened Maggie's resolve. The truth was that she wanted the emeralds, not so much for their beauty and value as because they were from Rafe. "Very well," she said in a low voice. "If you really want me to keep them I shall."

"I would like to give you a great deal more."

His words triggered a rush of fury. Why did he have to say that and spoil everything? She rose to her feet, leaving both jewels and an indignant Rex on the bench. "I don't want you to give me anything more," she

snapped. "This is already too much. Take those
damned emeralds away and give them to a woman who
will express her appreciation in the way that you
want."

Back rigid, she stepped into the sunshine and
plucked a rose from one of the bushes. As she broke
thorns from the stem, she told herself that she was *not*
going to lose her composure.

It was another resolution doomed to failure. Rafe
came up behind her and rested his hands on her shoulders. Though there was nothing overtly sensual in the
contact, his nearness undermined her good intentions
with dreadful ease.

In his deep, mellow voice, he quoted, " 'Come live
with me and be my love, Then we will all the pleasures
prove . . .'"

She yanked away, turning only when she was safely
out of his reach. "Damn you, Rafe Whitbourne, we've
been over this before! I won't be your mistress."

He could have followed her and used all the intoxicating weapons of the senses to try to change her mind,
but he didn't. Instead, he said quietly, "I'm not asking
you to be my mistress. I'm asking you to be my wife."

Maggie had believed that matters could not get
worse, but she had been wrong. Rafe was offering the
deepest desire of her heart—and his words triggered a
numbing wave of fear and grief.

Not daring to investigate the roots of her distress,
she said tightly, "You do me a great honor, your grace,
but we both know that when men like you marry, they
choose rich, beautiful, eighteen-year-old virgins." She
gave a brittle laugh. "I am none of those things. High
adventure can be like a drug—don't let a few days of
excitement warp your judgment."

In spite of her flat refusal, Rafe felt a flicker of
hope. Margot had said nothing about not loving him,

which was why she had refused Robin, and which was the only reason that really mattered.

"I'm not 'men like me'—for better and worse, I'm the one and only Rafael Whitbourne," he said in his most reasonable tone. "I also have quite enough money for any two people, or even any hundred people, so fortune is not an issue. Beauty? That is in the eye of the beholder, and in my eyes you are the most captivating woman in the world. You always have been. You always will be.

"As for age"—he closed the distance between them and caught her gaze, willing her to believe—"the only eighteen-year-old I ever met who didn't bore me to paralysis is you—and the woman you have become is even more irresistible than the girl you were."

When her lips parted to reply, he touched his forefinger to them. "That being the case, why won't you marry me?" He thought he saw a flash of something dark and anguished in her eyes before she masked her expression.

Brushing his hand aside, she said coolly, "Because I know myself too well, Rafe. I could never share you with another woman. The first time you had an affair, I would turn into a raving shrew and make us both miserable. I suppose you might be able to conceal your other women from me, but I will never live a lie, be it ever so charmingly told."

"I didn't want a fashionable marriage when I was twenty-one, and I don't want one now," he said emphatically. "If we marry, I swear that I will never give you cause to doubt my fidelity."

Shrugging off his avowal, she said, "Everyone makes mistakes, Rafe. You don't have to marry me to atone for believing Northwood. I enjoy my independence, and have no desire to give it up."

"Are you sure? No one whose hands are clenched is

thinking clearly, and this is too important to decide while upset."

With a choked sound between laughter and tears, she looked down and saw that her hands were white-knuckled fists. Carefully she straightened her fingers and saw that they were trembling. "The love we had when we were young was very real, and very special," she said unsteadily, "but we can never go back to it. Accept that it's over, Rafe."

He took her left hand and gently massaged the crescents that her nails had dug in the palm. "Why go back when we can go forward? Surely now we can bring a depth and wisdom to loving that we could not have done all those years ago."

She bit her lip, then shook her head.

"Can't we even try?" he said intensely. "Life doesn't offer many second chances, Margot. For God's sake, let's not throw this one away!"

She dared a quick glance at his face and saw that the layers of civilized detachment had been stripped away, leaving him open in a way that she had not seen since the morning he had ended their betrothal. Wishing that she could match his courage, she broke away and retreated to the fountain in the middle of the garden. In the center of the pool, a worn stone cherub held aloft an urn from which the water flowed. Staring at the cherub as if it were the most beautiful sculpture she had ever seen, she said bitterly, "You're deceiving yourself, Rafe. There *are* no second chances, in life or in love."

There was a long silence. She began to hope that he finally understood, and would stop trying to change her mind.

She should have known that he would not surrender so easily. He came to stand beside her, saying, "Don't keep retreating, Margot. You said yourself that it was a mistake to run away thirteen years ago. I won't let you do it again."

The undercurrent of her fear became stronger. "Leave me alone, Rafe," she said sharply. "I know what I want, and it doesn't include marriage to you."

He steeled himself for what must come next, for he sensed that unless he addressed the full horror of her past, she would continue to give him superficial reasons why they would not suit. "I know what happened in Gascony, Margot."

When she whipped her shocked gaze back to him, he said with slow emphasis, "I know all of it."

"Robin told you?"

"Yes, when we were in the cell together."

"Damn him!" she swore, her eyes blazing. "He had no right to speak of that, and to you of all people."

"I convinced him that . . . I had a strong need to know."

"So that's what is really behind your proposal," she said savagely. "Guilt. It's generous of you to be willing to accept damaged goods for your duchess, but it's bloody not necessary. I can take care of myself perfectly well without your misguided charity."

A spasm crossed his face. "Is that how you see yourself—as damaged goods?"

She sank down onto the rim of the fountain and buried her face in her hands. Until now, only Robin had known the whole, ugly story. It was unbearable that Rafe, of all people, was also aware of her disgrace.

The sunny garden disappeared as dark memories threatened to overpower her. She forced her mind away from them, only to come face-to-face with the fact that her utter helplessness had been even more devastating than the pain. In some ways, her whole life since then had been about proving that she was not helpless.

Battling desperately to avoid the ultimate humiliation of falling apart in front of Rafe, she said harshly,

"More than damaged—shattered beyond repair. That's why I welcomed the chance to stay in France with Robin, why I wouldn't let even Lord Strathmore know my real name. Margot Ashton was dead, and I wanted her to stay that way."

"Margot Ashton didn't die—she became a remarkable, compassionate woman." Rafe's voice was very soft. "You have touched more lives, accomplished more good, than most people ever dream of. I won't deny that I feel tremendous guilt about how I treated you, but that's not the reason I want you for my wife."

Afraid of what he would say next, she raised her head and said wearily, "I don't want to hear any more."

Ignoring her remark, he seated himself beside her on the rim of the fountain. "When I was twenty-one I loved you with all that was best in me," he said soberly. "At the time, I was frightened of how much I was in your power, because I loved you more than pride and honor."

He plucked several strands of grass and absently rolled them between his thumb and forefinger. "After I lost you, only pride and honor were left, and I slid into all their traps. When I look back at the man I became, I don't much like him. If I was usually courteous, it was because it was beneath me to be rude. When I was sometimes arrogant, it was because being a duke gave form and structure to a life that was essentially meaningless." He turned and looked at her, his grave gaze holding hers. "*You* are what gives meaning to my life, Margot."

By exposing so much of himself to her, he was paradoxically making Maggie herself more vulnerable. Feeling more and more afraid, her gaze slid away so that he could not see her cowardice. "I don't want to be responsible for giving your life meaning."

"You don't have a choice." He twined the strands of

grass around his finger like a ring. "It will be true whether we marry, or whether we never see each other again."

With every sentence, he was undermining more of her defenses. The horror of Gascony joined the separate fear she had felt when he proposed to her, creating a torrent of panic. Unable to conceal her feelings any longer, she cried, "I haven't the courage to try again, Rafe! The idea of risking myself with you terrifies me. Varenne's threat to blow my brains out was child's play by comparison."

The blades of grass snapped between his fingers. After a long silence, he said, "My life has been easy compared to yours, but I do know something about fear—I've spent the last dozen years living a life shaped by it. Because I didn't dare risk the kind of pain I felt after losing you, I kept life at a distance, never allowing myself to get close to a woman whom I might love."

"Then you should I understand how I feel. Give up, Rafe, please." Her breath was coming in raw, painful gasps and she knew that she should refuse to listen any longer. Yet she was utterly unable to make herself leave.

"Not until I'm convinced this is a hopeless case," he said, his tone adamant. "Admitting that I love you terrifies me, yet I must risk it because even pain is better than the emptiness I've known for the last dozen years."

He turned to her, his gaze compelling. "After the riot in the Place du Carrousel you said that the only thing stronger than fear is passion. But you're wrong." With gossamer tenderness, he brushed a strand of hair from her cheek. "It isn't passion, but love, that is stronger than fear. I love you, and I think that you must love me at least a little, or you would never have shared my bed. The love exists—give it a chance to heal the wounds of the past."

She yearned for what he was offering like a woman dying of thirst yearned for water. Yet she could not accept. Ever since Rafe had come to Paris, she had experienced one brutal shock after another, and the barriers she had erected for survival were collapsing. The storm of fear intensified to hurricane force, threatening to shatter her beyond any hope of healing.

There was only one form of solace that she trusted.

She slid along the marble fountain rim, then twined her arms around Rafe's neck and kissed him with desperate hunger. His calm demeanor fractured and he crushed her hard against him. In the fierce embrace that followed, her fear retreated a little, driven back by the molten madness of desire.

He unfastened the back of her gown and dragged the garment down to bare her shoulder. But instead of kissing her again, he stopped, his hands shaking. "We should be talking," he said unsteadily, "not pulling each other's clothes off."

She opened her dazed eyes. "Talking won't help, Rafe. Passion will—at least for a little while." She slid her hand down his torso until she felt a ridge of warm male flesh. He hardened instantly under her palm.

His breath caught. "Oh, God, Margot . . ."

Unable to withstand her, Rafe drew her willing body to the sun-warmed grass. Their limbs twined together and clothing was stripped away so that yearning flesh could be kissed and touched. Beyond fear, she gave a shuddering sigh of relief when he entered her in a swift, powerful act of possession.

But instead of proceeding to the blazing, inevitable conclusion, he became still, his arms trembling with strain as he throbbed within her. "Not yet, love," he gasped. "I haven't finished talking about fear. Life has taught you to be afraid, but it doesn't have to be that way. Let me love you."

"Isn't that what we're doing now?" Determined to draw him down into desire, she rotated her hips provocatively.

He involuntarily drove deeper, then caught his breath and eased back a little, sweat shining on his face. "This isn't love, it's sex—glorious and intoxicating, but not the same as making love."

"Stop talking about love!" Furiously she struck out at him, her nails raking his shoulders and chest.

He caught her wrists and pinioned them to the grass with gentle implacability. "I have to," he panted, "because it was the failure of love that sent us both off on such joyless, fearful paths."

"This isn't a bloody parliamentary debate, Rafe!" More than ever craving oblivion, she contracted her interior muscles in a ravishing caress.

He groaned and his head fell forward, his black hair tumbling damply over his eyes. She tightened again, and thought she had won when a violent tremor pulsed through him.

But once more his control defeated her. Raising his head, he said huskily, "Let me love you, Margot, for passion will never give you anything but temporary relief."

"Perhaps you're right," she whispered, inexplicably wanting to weep. "But passion . . . is safer than love."

He braced himself above her, his wide shoulders blocking the sun, filling the world so that there was nothing real but him. "Safe isn't good enough."

Unable to bear his probing gaze, she closed her eyes and tried feverishly to recapture the mindlessness of passion.

Sharply he ordered, "Look at me!"

Though she didn't want to obey, her eyes opened.

She was appalled to realize that she seemed to have no will of her own.

More quietly he said, "You deserve more than simple safety, Margot. You've already suffered the pains of loving—let yourself feel the joy."

Piece by piece, her defenses had been flaking away, and abruptly the last of them disintegrated, pitching her into a maelstrom of fear, pain, and anger. She had survived devastation by never allowing herself to fully experience the horror of the past, but now the memories swept over her with a ferocity that splintered her spirit. *Her father's agonized death cry, and his blood spilling over her face. Clawing hands and the excruciating defilement that forever destroyed her innocence. Unspeakable acts that had been literally unimaginable to a sheltered eighteen-year-old girl.*

She cried out with terror, desire vanishing as brutal sobs racked her to the core. *She was cold, so cold, and absolutely alone. . . .*

Instantly Rafe released her wrists and enfolded her in his arms, using his body and spirit to shield her from the storm. "I love you, Margot!" he said urgently. "I always will. You don't ever have to be alone again."

She had known, in the very marrow of her bones, that if she ever faced the full horror she would die.

Yet she didn't. Rafe was around her, within her, his tenderness and strength protecting her, his forcefully repeated words of love a lifeline that saved her from annihilation.

Gradually the maelstrom of terror began to lose its power and her rasping breath eased. The past had not changed; her memories were still bitter, the scars still deep. Yet his love was dispelling the clouds of terror as inexorably as the sun burned off the morning fog.

Fear ebbed, leaving emptiness. Then slowly, like the flow of the tide, the hollowness at the center of her soul filled with love. The warmth of his caring banished the dark shadows and suffused her with light.

And with love came a rekindling of desire. It was not the desperate craving that had ruled her earlier, but a powerful upswelling of emotion in which love and passion were inseparable.

Though he had softened while holding her against the storm, they were still locked together as intimately as man and woman could be. She arched against him, letting her body speak to his. As passion rose again, she whispered, "I love you, Rafe."

He exhaled roughly as he moved into the primal rhythms of mating. There was no trace of the distance she had sensed in him the first time they made love. Now he was wholly with her, spirit as well as body.

As they tried to merge their separate bodies into one, his powerful thrusts created another storm, this one the white wind of desire. She cried out and clung to him as she spun out of control. Savage contractions blazed through her, searing outward from the place of their joining. Her cry was echoed by his heart-deep groan as he released his seed deep inside her.

The descent from ecstasy was slow, a swirl of tranquility and light. As her fragmented consciousness slowly returned, she found that Rafe was shaking as badly as she. She stroked his sweaty back until her breathing steadied. "How did you know that I felt so alone?" she murmured.

Rafe lifted himself on his elbows and studied her face, his strained expression revealing how much her emotional cataclysm had cost him. "Recognition, I suppose. When I looked back, I realized that fear of loss had made me withdraw from the hazards of deep emotion. Yet what I found was not safety, but loneliness. I guessed that it was the same for you."

"That's it exactly," she said slowly. "I never forgot what happened, yet I never let myself fully feel it, either. To survive, I had to retreat from the terror. By doing so, I cut myself off from everything—and everyone."

"You speak as if that's in the past."

"It is, because you wouldn't let me retreat this time. Thank you, Rafe." As she looked into his clear gray eyes, her mouth curved into a smile. "In case I didn't make myself clear earlier, I love you."

He returned the smile with entrancing warmth. "As I believe I mentioned forty or fifty times, I love you, too."

She laughed a little. "It appears that for once we are in agreement."

A shadow touched his face. "I'm sorry that I forgot myself so entirely that I didn't withdraw." He hesitated, then said, "I hope that . . . there won't be any unwanted consequences."

Joy blossomed within her, and a pleasing sense of female power. "Such consequences would not be unwelcome to me," she said serenely. "And surely you would like an heir."

He looked startled. Then, with dazzling suddenness, his face lit up, as radiant as the sun above them. "Does that mean you'll marry me?"

Tenderly she ran her fingers through his tousled hair. "If you're sure that you want a lady with a shady past, there is nothing I would like more than to be your wife."

"If I'm sure!" Laughing, he caught her in his arms and rolled onto his back so that she was sprawled on top of him. "I've never been more certain of anything in my life."

"You were right, Rafe. Love is stronger than fear, and it feels a whole lot better." She rubbed her cheek against his. "Bless you for being braver than I."

"It was a risk worth taking." He stroked her bare backside lovingly. "You were concerned that I would be unable to resist the charms of other women, but remember, it's said that a reformed rake makes the best husband."

She hesitated, then decided that there must be complete honesty between them. "Frankly, I've never believed that. I know that you meant what you said—but leopards and unchangeable spots come to mind."

"I have always liked women in direct proportion to how much they reminded me of you, but no one else has ever held a candle to the original Margot." He grinned. "Will you find it easier to believe me if I say that I have grazed in enough fields to know that the grass is *not* greener?"

"You've just convinced me." Laughing, she laid her head on his shoulder. "Why is it that an ignoble assertion is so much more persuasive than a noble one?"

"Human nature, I'm afraid."

As they lay languidly together, it occurred to Rafe that he'd better protect Margot from the sun, for her fair complexion would burn much more easily than his dark hide. Gently he deposited her on the luxuriant grass, then propped himself on one elbow so that she was shaded by his body.

"You were lovely by candlelight, and you're even lovelier in the sun." Delicately he touched one of the fading bruises on her ribs. In the last several days, it had gone from blue-black to yellow-olive. "I'll be glad when these have faded away." His voice tightened. "You're a miracle, Margot. What you survived would have destroyed anyone with less strength."

She caught his hand and clasped it to her heart. "Nothing is without value, love. From the day my father died until ten minutes ago, fear was a constant companion, as close as my own shadow. Yet curiously, I was not afraid of small things, because the worst that I could imagine had already happened. In most ways I became stronger, capable of actions that would have been unthinkable earlier. That's why I could be an effective spy."

He kissed her forehead. "My indomitable countess and soon-to-be-duchess."

Hesitantly she said, "I have a request."

"Anything," he said simply.

She considered a dozen ways to express what she meant before saying, "Robin is my family. He always will be."

Rafe gave her a wry smile. "And you don't want me to act like a jealous, possessive idiot of a husband. Fair enough. I like and respect Robin enormously. If I work on it a bit, I think I'll be able to convince myself that he's your brother. He will always be welcome in our home, and I genuinely hope that he is a frequent visitor. Is that what you wanted to hear?"

"Yes, my love." A silky object pressed sensually along her side, and she looked down to see that Rex had decided that it was safe to sprawl along her bare flank. With a grin, she asked, "How about Rex?"

Rafe laughed. "He's welcome, too. Every household needs a tomcat, and now that I've reformed . . ."

Her joyous laughter chimed through the garden as she lifted her face to Rafe's, running her fingers through his black hair, molding her body against him in the sheer delight of closeness.

As their lips joined again, she had a fleeting moment of gratitude that this garden was so very private. They had a lot of years to make up for.

Historical Note

Though the Congress of Vienna is well known, the Paris peace conference of 1815 is relatively obscure. Nonetheless, it was a vital event that finally concluded the Napoleonic Wars.

Though I have taken some liberties, the background events of the story are true. Paris in the summer and autumn of 1815 was a hotbed of conspiracies, assassination plots, and political crosscurrents. Lord Castlereagh was indeed kicked by a horse in mid-September, and for some days after, the important meetings took place in his bedchamber at the British embassy.

Both art and Bonapartist political prisoners became topics of great controversy, and the events at the Louvre and the Place du Carrousel are accurately depicted. The French, however, had the last laugh on this; while the final treaty sent the stolen art treasures in Paris home, no one thought to include the many fine works that had been sent to provincial museums.

Some of the top Bonapartist military men were executed, causing outrage throughout Europe. Marshal Michel Ney, "the bravest of the brave," died with great courage before a firing squad. With the aid of three British subjects, another high-ranking officer escaped from prison dressed in his wife's clothes, proving once again that art has nothing over life when it comes to farce.

The Congress of Vienna and the peace settlement of

1815 are sometimes called reactionary because the tsar's nonbinding Holy Alliance is confused with the Quadruple Alliance, which was the actual peace treaty signed on November 20th. It was the Holy Alliance that came to be used as a tool of reactionary forces, while the Quadruple Alliance had one splendid new idea: that in times of future trouble, the great powers would gather together and discuss the situation. This was the seed that flowered into the League of Nations and the United Nations in this century.

The statesmen who engineered the settlement were tough, pragmatic men who sought to have peace in their time, and who had to work with the materials available on a shattered continent. They succeeded better than any of them dreamed of: Europe did not experience another continent-wide conflagration until 1914.

Meanwhile, the British embassy is still housed in the mansion that Wellington bought from Pauline Bonaparte, the Princess Borghese, and I'm told that on great occasions her plate still graces the table.

New York Times Bestselling Author

Mary Jo Putney

Silk and Shadows

**A classic love story that has become one of
her most beloved and acclaimed
historical romances....**

He called himself Peregrine, and like the falcon he was
wild and free. He was superbly handsome, fabulously
wealthy, overwhelmingly seductive. He cut a dazzling
swath through Victorian London—and wove a web of
desire around beautiful and proud Lady Sara St. James,
pledged to wed another man.

In Peregrine's arms, Sara learned the meaning of forbidden
passion—and forbidding mystery. Only the burning power
of love could pierce Peregrine's chilling silence about his
secret past and hidden purpose—as Sara plunged into a
whirlpool of yearning and uncertainty with a man who was
everything a woman could want or fear...

"A fabulous, fabulous book. Bravo!"
—Mary Balogh

"Brilliant. It got under my skin as very, very few books have."
—Loretta Chase

**Available wherever books are sold or at
penguin.com**

Three romance classics in one volume from
New York Times bestselling author

JO BEVERLEY

THREE HEROES

0-451-21200-2

The Demon's Mistress

A wealthy widow hires a war-torn hero to pretend to
be her fiancé, but what will happen when he learns
the truth about the woman he has come to love?

The Dragon's Bride

The new Earl of Wyvern arrives at his fortress on the
cliffs of Devon to find a woman from his past
waiting for him—with a pistol in her hand.

The Devil's Heiress

No one needs Clarissa Graystone's fortune more than
Major George Hawkinville. Now he must ignore
the hunger in his heart as Clarissa boldly
steps into his trap.

N598